"I ain't got much to give you to take your mind off hurting, but I'm offering you what I got."

Max drew a sharp breath, and she realized she stood silhouetted by the moonlight falling through the frosted window. Now was not the moment to go timid, she reminded herself. This was her idea—in for a penny, in for a pound.

A push and a wiggle eased the nightgown over her hips, and she let it drop around her ankles. "Last time anyone saw me buck naked I was a baby," she said uncomfortably, resisting an urge to clap an arm over her breasts and a hand over her private parts.

He didn't say anything, didn't do anything. And she suddenly wondered if offering herself had been a terrible mistake. Worse, there was naught to do but go forward. Tentatively, she reached a hand to his hair, paused, then drew him toward her.

A sound erupted from deep in his throat, and his arms came around her waist so tightly she thought he'd crush her, and he pressed his face against her bare stomach. "Damn."

"It's all right," she whispered, stroking his head, holding him against her. . . .

SILVER LINING

Maggie Osborne

IVY BOOKS • NEW YORK

This book is dedicated with love
to two beautiful young ladies,
Chantel and Brittany Osborne

An Ivy Book
Published by The Random House Ballantine Publishing Group .
Copyright © 2000 by Maggie Osborne

www.ballantinebooks.com

Library of Congress Catalog Card Number: 99-091148

ISBN 0-449-00516-X

Manufactured in the United States of America

First Edition: January 2000

OPM   10   9   8   7   6   5   4   3

Prologue

"Oh Lordy, I'm dying."

Low Down stared into the man's swollen face and her nostrils pinched against the stink of oozing pustules. Clenching her teeth, she reached deep inside for a dollop of energy, lifted his head, pulled out his pillow and changed the case, then settled his head back on dry, clean linen before she leaned near his ear.

"You're starting to scab up, which means the worst is over. You're going to make it."

"No I ain't."

"Now you listen, Frank. I know you got a pouch of gold hid under a plank in your cabin. If you die, I'm going to steal those nuggets. You just think about that."

His eyes fluttered open. "How'd you know about my stash? That gold is for my funeral and a headstone!"

"Too bad. If you die, I'm stealing it. I'll jump your claim, too."

Leaving him struggling to sit up, she moved to the next cot on stumbling feet. Christ Almighty. When was the last time she had grabbed a couple hours of sleep or had eaten anything? She couldn't remember. And the men kept coming to the school—sick, delirious, needing help. Before she bent over the next cot, she looked around, blinking hard to clear her vision, hoping this time she'd discover that someone had come to help her.

Her boot heel slipped in a pool of vomit and she pitched forward, nearly falling across Max McCord.

1

Swearing, she fetched a bucket and flung the water at the vomit. It was all she had time for, the best she could do. Pulling a letter out of her trouser pocket, she looked down at Max. Like all of them, he was in a bad way. His face and eyelids were swollen, and he was beginning to stink like rotten meat. That meant he'd start oozing soon, which was good. If she could push, prod, and coax them through to this stage, they usually survived.

She waved the envelope under his nose. "See this?" It was addressed to a Miss Philadelphia Houser in his handwriting; she knew that because she'd taken the envelope from his jacket pocket before his clothing was burned. When she was sure he was coherent and watching, she tore the letter into pieces. "If you die, Miss Philadelphia Houser will never know about the big fancy house you built for her. She'll never know that you were thinking about her right before you got so sick."

A hard flush of fever and outrage made him look almost healthy. "Damn it! You had no right to read a private letter! No right to rip it to pieces! You . . . you . . ."

Leaving him sputtering furiously and weakly pounding the bed, she moved to the next cot. Five minutes, that's all she needed. Just five minutes of sleep, then a long pull of whiskey to get her moving again.

This one's eyes were closed and she wasn't sure he was breathing until she shook him and saw his chest heave. Leaning to his ear, ignoring the weeping sores and the stench, she whispered, "Can you hear me, you worthless no-good worm? This is Martha, your first wife. I'm waiting for you, you spineless lazy chunk of pig offal. Go on and die so we can be together for all eternity." His breath hitched and a shudder of recoil ran through his body. She decided that he might just make it.

"Low Down? Are you still in there?"

The food was here already? It seemed like she'd just fed everyone. Dragging herself to the door of the schoolhouse, she sagged against the jamb and jerked back from the sudden blaze of sunshine. Or maybe the sting in her eyes was caused by the drift of noxious smoke curling off a pile of burning clothing and bed linens.

Preacher Jellison stood well away, almost in the twin ruts that served as a road, his nose and mouth covered by a blue bandanna. He pointed to a wheelbarrow full of food. "I don't know how good this will be. Mr. Janson who was doing the cooking died last night. Olaf Gurner cooked this."

She nodded, too exhausted to inquire how Mr. Janson had died. Not the pox, or they would have brought him to the school a week ago.

"Are there any new bodies?"

Slowly she shook her head from side to side. And thanked God. She doubted she had the strength to haul one more heavy body outside.

"Good. That's three days in a row. Maybe the epidemic is burning itself out." Preacher Jellison studied her. "You look like crap, Low Down."

A ghostly smile twitched her lips. "In my case that's probably an improvement."

"Try to get some rest. I'll be back in the morning. Is there anything you need?"

"More carbolic and glycerine." She tried to dose each man at least three times a day. Who knew if it did any good. "And bed linens."

"We've used every sheet in Piney Creek, so we sent down to Denver for more. They should be here tomorrow or the next day."

Squinting through the yellow smoke rolling off the burn pile, Low Down watched the preacher head back to the main camp, nearly deserted now. When the epidemic ended, the men would burn the schoolhouse to the ground and very likely it wouldn't be rebuilt. Families with children had been the first to leave, and no one expected they would return. The pox had killed Piney

Creek's ambitions to become a town as surely as it had killed the men crowding the makeshift cemetery higher up the mountainside.

Too exhausted to move until she absolutely had to, Low Down lingered in the doorway, letting the thin sunshine warm her hands and face. Overnight, a powdery cap had appeared on the high peaks, and the hummingbirds had already departed for lower altitudes. Both events signaled an early winter this year.

Maybe she'd head south, she thought, slapping at a mosquito. Start looking for luck someplace warm and dry.

Behind her in the schoolhouse someone moaned and called for water. She heard the splash of vomit hitting the floor.

A man could shoot a squirrel out of a tree from a distance of sixty feet. But he couldn't vomit into a bucket or pee into a pot only two feet away. It was one of the great mysteries of life.

After sending a long look toward her tent, which she'd pitched above the creek near her diggings, she shoved herself off the doorjamb, pressed a hand to her eyes, then fetched the wheelbarrow and pushed the kettles into the schoolhouse. Before the stench hit her, she sniffed fish broth, which was not going to receive an enthusiastic reception, and venison stew, most of which would end in the vomit buckets.

"Stony Marks, get your butt back into that bed, or I'm going to break both your scrawny legs!"

A naked man oozing pus, with vomit dribbled down the front of his chest, had nothing to recommend him, she thought, disgusted. When this was over, she'd leave Piney Creek and go someplace where she hadn't seen half the male population naked and at their sick worst.

Like so many other things, prospecting wasn't working out for her. On the other hand, fortune was said to *favor fools, so maybe her turn was coming. Maybe some-thing good was waiting for her out there somewhere.*

"Time to move on," she muttered, giving the wheel-barrow a shove. There was nothing good waiting for her here.

Chapter 1

"Hip hip, hooray! Hip hip, hooray!"

Blushing furiously, Low Down scowled at the men saluting her and waving tin mugs of beer that Olaf had brewed for the occasion. As she'd never before been a guest of honor or been cheered, she didn't know how to respond or where to look or if she should raise her beer mug, too.

Feeling flustered, she turned her gaze down the mountainside toward the haze of smoke hanging above the ashes of the schoolhouse. Burning the school had been the first order of business; then everyone had climbed up to Olaf's cabin for a celebration dinner of fried trout and elk steaks, followed by spirited talk about rebuilding.

It was a gorgeous day to consider new beginnings. Blue gentian and thick clumps of purple aster spilled down the mountainside like jewels strewn among the boulders. Daisies danced along the valley bottom, chasing the creek, and the rabbit brush had spiked into golden bloom. High overhead an eagle circled against a bottomless sky, so graceful and wild and free that Low Down's chest ached to watch. Right now she wished that she, too, could fly so she could escape the speech it appeared that Billy Brown, Piney Creek's self-appointed mayor, was preparing to deliver.

Stepping up on Olaf's sagging porch, Billy pulled back his shoulders, thrust out his belly, and led the enthusiastic salute in Low Down's honor. If she'd known she would be cheered, if she had even suspected this would turn into the proudest day of her life, she would have bathed in the creek this morning and washed her hair and donned some clean duds for the occasion. Instead, the guest of honor wore an oversized men's shirt and denim trousers, neither of which were too clean, and mud-caked gum-rubber boots. While self-consciously stuffing a hank of hair up under her old hat, she noticed that everyone else had spiffed up.

Billy Brown wore an almost-new red flannel shirt under the bib of his overalls, and he'd combed his hair and trimmed his beard. In fact, all of her former patients were nearly as tidy as they had been before the women left camp at the beginning of the epidemic. It touched her that the men had done some laundry and combed some hair in her honor.

"First we need to thank Olaf Gurner for today's fine repast and for stepping up to the stove and feeding our sick after Jacob Jansen drowned," Billy Brown said, beginning his speechifying. A chorus of good-natured insults erupted, directed at Olaf's fish broth, followed by a round of hearty applause.

"There are sixty-four of us here today," Billy Brown continued, his expression turning sober. "Six weeks ago Piney Creek had a population approaching four hundred souls. Men were finding nuggets; this place was thriving. Then the scourge hit."

Along with the others, Low Down shifted to gaze down at the camp. The empty storefronts made her think of a ghost town. No music tinkled from the saloon doors. Even the assay office was boarded up. A light breeze chased a paper scrap across a trampled section of yellowing grass where campfires had burned before rows and rows of tents. Already wild roses had sprouted where the tents had been. Low Down turned back to Billy Brown with the sad conviction that Piney Creek would never fully recover from the epidemic.

Billy frowned at the bottom of his tin mug. "I guess you men and the men up there in the cemetery braved the pox and stayed for the same reason I did. To protect your claim."

Lifting his head, he stared hard at Low Down. "But one person stayed who didn't have to."

"Well, I had a claim to protect, too," Low Down murmured. It seemed that a guest of honor ought to be a bit modest.

"You ain't found enough gold dust to support a chipmunk," Jake Martin said, leaning to spit a stream of tobacco juice at an anthill. "You coulda left your claim without a backward glance."

"God heard our prayers and gave us an angel of mercy who didn't desert us in our darkest hour."

The breeze blowing off the high peaks felt cool against the heat of embarrassment rising in her cheeks. She wished Billy Brown would end his speech right here. At the same time she secretly hoped he'd say more good things. Compliments were as rare as finding a nugget in her pan. She remembered every one that had come her way.

"This person stepped forward to fill our desperate need at great risk to her own health and life."

"Well . . ." A guest of honor ought to tell the whole truth even if it put a dent in Billy's speech. "I had the pox as a kid, and someone said you can't get it twice."

Coot Patterson rolled his eyes, then glared at her. "Nobody knows that for sure. Maybe it's true, and maybe it ain't. The point is, you stayed and took care of us when you didn't have to and nobody expected you to. Now shut up and quit kicking at the nice words ole Billy is saying."

"Will you people stop butting into my speech?" Billy Brown snapped. "Now, where was I? All right. Everybody here knows I'm talking about Low Down. If she hadn't fed you, cleaned you, nursed you, most of you would be pushing up grass right now. There weren't no other volunteers, that's for sure."

The cheers almost deafened her, and she didn't know what to do with her hands or where to turn her eyes, and her lips were twitching in a peculiar way. Being a guest of honor was a nerve-wracking affair.

"There's no way to adequately repay you for sticking by us and keeping most of us alive. But every man here agrees that we won't rest until we've expressed our gratitude. We want to do something for you, Low Down. Something big and something nice. Something as important and lasting as what you did for us. So you tell us what you want, and by damn it's yours. Anything at all, you just name it."

Heads nodded, and the men gathered in front of Olaf Gurner's cabin smiled appreciation at her and waited. Cheeks flaming, Low Down waved her beer mug in a gesture of dismissal.

"Hell, boys, I just did what anyone would do, that's all." She tugged the ragged brim of her old felt hat and fidgeted beneath the weight of so much unaccustomed attention. "You've thanked me enough. I never had a party in my honor, and I'll remember this all my life."

"No, sir, a party isn't near enough." Stony Marks pushed forward. "You worked like a dog. You fed us, washed us, forced that vile medicine down our throats. By sheer force of will you made some of us live who would have died if you hadn't bullied us, threatened us, maybe sweet-talked some of us that I don't know about." He waited for the hoots and chuckles to die down. "But we couldn't have survived if it hadn't been for you, and that's a fact. There must be something you've always dreamed about and wanted. Maybe something you never expected to get. We want to give it to you. We owe you."

Now Frank Oliviti stepped forward, gratitude soften-ing his wrinkled gaze. "First, I want to thank you for not stealing my gold like you threatened." Low Down grinned, waiting out the laughter. "If you want a house instead of that ratty little tent you got, we'll build you a fine cabin and furniture to go with it. Whatever you want, it's yours."

"If you've always hankered for a pi-ano, we'll go to Denver, buy one, and haul it up here," Billy Brown agreed. "You just tell us your fondest wish, no matter what it is, and we'll make it come true."

Max McCord was next to urge her to accept their gratitude. "Maybe you always wanted to stay in the finest hotel in Denver and eat oysters and drink cham-pagne in a suite. You just say so, Low Down, and we'll make that dream happen."

He didn't look like the same man she'd fed and washed and browbeat. Today Max McCord was so handsome that the sight of him made her feel peculiar inside, like her stomach was on fire. Frowning, she noticed the pox had left a few pits along his jawline, but he wasn't as scarred as some or as vain as the men growing beards to hide the marks. He was clean-shaven, his dark hair trimmed to collar length, and he wore fresh denims and a plaid wool shirt that was almost the same blue as his eyes.

It was while she was staring at Max McCord and wondering about the hot, uncomfortable tightness in her stomach that the idea came to her. There was only one thing in the world that she really, really yearned to have. She doubted it was the kind of thing the prospec-tors had in mind, but they were urging her to name her fondest wish. They wanted her to have something spe-cial that she'd never expected to get. But . . .

Preacher Jellison walked up beside her and hooked his thumbs under his suspenders. "These are proud men who owe an honest debt, and they won't rest until they've repaid you. So let them," he advised. "Everybody wants something, Low Down. Now's your chance to have it."

Squinting, she gazed down at the sunlight glittering on the serpentine surface of the river coiling through the valley. This morning she'd seen a family of foxes at the water's edge. The kits were summer-grown, almost ready to leave for territory and dens of their own.

"There is one thing," she said finally. Pulling a hand down her face, she tried to steady her thoughts. "But I don't think . . ."

"Let the men decide. Whatever you want, no matter how far-fetched you think it is, you've earned it, and these men are committed to giving it to you."

Sudden hope, hot and fierce, struck her with enough force that she swayed on her feet, feeling light-headed. Everyone was saying that all she had to do was ask and her dream would come true. This was her chance, maybe the only chance she would ever have. And like the old saying went: If you don't ask, you won't receive.

Billy Brown had been watching, and he knew when she made up her mind. A broad smile widened his beard. "Shut up, everyone. She knows what she wants. What's it going to be, Low Down?"

"I don't know about this," she said in a low voice to Preacher Jellison. He smiled, squeezed her arm, and urged her to state her wish.

Oh Lord. Well. This opportunity wasn't going to knock twice. Squaring her shoulders, she drew a deep breath and felt the fires in her stomach burn hotter. An expectant hush stilled the men's voices, and they looked at her with encouraging smiles.

"I want a baby."

"Excuse me?" Preacher Jellison stepped back and stared.

"A baby. That's what I want."

Dead silence met her announcement.

She heard leaves rustling on the aspens, heard the

crash of utensils against plates as Olaf dropped a pile of dishes. The silence was so complete that Low Down imagined she heard ants digging tunnels, imagined she could hear her hair growing.

Billy Brown pulled his hat from his head and raked stubby fingers through the thin strands that lay like fence pickets across his scalp. "Well." He glanced at the men staring at Low Down with blank expressions. "This here is a surprise, but nothing we can't handle. Right, boys?" He thought a minute. "There must be some orphans in the camps. We could—"

"No, I don't want someone else's baby. I want a baby of my own." At least no one was laughing at her.

"Aw hell, Low Down." Frank Oliviti frowned. "Are you saying you want one of us to . . . ?" A mottled red flush climbed the back of his neck, and he kicked at a clump of columbines. "Damn it. Are you sure you wouldn't rather have a bag of gold?"

She hadn't peered into a mirror in months, but judging from the way every man took a step backward, she decided she must look like hell. And she wasn't a beauty to start with. Nevertheless, she hadn't expected them to be so appalled at the prospect of bedding her. It was damned insulting, that's what it was.

Who the hell were they to be so particular? She'd seen most of them buck naked, and she didn't recall grabbing her heart and swooning over any perfect sculpturelike bodies.

"You asked what I wanted, and I told you," she said, raising her chin and narrowing her eyes. "If you didn't mean what you said, that's fine. I didn't expect anything anyway." She glanced at the angle of the sun. "Let's finish our beer and go back to the diggings. We've still got a few hours of good work light."

"Now, just hold it a minute." Billy Brown faced the men from Olaf's porch and raised his hands. "All right, boys, this ain't what we expected." A chorus of low swearing erupted. "But we did mean what we promised." A threat glittered in his gaze. "We voted on this. We agreed we'd give Low Down whatever she wanted. We made a commitment, and by damn, that hasn't changed."

A rumble of muttering and mumbling rose and fell, then silence returned. A resigned voice inquired, "So what happens next? How do we decide who has to do it?"

"A volunteer would simplify matters a whole lot." Billy skimmed a hopeful eye over the men, none of whom would look at her. "Do we have a volunteer?"

When no one stepped forward, Low Down felt a wave of heat flood her cheeks. Even her eyes felt hot. "To hell with all of you," she shouted, twisting pride and humiliation into a knot of anger. "I don't want to sleep with any of you either, so just forget it!" She'd never felt so offended in her life.

Worse, she had relied on the wrong proverb. The one she should have remembered stated: Promises are like piecrusts, made to be broken. They hadn't meant it when they told her to pick the thing she wanted most and she could have it.

Preacher Jellison grabbed her arm as she spun to storm down the mountain and back to her tent. "Let me go!"

This was no longer her proudest day. All she wanted to do now was pack up her few belongings, get out of Piney Creek, and pretend these last minutes of stupidity on her part and insult on their part had never happened.

Preacher Jellison held her at arm's length, keeping his body away from her kicking feet and flailing fist. "Shame on you, gentlemen. The angel of mercy who put herself in grave peril to save your worthless hides . . . ." Pausing, he took a minute to stare into the unhappy gaze of every man present. ". . . wants a baby."

Billy Brown rose to the occasion. "And by God one of us is going to give her one," he promised grimly, speaking between clenched teeth. "We are going to re-pay the debt we owe. Aren't we, boys?"

They looked at her now, sliding sidelong glances of speculation in her direction before they looked up at Billy Brown again. A long sigh of resignation skittered down the mountainside like an ill wind.

Stony Marks stepped forward. "I think Low Down is a good-hearted woman, and she might be right tolerable if she was cleaned up some," he said gamely. "But much as I'd like to honor our debt and do my part to repay her for keeping my butt alive, I can't be the man who does the poking. I'm married." He looked to Preacher Jellison to back him up. "It wouldn't be right to ask a married man to sin against his innocent wife."

"Well, damn. He's got a point, Billy." Preacher Jellison tightened his iron grip on Low Down's arm. She tried, but she couldn't pry off his fingers.

"Damned if he don't," Billy Brown agreed unhappily. "But we can cope with this development. You married men step over there beside the big spruce." He counted the bachelors remaining in front of Olaf's porch steps. "All right. We got twenty-three contenders."

"We got twenty-four," Jack Hart said sharply. "Mc-Cord, get over here. You ain't married."

Max McCord appealed to Billy Brown and Preacher Jellison. "I'm as good as, since I'm pledged to marry in two weeks, and I'm leaving tomorrow."

"Yeah, well, you ain't wed yet. You wouldn't even be alive to think about getting married if Low Down hadn't nursed your sorry butt back to life. So get on over here with the rest of us!"

For the span of a heartbeat, Low Down thought Mc-Cord would refuse. Since she'd read his letter to Miss Philadelphia Houser, she would have understood. But he marched forward with a frown and joined the men waiting in front of the steps. The bachelors glared at the married men, who had helped themselves to more beer

and who grinned back. Then everyone scowled up at
Billy Brown, waiting for whatever would happen next.

"I'm asking one last time for a volunteer," Billy Brown
said in a coaxing tone.

The only thing Low Down heard was her own teeth
grinding together as she considered taking a bite out of
Preacher Jellison's arm and breaking free. To hell with
them all.

Except she wanted a baby. And they had promised.

"It isn't you," Albie Davidson said, spreading his arms
and giving her an apologetic look. "Well, it's you, but
what I mean is, I just can't think of you as a woman.
You're one of us, you know? One of the boys."

"You're all bastards," she shouted, struggling to jerk
free of Preacher Jellison's grip.

Preacher Jellison hissed at her. "This is what you want.
Now stop fighting and take whatever you're given. The
Lord works in mysterious ways."

She couldn't argue with that. Because the Lord had
sent an epidemic down on Piney Creek, she had a chance
to get the one thing she longed for. That is, if one of
these bastards agreed to sleep with her and if she could
stomach sleeping with him. At the moment, that was a
big if. She hated them all. But she reckoned she'd put up
enough of a fight to appease her injured pride so she
didn't stomp off in a huff when Preacher Jellison released her.

"Hold everything," Preacher Jellison called suddenly,
his gaze going sharp. "What did I just hear?"

Billy Brown sighed. "Albie is going to place twenty-
four marbles in a hat. I'll scratch an X on one of them.
Whoever draws the marble with the X has to poke Low
Down."

Preacher Jellison strode forward, his florid face clamping into a thunderous expression. He climbed up to Olaf's
porch and elbowed Billy Brown aside.

"What are you pathetic sinners thinking of? You don't

thank God for sparing your lives by committing a sin with His angel of mercy. No sir! I won't stand for that, and neither will the Almighty. Whoever draws that marble with the X marries this woman! I'm warning you. Anything less than marriage is just begging God to smite you with disaster. God didn't save your butts to have you spit on His commandments!"

"Oh my gawd," Billy Brown said, staring in disbelief. "Marry her? Lord A'mighty, this just gets worse and worse."

"Now wait a damned minute," Low Down shouted over the roar of protest. Shock widened her eyes. "I never said anything about marrying or a husband! All I want is a baby!" Preacher Jellison was turning this into something she'd never intended and didn't want. Shouting to get his attention, she fought to be heard. "No husband. Just a baby!"

The preacher pulled a worn Bible from his jacket pocket and waved it above his head for all to see. "Would you offend God by heaping sin on your angel of mercy?" He flung a pointing finger at Low Down.

"Honestly, I don't mind having a little sin heaped on me. Just enough to get a baby, and I don't think God would object to that too much. I don't want to do this if it means getting married. I just want a baby, that's all." Her voice trailed when she realized no one was listening. All attention was focused on the preacher.

"Does this good woman's child deserve to be born a bastard? Is there any son of a bitch here who truly believes that piling sin and shame on this woman and her child is the way to thank her? Is that your idea of expressing gratitude to the woman who saved your miserable lives?" Contempt curled his lip.

"Listen, on second thought, a pi-ano would be real nice," Low Down said loudly. She didn't know how to play a piano and had no place to keep one, but those problems could be worked out.

No one paid her a lick of attention. Preacher Jellison was gathering momentum and working up a lather, holding his audience spellbound with the thunder of his voice and the weight of his listeners' increasing guilt. By the time the last echo resounded off the opposite valley wall, the married men were in a fury of righteous indignation, shouting insults at the bachelors, castigating them as selfish weaseling ingrates who were going to call down the wrath of God on everyone if they didn't do right by the poor self-sacrificing woman who had risked her life to save theirs.

No fool he, Billy Brown seized the moment to pass the hat containing the marbles and every man in the single group glared at the married group, then did his duty and withdrew a colored glass ball. One after another they examined their marble, then headed for the beer barrel with a grin of relief.

Except Max McCord.

McCord stood as if he'd put down roots, staring at the green glass in his palm. All around him men slapped each other on the back, made jokes, and looked around to see who had drawn the marble with the X.

When Low Down couldn't bear McCord's frozen silence another minute, she turned her back on him and faced down the mountain. She hadn't expected that anyone would jump for joy to discover the scratched marble in his hand. She wasn't happy either. But she had secretly hoped the man she ended with wouldn't look as shocked and stricken as Max McCord.

She had mixed feelings about him. Part of her felt sympathetic that he wouldn't be able to marry the woman he loved. He had to marry her instead. Events had spiraled so far out of control there was no stopping them now. Preacher Jellison had everyone churned up and eager for a wedding. No one cared that she and McCord didn't want this.

Frowning down the mountainside, she thrust a hand

into her trouser pocket and closed her fingers around the copy of Max McCord's letter that she had written out from memory. She didn't know why she'd copied his letter. Well, yes she did. She liked to read it and pretend that someone had sent this letter to her. McCord had some beautiful words inside of him.

"Gather around, and somebody bring the bride and groom up front."

"We have to do it right this minute?" Low Down would have at least liked to wash her face and comb her hair. But the men cared only about repaying their debt right now in case God was watching and prepared for swift retribution if they faltered, and in case McCord might be tempted to shirk his duty if they permitted any delay.

McCord continued to stare at the marble like it was a miniature crystal ball revealing a future that sucked the marrow from his bones.

Coot Patterson and Stony Marks each took one of McCord's arms and dragged him forward. Frank Oliviti and Jake Martin led Low Down through the crowd. She felt as if she ought to say something to McCord, but she didn't know what. He looked dazed anyway, and probably wouldn't have heard anything she said.

She felt a little dazed herself and suddenly nervous. She wet her lips and rubbed her palms along her trouser legs. Damn, she wished she'd washed this morning and had put on some clean long johns and a better shirt. She wished things hadn't gone this far. She was going to regret the husband part, she just knew it.

"Wait a minute." Billy Brown pushed to the front, twisting a gold ring off his little finger. He thrust it into McCord's hand. "This belonged to my mother. It's for the bride," he added when McCord frowned like he didn't understand why he was looking down at a gold ring.

"Take off your hats and quit talking." Billy gave the men a hard stare and followed with a hint. "McCord's doing the hard part, carrying the major thrust of our gratitude, so to speak. But the rest of us ought to do something. Like chip in to help the happy couple set up housekeeping. Keep in mind what we all owe Low Down. And we also owe McCord for taking this like a man. Remember that it could have been you saying the 'I do's,' so give generously."

Preacher Jellison waited for the muffled guffaws to ebb, then he smiled at Low Down as if this whole wedding had been her idea instead of his, as if she and McCord were indeed a happy couple who sought his blessing on a joyful event. She seriously considered punching him in the stomach, but he began the ceremony before she'd made up her mind about doing it.

"Dearly beloved, we are gathered here together in the presence of these witnesses . . ."

It didn't take long to bind a man and woman together for the rest of their lives. In less than five minutes Preacher Jellison smiled and said, "I now pronounce you man and wife. You may kiss the bride."

Low Down and Max McCord reluctantly turned and stared hard at each other. Then McCord spun on his heels, walked through the crowd of men and continued on down the mountainside.

Low Down pushed her fists into her pockets and watched him stride away. She didn't really care if he kept going, jumped on his horse, and rode out of here. Getting married was a mistake that neither of them had asked for.

Fingering the letter in her pocket, she watched until McCord reached his diggings and ducked inside his tent, dropping the flap behind him.

She should have settled for the bag of gold or the stupid piano.

Thrusting out her hand, she squinted at the ring, bright and shiny against her sun-dark skin. Well, whatever happened, she'd keep the ring. They'd convinced her that she deserved something for emptying all those vomit buckets.

But she'd really wanted a baby, someone to love who would love her back. A real family of her very own. Like an idiot, she'd let herself get her hopes up.

"Olaf? Isn't it time to break out the whiskey? The bride needs a stiff drink. And I want to hear more about that generous chipping-in part."

No sense crying over spilled milk. She might as well have a few drinks, hear a few prospecting stories, and enjoy what was left of her wedding day.

Chapter 2

Max scrawled his name, then shoved a handful of pages into an envelope and set aside the plank he'd been using as a writing desk. The floor of his tent was littered with earlier drafts of the hardest letter he'd ever written, evidence of a long and difficult night. Sitting on the side of his cot, he rubbed his eyes, then stared at the wadded paper balls.

Someone had been fated to draw the scratched marble, that was a given, but he hadn't believed it would be him. His life was planned. Searching for gold had satisfied a long-time curiosity, but largely it had been a last hurrah before settling down, a summer fling with adventure while he could still indulge such whimsy without affecting anyone else.

Digging his fingers into his scalp, he swore and kicked at the wadded balls.

Everything he wanted had been within his grasp.

Ironically, if the celebration at Olaf's cabin had taken place twenty-four hours later, he would have missed it. He would have been riding toward the front range and an assured future. He had delayed his departure for a day he really couldn't spare from a sense of obligation to toast the woman who had saved his life. That simple decision had led to his betrayal of Philadelphia and the destruction of their lives and happiness.

"McCord? Are you in there?" Preacher Jellison kicked at the tent flap.

He pulled a hand down his jaw, feeling stubble and the effects of no sleep on top of a belly full of rot-gut whiskey. The last person he wanted to see was Jellison.

"McCord?"

"What the hell do you want?"

"I can go inside or you can come outside. What'll it be?"

The air inside his small tent was close and sour, dense with oily smoke from the lantern next to his cot. Swearing beneath his breath, he threw open the flap and stepped into the crisp mountain sunshine, blinking against the morning glare.

His tent sat atop a knoll above his diggings, about thirty feet from the creek bank. Last night he'd sold his claim to Coot Patterson for a jug of home brew, the worst stuff he'd ever swallowed. Holes burned in his stomach, and his head was filled with ricocheting cannonballs.

"If you weren't a preacher, I'd tear you apart piece by piece," he said on his way past Jellison.

Bending at the sandy edge of the creek, he scooped water into his hands and splashed his face and throat, letting icy drops roll down under the collar of his shirt. Then he rinsed the taste of rot-gut out of his mouth and spat.

"Would you feel any better if all you had to do was get Low Down with child and then abandon her? You don't impress me as that kind of man."

Standing, he dried his hands on his shirt, gazing downstream at the men standing in water and whirling their pans or rocking their sluices.

"All right," Jellison said to his back. "Maybe everybody rushed into a situation instead of chewing it over first. But don't forget that you're alive because Low Down was the only person willing to care for you when you were throwing up your guts and raving out of your mind."

"The same could be said about three-quarters of the

men left in Piney Creek. But it was me who had to marry her." The crazy injustice of it clawed at his chest. "We never agreed that one man would pay the price for everyone. That wasn't part of our decision."

"No, it wasn't. But it's done. Can't go back and change things now."

They stood beside the rushing water, listening to the calls and curses of the men working the creek banks. "I was going to be married in two weeks," Max said. "Two weeks later, I would have taken a lucrative position in the Fort Houser bank."

"Well." Jellison frowned down at his boots. "You can still be a banker, I guess."

"I doubt Mr. Houser will welcome me into his bank when he learns I've jilted his daughter."

The situation was unbelievable. Honor and duty were his guiding principles. This close to the wedding, he would have married Philadelphia if he had detested her because a man didn't renege on his promises, didn't humiliate a woman. In the time it took to draw a marble out of a hat, he had destroyed his good name, humiliated Philadelphia, shamed two families, and caused a scandal that would reverberate in Fort Houser for as long as he lived.

"In retrospect, maybe we should have let you stand with the married men," Jellison conceded.

Throughout the night, friends and acquaintances had stopped by his tent to state the same second thoughts. But no one had said it at the time, when it would have counted for something.

"Things don't always work out like we believe they ought to, son. The Lord works in mysterious ways."

Only the Bible dragging at the pocket of Jellison's frock coat saved the preacher's bones from taking a beating. Yesterday hadn't been the Lord's doing, it had been Jellison whipping everyone into a froth.

"Make no mistake, McCord, in the eyes of God, you

and Low Down are married. That was a real wedding. It's a shame about that other young lady, but now you have a duty to do right by the wife you got."

Eyes glittering, Max leaned over the preacher, itching with the need to bloody his knuckles on Jellison's face. "Don't lecture me about duty." He started to walk away, but Jellison's sharp voice stopped him.

"There's something you need to know. Low Down ain't much to look at, and she's rough as a cob. But she's a good woman. Honest and hardworking. A lot of women with no family and no advantages might have taken to the cribs, but not her. She's made her way with her hands, not on her back."

Low Down rose in his mind as he'd last seen her, standing beside him whispering her vows. Wearing a saw-brimmed hat leaking dirty hair, dressed in layers of shapeless, musty-smelling men's clothing. Her face had needed a wash along with the rest of her.

And then Philadelphia shimmered into memory, his beautiful lost Philadelphia. The fire burned hotter in his stomach, and his throat closed on a rush of bile.

"Low Down ain't just your wife's name, it's her condition. That woman has never had a lucky break, never had anything good handed to her. In my opinion, she deserves better than life's given her." Jellison waited for Max to inquire about Low Down's background, but he didn't. "Anyway, I'm hoping the something better is going to be you."

"There won't be any happily-ever-after, Preacher. Not for Low Down and not for me. Not for anyone." Nothing Jellison could say would make this situation any better.

Low Down hadn't figured in his thoughts throughout the long night, but maybe she'd had plans, too. Plans that didn't include being shackled to a stranger. There was a noose on both ends of the tie that binds.

"I only got one more thing to say. This situation ain't

Low Down's fault, so don't go blaming her. She didn't choose you. God put that marble in your hand. If you're fool enough to blame God and fight His plan, then good luck to you, son, because you're going to need it. Just don't go punishing someone else for something that isn't her fault."

Jellison didn't offer to shake hands before he strode away from Max's tent, and neither did Max. He lit his fire, hung a coffeepot over the flames, and stirred together a mess of biscuits.

The talk about fault went to the heart of the matter. He wanted someone to blame, someone he could pummel and punish for the catastrophe wreaked on him and Philadelphia and a future as sparkling as the sunshine striking diamonds off the surface of the creek.

But who? Granted, Billy Brown should have halted the proceedings and called another meeting to discuss the twist their gratitude had taken. But Max couldn't imagine any man stating that he'd rather Low Down had let him die than poke her. In the end, they would have agreed that someone had to give her a baby.

Jellison made him the maddest because he'd introduced marriage. But naturally a preacher would insist on marriage. It could be argued that Jellison would have been derelict in his duty if he hadn't raised the specter of sin and damnation.

Low Down? She had set a train in motion, impossible to halt once the wheels began to grind. But everyone present, including himself, had urged her to name whatever she wanted most. No one had mentioned any restrictions. No one had added, "as long as what you want is reasonable."

Standing abruptly, Max ground his teeth together and glared down at the skillet of burning biscuits. A terrible wild darkness filled his chest with an intolerable pressure that would burst through his skin if he didn't do something. Losing control, he kicked the skillet off the flames, kicked it down the incline and kept kicking until the pan sailed hissing into the creek.

Then he jammed shaking hands into his pockets and discovered he still had the green marble. Holding it to the sunlight, he swore and ran his thumb over the scratched X that had made a jilted bride out of Philadelphia and a bastard out of him.

In the end, this small glass marble was all he had to blame. The utter ridiculousness of it struck him hard and stopped him from flinging the marble into the rushing creek. He rolled it between his fingers and finally decided he would keep it.

Whenever he was arrogant enough to believe that he was the master of his fate, or anytime he became so puffed up as to think he might deserve a little happiness in life, he would look at the green marble as a reminder that he was wrong.

When he could finally bring himself to do it, he went in search of his new bride. The men he passed gave him a thumb's up sign or a nod of sympathy but none met his eye directly. He understood. In their shoes, he would have felt uncomfortable, too, that one man bore the burden for all. There was some satisfaction in knowing the men recognized the injustice that had been done him.

He might have walked past Low Down's claim, mistaking her for a man, if he hadn't recognized the clothing she'd worn yesterday. Halting at the top of the rise, he crossed his arms over his chest and silently took stock of the stranger who was now his wife.

First, she gave no indication that she knew he was present, indicating she was neither observant nor cautious. A kinder viewpoint might have been to grant her a high level of concentration and intent focus. She stood at the edge of the creek, squatting over the water, swirling her pan just beneath the surface to wash away dirt and loose matter. When she raised the pan to pick out rocks and gravel, he saw that her hands were red from the icy water and rough-looking even from a distance.

Philadelphia's small hands were white and soft, the nails beautifully shaped and buffed to a pink sheen.

Low Down's ugly hat shaded her neck and face from the sun and a cloud of mosquitoes, but one long coil of gray-brown hair swung down the back of her wool vest. With something of a shock, Max realized the grayish color was mud and dirt. Heaven only knew what color her hair might be when it was clean.

The night before he'd left for the mountains, he had stood on Philadelphia's steps and watched the light from the porch lamp cast a golden halo around her curls. Her skin and hair had smelled like roses.

Blinking, he watched Low Down examine her pan and poke a finger at the sandy residue. With a sound of disgust, she tossed it out, then stood, stretched, and reached for a shovel to refill the pan with a new load of hope.

She was tall, something he hadn't really noticed yesterday, only three or four inches shorter than he, which made her about five foot eight. Not small and delicate like Philadelphia.

"How long you going to stand there gawking? I thought you were leaving today," Low Down said. She hadn't looked at him once and didn't now.

So she wasn't as unobservant as he'd supposed. He also noticed the Colt strapped to her waist and realized she wasn't incautious either. Dropping his arms to his sides, he walked down to the water's edge and inspected her sluice. She'd set it up efficiently, but he didn't notice much color glittering along the ridges. A little dust maybe, but no nuggets.

"We'll leave in the morning." He wanted his letter to reach Fort Houser before they arrived. "I figure we'll ride out at sunup."

She squatted over the water again and plunged her

pan beneath the surface. "We? Come on, McCord. You ain't taking this marriage seriously, are you?" She made a derisive sound at the back of her throat. "Everybody knows the ceremony was a sham." She concentrated on swirling her pan as if the matter was closed and there was no more to say.

"The wedding was real, and you know it," he stated in a flat voice. "Like it or not, you and I are married."

She didn't look up immediately, but she stopped circling the pan and she lifted her hands out of the icy water, making sure he noticed that she wasn't wearing the ring Billy Brown had provided. "Go home to Miss Houser," she said in a low voice. "Just ride out of here. Neither of us wants to be married, so just go."

He leaned against a granite boulder facing the willows and cottonwoods crowding the opposite bank, and he wished to Christ that he could do what she suggested.

"And do what? Marry Miss Houser and make a bigamist out of myself?" And then spend the rest of his life living in fear of exposure and dreading what the truth would do to Philadelphia and their families and any children they might have if the marriage to Low Down ever came back to bite him.

She rocked back on her heels, dipping her butt in the cold water, and she glared up at him with hazel eyes that were an odd mixture of green and brown.

"We're married," he said again. Maybe if he said it enough times, he'd start to actually believe it. "We have to decide where we go from here."

"For starters, I'm not going anywhere with you." Standing up, she slapped at the water dripping off the butt of her trousers, then she picked up her shovel and leaned on the handle. "Don't get me wrong, McCord, I've got nothing against you. I just don't want the aggravation of a husband, not you or any other man. Plus, you already have a wife lined up and waiting. She doesn't have to ever know what happened yesterday."

She waved one red-cold hand. "Or, if you think you need to, ride up to Wyoming and petition for a divorce."

Work had slowed all along the creek, and the men found reason to face in the direction of Low Down's claim. Those down wind made no pretense about straining to overhear the conversation. The noise of shovels and voices had ceased.

Max drew a breath. "It's not easy to obtain a divorce; very few are granted." He waited, then said the rest. "There's also a matter of duty." When she frowned, he realized he had to spell it out. "The men's gratitude. Their expectations."

"Oh. That." Her laugh was so false that he scowled. "Having a baby was a dumb idea." She smiled down at layers of men's clothing then tugged at the neck of the faded long johns bunched above her shirt collar. "Can you imagine me as a mother? Now that I've had time to think about it, neither can I."

Considering that he didn't know her at all, it impressed him as odd that he knew she was lying. But he'd watched her as she struggled to decide whether to ask for the one thing she wanted most. She wanted a baby and had wanted one for a long time.

He pinched the bridge of his nose between his thumb and forefinger. Unbelievably, not only had he been forced to marry this woman, but now he found himself in the ludicrous position of having to persuade her to honor their vows.

"Low Down . . ." He let the words trail, wondering if she had a real name. "I'll go to my grave resenting what happened yesterday. But I agreed that you deserved whatever you wanted as a token of our gratitude. And I put myself in the group of men who would draw a marble out of the hat." In retrospect, stepping forward had been the deciding act of his life. And the stupidest. "It's important to the men you saved that you have that baby. And they expect me, as a man of honor, to do what I agreed to do." He flat could not believe he was saying this. His voice hardened. "If you've changed your mind about a baby, or if it was a frivolous choice, then damn you." He stared at her. "Your foolishness wrecked several lives."

Her mouth dropped open, then snapped shut, and she studied him intently. "Are you saying you intend to give me a baby?"

"That's my duty." Thrusting his hand into his pocket, he curled his fingers around the green marble and gripped it so hard that he felt the curve bruise the bones of his palm. "A McCord does not shirk his duty."

"Well, I'll be a son of a bitch!" Rubbing her cheek, she considered him with a thoughtful expression. Once the idea took hold, she flicked a hopeful glance toward her tent, and Max hastily raised a hand.

"Not right this minute," he said quickly in case that's what she was thinking. At the moment, he couldn't imagine ever desiring this scruffy woman. But even if she'd been beautiful and perfumed, a sloe-eyed temptress, he couldn't conceive of bedding her at noon-day with sixty-plus men watching and listening. Frowning at the men lining the creek banks, he imagined a slump of disappointment rippled through the ranks, and wondered uneasily how much of this discussion they could overhear.

"Well, then when?"

"When the time is right," he hedged, having no idea when that might be. But it wasn't now.

She nodded slowly, thinking it over. "All right. I guess we're stuck anyway, so I might as well get a baby out of the deal. What I said earlier—" she waved a hand "—I was just jawing. I really do want that baby. But I don't want a husband. Could we agree to this? Once I get pregnant, we're both off the hook. You go your way then, and I go mine. We're quits."

The baby was the crux of the matter for both of them, not the marriage which neither wanted. Already

Max's mind had leapt ahead, feverish with hope that Philadelphia would understand the circumstances and wait for him to arrange a divorce.

No, she wouldn't.

Low Down lifted the shovel handle and poked the bucket at the ground. A pink flush traveled up her throat. "How long do you think it will take to get me pregnant?"

Philadelphia would have chosen a euphemism instead of saying pregnant straight out. But Philadelphia was a refined lady. Low Down was about as refined as her muddy, shapeless gum-rubber boots.

Uncomfortable with the question, Max rubbed his chin, fingering the pox marks along his jaw in a gesture that was becoming habitual. "I don't know."

"I mean, how many times does it take?" From the corner of his eye, he noticed her cheeks had caught fire and were now as scarlet as her hands. "How many times do we have to, you know, do it?" Throwing down the shovel, she planted her fists on her hips and swung away from him. "I'm trying to ask if we can get this done before you leave so I don't have to leave with you."

Oh Lord. Feeling inadequate for this conversation, he covered his eyes, then dragged his fingers down his face. It hadn't occurred to him that she'd be an innocent. As if she'd guessed his thoughts, she whirled around and narrowed her eyes into slits.

"I've been with a man, and I'm not as stupid as you're probably thinking. But it was a long time ago, and I didn't ask about babies or how many times it took to get one. And I've never known a woman well enough to ask such a thing."

He hadn't believed her face could get redder, but she suddenly looked as if she had a severe sunburn. Feeling the heat in his own throat, he suspected he looked the same. Standing away from the boulder, he hooked his thumbs in his back pockets and focused hard on the water rushing past his feet.

He cleared his throat loudly. "Do you know how to tell if you're pregnant?"

"Well, of course," she snapped. "I do know that much."

"Getting pregnant has nothing to do with how many times two people, ah, do it." He cleared his throat again. "Sometimes it only takes once. Sometimes months and months can pass." He didn't want to consider that possibility.

Hopefully, she'd be more appealing after a bath and a hair wash, and when she was dressed in a clean, frilly nightshift. Sliding a sidelong glance toward the spot where she was pacing along the creek, he tried to peer past the baggy loose clothing she wore. Then he swore between his teeth. He couldn't believe he was even thinking about taking her to bed. "In fact," he muttered, hating it, "most of the time getting pregnant takes a while."

"Damn," she said unhappily. "So there's no choice, I have to leave with you. Well, hell." She kicked the side of her sluice. "I had plans."

The sour burn of bitterness squelched any reply he might have made.

"So. Where are we going? South, I hope?"

"West."

"That doesn't tell me anything."

"Fort Houser is about a four-hour trip by wagon out of Denver." The town had never been a fort, actually. Joseph Houser, Philadelphia's grandfather, had bestowed the name in hopes the army would take notice, build a stockade on the site, and protect his interests and holdings. The army had bypassed Fort Houser but so had marauding Indians. In the ensuing years, Joseph Houser's dream had blossomed into a growing, prosperous town.

"The winters get cold out there on the plains," Low Down commented sourly.

Now that he'd covered the basics, Max couldn't think of much more to say. He instructed her to be packed and ready to leave Piney Creek by six the next morning. She mentioned that she'd use the rest of the day trying to sell her claim, but she doubted anyone would buy it. He inquired if she needed assistance packing, and she stared at him as if he'd lost his senses.

"Well," he said after a minute. Pulling his watch out of his pocket, he consulted the time as if he had somewhere to go and something to do. "I guess I'll . . ."

She picked up her pan and carried it into the water, slapped at a mosquito on her throat, then squatted. "I caught a trout this morning, and I've got some wild onions to cook with it. You want to come to supper?"

Her back was to him, and her hat brim covered the nape of her neck and the sides of her face.

"I've already made plans," he said hastily, the lie stiff on his lips.

A shrug adjusted the long coil of dirty hair. "Suit yourself."

He'd climbed the incline before she glared over her shoulder and called up to him.

"McCord? Remember yesterday when I promised to obey? Well, I lied. I won't obey any man." She turned back to the creek and plunged her pan into the swiftly flowing cold water. "The other vows were lies, too."

Standing in the tall grass at the top of the bank, he watched for a moment, thinking what a strange creature she was.

Years ago when he'd been young enough to believe such matters lay within his control, he had described his future wife to his brother. She would be small and dainty and beautiful, blond and blue-eyed. Her nature would be as sweet as the scent of her hair and skin. She would be accomplished in the womanly arts and would entertain him in the evenings with music and song. Together they would make strong, handsome children.

He hadn't known it then, he thought, gripping the marble, or maybe he had, but he'd been describing Philadelphia.

Instead, he had married a woman as far from his ideal as it was possible to get.

Right now, "low down" described his condition, too.

Chapter 3

Low clouds hung in the valley folds, and ground mist floated around pines and brush creating a damp gray world that matched Low Down's mood when she stepped out of her tent.

Things were progressing as expected, which was to say that she had lost control of her life. In about an hour she would head west for no other reason than because that was where her new, unwanted husband wanted to go. Had he troubled himself to inquire if she had someplace she would rather go, like south? No, he had not. Had he explained why they had to travel west instead of heading somewhere warm for the winter? Well, she could guess that Philadelphia lived in her grandfather's town and Max wanted to see her, but he hadn't explained. Not a word. It was just pack up and be ready to leave at sunup.

Already she saw confirmation that she had to obey in certain matters, like it or not. If she wanted a baby, she had to follow wherever her husband's privates went, regardless of where she might want to go.

Swinging her leg back, she started to kick something on the ground but stopped in time when the mist swirled around her boot revealing that the object she'd been about to kick was not a stone. Sinking down on her heels, she discovered a speckled blue metal cup in almost-new condition. Just beyond the cup sat a coffeepot that hadn't been used enough to blacken the bottom. Next to

35

the pot were two clean bandannas hardly even faded. And then a real prize, a small pouch holding six fair-sized nuggets. The nuggets had to be from Frank, she guessed, blinking hard.

Between her tent and her campfire, she found a set of stirrups, a saddle blanket, a new hat with only one hole in it, a bone-handled comb with most of the teeth intact, a barely used toothbrush and a mostly full tin of tooth powder, a silver spoon, a pocket watch in a leather case, a pair of neatly mended wool socks, a well-thumbed songbook to add to her collection, and leather gloves in much better condition than her own.

And that wasn't all. Someone had started her fire and coffee and left her a skillet sizzling with fried venison and potatoes.

Clutching her treasures in her arms, Low Down sat on a log near the warmth of the fire and whispered a word of gratitude for the mist. It would have embarrassed her half to death to have anyone see tears in her eyes, and they would have seen because she sensed the men nearby in the chilly mist.

"Thank you," she shouted when she could trust her voice.

"You didn't have to do this. Chipping in at the wedding was more than enough." As far as she knew, Max wasn't aware of the pouch Billy Brown had presented her after Max had stomped away, and she didn't plan to tell him about it. "I'll think of you every time I use these wonderful things."

No one answered, but the mist seemed less gray and the sky brighter than it had a minute ago. When she sensed the men slipping away, she poured coffee into her new speckled cup and inspected her gifts one by one, taking her time to admire each item thoroughly. She wasn't a weepy woman, so it irritated her that her eyes kept fogging over, but hell, she couldn't recall the last time someone had given her a gift, and here she had more than a dozen.

The new hat went on her head and her old hat plopped on the fire. New socks replaced old. She carefully tucked the watch into her pocket, and she chose the least-faded bandanna to tie around her throat. Then, feeling very grand, she stirred a sugar cube into her coffee with the silver spoon, and afterward she meticulously polished the spoon on her shirttail before she tucked it safely into Frank's pouch of nuggets. She added the pouch to the leather cord tied around her neck, which already supported the chipping-in money and the gold dust she had panned out of Piney Creek.

After she washed her skillet and plate in the creek, she tested the toothbrush and enjoyed the luxury of tooth powder, something she'd been out of for a couple of weeks. The powder had a faintly peppermint taste that she liked a lot.

By the time Max showed up, just as the morning sun was burning off the ground mist, she'd finished attaching her gift stirrups and had slung the new saddle blanket over Rebecca's back.

"I thought you'd be ready by now," he remarked impatiently.

"Well, pardon me." She slid him a glance, trying to determine if he was looking over her belongings, figuring they were now his. On the other hand, it occurred to her that Max McCord might not think her paltry possessions worth claiming.

His hat was comfortably worn, but there were no holes and the brim was smooth. His denims weren't patched or thin in spots, nor were his jacket or waistcoat. His boots looked practically new. And his horse. Low Down had never owned a ride as fine as the mustang Max sat atop.

"What's her name?" she asked, admiring the shine of sunlight on the mare's fiery coat.

"Marva Lee. Are you ready to go?"

"You can see I still have to strap down my saddle-bags." And tie on her bedroll. The tent she would leave behind; maybe someone could use it. If events progressed the way they were supposed to, she'd be sharing Max's tent.

When she finished loading, she checked the site to see that she hadn't forgotten anything, then pushed back her hat and gazed down the slope at her diggings. A lot of hope had run through that sluice.

Tilting her head, she studied the sugary early snow frosting the high peaks, listened to the tumble and splash of the creek. Finally she dropped her gaze to the men pretending to work along the banks, pretending not to watch her and Max prepare to leave. Some of them she liked, some she didn't. But they'd always treated her squarely.

She cupped her hands around her mouth and shouted. "Good-bye all you gold grubbers! Just remember, I've seen you naked and none of you got do-diddle to brag about!" Laughter ran down the banks, and she grinned. "Strike it rich, boys!"

A chorus of good-luck wishes rolled down the creek banks and once again Low Down felt her throat getting tight and her eyes shiny. Damn it anyway. One era of her life was ending, and a new uncertain phase was beginning. She didn't know how she felt about any of it.

"Are you sure that mule can keep up?" Max asked from behind her.

"Rebecca's old, but she's like me. Sturdy, capable, and mean when riled." Low Down swung into the saddle. "Are you going to say good-bye to the boys?"

"I said my good-byes last night."

Drank them was more likely, Low Down thought, examining his bleary eyes and the paleness beneath his sun-darkened face. Men could do that. Sit and drink together without passing a sentence, then get up and go in the belief they had said all that needed to be said. Women required the words. But Max knew that, she suspected, pressing her hand against the pocket where she kept her copy of his letter.

Suddenly and for no reason at all she felt a surge of anger. "Well? What's the hold up? You know where we're going, so you'll have to lead off. I sure don't know where we're going. Nobody asked me about it. All I know is we're headed west, not south. I never heard of any place called Fort Houser, and I don't want to go there, but I have to because I'm married now, like it or damned not." She leaned a forearm on the saddle horn and returned the stare he was burning down on her. "So?"

"One thing," he said after a minute. "Did you bring the wedding ring?"

"I've got it." She wasn't going to reveal where she kept her valuables. Her long johns, shirt, vest, and jacket were bulky enough that he couldn't see the pouches tied beneath her clothing. He wouldn't even suspect.

"I'd appreciate it if you'd wear the ring from now on."

He phrased the request politely enough, but Low Down knew a command when she heard one, and she thought about that during the rest of the day as she and Rebecca followed him down rough-and-rugged terrain.

Since she had informed him that she would not obey, and she meant it, her instinct was to fling the wedding ring down a ravine so she could honestly announce that she no longer had the ring and thus couldn't wear it. But impulse was not her guiding principal. Proverbs were. And the proverb that applied here was probably: They that are bound must obey. Marriage came under: Act in haste, repent at leisure. God knew she was bound, and she was repenting.

When they stopped for the night, early enough that they still had light to set up camp, she thrust out her chin and asked why he wanted her to wear the ring

since neither of them considered their marriage anything close to the genuine article.

"The marriage is real all right," he said in a resigned
voice after he'd tethered Rebecca and Marva Lee to a
picket line and then returned to the fire Low Down had
started.

"Maybe I don't see it that way." Making coffee was
the first thing she did, even before she laid out her bedroll or thought about food. This time the coffee wouldn't
be much good since the gift pot was practically new and
you needed a seasoned pot for truly decent coffee. She
poured hers into the speckled blue cup and left Max to
get his own. No sense starting a bad habit by waiting
on his butt like she was a real wife.

He rolled up a log and sat across the fire from her.
"My family is going to expect that you'll be wearing a
wedding ring."

Low Down's hand jerked and boiling hot coffee
slopped unnoticed on her denims. "You have a family?"
She gaped at him. "And we're going to see them?"

"My family owns a ranch outside Fort Houser." For
a long moment he gazed into his coffee cup, then swallowed half the liquid. "My mother split the ranch into
quarters last year after my father died. My brother, Wally,
lives in the main house with my mother. My sister and
her family have a place about a mile south. My quarter
is north."

It hadn't entered her mind that he would have family
or that she would get to meet them. Or have to meet
them, as the case might be. This was a truism about husbands that she'd overlooked because she hadn't thought
about it at all. You married their families, too.

But . . . good Lord. Suddenly she sort of had a family.
The revelation amazed her.

"I've been thinking about this," Max said, frowning
at her across the flames blackening the bottom of the

new coffeepot. "You and I know what we've agreed to. But I doubt others would understand."

"You don't want your family to know we're going to divorce after I get pregnant," Low Down stated bluntly.

A flush of discomfort climbed his throat, or maybe it was only the flames reflecting on his skin. "I explained the circumstances in a letter to my mother, but I didn't mention a divorce as we hadn't agreed to that yet." He ground his teeth hard enough that knots ran up his jawline. "My family will expect us to treat this as a genuine marriage."

Picking up a stick, she jabbed at the fire. "What exactly does that mean?"

"We'll move into my house," he said, turning his head away from her. "And set up housekeeping."

The house he'd built for Philadelphia.

"My family will expect us to attend Sunday dinner, and other family events. They'll expect us to make the best of the situation and try to make a success of our marriage."

"We made our bed and now we have to sleep in it? Like that?"

He circled his coffee cup with his hands, his face turned toward the growing darkness beyond the fire. "I'll understand if you don't want to mount a pretense for the sake of my family. But I'd appreciate it if you would."

"We'd be living in a real house," she said, thinking about that. Her fingers dropped to the letter in her pocket, and she remembered everything he'd written. He had wanted to surprise Philadelphia with the house but hadn't been able to resist describing it. To Low Down, his description had made the house sound like a palace.

Living in a real house . . . she'd been camping out of a tent for so many years that the idea of a house enthralled her even if it had been built for another woman.

She thought about upholstered chairs and a mattress to sink into and maybe even rugs between her feet and the chill of a winter morning.

"My place is about three miles north of the main house. If you need advice about housekeeping chores, my mother and Gilly are both near enough to help."

Her chin stiffened. "Well, hell. I guess I can cook and scrub a floor without asking for instructions." Immediately she thought of the old saying about the devil wiping his buttocks with poor folk's pride, and she swallowed hard. "On the other hand, there might come a time when I could use a little guidance."

Years had passed since she'd done any housework. Maybe there were things she'd forgotten. Still, how would it look to Max's mother and sister, her new family, if she had to request assistance with chores they would assume every woman knew? What kind of impression would that make?

Dropping her head, she rubbed her forehead. How had she jumped from refusing to pour his coffee to wanting to impress his mother and sister? This was getting complicated.

"I'll cook our supper," she announced abruptly. She had intended to open a can of beans for herself and leave him to fend for himself. A small slap back for his refusal to share her trout last night. But this news about his family changed things. "It won't be anything fancy, just beans and bacon and biscuits."

"There's something else we need to discuss." This time there was no doubting the color rising in his face. He ran a glance over her, starting at the crown of her new hat and traveling down to her scarred, old riding boots. "I think we should stop for a day in Denver." Tilting his head, he studied the stars starting to poke holes in the sky. "I think we should buy you some dresses and hats. And give you a chance to have a bath and clean up a little."

Pride scratched her ribs, and her cheeks flamed. He was ashamed of her. Well, what did he expect? He hadn't plucked her out of some sweet-smelling parlor, after all. A mining camp didn't exactly offer the best facilities for cleanliness, and no one cared anyway.

More to the point, she thought suddenly, what would his mother and sister expect? She was beginning to form two definite impressions about her new family. First, their opinion mattered greatly to Max. And second, her newly acquired mother and sister were probably cultured ladies with fancy dresses, fancier manners, and high standards that Low Down couldn't possibly reach up to.

Her heart sank. If there was one thing worse than having no family at all, she suspected it would be having a family that was ashamed of her. A glimpse of the future flashed across the back of her mind, and it didn't feel good.

Well. Time flies. His fancy family wouldn't have to put up with her for long.

Silently she fetched her skillet and a slab of bacon and the biscuit fixings. She didn't say anything while she worked on supper. But she peeked at him, wondering if his family resembled him.

If so, the McCords were a handsome bunch. If she'd been the type of woman to swoon over a good-looking man, Max McCord would have been the man. She guessed she'd never shared a campfire with one who was better-looking. The summer sun had tanned his skin to a golden bronze that made his eyes seem bluer by contrast. His nose was thin above a wide stubborn mouth with sharply defined contours.

As she'd always thought of wrinkles as the punctuation marks of life, she studied his face carefully. The dashes radiating from the corners of his eyes suggested that he was a serious man, but the broad commas framing his mouth also told her that he could laugh.

The next thing of interest was his hands. Max's hands were hard and square, work hands, she noticed with satisfaction. She had work hands, too.

Finally she considered his overall impression, recalling the first time she'd noticed him. She hadn't been surprised to find him in a gold camp. He was tough enough to hold his own, not afraid of hard work. But there was also a hint of the dreamer about him, a man who could imagine gold in rushing water, who might see pictures in a puffy sky. A man who could describe a house to a woman and make it sound like a poem.

"I ain't worn a dress in years," she said, lowering her gaze to the balls of biscuit dough she was forming between her palms. "But I'll do it to please your ma. Is there any other damned thing you want to change about me, or are we finished with this?"

Standing, he placed his hands in the middle of his back and stretched. "You could stop swearing and saying ain't."

Oh she could, could she? She could also give him a demonstration of some real cussing, climb on Rebecca, and head south. Marriage wasn't something she'd asked for or wanted. Already she hated having a husband.

But she did want a baby.

And having a family was the best gift she could imagine. Even if the McCords turned out as she suspected they would, lofty and judgmental, still it would be wonderful to be able to say: "My family."

"You know, I just knew it would come to this." She jabbed a fork into the bacon slab and turned it over in the skillet, not caring that grease splattered into the flames. "You want to change how I look and how I talk and I don't know what all else. And I'll do all that, to get what I want. But maybe there's a few things about you that I don't like either."

"I imagine there's plenty of things you don't like about me," he said, walking into the deepening shadows to fetch their bedrolls. He flipped hers out on one side of the fire, and unrolled his on the other side. "I'm willing to make accommodations where I can, if I can. We should both remember that we only have to put up with each other for a short while."

"Well you can start by not behaving like this situation is all my fault." She dumped a large can of beans on top of the bacon. "I didn't make you pick the green marble. I wasn't even hoping that you would." Maybe that wasn't quite the unvarnished truth. Maybe she'd passed a thought that if she had to sleep with someone to get a baby, it would be nice to sleep with a man like him who was easy on the eyes.

"I'm not saying you're completely to blame, but no one ever imagined that you'd want a baby."

She glared through the darkness, unable to distinguish his tall frame from the surrounding pines. "You could have swallowed your pride and refused to draw from the hat." The others would have scorned him and made him feel like a welsher and about as tall as a cork, but he could have done it. Of course, no man worthy of the name would have.

He stopped at the edge of the firelight and his shoulders stiffened with offense. She noticed he clenched his fist around something in his pocket.

"Without honor and integrity, a man has nothing."

A long breath raised her chest. "All right, I guess you couldn't refuse. But that's not my fault."

"No it isn't," he agreed, surprising her. But his tone plainly stated it was her fault for wanting a baby in the first place.

"Look," she said, sounding and feeling defensive, "I'm sorry things worked out that you can't marry Miss Houser." Leaning to the fire, she spooned out beans and bacon and thrust a plate in his direction. And then she said something she hadn't planned, hadn't even known she was wondering about. "Do you love her a lot?"

"I would prefer not to discuss Miss Houser." He sat on the log and balanced the plate on his knees.

"I've never loved anybody, so I don't know much about that kind of thing." And it was none of her business. But to her irritation, she couldn't back off the subject. "Did you write a letter to Miss Houser, too?"

She didn't think he would answer, but he finally said, "That would be cowardly. I need to tell her about this in person." As if he'd lost his appetite, he pushed the beans around on his plate.

Low Down pushed the beans around on her plate, too. "I guess Miss Houser is going to be mighty upset."

Then, surprising her again, he told her about the bank position that would be withdrawn now. Privately, she thought that was probably a good thing. He didn't have a banker's hands.

"There will be a scandal. You and my family will suffer for it," he said, lifting his gaze to her. "I've jilted the daughter of Fort Houser's leading citizen less than two weeks before the wedding. I'm going to be labeled a son of a bitch, and you're going to be seen as an unscrupulous temptress. At least in the beginning."

Her eyebrows soared. "*Me?* A temptress?" It was the most thrilling thing she'd ever heard. And the most ridiculous. When she stopped laughing, she gave him a grin and a shrug. "Hell, I don't care what people think about me."

"I care. A man spends a lifetime building a reputation he can be proud of. Then, just like that, it's gone." He snapped his fingers. "That's a hard thing."

Tilting her head to one side, Low Down examined him across the campfire. The part of her that responded to people in need wanted to reassure him and make things right, but she didn't know how.

"The job at the bank . . . was it something you always wanted?" She tried to imagine him fancied up in a banker's frock coat and tall hat and couldn't pull the picture into her mind. But the way he sat on a horse and the tall lanky look of him fit her image of a rancher. She could easily visualize him bucking hay, riding fence lines, tending his land and stock.

He didn't answer, and she didn't push. "The beans are good enough," she commented after a period of silence. "But the bacon could have cooked a little longer."

They finished eating without speaking, then Max washed up the dishes in the stream beside their camp. He did it in a way that made Low Down think his mind had traveled miles into the distance. She thought hard; then, while his back was to her, she reached up under her shirt and vest and slipped the silver spoon out of the pouch.

When he returned to the fire, she glanced up at him and offered in a hesitant voice, "Would you like to see something pretty? It might make you feel better."

"What?" Frowning, he blinked down at her as if he'd forgotten about her until she spoke.

"Look." Holding out the spoon, she turned it between her fingers, delighted by the way the firelight reflected in the bowl as if she held a spoonful of fire. "Isn't it lovely?"

"It's just a spoon," he said without interest. Continuing past the campfire, he sat down on his bedroll and tugged at his boots.

Face flaming, Low Down hastily shoved the spoon into her pocket, then busied herself setting up the coffeepot for morning. How could she have been so stupid? He'd probably grown up eating off silver spoons. A silly old spoon wouldn't be anything pretty or wonderful to him.

"Max?" she called none too quietly once she was settled inside her own bedroll. "Are you asleep yet?" His name felt awkward on her tongue and entirely too familiar. But calling him Mr. McCord wouldn't have felt right, either.

"What is it?"

"I don't want to do this," she said, peering up at the stars. They were too different, too far apart in every way. "I think we should part company right now and go our separate ways. I don't want to meet your family; they won't like me. I don't want to live in another woman's house. I don't want to be married to you, and you don't want to be married to me."

"Don't you understand? It's too late."

"What if I just rode away? You could tell your family that I ran out on you."

"We'd still be married. Miss Houser and her father would still detest me. I'd be a shirker in the eyes of the men who trust me to repay you for saving our lives. They expect one good thing to result from this disaster." A long silence ensued. "If you really want to run off, I can't stop you. But when I step back from the personal consequences, I can say that you deserve the baby you want."

He'd surprised her again. On the other hand, considering his prickly feelings about duty and honor, she supposed she could understand why giving her a baby was important to him. He had said he would, and he'd made a commitment to the other men to see this through no matter what.

"You were right about me blaming you," he added, talking to the black sky the same as she was doing. "I agree that has to stop. While we're married we should at least treat each other cordially."

"I'm not a very cordial type," she admitted, thinking it over. A person who strewed roses usually stepped on thorns. She'd learned that lesson years ago. It was better to let people know right fast that she gave as good as she got. This wasn't exactly a cordial attitude.

"I've noticed. And right now you have no reason to believe that I'm cordial, either. But I think we'll get through this easier if we treat each other politely."

"What I know about polite wouldn't stuff a thimble."

His silhouette was just visible on the far side of the embers, arms crossed behind his head, his nose pointed toward the stars.

Low Down didn't speak again. Neither did she fall immediately asleep. Lying on her side, she watched the embers fade from orange to ashy and castigated herself for being so fricking wishy-washy. It was disgusting.

How many times had she insisted that it wasn't a real marriage or that she didn't want to be married, or suggested that he ride away or she ride away? And then at a word from him, she spun herself around and was suddenly willing to give this stupid tragic marriage a try? He must think her convictions lasted all of two minutes. She was beginning to think so, too.

Wrenching over on her stomach, she yanked the blanket up to her shoulders and squeezed her eyes shut. But her thoughts wouldn't settle down.

Just once in her life, she wished a man's voice would soften toward her as Max's voice softened when he spoke Philadelphia Houser's name. Well, it didn't matter. A person couldn't really miss what she'd never had.

She focused her restless thoughts on the baby. That's what kept her from riding away as everything sensible urged her to do. A baby. Her very own family to love. To have a baby, she'd put up with almost anything. Even a husband.

Chapter 4

⟨❧━━━━━━━━━━━━━━━━━❧⟩

Max's state of mind dropped as rapidly as the altitude. All the way down the mountains, he rehearsed what he would say to Philadelphia and her father, testing one approach after another. No matter how he arranged the words, the end result was mortifying.

He had ruined Philadelphia and discarded her. That's what she would hear. Howard Houser would hear that his daughter had been humiliated and shamed at the brink of the altar, and further that Max had spit on the job at Houser's bank. Houser might not shoot him on the spot, but there would be retribution.

Until today, Max hadn't allowed himself to accept that he had ruined Philadelphia. Now a beautiful memory ate at his mind like acid, and what had seemed so right at the time was unforgivable.

He hadn't planned to take advantage, had later been shocked that emotions had escalated to such a high peak during the last night before he departed for Piney Creek. Neither he nor Philadelphia were the type of people to disregard honor or convention, yet it had happened.

If he had behaved with more restraint and less urgency, if they hadn't been alone in the gazebo, if Philadelphia's hands and lips had echoed her soft murmurs of protest. If he hadn't wanted to reassure her about his leaving, if she hadn't wanted to persuade him to stay. Afterward, she had lain in his arms and wept and wor-

ried aloud about whether he could ever respect her
again. And he'd silently flogged himself for acting the
cad and stealing her wedding night from her.

How right he had been. When she eventually married, she would begin her marriage in deceit. And he
had done this to her.

"Supper's ready," Low Down called behind him.

Hunched over, staring out at the Great Plains, he
spent another minute gazing out at the distant lights of
Denver winking like fireflies in the dusk.

Now the question was, Could he ever respect himself
again? Self-recrimination and disgust made him doubt it.

Eventually he turned toward the campfire, his shoulders still bunched in knots, his hands deep in his pockets. He watched Low Down stirring a pot over the
flames and for an instant he hated her. The next time
she offered to ride off and leave him, he'd tell her to go
and good riddance.

Squeezing his eyes shut, he rubbed a hand across the
pox marks on his jaw.

If he let her ride away, nothing would change. He'd
still be married to her. He'd still have to face the painful
scene with Philadelphia and her father. If he drove Low
Down away, all he'd accomplish would be to carve one
more dishonorable act on the ledger of his life. Sixty-
three men trusted him to do what he had given his word
to do. If he failed, those men would haunt his conscience for the rest of his life. Damn it to hell.

Silently, he approached the fire and accepted the plate
Low Down handed across the flames. Tonight she'd
made a stew out of jerky and wild onions and mush-
rooms. She could have prepared pheasant under glass
with foie gras on the side and he wouldn't have tasted a
thing.

"Is something wrong with your supper?" she asked
when she finished eating and noticed that he had barely
begun.

"The stew's fine."

"It's too salty, isn't it?"

"I have a lot on my mind, that's all."

The firelight softened her expression and made her skin look smoother. She might have washed her face, and it looked like she might have pulled a comb through the fringe of hair falling across her forehead. He wasn't certain and didn't care. All he could think about was Philadelphia. He would write her from Denver and inform her to expect him the following evening. He would also request that Mr. Houser be present.

"I guess we'll ride into Denver before noon tomorrow," Low Down remarked, pouring herself a cup of coffee. He nodded and made himself swallow a bite of the salty stew. After a minute or two, she made another effort at conversation. "I know a secondhand place where I can buy some dresses and a hat."

A full minute passed before her comment penetrated but when it did he scowled. "I don't want you buying secondhand."

Instantly she bristled. "No man tells me how to spend my money!"

"Dressing a wife is my obligation, not yours." How many times had he watched his father defer to his mother with a shrug and a look that said, It's your land, you decide. He had seen firsthand what a woman's money could do to a man's pride.

Low Down's chin jutted, and her eyes narrowed. "I'll pay for my own clothes, thank you very much."

"The hell you will," he snapped, setting his plate on the ground. "We agreed to treat this as a real marriage for however long it lasts. That means you don't humiliate me by behaving as if I can't provide for a wife! While we're together, I'll pay for whatever you need."

Easing back on the log, she stared hard at him. "I swear, you have enough pride for six men. What if I told you I had a little pride, too. It's not my intention to humiliate you, but I don't want to be obligated, either."

"This is not negotiable, Low Down. I'll provide." Hating it, he remembered Jellison telling him to do right by the wife he had. And by God, he would. He wasn't going to have Low Down weighing on his conscience, too.

"I thought we agreed to be cordial. Even I know that tone isn't cordial. So. Are you mad at everybody and everything, or are you back to blaming me for everything under the sun?"

Part of the difficulty was that she didn't understand. By her own admission she had never loved anyone. She'd never lost someone with whom she had planned to spend her life. She'd never had a good name to lose. Didn't care what her neighbors thought of her. And someone called Low Down wouldn't comprehend what it did to a man to recognize that he'd dishonored the principles he lived by and held dear.

Thrusting a hand into his pocket, he caught up the green marble and gripped it hard.

"I thought you said you'd never been to Denver," he said abruptly, changing the subject.

He had to stop blaming her. In the end, their marriage was everyone's fault and no one's fault. If he continued to see the collapse of his life every time he looked at her, he would never be able to make love to her and be rid of her. If ever there was a misnomer for an act, it was "making love." He and Low Down would never make love. He would do his duty, and she would permit it.

"I didn't say I hadn't been to Denver. I said I'd never heard of Fort Houser." Standing, she stretched then picked up their plates and shook off the scraps. "I spent a year in Denver a long time ago. That's how I know about the secondhand place." Turning her head, she glanced toward the lights twinkling on the plain. "I worked in a laundry down in Chink Alley. Most folks think Chinamen do all the washing and ironing, but that ain't—" she paused and inhaled deeply "—that isn't always so. And some think a Chinaman would cheat you as soon as look at you, but the Chinaman I worked for treated me square. I had no complaints."

"You worked in a commercial laundry?" She was so different from any woman he'd known that she was incomprehensible.

"It was honest work," she said sharply, taking offense at his expression. "I've done a little bit of everything in my day. I even worked on a ranch way back when. That was down in New Mexico. I helped with the cooking and cleaning in the main house, so it isn't like I learned much about tending cows. But I did learn that ranching isn't an easy life."

He poured another cup of coffee and watched her clean the plates and spoons they'd used. "I've never known a woman like you," he said finally. Women didn't live the life she described.

Her laugh was husky and appealing in a way he hadn't expected. And when she smiled, her eyes caught a sparkle of firelight. "I've heard that before."

"Last night, you said you didn't want to live in another woman's house."

"I thought about that today," she said, not looking up at him. Since they hadn't camped by a stream tonight, she wiped off their plates with sand and a moistened rag. "That house is always going to be Miss Houser's place."

"Miss Houser would never have been happy living on the ranch. Eventually, I would have had to build a place in town." He didn't know why he was telling her this, except possibly he wanted to make up for blaming her again. Or maybe the reason was less noble; maybe he just wanted to talk about Philadelphia. "I realized that after I wrote the letter you read, while I was recovering from the pox. The house was a mistake."

She stopped scrubbing the stew pot and blinked at him. "You built her a house knowing she wouldn't like it?"

"We disagreed on where we should live," he said, staring into the flames beginning to die under the coffee-pot. "Philadelphia preferred to live in town near her father and her friends." And she had believed it more seemly for a banker to be part of the town society and community. "I prefer to live on the ranch where I can continue to manage my land and stock." Where they resided wouldn't be a problem now, nor would the difficulties of juggling banking with ranching.

"See, now there's another problem with husbands," Low Down said, speaking earnestly as if Max had agreed it was a given that husbands were problematical. "She wants one thing, you want another, and so you just go ahead and do it your way. That's what husbands do, and it's one of the reasons why I didn't want one."

"When two people disagree, someone has to make a decision."

"Yeah, and it's you, and you decide your way."

"Look, the reason I mentioned the house was to tell you that Miss Houser wouldn't have liked living five miles outside of town. You don't have to think of the house as another woman's." That wasn't entirely true, as every room had been designed with Philadelphia in mind. At the moment, he regretted raising the subject at all. "Miss Houser never saw the house or stepped foot in it." Another change of topic was needed. Looking at her across the fire, he said, "Tell me about you."

"There's nothing to tell." A shrug lifted her shoulders.

"How old are you?"

"Twenty-eight. How old are you?"

"Thirty-one. Where are you from?"

"Now that one's harder to answer." After stacking the dishes in a pile, she reached for her coffee cup. "When I was about four, I was sent west on one of those orphan trains. The journey originated in New

York City, so that's probably where I'm from. Who knows?" She frowned down at the wedding ring on her left hand. "I was adopted by a family in Missouri, so I usually say I'm from there. I ran away when I was thirteen, and I've been drifting around on my own ever since. End of story."

Max tried to guess what questions his mother would ask about his new wife, what she would expect him to know. "So you have no family?"

"I never thought of the Olsons as family, and they didn't think of me that way. They had four kids of their own and three adopted. We were a labor force, that's all." Lifting her hands, she examined her fingertips. "For years I had cuts and scrapes and little scars on my fingers from pushing a needle through leather. At the Olson's shop, we made leather goods. Chaps, vests, hats, boots, you name it. But tanning the hides was the worst. I don't ever want to do that again." Alarm flickered in her eyes. "You don't skin cows on your ranch, do you?"

"No." He thought about his sister and Philadelphia and their genteel upbringing and could not imagine them scraping a cow hide. "Did you go to school?"

"Not regular. But I can read and write," she said defensively. "And I know things they don't teach in school. I know how to survive off the land. I can hold my whiskey as good as any man. I know how to stretch a dollar. I ain't afraid of hard work."

As if the conversation had made her angry, she stood and strode into the darkness. Max heard her muttering to Rebecca and Marva Lee while he considered what she had told him and matched her comments to Preacher Jellison's remarks.

He had no idea what his mother and sister would make of her. If it came to that, he wasn't sure what he made of her.

Whatever else she was, he accepted that she was capable and self-reliant. Both nights she'd carried her share of the work as they set up camp. Without discussing it, they had split the tasks as if they'd traveled together before and knew each other's habits well.

Her voice came out of the darkness from somewhere near the picket line. "When are we going to get to the poking?"

Subtle and modest she was not. Max gazed into the flames burning low above the embers. "Maybe tomorrow," he said after clearing his throat.

"Sooner begun, sooner done," she called in a snappish tone. He didn't want to think about it.

Long after Low Down lay wrapped in her bedroll, he sat beside the fire pit staring at the coals and thinking about the next few days.

Denver had grown and changed since Low Down had last passed through. There were more hotels, more saloons, more shops, more trees in the residential areas, more everything. The last time she'd been here, drovers were yee-hawing a herd down the main street, and gunshots were as common as horse apples.

Now there seemed to be an oyster bar on every other corner, and more silk hats than caps or Stetsons. Hustlers worked the board sidewalks and called to passengers in hacks and fancy carriages. Construction crews seemed to be everywhere. She wouldn't have recognized the place.

"I've never stayed at the Belle Mark, but I've heard it's clean and comfortable," Max said, raising his voice above the rattle of a passing beer wagon. Pointing toward Fourteenth Street, he turned away from the noisy mayhem of downtown.

If he hadn't stayed at the Belle Mark, then where did he usually stay when he and his family visited Denver? Wherever it was, he didn't want to be seen there with her.

By now she ought to know better than to allow this

kind of assumption to undermine her confidence. Such
as it was. Besides, she knew she didn't belong in fancy
diggings, and Max knew it, too. A plain old cheap-side
boardinghouse was good enough for her, and that's undoubtedly where they were headed. As long as the room
had a real bed and clean sheets, she'd think she was
sleeping in a palace.

Her mouth fell open when she saw the Belle Mark.
This was not a boardinghouse, and staying here wouldn't
be cheap. The Belle Mark was four full stories of red-
stone elegance. The front door gleamed with brass fit-
tings and a green-and-white-striped awning extended to
the street. She couldn't get over it. Never in her life had
she stood beneath an awning.

Next she noticed a man dressed in a green uniform all
shiny with brass buttons and gold epaulets standing at
the foot of the awning, smiling at passing carriages with
an expression that invited passengers to stop and step
inside. He flicked a glance toward Max and Low Down,
noted their horses and travel-worn appearance, then
turned away without interest.

"Max?" She rode up beside him, frowning at the
man in the green uniform. The uniform and cap and the
man's superiority intimidated the bejezus out of her. "Is
that man the owner of the hotel?"

"He's just the doorman." While she continued to
stare at the details of his uniform, Max added, "His job
is to open the door for patrons of the hotel."

Lordy. The man was togged out like a general in a
foreign army, and all he did was stand in the awning's
shade and open the door? He looked like he ought to be
deciding who would live and who would die.

She noticed how he deliberately ignored them. "You
know, this place is just too fancy-dancy. There used to
be a boardinghouse down on Walnut Street that took
overnight lodgers. Let's go there."

"After a summer of living in a tent, I'm ready for a real hotel."

There he went, deciding things his way. Already she recognized the set jaw and closed expression that stated he had made up his mind and no argument from her would change his decision.

Fuming, she shifted in her saddle and searched for a way to deal with the situation since she had to accept it. "All right," she said finally. "You go inside and get us a room, then let me know the number and I'll come along later." Maybe there was a back entrance without an inflated swell in a uniform passing judgment on all who walked beneath his awning.

For a moment she believed Max would accept her suggestion and a rush of relief made her feel light-headed. Nothing but embarrassment lay under that awning. Max would hate being seen in a place like this with such a sorry specimen as her, and she would feel ashamed because she knew she looked like the devil. Hell, she looked so disreputable and wrung out that sixty-three men had refused to share her bed. And the sixty-fourth wasn't chomping at the bit for his opportunity, she thought, sliding a look up at Max.

"We're honorably married," he said slowly, his gaze fixed on the man in the green uniform. "I'm not going to have my wife slipping in after registration like some dollar-a-night doxie." His shoulders pulled back and squared, and his eyes went as hard as blue stones. He was going to insist that the two of them walk past the man in the green uniform and stroll on inside as if they had as much right to be there as anyone else.

Maybe he had that kind of backbone, but she didn't.

Low Down swung off of Rebecca and thrust the reins up at him. "I'm going to buy me some dresses," she announced, anxious to escape. "I'll find you later." She'd already taken a few steps toward California Street before he called to her in an exasperated voice.

"Have the bills and your parcels sent to the Belle Mark."

Low Down nodded and hurried toward the noisy rush and bustle of traffic. A few years ago, no one would have given her a second glance. Now, with Colorado a state and Denver the capital, with the new air of cosmopolitan growth, Low Down found herself the object of disapproving stares from the windows of carriages and from ladies passing on the street. Well, that didn't bother her. Since when did she care what anyone thought of her?

But she paced up and down in front of the Colorado Merchant's Bank for twenty minutes before she could make herself raise her chin, square her shoulders, and push open the doors. Almost immediately a frosty-eyed gentleman strode toward her wearing an expression that said his bank wasn't for the likes of her. She bit her lips and thrust out her chin. "I got some money I want to invest. Or ain't my money as good as everyone else's?"

In the end he was a banker. The word "money" rearranged his opinion regarding how a respectable woman ought to look. She could have smelled of worse things than mule and perspiration and he would still have smiled when she untied the thong around her neck and showed him the chipping-in money, Frank's nuggets, and her heavy pouch of gold dust. The banker led her to an office off the lobby, and before they finished doing business, he'd even called her "ma'am" once or twice.

With her valuables safely seen to, Low Down was free to attend to the distasteful chore of acquiring dresses. To her surprise, there were ready-made shops along Fifteenth Street displaying dresses in their windows. She walked along the storefronts, peering at gowns targeted to high society right down the scale to dresses fit for ordinary women. By angling her head at an awkward tilt, she caught a glimpse of a few price tags and gasped. The prices matched the high-faluting array of ruffles and bows and braids and ribbons.

She could only think that Max hadn't known the cost of female fashion when he'd insisted on paying. Certainly she hadn't. And she was no more inclined to waste his money than to waste hers. Waste not, want not.

The secondhand shop was where she remembered it, thank heaven, on a side street mired in horse droppings, where the sanitation arrangements still consisted of hogs wandering free between the buildings. The pungent odor of boiling malt wafted from the brewery, and the saloon on the corner still offered nickel beer. The city fathers probably wouldn't agree, but it was comforting to discover that some things hadn't changed.

She didn't have to wind up her courage to walk into the secondhand shop, and it didn't bother her when the woman behind the counter looked her up and down then rolled her eyes in disbelief.

Low Down grinned. "I need the works, starting from the skin out. Undies, stockings, shoes, a couple of dresses, a coat, a hat, gloves, a bag."

"Honey, you need a scrub bath, a hair wash, and a bonfire for them duds you got hanging on yourself." Cupping her hands around her mouth, the woman shouted toward a door at the back of the store. "Mazie? Get on out here. We got us a real challenge to deal with."

A deep sigh started high in Low Down's chest and emerged as a breath of relief. She'd come to the right place.

The sun was sinking toward the mountains west of town before she returned to the Belle Mark, her feet dragging with reluctance as she approached the dreaded man in the green uniform.

She was so intent on planning how she might sneak past him that she didn't immediately notice a well-dressed gent sitting on a bench beneath the awning smoking a cigar. When she realized it was Max, she stopped in her tracks and her mouth dropped.

He wore a low crowned hat over freshly barbered hair, and a dark suit set off by a snowy boiled shirt, maroon vest, and neat dark tie. His boot tops were polished to such a high shine that he could undoubtedly see the underside of the awning when he looked down.

"Well, my gawd," she said softly, walking up to him. "Maybe you have the makings of a banker after all." A whiff of bay rum caught her attention and the rich scent reminded her that maybe she should have purchased a small bottle of lady's fragrance. Such a thought made her smile. She had never owned perfume or ever imagined that she might want to.

Max stood and removed his hat as polite as you please, and that was another first. Men didn't usually doff their hats to Low Down. She didn't look, but she hoped the snooty man in the green uniform was watching.

Max extended his arm. "I'll escort you to our suite."

"A suite? Well la-ti-da," she said lightly, trying to sound like the idea of a suite didn't make her nervous. And she accepted Max's arm as if they were sharing a joke. She could tell he felt as ridiculous offering his arm as she felt about taking it. "Are all ranchers as rich as you?"

"This is a one-night extravagance."

Everyone in the vicinity watched them enter the Belle Mark, or so it seemed. Inside, Low Down cringed and shrank from waves of silent condemnation. And suddenly she was glad for Max's rock-solid arm because she needed something to cling to during the endless walk through the lobby and then up the grand staircase.

For years she had operated under the theory that if she kept her eyes downcast and didn't glance up, then no one would notice her. Therefore, she didn't see much of the lobby except the marble floor followed by a crimson-and-gold carpet that flowed up the staircase. But she managed a sidelong impression of shining brass and mirrors and frothy arrangements of ferns and elegantly dressed people perched on expensive furniture. Piano music shimmered from a nearby room, the tune so soft and sweet that it made Low Down's chest tighten.

Once Max led her around a curve and out of sight of the lobby, she released a breath of relief as if she had slipped safely through a gauntlet. Now she could look around.

"Oh look! There are brass numbers on each door! And crystal globes on the lamps!" The carpet runner displayed a riot of dark-colored flowers and was lovely enough to frame, and there were towering arrangements of fresh lilies on every stair landing. "I ain't never been in a place like this," she whispered to Max, too excited and awed to remember not to say "ain't." "And I never will be again. Ain't it just amazing?"

"Your parcels are inside the room," he informed her, bending to insert the key in the lock. He pushed the door open, then consulted his pocket watch. "It's five o'clock now. I made dinner reservations at the hotel dining room for eight. I'll return around seven-thirty. Will that give you enough time to—" he touched his tie and fumbled for words "—freshen up?"

Her impulse was to ask where he was going, but that was none of her business. And she was disappointed that he wouldn't be present when she examined her purchases. She didn't trust her judgment and would have liked his opinion about her new dresses. Oh hell, what was she thinking of? Men knew even less about fashion than she did.

"I'll be ready," she promised, watching him close the door behind him. The air where he'd stood smelled of bay rum and cigar smoke, and she inhaled deeply, wondering if he would keep his promise about doing some poking tonight.

Heat rushed into her cheeks, and she shoved the

thought aside. Besides, he hadn't really promised it would happen tonight. He'd only said maybe.

The first thing she noticed when she stepped out of the foyer and into the suite was the pile of packages she'd purchased. Boxes and bags completely covered a blue-striped sofa and spilled onto the floor. No wonder Max had seemed so terse. He must be angry about how much money she'd spent. She'd been upset herself when she saw the final bill. The only thing that helped was guessing what her duds would have cost if she'd bought them new from the ready-made shops.

Then her eyes widened as the impact of the suite overwhelmed her. A longing came over her to bounce around the room and sit in every elegant chair, examine every bibelot on every elaborately dressed table. But she wouldn't have touched a single item on a dare, not even if someone had offered to pay her. She was terrified that she'd break something or get something dirty. This was a look-at-only room, not intended for actual use.

And look she did, but from the center of the carpet, a safe distance from any items she felt tempted to touch. Once she'd seen and marveled at everything, she explored further and discovered an indoor water closet. Sure enough, when she pulled the handle, the water in the bowl swirled and gurgled away. She tried it several times, laughing and shaking her head in amazement.

Next to the water closet was a larger room containing a tub and a sink. After testing the tub spigots, she discovered the hot water was only tepid, but that didn't lessen the miracle of having running water right at her fingertips to turn on or off anytime she liked. No one had to haul it inside or heat the buckets at the stove. She'd heard about luxury like this, but she'd sure never expected to experience it for herself.

Leaving the water running and the tub filling, she examined the bedroom next. Someone, probably Max, had put their saddlebags in the closet. The clothing he'd worn earlier today hung on a rod, freshly washed and ironed, ready for tomorrow. None of her clothing hung there, but that didn't surprise her. Max expected her to wear her new lady things to meet his family.

Worried about the water running in the tub, she returned to the bathroom where she curiously studied Max's shaving items with her hands clasped behind her back so she wouldn't accidentally disturb his things.

Finally, she stiffened her backbone, drew a deep breath, and forced her gaze to the mirror above the basin. The dreaded moment of revelation had arrived.

"Oh my gawd!"

Shock darkened her eyes, and she cursed for a full minute. Even for her, she looked bad. There was a relatively clean oval that started at her forehead, curved in front of her ears and ended at her chin. Beyond the oval lay a summer's worth of grime.

Her skin was golden-brown from the sun and wind-chapped. Her eyelashes were stuck together in clumps.

And, oh Lord, her hair. Her hair was so gray with dust and dried mud that she looked like an old woman. And her clothing. She'd been living in these duds for a while, and they looked it. Probably smelled like it, too.

"Well, damn!"

What she needed was a jug of brew to steady her nerves, and a miracle.

Thank heavens she'd refused to look into the mirror at the secondhand shop. Instinct had warned her to save the shock of seeing herself until she was alone, and she was glad she'd waited. Because now she had a chance to do something about it immediately.

No wonder none of the men in Piney Creek had wanted to sleep with her.

"Stop that," she said in a low voice, turning her eyes away from the mirror. She needed to stop stewing over that bottom moment in her life when the hat was passed and the men had reached inside, their mouths turning down in dread. All remembering did was make her feel bad.

And she didn't want to feel bad tonight. She wanted to enjoy a real tub bath and the squeak of clean hair. She wanted to wring every tiny drop of pleasure out of staying in a suite—a *suite*, if you please. The queen of England didn't have it any better than this.

After her bath, she had to figure out how her new clothes went together, a chore she was determined to make pleasurable and not frustrating and annoying. Then she had supper to look forward to, a meal she didn't have to cook, and maybe more music, something lively, she hoped. The best tunes were the ones you could tap your toes to.

And finally, to top off this unbelievable experience, maybe tonight would be the night for a poke. And maybe a baby would result. Wouldn't it be grand to conceive a baby during her one and only night in a real hotel suite? Now that would be a fairy-tale story to remember all of her days.

Laughing softly, she slid under the water and lay on the bottom of the deep tub, blowing bubbles up to the surface.

Chapter 5

Max let himself in the door, absorbed with thoughts of the letter he had posted to Philadelphia and her father, turned toward the living room, and stopped short.

Low Down waited near the window, wringing her hands together and peering at him with an anxious expression. He knew it was Low Down because he expected to find her in the suite, but if this woman had walked past him in the lobby, he would not have recognized her.

As this was the first time he'd seen her when she wasn't wearing a hat, what he noticed immediately was her hair, a warm reddish brown, which she had smoothed back into a glossy knot at the nape of her neck. His sister, Gilly, would have referred to the style as work hair. But Max believed an explosion of frilly curls looked faintly ridiculous on a tall woman, and he silently applauded her wisdom in avoiding an elaborate arrangement. In fact, the simplicity of the style imparted a surprising hint of dignity.

No amount of scrubbing could have converted her tanned face and hands into the creamy paleness so coveted by women of fashion, but tonight she glowed with the same shiny golden health and vitality that he associated with his mother. That also surprised him. Previous to this moment, he would not have believed that Low Down had anything in common with his mother.

"You're staring at my face," she murmured, raising

both hands to her cheeks. "I rubbed some lamp oil on my . . . but the oil was too shiny, so I rubbed it off again, but it wouldn't come off completely, and my face is still shiny, damn it, but I don't have any powder. . . ."

Now he placed the scent he had detected: lamp kerosene beneath a strong soapy smell that reminded him of wash day at the ranch. And he noticed the clean natural arch of her eyebrows, and the feathery length of her lashes. Her nose was undistinguished, just a nose, and he couldn't tell whether she'd rouged her mouth, as her lips were pressed into an anxious line. If she didn't have powder, she probably didn't have rouge either, but tonight she looked like a woman.

Finally, he examined the ugliest dress he'd observed in a while, certainly not one his sister or Philadelphia would have chosen for an evening out. A shopkeeper's wife might have selected this dress for Sunday meeting; it was high-necked with plain sleeves to the wrist and boasted nothing whatsoever to distract the eye, no trim or fancy tucks that might be considered attractive. Moreover, the fit was wrong. The molded bodice clung too snugly, the waist hung too loosely, and he suspected the skirt required a larger petticoat frame in order to hang properly.

But his gaze lingered on the tight bodice that revealed full rounded breasts that astonished him. He'd had no inkling, none at all, that a beautifully statuesque figure existed beneath Low Down's sloppily loose, shapeless vest, shirt, and long johns. If he'd thought about the subject at all, he would have guessed that she was straight up and down with no curves.

"Will you say something, for God's sake? I'm a nervous mess. Do I look proper enough to eat supper in a hotel dining room?"

He made a twirling motion with his forefinger. "Turn around," he ordered in a strangely husky voice.

She rolled her eyes, then slowly turned for his inspection. Just as he'd suspected. The seat of the dress had begun to shine and show wear, and the poof looping over the bustle was a slightly different color, suggesting it had been replaced at some point.

"Damn it, Low Down! You bought seconds after I told you not to!"

"The important thing about that conversation was not what I bought, but who paid." Her wedding ring caught the lamplight when she smoothed a hand along the draped material at her waist. "This is a perfectly good dress, hardly worn at all. There was only one small tear under the arm, and I fixed that. Now tell me the truth. Can I be seen in public without people laughing at us?"

This was the woman who continued to swear that she didn't care what people thought of her, Max thought, suppressing a sigh. But she'd been truthful when she warned him that she wouldn't obey.

"You'll be fine," he said, deciding not to make an issue out of buying seconds. The hour was too late to send her out on another shopping expedition.

"Thank God!" The air ran out of her as if she'd been holding her breath. "I have another dress in case you didn't approve of this one, but it would have taken forever to change. You can't imagine the contortions required to put together a rig like this." Her hands fluttered up in helpless exasperation. "I thought I never would figure out this bustle contraption. Why fashion wants women to look like they have a butt the size of a wagon, I don't know, but I can tell you it sure feels strange. And a corset!" Letting her head fall backward, she blinked at the ceiling. "No person can wrench their arms around to lace it up by themselves. You have to twist the thing around front, lace and tie it, then twist it back around, and then you get pinched spots and you can hardly breathe. And I'll tell you something else I learned. You better put your stockings on first because you sure can't bend over while you're wearing a corset, lest ways not this one, so you have it take it off, put on your stockings and start all over."

No woman, not even Gilly, had ever mentioned a corset or stockings in his presence. And he could sooner imagine the women of his acquaintance doing somersaults through the lobby of Howard Houser's bank than he could imagine them commenting about butts as big as wagons.

Max cleared his throat and removed his gloves from his pocket. "If you'd like to fetch a shawl, gloves, and your bag, we'll go down to dinner. You did buy a shawl, gloves, and a bag?"

"I have two shawls. This is the evening one." She lifted a length of fringed paisley from the back of a chair and whirled it around her shoulders like a cape. Grace was not her strong suit. "And this is my evening purse," she said, showing him a drawstring bag that made a light clinking sound when she lifted it. He couldn't imagine what she would carry that might clink. "If I hold it facing this way, no one will notice that some of the beadwork is missing." She seemed proud of this point.

"Maybe we should sit down and have a drink before we go downstairs." Right now he wanted a whiskey.

Horror widened her eyes. "No! We can't sit on those chairs." Color rose in her cheeks. "They're just to look at." When he lifted a baffled eyebrow, she hurried past him on the way to the door, trailing the scent of soap and kerosene. "What if we accidentally left a smudge or a scratch or spilled something, and someone discovered it and threw us out of here?" Turning, she leveled a hard warning look at him. "This is the only time I'm ever going to stay in a place like this, and I don't want to ruin it by getting thrown out. So don't sit on those chairs!"

She disappeared into the corridor, wobbling a little on what he assumed were nearly new high-heeled shoes.

Max rested his forehead in his hand for a moment, then went after her, catching up at the landing.

"Maybe I better take your arm again," she muttered, eyeing the staircase. "If I fall down the stairs," she added in a low dry voice, "and end up sprawled at the bottom in front of all those swells, I'm going to pretend that I'm dead. You tell someone to haul me off to the nearest boardinghouse, then go have your supper."

If someone had told him this morning that he'd find something to laugh about today, he would not have believed it.

She glared at him, then slowly a smile appeared. "That's the first time I've heard you laugh."

When he placed his hands on her shoulders and turned her to face him, it was also the first time he had touched her. Beneath the soft paisley shawl, she was as solid as granite.

"Listen to me," he said, looking into her eyes. "You're not going to fall down the stairs. And no one is going to pay any attention to us. No one is going to throw us out of the hotel. Stop worrying." He recalled her comment that she'd never stay in a place like this again. Very likely she was correct. "Enjoy the evening."

"I don't belong here," she said, sliding her eyes away from his. "If Mrs. Olson—the woman who adopted me—if she could see me now, she'd tell you so."

"Just for tonight, pretend that you do." He extended his arm, and she gripped it with surprising strength. "Ready?" She nodded, lifted her skirts, and they slowly descended. Low Down kept her gaze on the floor until they reached the dining room, then she raised her head for a quick look around and he felt her draw a deep breath.

"It's so beautiful! Well, take a look at that!" she

whispered, leaning close to him. "There's the man in the green uniform!"

"No," Max said, careful to keep any hint of amusement out of his voice, "that is the maître d'. He'll seat us."

When the maître d' held her chair for her, she looked at Max with wide, amazed eyes, then, when he draped a napkin across her lap, she clapped a hand over her mouth and laughter sparkled in her gaze.

"Would you care for a drink before dinner, sir?"

He wasn't certain, but he thought it possible that Low Down was strangling. "Are you all right?" he inquired, leaning toward the candles in the center of the table.

"I'll have a whiskey," she gasped.

The maître d' arched an eyebrow as if her request for whiskey explained the awful dress and her crimson face.

"The lady will have sherry, and I'll have a whiskey," Max said in a firm voice.

"Oh Lordy," she gasped when they were alone. "I couldn't believe it when he put the napkin across my lap! Did you ever hear of such a thing? And then he draped one across your lap, too!" She fanned her fingers in front of her face. "I swear I didn't know whether to laugh or belt him one for being so familiar. Oh, Max. Did you ever see anything like this room? There's fresh flowers on every single table, did you notice?" Dropping her hand, she fingered the edge of the cloth, then informed him, "This is real damask. When I worked for the Chinaman, we washed a lot of tablecloths like this. If you think my new duds are expensive, you should check what a damask tablecloth costs. It's enough to make your eyeballs bulge."

"I didn't think your new clothing was particularly expensive." He knew for a fact that Philadelphia had spent more on one hat than Low Down had spent for her entire new wardrobe.

Now she noticed the array of silver gleaming against the damask and her hands dropped to the beaded bag in her lap. "I guess I didn't need to bring my spoon."

Her comment revealed more than she could guess about her background. Only the cheapest boardinghouses required a lodger to furnish his own eating utensils.

"Remember? I showed you my spoon. It's real silver, just like these." Pride and defensiveness firmed her tone and her chin lifted as if she were challenging him to say something.

"I recall your spoon was very pretty," he said, feeling at a loss.

But she seemed mollified. "Yes, it is. It's one of my prized possessions." Frowning, she touched a gloved finger to the row of forks. "Why do we need so many extra forks and spoons?"

He started to explain, then gave up and advised her to watch and follow his lead when it came to choosing her utensils.

Once their drinks arrived, and he'd smiled at Low Down's contempt for sherry, he relaxed and enjoyed the excitement dancing in her hazel eyes. Earlier today, he had dreaded everything about the idea of spending a night in a hotel with her. But, oddly, there was something interesting, maybe touching—he couldn't pin down the precise reaction—about sharing another person's firsts. The first glimpse of an elegant hotel lobby and a suite. Her first foray into the world wearing a dress, at least in recent years. Her first awed impression of the maître d'. Her first taste of sherry; her bafflement and then pleasure at the sight of a full setting of silver.

To extend her day of firsts, Max ordered fried artichokes, duchess potatoes, and lobster salad. For dessert, he chose peach canapés, prepared in a chafing dish beside their table, enjoying her amazement and wide shining eyes.

After the canapés, she politely covered a satisfied burp

with her fingertips, then leaned forward to confide, "I loved everything except the coffee. This is the weakest coffee I ever tasted. They must have a new pot that ain't—isn't—broken in yet." An anxious look appeared in her eyes. "I want to remember all of this, every little detail. What was the name of the pastry meat again?"

"Beef Wellington."

"And lobster! I could eat a barrel of that. I'll bet that lobster cost the earth." When he told her the price of the lobster salads, she fell back in her chair and stared at him in shock.

"Max, seriously. Are you rich?"

The question made him laugh. "My family is comfortable, I suppose you could say. Land rich and cash poor. Staying here is a treat for me, too, and I'm paying for it with some of the color I panned out of Piney Creek."

A frown puckered her brow. "Don't you need that money to buy cows or something?"

"This time of year ranchers sell cattle. We buy in the spring."

"Since you're sort of rich, I should have bought a feather or a cloth flower to stick in my hair," she mentioned, sliding a peek toward the other tables. "The shop lady said so, said I needed earrings, too, but I didn't want to add to the cost."

"You look nice just as you are."

She would never be a beauty, would never be a woman who attracted attention for her appearance or style. But if she had looked like this four days ago, she wouldn't have lacked for volunteers to father her baby.

"You don't mean that," she said with a look of naked pleading that begged him to assure her.

"I do," he said stiffly, uncomfortable with the turn the conversation had taken. He decided she was easier to deal with when she had the chip on her shoulder and her chin thrust out. Uncertainty and vulnerability were not qualities he associated with the woman who had cursed, kicked, shouted, and willed him to survive the pox. A deeper glimpse into her character wasn't something he welcomed.

After placing his napkin beside his plate, he glanced toward the door. "Would you like to take a walk? It's warmer at this altitude, and it's a pleasant night. If you like, we could walk up to Broadway and view the electric lamps." When she didn't appear enthusiastic, he offered another suggestion. "Or perhaps you'd care for another cup of coffee. We can stay here and enjoy the music. Or take our coffee into the lobby."

She crossed her arms on the table and tilted her head to indicate the string quartet at the back of the dining room. "The music isn't too lively."

"Lively music isn't considered beneficial to digestion."

"And a walk . . ." She hesitated, then spoke in a rush. "Actually, if you don't mind too much, I'd like to get the poking over with." Circles of color burned on her cheeks. "The longer we put it off, the more nervous I'm getting about the whole thing. And the way I figure, tonight would be a good time. I might not look this good again."

Of course, he had known the moment was coming. He couldn't avoid it forever. And he'd halfway promised that tonight would be the night they made the first attempt toward the baby she wanted. Suddenly he felt the presence of the Piney Creek prospectors. A prickle along his neck raised the uncanny impression that if he looked over his shoulder, he'd see the miners standing behind him, waiting to hear him deliver the correct answer.

"We could do that," he said reluctantly, frowning and tugging at his collar.

"Good!" A relieved smile curved her lips, and for a moment she looked almost pretty. "Let's get to it, then."

This time as they crossed the lobby and climbed the staircase he was glad she kept her head down and her gaze fixed on the floor. He didn't want her to note his unwillingness, even though he couldn't imagine that she'd fooled herself into believing he was eager to bed her.

The first thing he did upon entering the suite was walk directly to the drink cart and pour himself a generous splash of whiskey. The scent of soap and kerosene announced she'd followed.

"I'll have one of those, too."

He gave her the whiskey he'd fixed himself and poured another.

Raising her glass, she tipped it against his. "I sure hope this works the first time." After she'd drained half the whiskey, she stepped back from him and pressed her lips together. "How do you want to go about doing it?"

He was doing a lot of throat clearing tonight, especially in the last few minutes. "Why don't you go into the bedroom and get ready," he suggested uncomfortably, turning the whiskey glass between his fingers. "I'll join you in a few minutes."

"You mean I should get out of this rig before you come, so we don't waste any time. All right." Their shoulders collided as they both turned to the drink cart, and she jumped back as if he'd scalded her. Max stepped aside and let her pour a refill. She tossed down the whiskey and filled her glass again. "Can I trust you not to sit on the chairs while I'm in the other room?"

This was not the moment to argue about sitting on the chairs. He nodded and filled his whiskey glass to the brim.

"I didn't like that sherry," she said, carrying her whiskey toward the bedroom. At the door, she straightened her shoulders and turned back to him. "There's a couple of things I need to say before we get started."

Of course, he thought with a sigh. This was not a woman who regarded silence as a virtue.

"First, I want to thank you for taking your duty seriously and for living up to your promise to the boys and to me."

"Do we have to talk about that?" Even from across the room and in dim light, he noticed her fingers were shaking.

"I told you already that I did this before a long time ago. I didn't like it much, and I wasn't good at it, so don't get your expectations up. Just do what you have to do and don't dawdle around."

Without thinking, he sat down and crossed his ankles on the ottoman. "Damn it, Low Down, tonight won't be the first time I've been with a woman. I don't require instructions."

"I knew I couldn't trust you about this! I just knew you'd sit on a chair!" Her chin came up and her eyelids narrowed, and for the first time tonight she looked like the woman he'd known in the schoolhouse. "As for the other, all I'm saying is get to it and get done with it." Whirling on her heels, she slammed into the bedroom, but not before she gave him a stony look and muttered something about getting thrown out of the Belle Mark and it would be his fault.

Never in his life had he felt less like making love.

Rising, he walked to the window and pulled back the drapes, gazing down at the young trees lining Fourteenth Street. A set of carriage lamps appeared, then passed his line of sight.

If his life had proceeded according to plan, he would have married Philadelphia in a matter of days. Instead, he was about to take another woman to bed. He lifted the whiskey glass to his lips with one hand and gripped the green marble with the other. Nothing about this felt right or honorable.

"Max? I'm ready."

Turning from the window, he caught sight of a billow of nightgown, then heard the bed springs squeak.

Grimly, he drained his whiskey glass, then rubbed his

palms against the legs of his trousers. The only thing
that could make this situation worse was if he couldn't
perform at the critical moment. On that issue, he had to
trust that his body wouldn't know that his mind was unwilling. Or that he was damned near as nervous about
the next few minutes as Low Down appeared to be.

Feeling the men of Piney Creek pushing from behind, he crossed the living room and walked into the
bedroom. She had pulled the shades and the draperies
and extinguished the lamps. He couldn't see much of
anything.

Maybe that was best. Stepping out of the shadowy
light spilling through the doorway from the living room,
he took off his jacket and vest and removed the studs
from his shirtfront and cuffs, then looked around for
the bureau.

"The dresser is right behind you."

She was watching. Frowning, he placed the studs on
top of the bureau, then peered toward the bed. All he
could see was a pale blur that might have been the
sheets or might have been her nightgown. She'd seen
him stark naked when he was ill, so why undressing in
front of her made him uncomfortable was a mystery,
but it did. Before he stepped toward the bed, he removed his tie and his trousers but decided to leave on
his shirt.

"Damn it!" Grabbing his toes, he hopped around on
one foot, cursing.

"What happened?"

"I stubbed my toe on the bedpost," he said between
clenched teeth. His next thought was the memory of
Preacher Jellison promising God's retribution if the men
didn't do right by Low Down. His stinging toe felt like
a warning.

Stumbling to the side of the bed, he sat heavily on the
edge, massaging his toe and wishing he were a hundred
miles away. At length, he pulled back the sheets, plumped

up the pillow, then slid into bed and sat against the head-board. Now she had her back to him and was curled into a ball.

"I'm not taking off my nightgown, so if you were thinking I would, forget it," she stated in a muffled voice.

She'd crunched down and pulled up the sheets and all he could see of her was the back of her head.

"Do you plan on helping things along any?" he asked, exasperated. It would have been more conducive to the moment if she'd taken down her hair, and if she didn't feel so strongly about removing her nightgown, and if she'd at least face him.

Her answer was so long in coming that he began to hope she'd fallen asleep. "Why do you need help? Can't we just get this over with?"

"Contrary to some women's belief, a man needs a little stimulus to make things work." The back of a woman's head wasn't the most alluring view he could think of.

"Well, what kind of help do you have in mind?" came the muffled question. "This sure sounds like daw-dling to me."

"Well, I'm sorry, damn it, but sometimes poking requires a little buildup. If that seems like dawdling, that's just too bad, because there's nothing I can do about it!" Anger was not going to improve the situation. After drawing a breath, he ground his teeth together, slid under the covers, hesitated, then curled around her body. She made a hissing sound between her teeth, and he inhaled a whiff of whiskey fumes and the strong scent of kerosene.

On the positive side, her warm firm buttocks pressing against his groin caused an involuntary stirring that was powerfully encouraging.

"It would help if you'd try to relax," he said against the nape of her neck. Her hair, at least, didn't smell like kerosene. The silky coil beneath his nose smelled clean and soapy.

"Now, how can I relax?" She spoke into her pillow and held herself rigid. "I don't know what you're going to do next."

He didn't know either until he heard his answer. "I'm going to reach up under your nightgown and touch your skin. Think of it as preparation, not as dawdling."

Placing his hand on the nightgown covering her thigh, he paused to let her get used to his touch, then he moved his fingers and began to inch up her nightgown in what he intended as a provocative and hopefully seductive act for them both. He inched at the material, kept inching at it, pulling at it, tugging on it, until a sizable wad had bunched up between his hand and chest. What the hell? "How big is this thing?" There was no end to the nightgown, no hem that he could find and heaven knew he was trying.

"The big one was the cheapest."

Throwing back the covers, he blinked and tried to see what he was up against. At once he realized the nightgown was a hugely voluminous tent with a drawstring tied at her throat. Where he'd gone wrong was pulling sideways instead of straight up, and that was not going to work. He'd still be inching along when the call to judgment sounded. "There must be thirty yards of material here." He'd never seen such a voluminous nightgown or even suspected such a thing existed.

She rolled on her back inside the nightgown and heaved a sigh. "I can see that I'm going to have to take a hand in this or we're never going to get it over with."

"Well, thank God. A little help would be greatly appreciated," he said, staring down at her. "Could you start by taking that damned thing off?"

"No," she said emphatically. "Get back under the covers."

Her stubbornness about the damned nightgown meant

he'd be working blind. All right, if that's how it had to be, he'd cope. Once he was alongside her again, he felt her hands tugging at the nightgown under the sheets and thanked heaven for small favors. Then she rolled back on her side and sort of wiggled, which he interpreted as an invitation to curl around her and begin again.

This time her bare buttocks pressed against him and his reaction to skin and heat and curve was immediate despite the huge wad of material bunched at her waist. Closing his eyes, he tentatively stroked a hand over her bare hip, surprised by the taut smoothness of her skin. On the upward stroke of his palm, he continued tracing the curve of her waist, then slid his hand up under the cursed nightgown almost to her breasts.

"This feels very much like dawdling," she whispered in an oddly breathless voice. But she didn't shove his hand away as he'd given her an opportunity to do.

Seizing on the lack of protest, he continued his exploration, amazed that he had ever supposed she had no curves. Her hips narrowed to a small waist and farther up he found the swell of her splendid breasts. Soft, yielding warmth filled his palm, and her body shifted against him as if she'd shivered. Wishing he could see even a patch of actual skin, he brushed his fingers lightly across her nipple until he felt it bud and stiffen. Then he slid his palm down her belly and stroked the nest between her legs until she made a strangled sound and pushed his hand away.

"That's enough dawdling," she gasped, rolling onto her back.

His own breath was ragged as he lifted over her, wishing she was naked, half feeling that he was making love to a nightgown instead of a woman. After slapping aside his shirttail and shoving a bulky roll of nightgown away from her thighs, he entered her, then froze when she stiffened abruptly.

"What's wrong?" he asked in a husky voice, peering down at her. "Am I hurting you?"

"No. It's just that I don't know what to do with my knees," she whispered. Now that his eyes had adjusted to the darkness, he could see her staring up at him. "Or where to put my hands, and I don't know if I should close my eyes."

"I thought you said you'd done this before." He was whispering, too, and had no idea why.

"I also said I wasn't any good at it."

"Raise your knees." A film of perspiration heated his brow, and a tiny voice deep in his head congratulated him on having the control to stop the proceedings and issue instructions. "Put your hands on my shoulders. Open or close your eyes, whatever you want."

"That's a good idea. This is a lot more comfortable," she confided in the same breathless whisper after she'd raised her knees. "You can go ahead now."

"You're sure? There isn't anything else you'd like to discuss at this crucial moment?"

"If it won't make you nervous, I think I'll watch."

It did make him nervous. He couldn't really reach stride until she turned her head to the side, then he rushed toward crescendo before she looked at him again. In the end he forgot to notice if she watched, losing himself in the sweet mysterious force of a ritual that had begun at the dawn of time.

Afterward, he lay beside her in the darkness, catching his breath and feeling strangely unsatisfied.

"Max? Thank you," she said softly, her head turned away from him. "This was an amazing day, the most wonderful day in my life. I'll never forget a single detail."

Tossing back the sheets, he padded across the room and found his jacket and his cache of cheroots. In the flare of the match, he noticed that the pins had come loose from the coil on her neck and long strands of dark hair spread across her pillow. He waved out the match with an irritated gesture.

"Do you mind if I smoke?" he asked, coming back to bed. As he'd already lighted the cheroot, the question was moot.

"I like the smell of a cigar," she murmured drowsily.

After propping his pillow against the headboard, he smoked in silence, thought about what had transpired, and questioned the anger building in his chest. It wasn't difficult to identify the source. He had betrayed a woman who didn't know yet that he wouldn't be marrying her, a woman he had intended to remain faithful to for the rest of his life. Guilt twisted into a knot behind his rib cage.

He hadn't done well by Low Down, either, he realized, frowning into the darkness. He'd done his duty and nothing more. He hadn't kissed her, had shown her no particular tenderness. He'd indulged just enough foreplay to ensure that she was ready for him, and then he'd proceeded with little thought for her satisfaction or pleasure. That wasn't how a man expressed gratitude for his life; it was how he coupled when he was paying for his pleasure.

Lowering his head, he rubbed the bridge of his nose between his thumb and forefinger, regretting everything about the last twenty minutes.

Low Down.

His head snapped up, and he stared at the sleeping form beside him.

He'd been married to this woman for four days, he'd just made love to her, and he didn't know her name.

Appalled, he dropped a hand on her shoulder and gave her a shake. "Wake up."

She bolted upright, instantly alert, her hands slapping at her waist where her Colt would normally have been strapped. "What's the matter? What's wrong?" she said, starting to swing out of bed. "Are they throwing us out of the hotel?"

Max caught her arm. "Nothing's wrong. I'm sorry I woke you, but I have to know something, and the answer won't wait until morning. What's your real name?"

"You woke me up to ask my name?" After a minute, she laughed and eased back into bed. "Louise Downe."

"How did you get from Louise Downe to Low Down?" The instant he asked the question, he knew he didn't want to know the answer.

"Well, you remember how I told you about Mrs. Olson?" She covered a yawn. "When I was little she used to shout at me. She'd say, come here you low-down, good-for-nothing little piece of . . . well, you can guess the rest. I got it in my head that Low Down was my name. Then, after I ran away, I heard a man from Washington talking about being low down on a totem pole. That seemed to fit, too. And so—"

"I don't want to hear any more." After a minute he opened his arms. "Come here."

"What?"

There wasn't much he could do to make up for a performance that had been perfunctory at best, but he could end an intimate act in a more honorable fashion than rolling away from her as if he'd paid for her favors.

Reaching, he guided her head to his shoulder, sensing her surprise and hesitation. At length she relaxed against him, and eventually he felt the soft rise and fall of her magnificent breasts against his side and knew she'd fallen asleep.

He finished smoking the cheroot, his thoughts a dark kaleidoscope of shifting images. Philadelphia. His summer in the mountains. The ranch. The period in the schoolhouse when he had believed he would die. And the stranger in his arms, his wife.

There was no way out of this mess. No way to set things right with Philadelphia or her father. No way to shield his family from scandal and shame. Tonight he and Low Down had sealed their misfortune by beginning a marriage neither of them wanted.

But he'd done his duty. Preacher Jellison and the men at Piney Creek must be laughing their butts off.

Chapter 6

A rough spot on the wooden wagon seat snagged Low Down's skirt when she twisted around to peer back at the Belle Mark. She had arrived there yesterday as one person and departed today as another. She looked different; she felt different, and maybe she was. Maybe she was pregnant. Her heart lifted at the possibility. On the other hand, he who lived on hope dined on scraps. It was better not to hope too much. Just wait and see.

When Max headed the team north and she could no longer make out the green-and-white-striped awning, she turned her attention to the items packed in the wagon bed.

"Mostly provisions and supplies for the ranch," Max explained. "And a few gifts for the family."

"What kind of gifts?" she inquired, anxiously smoothing her skirts before she checked on the hat pin that anchored her hat to her hair. A person had only one chance to create a good first impression, and she wanted Max's family to approve of her. On the other hand, why should they?

Max glanced back to make sure he wasn't driving too fast for Marva Lee and Rebecca who were tied to the tailgate.

"I bought Gilly's husband, Dave, new strings for his guitar and a hatband. My brother, Wally, gets a silver belt buckle and a book of house plans in case he decides someday to build on his quarter. The bolts of cloth are for Gilly and my mother."

"What kind of material did you choose?"

"Velvet."

Low Down whistled. "Son of a bitch. That must have cost a pretty penny!" When he turned his head to frown, she lifted her hands. "I'm sorry. I'm not swearing as much as I used to." Changing herself was not easy. Old habits died hard. "What else did you buy?"

"I bought Ma a new set of account books." Max kept his eyes on the twin ruts in front of the team.

Learning what gifts he'd chosen gave her a small glimpse of her new family. "What did you buy Gilly and her daughter?" she asked. She had been especially interested in Gilly and Sunshine since Max had told her about them.

"There's a doll for Sunshine, and a box of lace-edged handkerchiefs and a book of sheet music for Gilly."

"Sheet music?" She considered for several minutes, then finally decided to confide in him. "I collect songbooks myself."

Surprise lifted his eyebrows. "Then the piano wasn't as far-fetched a suggestion as it seemed at the time."

"I don't play the pi-ano, I just collect songbooks."

"Why?"

"Because I enjoy the stories." She liked to surprise him, but suddenly she felt uneasy. His expression suggested that other people didn't do this. "Take that song about 'Grandfather's Clock,' for instance. It stopped ticking when the old man died." She gazed into his eyes, as blue as the powdery sky. Then, since she'd come this far, she plunged ahead. "Don't you think that's sad and touching?"

"I guess I never thought much about the words."

"Another example is 'Shoo, Fly, Don't Bother Me.' That's a funny one. Anyway. The song stories are short, and most of the time they offer a lot to think about. I've thought of a dozen ways that old grandfather might have died and stopped the clock. Or, take 'Silver Threads Among the Gold.' I mulled over that song for days after I read the words. Pondering growing older and asking myself if I'd done all the things I wanted to do. That's when I first started thinking about a baby and getting to it if I was ever going to."

She stopped short. Neither of them had referred to last night, and she didn't think they should. There was a time to speak and a time to be silent, and she figured what happened behind a bedroom door demanded silence. Max had done his duty; that was the important thing. Now they would wait to discover if he needed to do it again.

She slid a sidelong glance at his profile then pushed at the fingers of her gloves, trying to make them fit better. Oddly, the motion made her uncomfortable, made her think about last night. Not talking about last night was easy. Not thinking about it was the hard part. It seemed that nearly everything recalled some detail. The firm manner in which he held the reins between his hands. The breathless way her corset squeezed her ribs. The smell of shaving soap that occasionally wafted in her direction.

She gave her head a shake. "Well. That's why I collect songbooks. I like to read the stories and then think about them."

"If you like stories, why don't you read books?"

"Hoo boy, now that's a good one!" She slapped her thigh and laughed. "First, books cost too much money. Second, well, what would you think if you saw someone like me reading a book? You'd think I was putting on airs, sure enough. No, the songbooks are good enough. I like them." And she had a new one from the boys at Piney Creek that she hadn't read yet. It was a treat to look forward to. And maybe if things went well between her and Gilly, Gilly would be willing to trade some of her books.

Max rubbed his eyes, then dropped his hand back to the reins.

"Pretty day today," Low Down remarked after another mile had rolled beneath the wheels.

"I suppose so."

To the west, the Rocky Mountains drew a jagged purplish line across the horizon. Some of the peaks were snow-capped, but here on the slope of the plains, autumn had just begun to hint at the brilliant display to come. The grasses had faded, and Low Down spotted a few pale leaves among the tall cottonwoods clumped across a rolling landscape. They passed men raking hay out of stubbled fields, and soon the ranchers would move their cattle down to winter pastures.

"Every turn of the wheels makes me more nervous," she admitted after another mile had passed in silence. She was wearing herself out with the anxiety of wondering if Max's family would accept her during the brief time they would be married. Of course, it didn't matter, and she didn't care.

"Stop worrying," he advised.

She couldn't help it. What if his family hated her on sight? After all, she was the one who had wrecked the wedding plans.

"Oh damn." Flinging out a hand, she gripped Max's tense arm. "I'm sorry. I forgot all about tonight. You're going to see Philadelphia and her father." She stared at him, feeling the steely tautness of the muscles beneath her fingertips. He must be dreading tonight as much as— more than—she dreaded meeting his family. "Max . . . I wish—"

"Low . . . Louise. I don't want to discuss this."

Louise? Suddenly she remembered him waking her to ask her name. And then, her shock when he had pulled her into his arms. The back of her neck grew hot, and she turned her head away, busying herself by slapping at her skirts, checking her hat, pushing at the fingers of her gloves.

"Does your family like Philadelphia?" she inquired in a low voice, furious with herself that she'd ask such a dumb thing. "I guess they do," she said when Max didn't answer.

"Do we have to talk? I have a lot on my mind right now. I need to do some thinking."

"About what you'll say tonight to Miss Houser and her father. I understand. Silence is golden." Twisting her fingers in front of her mouth, she made a motion like she was locking her lips and throwing away the key.

For the next hour neither of them spoke. Low Down gazed at the fields and trees and streams and distant mountains. She fussed with her skirt and hat and gloves and bag and laced her shoes again. She swayed on the wagon seat, occasionally bumping against Max's shoulder and thigh. The trip seemed interminable.

"How much farther?" She spotted a town ahead and hoped it was Fort Houser, named for Philadelphia's grandfather, who had founded the town. She suspected Max believed she hadn't paid attention when he told her about Philadelphia's high-faluting family, but she had.

"That's Fort Houser," Max confirmed. "We'll bypass the town and go directly to the ranch."

She supposed that made sense. He wouldn't want word flying back to Philadelphia that he'd returned home accompanied by a woman. Philadelphia should hear the bad news from him.

"We'll be home in less than an hour."

Home. To a real family. Lordy, she hadn't been this nervous in years.

"I don't care if they like me or not." She placed a hand on her stomach and strained to see into the distance, looking for a ranch house among the stands of cottonwood and willows. "It won't be for long, any-way. For all we know, I'm pregnant right now."

"That would be good," Max said, speaking between his teeth. He, too, sat straighter and stiffer on the wagon seat. It occurred to her that he probably wished he didn't have to bring her home to his family. The more she thought about his being ashamed of her, the angrier she became. She hadn't asked for these complications. It wasn't her fault that she couldn't live up to the McCord family standards.

Turning on the wooden seat, she narrowed her eyes on his expensive hat, scanned the rich gloss of his leather jacket. She'd bet the earth that none of the McCords had ever gone to sleep hungry, or insulated their boots with old newspaper.

"I'm sorry that I'm not some fancy-dancy butterfly wearing a velvet dress to meet your snooty family. But I have my good points! And just remember, it wasn't me who insisted on marriage, and I didn't choose you!" Flouncing back into place, she crossed her arms over her chest and glared at the road.

"What the hell are you talking about?"

She felt his stare like a scald on the side of her face. "It ain't my fault that I don't have a grandfather who founded a town. Or that I can't play the pi-ano."

"Louise—"

"I am what I am, and damned if I'm going to apolo-gize for it! I don't care what you or your family think of me." As always, her beloved proverbs came to her res-cue. "Every tub must stand on its own bottom. That's how I've always lived, standing on my own bottom." She was working herself into a respectable state of anger. "I don't need you or your judgmental family."

"You may not need a family," Max said in a resigned voice, "but there they are, waiting for you on the porch. Someone must have seen us coming down the road."

"What?" Her head jerked up, and she discovered they

were approaching a sprawling two-story house with a multitude of outbuildings scattered behind. An enormous elm shaded a veranda that skirted the front of the house like a ruffle.

Low Down's gaze lifted to the gingerbread cutouts adorning the eaves, noted freshly painted green shutters framing the windows, then she drew a deep breath and forced herself to examine the people waiting on the veranda. They looked back at her as the wagon turned into the yard.

As she'd guessed, the McCords were a good-looking family and as impressive as the house. Gilly, small and pretty and stylish, stood beside a handsome sandy-haired man who must be Dave Weaver, her husband. Between them was a tiny version of Gilly, holding her mother's hand. To the left was a shorter, softer version of Max. That would be his brother, Wally. And standing apart from the others was a ramrod-straight woman, still handsome, wearing an expression that revealed no hint of her thoughts as she watched scandal spin into her yard and draw to a halt.

No one moved or spoke as Low Down swung down out of the wagon, forgetting to wait for Max to come around and offer his assistance. Abruptly aware that she hadn't behaved like a proper lady, she froze beside the wagon in a flutter of uncertainty, returning the scrutiny of her new family. Wally and Dave gazed at Max with sympathy narrowing their eyes. Gilly stared straight at Low Down, her eyes wide with—what?—curiosity? Dismay?

Then Max appeared beside her as his mother came marching down the steps, an ice-blue gaze fixed on her son until she reached the wagon. She examined the pox marks on Max's jaw, but she spoke to Low Down first.

"I'm Livvy McCord, Max's mother. And you must be . . . ?"

Livvy McCord loomed large. There wasn't a doubt in

Low Down's mind as to who ran the McCord household and probably always had. This was a formidable woman. Not a single wrinkle creased the woman's stiffly starched white blouse or her plain black skirt. And though a light breeze stirred the roses climbing the veranda trellis, not a strand of Livvy McCord's gray and auburn hair dared stray from the tidy bun crowning her head.

"I'm called Low Down." Though she cleared her throat, her voice emerged a mere degree above a whisper.

"Not here you're not," Livvy McCord said sharply, her eyebrows coming together. "You must have a name. What is it?"

"Louise Downe."

Not many women stood as tall as Low Down, and Max's mother reached only to her eyebrows. Nevertheless, she would have sworn that Mrs. McCord towered over her.

Still not looking at Max, his mother took both of Low Down's hands in hers. "First, I thank you from the bottom of my heart for saving my son's life. In his letter, Max said you were the only person willing to nurse the men who fell ill with pox. They would have died without your care. Is that true?"

Low Down cleared her throat again. "I guess it is." She cast a glance toward Max, who focused on the people still waiting on the veranda. Knots ran along his jawline.

"We have an unfortunate situation here," Livvy McCord said, speaking slowly, "and a lot of people will suffer for it. But you earned the right to ask for whatever you wanted, however ill-advised your choice might be. And you," she said, turning finally to Max, "did the right thing, regardless of the consequences. No honorable man could refuse to draw a marble from the hat, not after you agreed to repay this woman for your life by granting whatever she wanted. You did what you had to do."

Mother and son gazed at each other, then Max enveloped his mother in a hug. Their embrace broke the paralysis of the people on the veranda and the rest of the family spilled into the yard.

Low Down met Gilly and Dave Weaver, who regarded her with frank curiosity and expressions that reserved judgment. Their daughter, Sunshine, smiled shyly and peeked up through long, dark lashes. And she met Wally, who gave her a solemn nod before he pounded Max on the back in a roughly affectionate greeting.

"You sure did it this time," he said, giving his brother a rueful grin.

Max returned a weak smile, then stepped forward to embrace Gilly and Sunshine and shake Dave Weaver's hand.

When the introductions and greetings ended, Livvy McCord sent the others inside but kept Max and Low Down beside the wagon. "We need to talk." Her eyes, as blue as Max's, steadied on Low Down. "I apologize for the necessary bluntness of this conversation. But time is of the essence. If anything is to be done about this situation, a solution must be found before Max speaks to Mr. Houser tonight."

"Bluntness ain't going to offend me. Hell, speak as freely as you want." After all the polite greetings, some plain speaking would be welcome.

Livvy McCord studied her for a long moment, and Low Down realized she'd said "ain't" and "hell." A suspicion that she wasn't making a wonderful first impression tugged her spirits down.

"As Max described the circumstances of your marriage, I sense the ceremony occurred quickly and impulsively. Correct?"

"Yes, ma'am." Low Down decided she could be blunt right back. "I wanted a baby, not a husband. Things plumb got out of hand, and suddenly we were standing there being married. That was the preacher's idea, not mine. I guess you wouldn't agree about having a baby out of wedlock, but that's all I wanted."

"I believe it's immoral and wrong to deliver a child without benefit of marriage." But a hint of relief softened Livvy McCord's expression. "However, now that I understand your position, I believe we can resolve the current difficulties."

"Ma, there's no way to work this out." Hooking his thumbs in his back pockets, Max frowned toward the barn and a corner of the bunkhouse showing near a stand of cottonwoods.

Livvy glanced at Max then back to Low Down. "I'm sure you're aware that Max was to be married in ten days." When Low Down nodded, she drew a breath and continued. "Perhaps you'll agree that it isn't fair that Miss Houser will be humiliated and thrown into a scandal through no fault of her own."

"I told Max time and again that we should just pretend the marriage never happened," Low Down said solemnly. She had an idea where Livvy McCord was heading with this conversation.

"Excellent!" Color flooded Livvy's face, and her eyes brightened. "Then you wouldn't object to dissolving the marriage between you and my son?"

"Not at all." Low Down had no idea why she'd hesitated a beat. She also thought Max might jump in and tell his mother that they had planned to divorce after she got pregnant anyway. But Max didn't, so she didn't mention it either.

"Wonderful." Livvy addressed the next remark to Max. "It would create a far lesser scandal to postpone the wedding to Miss Houser than to jilt her practically at the altar. You can go to Wyoming and petition for a divorce at once. With a little luck, we can keep the purpose of your Wyoming trip secret, and no one need ever know about your marriage to Louise or the real reason for postponing the marriage to Miss Houser."

"Makes no never mind to me," Low Down offered. A twinge of regret pricked her skin, but it had never been her intention to cause Max any trouble. Besides, she might be pregnant already.

As far as she was concerned, the problem was now solved exactly as she had suggested in the first place. But Livvy McCord wasn't finished.

"There are many homeless children," she said, "and I will help you facilitate adoption. Max will see to it that you don't lack for funds to raise a child."

"That isn't necessary," Low Down protested. Now probably wasn't the moment to explain that she wanted her own baby, not someone else's.

"It is necessary," Livvy insisted. "You were promised a child, and you'll have a child." She looked from Low Down to Max and drew a breath. "There are many details to be settled, but I believe we've found a solution that will at least cushion the scandal if Miss Houser and her father agree, and I can't think why they wouldn't. Unless . . ." She hesitated, then firmly squared her shoulders.

"I detest asking such an unforgivably intimate question, but I must. There's one thing that might . . . is there any chance, any possibility at all, that Louise might be with child? Did the two of you . . . what I mean is, did you . . . ?"

To her astonishment, Low Down felt her cheeks burn red and noticed that Max's face had also flushed scarlet. Even Livvy McCord's cheeks showed high color. "Yes," Max answered in a strangled voice.

"That's why I'm willing to dissolve the marriage and leave," Low Down added, hoping to reassure. "Max did his duty. So I'm willing to call things even, and I think the boys in Piney Creek would be satisfied that Max kept his end of the bargain."

Far from being reassured, Livvy McCord looked

stricken and her shoulders sagged. "I was afraid of this," she said in a low voice. "If there's any possibility that you might be with child, then we can't dissolve this marriage." Raising a shaking hand, she covered her eyes. "No son of mine is going to desert a woman who may be carrying his child. Divorce is no longer a consideration." She dropped her hand and blinked up at Max. "That's it, then. There's no way to sidestep what's coming." Turning, she lifted her skirts. "We might as well go inside and have some of Gilly's chocolate cake."

"Mrs. McCord, wait." Low Down took a step forward. "I might be pregnant or I might not. Either way, I'm willing to ride out of here right now, and Max can get a divorce or pretend the marriage never happened. I never wanted to cause anybody any trouble. I just wanted a baby."

Livvy turned on the steps. "The marriage between you and my son has been consummated; it's valid. You are now part of this family, Mrs. McCord. There will be no more talk of divorce or riding away." Her gaze narrowed. "You made this bed, now you lie in it."

His mother saw the situation as Max had predicted. Low Down had to accept the marriage and stop thinking about riding away. She gripped her secondhand purse with both hands and turned to Max. "I'm sorry," she said in a low voice.

"Like you said, you didn't put the marble in my hand." Removing his hat, Max pulled a hand through a tumble of dark curls, then he took her arm and led her inside to the parlor.

The room was elegant enough to widen Low Down's eyes and formal enough to suggest that it was used infrequently, perhaps only for special occasions.

At present, the tension in the faces of those who watched Max lead her inside told her that Livvy McCord had announced there was no way to get rid of her, no way to rescue Miss Houser, no way to avert the scandal rushing down on them.

Livvy stood before the unlit fireplace and waited until Low Down had perched uneasily on the edge of a mauve-dyed horsehair sofa. "Welcome to the McCord family," Livvy intoned solemnly. She spoke politely, but coolly. She sounded resigned.

The others also murmured words of welcome. But Low Down was conscious that Gilly politely examined her tight bodice, her worn secondhand shoes. When Gilly's gaze lifted to Low Down's hat, she noticed her new sister-in-law's lips turn down in something that might have been a delicate shudder.

Wally and Dave nodded to her, and she suspected they were comparing her, point by point, to Philadelphia Houser. She could guess how she fared in that contest. Sunshine seemed to be the only person present who had not formed an opinion.

"When is your meeting with the Housers?" Livvy asked Max.

"At five this afternoon."

Low Down glanced at the mantle clock.

"You'll need to leave in about an hour." Livvy gazed at her family. "Mrs. McCord saved Max's life. She's one of us now, and we'll stand by her. This situation is unfortunate for everyone, but no one is at fault." Her gaze brushed Low Down.

Low Down was fascinated by the way Livvy McCord decided things as if she hadn't recently emerged from widow's weeds, as if she had always been the head of the household. Or maybe that was what being a mother was all about. Trying to solve the problems of her children, trying to protect them. This was the first time that she'd seen a caring mother in action.

"We'll have some of Gilly's cake, then you boys help Max unload the wagon," Livvy suggested, stepping toward the plates and napkins laid out on the sideboard.

"Did you buy a mule," Wally asked after he had a plate of cake balanced on his knees, "or does she belong to Mrs. McCord?"

For an instant Low Down thought Wally referred to his mother. A mild shock shook her hand when she realized he meant her.

The conversation turned to Max's summer in the Rockies, then Max inquired about the ranch. If not for the tight faces and an edgy undercurrent of tension, Low Down might have believed everyone had forgotten about Max's upcoming appointment.

As if her thoughts had cast a signal, the men abruptly rose, thanked Gilly for the cake, then filed out behind Max to unload the wagon and see to Marva Lee and Rebecca. Low Down wished she could go with them.

"We might as well have our coffee in the kitchen," Livvy said, picking up cake plates.

Low Down jumped to her feet, but Livvy and Gilly had already collected the plates and she had only her own to carry to a large, sunny, well-equipped kitchen. Not wanting to be in the way, she sat at a long table and tried not to think about how foolish she felt wearing a hat when Livvy and Gilly were not. Tried not to think about her ill-fitting gown, or the corset that was squeezing the breath out of her.

"What's your mule's name?" Sunshine asked solemnly.

"Rebecca." At least someone wanted to talk to her. "How old are you?"

"I'm five. I can read and write my name."

After scraping and stacking the plates, Gilly took the chair across from her. "I'm sorry. I hope you won't take this the wrong way, but I keep thinking about Philadelphia, Miss Houser, that is, and how terrible this will be for her. I can't imagine how I would have felt if I'd been jilted at the last moment."

Livvy set cups of coffee in front of them, gave Sunshine a glass of milk, then sat down. "I feel sorry for

Philadelphia, but I'm more concerned about what Howard Houser will do."

"Oh, Mama. Not business again."

"Houser's bank holds the mortgage on Max's place."

Low Down frowned. "You don't think—"

"I hope I'm just borrowing trouble." Livvy studied Low Down's hat and her dress. "My daughter and I prepared Max's house. We made up the beds and stocked linens and food. But I think the two of you might as well stay here overnight. I doubt you feel up to getting organizing right now. You must be tired."

"I'm sorry about the trouble, ma'am," Low Down said, stirring a spoon around and around her coffee cup. "And I'm sorry I ain't the kind you wanted your son to marry." She was too nervous being alone with them to remember about ain't. "I'm sorry about Miss Houser. I'm sorry about damned near everything you can think of. I don't know what else to say."

"You strike me as a straight-talking woman," Livvy said into the ensuing silence. "So I'll admit this isn't the kind of marriage I wanted for Max. What mother would? A man should choose the woman who will be his life's partner and the mother of his children, not have the choice thrust on him."

"You must feel the same way yourself," Gilly added softly. "It must seem very odd to have a husband chosen by lot rather than by inclination. What a terrible situation for everyone."

Genuine sympathy glistened in Gilly's pale greenish-blue eyes, and Low Down suppressed a sigh. She had never known how to respond to tenderhearted women.

Sunshine clasped her small hands around the milk glass and looked up at Low Down. "Did you do something bad?"

"Why would you ask that?" Livvy inquired, frowning.

"Because Aunt Low Down keeps saying she's sorry."

"No, your aunt did not do something bad. And her

name is not Low Down. We will call her Louise and think of her as Louise. That includes you," she said to Low Down.

"It's going to be hard to think of myself as Louise." She'd known Livvy McCord only a couple of hours and already Livvy was demanding changes. She wasn't sure how she felt about that.

"Since it doesn't seem like the men are coming back anytime soon, we might as well start some get-acquainted talk." Livvy took a well-seasoned, black-bottomed coffeepot off the woodstove and refilled their cups. "Naturally we're curious about your background, where you were raised, who your family is."

For one long shameful moment, Low Down considered painting a pink gloss over her past. But these people were her new family, and they deserved better. So did she. Lifting her chin and gripping the coffee cup between her hands, she drew a deep breath then told her new mother and sister-in-law the unvarnished truth about herself beginning with the orphan train.

At the end of her story, they stared at her in wide-eyed silence.

When the grandfather's clock in the hallway chimed the half hour, Livvy and Gilly blinked. "Max must be walking up to the Houser's door right now," Gilly said in a low voice.

He'd ridden away without saying good-bye to anyone. Low Down lowered her head and gazed at the gold wedding band circling her finger. She'd believed he would check on her before he left.

After a minute she realized she was being foolish. She'd never required looking after, and she didn't now. She turned her attention back to Livvy McCord and her daughter, both of whom were staring at her as if she'd sprouted antlers.

Low Down squared her shoulders and forced a shy smile to her lips. "I know you ain't too happy about me. But I'm so glad to be part of a family. I used to wonder how it would feel to sit at a kitchen table with a ma and a sister and a niece and just talk about things. It feels nice."

"Would you tell the part about the Chinaman and the laundry again?" Sunshine requested, enthralled.

Low Down laughed and retold that part of her history.

Chapter 7

A terrible situation was about to get worse, Max thought, biting down on his back teeth as he tied his horse to the hitching post outside the Houser residence. There wasn't a thing he could do about it.

He'd awakened this morning feeling guilty and bowed with regret. Making love to Louise had been a mistake. The honorable thing would have been to wait until after he'd told Philadelphia that he couldn't marry her.

If he had waited, then he might have accepted his mother's surprising suggestion that he and Louise divorce immediately. He would have bet everything he owned that Livvy McCord would never advise a divorce under any circumstances, yet she had.

But if he'd divorced Louise without attempting to give her the baby she wanted, then he couldn't count himself as a man of integrity. Forever afterward, each time he made a promise he'd hear the men from Piney Creek shouting inside his head, telling him that he couldn't be trusted, that his word wasn't worth a plug nickel.

No matter what he did or didn't do, he seemed to make the wrong choice and ended by making the situation worse.

Standing beside his horse, delaying the long walk up to the door, he thought about the interminable ride to Fort Houser. If his plans had unfolded as they should have, he would have arrived at the ranch alone and received a joyous welcome. Instead, he'd brought shame and an un-suitable wife to his family.

He'd known the McCords would treat Louise cor-dially, and they had. But he'd sensed his sister's dismay, had read sympathy in Wally's and Dave's uneasy grins. He'd heard his mother step out of character and offer a suggestion that ran against everything she believed.

Thrusting a hand into his pocket, he gripped the green marble hard enough to bruise his palm, and he frowned at the Houser mansion, wondering if he imag-ined the curtains twitch beside the door.

This would be the last time he walked up those steps and knocked at that door. The last time Howard Houser called him son and shook his hand with warmth. The last time that his beautiful Philadelphia would gaze at him with a loving mischievous sparkle in her blue-green eyes or dimple into a smile for him alone.

The marble was such a small and insignificant thing to have had such a devastating impact on his life. How was that possible? To wreak this much damage it seemed that something much larger and more dramatic was required.

The heavy carved door swung open as he lifted his fist to rap, and Mr. Houser's man, Ridley, beamed at him. "Welcome home, Mr. McCord. You're expected in the family sitting room." Smiling broadly, Ridley took Max's hat.

Then he heard her voice. "I won't wait another minute!"

She ran into the foyer in a swirl of rose-colored silk and bouncing gold curls and threw herself into his arms, not caring that she might shock Ridley. A week ago Max would have laughed and been charmed by her scan-dalous eagerness to see him. Today his chest tightened until he thought his ribs would crack.

"Oh Max. Thank heaven you're home!" Her arms circled his waist, and she gazed up at him with tears sparkling on her lashes. "When I learned you were so ill, I was desperately afraid you would die. I didn't know what I would do if that happened! Thank heaven, thank heaven!" Raising her fingertips, she lightly touched the tiny scars on his jawline, and he noticed the high color burning on her cheeks before she spun away from him. "You must see the wedding gifts. Every surface in the parlor is covered with wonderful things! No, you'll want to see Father first. Come with me, then. We'll have sherry, and dinner, and *then* we'll examine the gifts." She stopped and cast him a long lingering look that he couldn't read. "I have so much to tell you." And then she hurried toward the double doors leading into the family sitting room where her father waited.

A sweet rose scent lingered where she had touched his skin. But this was a Philadelphia he hadn't seen before, spinning from one topic to another, whirling from one door to the next. Then it occurred to him that of course she would be nervous. This was mid-September; they hadn't seen each other since the end of May. She believed they would marry within days, without a real opportunity to become reacquainted. Or was it more than that? He recalled thinking her last letters had seemed strained.

Wishing himself anywhere but here, wishing with every fiber of his being that he could reach into the hat again and this time draw an unscratched marble, he followed her into the family sitting room and shook hands with Howard Houser.

"Welcome home, son." Howard accompanied his greeting with what Max thought of as a banker's two-handed grip and direct sincere gaze. "You look tanned and fit after your final frivolous summer as a bachelor. Sit down, sit down. Ridley, bring glasses and the sherry decanter. And yes, my dear," he said to his daughter with a smile. "With the wedding so near, you have my permission to sit beside Mr. McCord on the settee." To

Max he winked and added, "Judging by a torrent of tears and sighs, I believe someone missed you a great deal this summer."

Rather than look at Philadelphia, Max gazed at a room he would never see again, a room he had always liked. All the worn and most comfortable furniture had found its way here after Mrs. Houser died. Unlike the mansion's other rooms, no effort had been made to co-ordinate color or style here. Yet the mismatched fur-nishings and crowded wall hangings fit together in a way that offered welcome and comfort.

"I don't care for anything to drink," Max said, stand-ing abruptly as Philadelphia sat beside him and her skirts overlapped his legs. It wasn't possible to say what he had to say with the scent of her in his nostrils, with the warmth of her scorching him. He moved to stand before the unlit fireplace, leaving her with a puzzled frown drawing her brow.

Even frowning, Max decided she had never looked more beautiful than she did tonight. Her golden curls caught the lamplight and glowed like a halo around her milky complexion. The pink burning on her cheeks spoke of her pleasure and excitement at seeing him as did the moist shine in her eyes. The same shine had glistened in her eyes during their last evening together. He'd never forget how she had looked in the moonlight streaming through the fretwork edging the gazebo. Never forget opening the long row of buttons that ran down her back, and then the touch of her silky bare skin against his palms.

Oh God. Leaning his elbow on the mantelpiece, he covered his eyes with his hand. This was the worst mo-ment of his life.

"Max?" she murmured in a puzzled voice. "There are a dozen details about the wedding that require your opinion before I make a decision." He heard her falter. "You seem . . . I don't know . . ."

With his mind's eye he observed how tonight should have been. Philadelphia bubbling with questions about his summer in the mountains and his relating amusing stories. After dinner Howard would take him into the library for a cigar and conversation about the bank and the position Max would fill there. Discussing plans for the future would tack wings on the hours and make them fly until the longed-for moment when Howard discreetly allowed the couple an hour alone. Then Max would draw his bride into his arms and briefly discuss the wedding before he demonstrated how much he had missed her.

"Well, son, did you find what you were looking for up there in the mountains?" Howard handed Philadelphia a glass of sherry, then sank into his favorite chair.

"We need to discuss the period when I was sick with the pox." In about three minutes the smile would vanish from Howard Houser's mouth. The shine would fade from Philadelphia's eyes. "I would certainly have died if not for the ministrations of a woman named Louise Downe."

"Your mother sent us a copy of some preacher's letter relating how deathly ill you were." Philadelphia's full mouth pushed into a pretty pout. "It's your own fault, you know. I told you not to go up there. I begged you to stay here with me."

None of her arguments or wiles had changed his mind about prospecting for gold as his father had done years ago.

"You will never know," he said, remembering the taste of her mouth, how her skin had gleamed in the moonlight, "how much I wish I had stayed." A hint of satisfaction flashed in her eyes, but Howard sat a little straighter as his instincts flared.

When Max reached the point in his story where the surviving men agreed to give Low Down whatever she wanted as a token of their gratitude, the warmth departed Howard Houser's eyes. He frowned and set aside his sherry. He couldn't know what was coming, but he sniffed something unpleasant, something momentous.

Max ended the story by speaking directly to Philadelphia, watching her face turn ashen, cringing inside as she stiffened and her expression grew taut with horror. "I'm sorry," he said hoarsely, after describing his wedding on the side of a mountain.

Her hands lifted, palms out as if warding off a blow. "No!" She drew the word into a long wail. "No, this can't be true."

"You son of a bitch," Howard shouted, coming to his feet. "You could have walked away. What kind of no-good bastard would place himself in the running to marry one woman when he's days from marrying my daughter? How in the hell could you do that?"

"Oh no. No," Philadelphia whispered, staring at him in shock and disbelief. "You didn't. You couldn't have. No. You wouldn't do this to me."

"I ought to kill you, McCord! No one humiliates me or my daughter!"

"There was no choice."

Silent tears streamed down Philadelphia's face. She trembled all over, and her hands shook so violently that sherry spilled unnoticed down her dress. "Good Lord above. What will I do?"

"I'll ruin you, you spineless piece of offal! Ridley! Bring my shotgun. So help me God, I'll blow you to kingdom come!"

"Oh Max. You don't know what you've done." Slowly Philadelphia rose to her feet, the sherry glass slipping from her fingers. Her arms rose to cross her breasts, she clasped her shoulders, and a long animal sound keened from her lips. Both men fell silent, frozen by her anguish.

"What am I going to do? Oh Lord, what am I going to do?" She gazed at Max with wet, panicked eyes. Agony thinned her voice. "I'm with child."

Her eyelids fluttered and she crumpled to the floor in a billow of pink silk.

Ridley sent the cook's helper to fetch Livvy McCord while the housekeeper tucked Philadelphia into bed. Max found an ax in the backyard and split logs into kindling, working like a man possessed. Grinding his teeth, he swung the ax above his head then down on the log, feeling the shock of contact ripple up his arms and into his shoulders.

She was carrying his child, and he couldn't do right by her. Couldn't marry her. Couldn't save her from disgrace, humiliation, shame, or a reputation ruined beyond redemption.

Swearing steadily, he placed a boot on the log and twisted the ax until the wood split into two pieces. He wanted to shout at God or fate or whatever malicious power had guided his fingers to the green marble. He wanted to smash and destroy and turn back the clock and make everything end the way it should have.

Ridley's expressionless voice called through the darkness. "Mr. Houser wishes to speak to you before Mrs. McCord arrives."

Before he returned inside, he took a moment to run his fingers through his hair and compose himself. The answer was obvious. He simply had to divorce Louise without delay. But the baby would be born before a divorce was granted. Cursing, he shrugged into his jacket. No matter what happened, he'd smeared a stain of scandal on Philadelphia which would follow her to the grave. She didn't deserve that. She didn't deserve any of this. Her only crime had been to love him.

"Did you know my daughter was pregnant when you married that other woman?" Howard demanded when Max returned to the sitting room.

"Of course not."

"But you knew pregnancy was possible, you son of a bitch," Houser snarled.

Max braced a hand on the mantelpiece and stared into the unlit fireplace. "If she'd told me, if she'd even hinted, I would have left Piney Creek at once. We could have moved up the date of the wedding and this disaster wouldn't have happened." That was the tragedy. None of it had to have happened.

"Pregnancy is hardly the type of news a decent young woman mentions in a letter. And don't even hint that my daughter is in any way to blame for what you did to her! You ruined her, betrayed her, and jilted her. You've destroyed her good name and brought shame on this family!"

Max dropped into a chair and sank his head in his hands. "I'm totally responsible." There had been a moment after Ridley had fetched the shotgun that he'd believed Houser would pull the triggers, and he hadn't attempted to defend himself.

"You're damned right you're totally to blame." Howard threw a glance toward the shotgun leaning against the fireplace. Then he flexed his fingers and tossed back a whiskey. "She could have had any man in this county. But, no. She wanted you. Every beau she ever had would have given her the moon and the stars if she'd asked. But not you. I told her she was making a mistake. I told her, Think about the house he's building you. Do you really want to live outside of town? On a ranch? Does he care about your wishes? But at least I thought you were a decent man. I would have sworn Max McCord wouldn't force a respectable woman to abandon her innocence and morals." He made a spitting sound. "You'll pay for this."

Every day for the rest of his life. He would never forget how happy she had been to see him, followed by her devastation and agony when she understood that he could not marry her and she was truly ruined.

Ridley had taken Livvy's cape in the foyer, but she still wore her hat and gloves when she hurried into the sitting room, her skirts crackling around her boots. She threw Max a quick questioning glance, then turned sympathetic eyes to Howard Houser.

"I'm terribly sorry, Mr. Houser."

"You don't know all of it, Mrs. McCord. Your swine of a son ruined my innocent daughter." Houser's face was on fire and his hands trembled.

"Philadelphia is pregnant," Max said, forcing the words across his tongue.

"Oh my Lord!" Livvy's knees collapsed and she dropped onto the settee as if her bones had melted. Shock widened her eyes.

"He should be horsewhipped, then tarred and feathered and run out of town on a rail!"

"Oh Max."

"I'll leave for Wyoming in the morning." He clawed a hand through his hair. "Philadelphia can go back East. I'll join her there, and we'll marry as soon as the divorce is final."

"Max, stop and think. What if Louise turns up pregnant?" Livvy asked softly. "Will you divorce one pregnant wife to marry another?"

Howard Houser's lips curled in revulsion. "You were bedding another woman while my daughter was trying on her wedding gown? You son of a bitch!"

At some point Howard Houser had switched from sherry to whiskey and had consumed enough that he swayed on his feet. "You're never going to touch my daughter again, you hear me? I'll see you in hell first. I'd rather have a street sweeper for a son-in-law than you!"

Livvy narrowed ice-blue eyes. "Put away the whiskey, Mr. Houser. We aren't going to settle anything if you're drunk."

"And just what in the hell is there to settle, Mrs. Mc-Cord? My daughter is ruined, our two families are disgraced, there'll be enough scandal and gossip from this to entertain Fort Houser for years. I'll send Philadelphia somewhere to have your son's bastard where at least she doesn't have to endure public shame and humiliation. And then what? If she brings home a baby, you know damned well what people will think and say! So she loses her home as well as her good name."

"That won't happen." Livvy's back straightened and her shoulders stiffened. She turned a hard stare on Max. "A McCord created this mess, and a McCord will make it right."

"I'll move the earth to make that happen," Max said, dragging his fingers across the pox marks on his jaw. "But I can't make it happen soon enough. The baby will be born before the divorce is final."

"I'm not talking about you. I'm talking about Wallace."

His head snapped up. "Wally?"

But she was already explaining to Howard Houser. "We put out the story that Philadelphia realized very late that it was Wally whom she loved and wanted to marry. She told Max in a letter and broke off the betrothal. When Max learned her true feelings for his brother, he placed himself in the draw to marry Louise. After he returned to Fort Houser, now a married man, Philadelphia and Wally felt free to elope to Denver."

Both men stared at her.

"This baby will arrive too soon," Livvy continued, frowning. "That can't be helped and it will cause talk. But if we handle our story correctly, we can at least plant the belief that it's Wally's child. That will help some."

Howard lit a cigar and waved out the match not taking his eyes off Livvy. "Philadelphia wouldn't have to go back East."

"She won't have a child out of wedlock. She'll be married and the child will have a name."

"The scandal gets cut by half. My daughter doesn't get jilted. If the story is handled right, it'll appear that she gave this bum the boot."

Max leaned against the fireplace and covered his eyes. Christ. He didn't want to drag Wally into his problems. Didn't want to imagine Philadelphia married to his brother or to anyone but himself. "There must be another solution."

"You shut up," Howard snarled. "You have no say in this." He turned back to Livvy. "Can you guarantee that Wally will agree to marry her and raise his brother's bastard?"

Livvy lifted a shaking hand to her forehead, but pride kept her spine straight. "Yes," she said firmly. "The McCords know their duty. If the shoe were on the other foot, I'd expect Max to step forward and do right if Wally couldn't."

And he would have, because that's how the McCords were. Reaching into his pocket, Max curled his fingers hard around the marble. The tiny glass ball cast ever widening circles, swamping others as well as himself and Philadelphia.

"Now the next question is, will Philadelphia accept Wally?" Livvy asked.

"You can depend on it," Houser stated harshly. "What choice does she have?" The next words sprayed Max like bullets. "Now, get out of my house. I never want to see you again," he snarled. He turned to Livvy as she stood and smoothed shaking hands over her skirt. "I'll expect you and Wallace to be at the bank tomorrow morning at seven o'clock sharp. We'll work out the where and when of what has to be done."

In silence Max helped his mother down the steps and walked her to the wagon she'd driven into town. A beating would have been easier to endure than what he had just been through. For the first time in his life he felt as if his manhood had been stripped from him. And he'd been helpless to offer any defense.

"There'll be frost tonight," Livvy remarked, pulling her cape close around her before she climbed up on the wooden seat.

Max lit the lanterns hanging on the wagon. "I feel crazy inside. I want to go to the Red Shoe and get as drunk as I've ever been. Smash things. Get in a fight. But it won't change one damned thing."

"I know." She took the reins into her hands, then gazed down at him. "You did wrong, Max. It takes two to pull the taffy, but mostly you're to blame. Not for marrying Louise, that you had to do. But for taking advantage of a young woman's innocence and leaving her vulnerable to shame and ruin. Now Wally will be in the same unjust position you were. Forced to marry a woman he didn't choose."

He swore and hit the wagon slats with the heel of his palm. "How do I make this right with her? And with Wally?" How could he bear watching them together?

"I don't know. I suspect you can't. But I'm glad your father isn't alive to see this," his mother said softly, then she lifted the reins, clucked her tongue, and drove into the darkness.

Feeling as miserable as it was possible for a man to feel, Max swung up on his horse and followed behind her.

Red-eyed and exhausted from crying, Philadelphia pressed her face into the pillow and struggled to accept the unthinkable. What was she going to do? The question revolved in her mind like a wheel circling round and around.

Obviously she couldn't remain in Fort Houser. The disgrace and humiliation would kill her. Like other ruined young women, she would announce that she was going East to enjoy a long visit with an aunt, a cousin, or some other distant relative. Girls in trouble always went East. Most often the girl returned six or seven months later with an infant supposedly borne by the aunt, cousin, or relative who had died at the birthing. This was the usual story. Then, the girl or her mother raised the child and doggedly maintained the fiction of its origins.

But everyone knew. And whispered and gossiped and felt infinitely superior. And the girl who went East was never again respectable no matter how virtuous or above reproach she might become. Her reputation and her future were irrevocably destroyed. Decent women did not call; decent men did not come courting.

"Oh God, oh God, oh God!" Philadelphia pounded her pillow with her fists. She was not equipped to cope with a situation that could not be fixed or manipulated in the way she wanted. Frustration and panic collided in her mind.

She did not *want* to be pregnant. She did not *want* to be sent back East. Max was supposed to fix this problem by marrying her. Furious and frightened she ground her forehead into the pillow. What was she going to do? What was she going to do?

Damn Max McCord. Damn him to hell.

Rolling on her back, she stared at the dark ceiling and touched her fingertips to her stomach, tracing the slight bulge beneath her nightgown. It was still there. A dozen times a day she stroked her stomach expecting to discover the little bulge had vanished. And each time her fingers encountered the unwanted curve, a frisson of shock and disbelief stunned her for a moment.

She couldn't believe this had happened. To her! Young women like Philadelphia Houser did not get pregnant out of wedlock. The scandal would be enormous. Simply enormous. Those who envied or disliked her would receive great satisfaction and pleasure in gossiping about her fall from grace and respectability. They would say things like: "Her grandfather must be twisting in his grave." Or, "How low the mighty have fallen." "That Philadelphia Houser finally got her comeuppance." She couldn't bear it.

The clock in the downstairs foyer had chimed the midnight hour before her father rapped at her bedroom door, then stepped inside. "I assumed you'd be awake."

She sat up in bed and cried, "You have to fix this! Daddy, you have to make Max marry me!" Fresh tears burned her eyes, and she covered her face and sobbed. "He can't do this! He can't abandon me now, he just can't!"

When her father didn't rise from the chair next to her bed and take her into his arms to comfort her, she peeked at him through her fingers. Even in the dim light falling through the door from the hallway sconce, she recognized the anger clamping his mouth and steeling his eyes. How dare he be angry with her? His pride was nicked, but her life was ruined. Resentment trembled through her body. It wasn't fair that she had to manage him and turn his anger into sympathy before they could even discuss how he would fix this problem and save her.

"I'm sorry I disappointed you," she murmured, speaking through sobs, saying what she knew would appease him. "Please Daddy, please forgive me. I'm so sorry, so ashamed."

"You should be," he snapped.

"What?" Shocked, she dropped her hands and stared. He was supposed to sigh and shake his head, then comfort her and call her his good girl.

"Here." He tossed a handkerchief on the quilt. "Dry your eyes and blow your nose. Compose yourself because we have matters to discuss."

"You smell like whiskey!" He'd been drinking. That explained why he wasn't reacting as he should and usually did.

"McCord took advantage of you, and he'll pay for that. But I also know that Max McCord is a decent man. If you had said no and meant it, you wouldn't be in this trouble now."

Fire rushed into her face. "You're blaming me?" She couldn't believe it. "Me?"

"The woman sets the pace. You're as responsible as McCord."

Fury glittered in her eyes. It would be a long time before she forgave him for suggesting she bore some fault.

"I'm also to blame." Falling silent, he rubbed the bridge of his nose. "I spoiled you after your mother died. Maybe I should have remarried. Maybe if there'd been a woman in the house, someone with whom you could discuss woman things . . ." He dropped his hand to his lap and looked at her. "I can't fix this the way you want it fixed. I can't make the pregnancy disappear. I can't free Max to marry you in the next few days. Neither of those things will happen."

One more shock rocked her universe. He'd always been able to correct whatever problems disturbed her world. Deep inside she'd believed that somehow, someway, he'd fix this problem, too. Panic leapt into her eyes.

"What am I going to do? Everyone knows we don't have any relatives back East," she said, her voice spiraling toward hysteria. "But I can't stay here." She was being driven from her home. It was unbelievable. "And you know what everyone will think, don't you? They'll think Max refused to marry me because I was pregnant! They'll say . . . Oh heavens, I can't bear it. Daddy, you have to do something. You have to help me!"

"Listen to me." Finally he took her hand and held it between both of his on the edge of the bed. "You'll marry Wally McCord the day after tomorrow. The two of you will elope to Denver."

She blinked hard, thinking she couldn't possibly have

heard correctly. But he continued talking, relating a fantastical story about how she had always loved Wally instead of Max, and fortunately, she had recognized the true object of her affections in time, before she married the wrong man.

"Wally?" she repeated dumbly. Her brain ceased to process information. Surely he wasn't suggesting that she marry Max's brother.

"There will still be talk; that can't be helped. Gossips will imagine two brothers vying for the same girl. You and Wally meeting behind Max's back. Eloping. I don't know yet how to explain the woman Max married, but we'll come up with something."

"I can't marry Wally," she whispered, staring at her father. "I hardly know him."

"You can marry him, and you will."

"Wally McCord?" She shook her head in confusion. When she tried to pull Wally's face into memory, she saw Max, younger and grinning, softer and more malleable, easygoing. Where had this idea come from?

"You have three choices," her father stated flatly. "You can do nothing, stay here, and face the disgrace and humiliation. Or you can go back East, have the baby, put it out for adoption, and still be the object of whispers and speculation. Lastly, you can marry Wally McCord, scatter a few lies to dampen part of the scandal, and thank heaven that he's willing to give your bastard a name. No matter what you do, there will be a storm of gossip. The way I see it, marrying Wally McCord is your best choice. I wish he wasn't a McCord, but he's all we have."

"But I don't want Wally," she wailed. "I want to marry Max."

"That is the stupidest, most foolish thing I've ever heard you say." Her father's fingers tightened painfully around her hand. "Remember this. McCord's pride was more important than you," he said bitterly. "Max didn't have to draw a marble out of that hat. If he'd cared one iota for you, he would have refused. And if he'd truly cared, he wouldn't have destroyed your innocence, then ridden out of here to spend the summer in the mountains."

This time when she burst into tears, he wrapped his arms around her and let her cry on his neck.

She didn't know how she could hate Max and want him at the same time, but she did. One thing she did know. It wasn't over between them.

Chapter 8

An open expanse of land, sky, and horizon settled Max's thoughts as the enclosed slopes and valleys of the mountains never had. Here on the high plains, a man could breathe. He could see what was coming.

Shifting his weight on Marva Lee, he let his eye follow a line of tall cottonwoods and wild plums banking a dry creek bed that flooded every spring. Long after he had crumbled into dust, the land would endure, cycling through the seasons with an ageless predictability. Usually this thought made his problems seem small. But today, his problems struck too deep.

Hoofbeats sounded behind him, and he straightened in the saddle, waiting for his brother.

Wally reined up, and silently they watched a steer just visible through a leafy stand of ripe chokecherries.

"The roundup starts the day after tomorrow?" Max asked finally. Ironically, the fall roundup had been a consideration when he and Philadelphia had discussed dates for the wedding.

"Right," Wally confirmed. "We'll bring all the cattle to Ma's place, then sort out which beeves belong to who. We figured we'd divvy up any unbranded stock."

Very likely this would be the last year they ran the four parcels as one ranch. Dave had already started fencing his and Gilly's land, and Max's hands were also putting up fence.

"You'll have to handle it without me this year," Wally

said, squinting at the ragged line of peaks shadowing the horizon.

Max clenched his teeth, and his thighs tensed, sending Marva Lee into a sideways dance.

He circled her back alongside Wally's roan. "I spent last night sitting in the barn thinking about . . . everything. I wish I knew what to say." Neither of them looked at the other. "Thank you and I'm sorry don't begin to cover it." He wanted to ask what had happened at this morning's meeting between Wally, Livvy, and Howard Houser, but pride got in the way.

"You'd do the same for me."

"I would. But that doesn't make any of this right. I keep going over and over it." He watched the steer hiding in the chokecherry bushes. "If I hadn't drawn a marble out of the hat. Or if I hadn't gotten sick. If I'd stayed here and hadn't gone to Piney Creek in the first place." That's why they had made love. She'd wanted to entice him to stay in Fort Houser and give up his summer in the mountains. Why hadn't he?

"Did you find what you were looking for up there?" Wally jerked his chin toward the line of mountains to the west.

"It doesn't seem important anymore."

He'd been trying to comprehend the longing in his father's voice when Jason McCord recalled the three years he'd worked the streams and mines near Central City. Those three years of searching for gold had been the defining years of his father's life, a passion Max had never understood.

If his father had been beside him now, Jason would have fixed his gaze on the mountains, and a half-smile of memory would have twitched his lips. He wouldn't have seen the steer or noticed the geese passing overhead in an arrow-shaped formation.

When Jason McCord finally came out of the mountains to join his family, the fire had gone out of him.

Max had wanted to know why. He'd wanted to understand the expression in his father's eyes when he turned his face to the far horizon. Now maybe he did. And oddly, it wasn't the gold as Max had always believed. It was the search itself and the dreams of a life changed. Jason McCord had left his dreams in the streams near Central City.

"Whatever you found up there . . . was it worth it?" Wally asked in a low, curious voice.

He didn't answer.

"We'll live with Ma in the main house," Wally announced abruptly, tapping the end of the reins against his thigh.

That decision surprised him. He'd assumed that Wally would move to town.

"This way she'll have Ma, Gilly, and Louise to help with the delivery or if anything goes wrong along the way."

Good God. He hadn't given Louise a thought since he'd left her in his mother's parlor yesterday afternoon.

"There are obvious disadvantages to me and Miss Houser—Philadelphia—living out here," Wally continued carefully, "but Ma and Mr. Houser agree it's the best choice. The progress of the pregnancy won't be as easily noted by every gossip. And this is one way to take some of the punch out of the scandal. Make it seem like there's no hard feelings between you and me."

Max squinted at a second squadron of geese heading south, then shifted in his saddle. "Are there hard feelings, Wally?"

Something hot flickered in his brother's eyes, a quick flame that died before the heat burned either of them. "All my life I've had to take your leavings," Wally said in a flat tone. "I never had a schoolbook that didn't have your scribbling in the margins. It was years before I owned a new shirt or a pair of boots that you hadn't worn first. As you outgrew a chore, it became mine.

Now I'm getting the bride you jilted, and you were there first. How do you think I feel?"

Max covered his eyes. "I wish to Christ none of this had happened."

"I've been thinking, too, and I've got a few things to say. If I have to do this, then I want to do it right. I'll try my damnedest to be a good husband to Philadelphia and a good father to her child. But I can't succeed if you get in the way, Max. As far as you're concerned, you and Philadelphia never happened. You walk away and don't look back. You give me a chance to make this marriage successful. Second, I want your promise that you won't come between me and the child I'm going to raise. You give up any claim, and you agree that the child is mine and will never know that I'm not his or her father."

Each word was a knife to the heart. Each request was necessary and fair. When he could, Max unclenched his jaw and spoke in a thick voice. "You have my word. And my gratitude."

He stayed on the range after Wally rode back to the main house, sitting slumped in the saddle, thinking about Wally's optimism. Somehow his brother had been able to set aside any bitterness or resentment, turn his attitude around, and talk about his intention to make a success out of a marriage to the wrong woman and about raising a child that wasn't his.

Max hoped to God that he could live up to his promise.

What Wally asked was not unreasonable. For the circumstances to be bearable, both Max and Philadelphia had to pretend there had never been anything between them. They had to forget that she carried Max's child. Anything less would be unfair to Wally and would generate deep resentment and trouble.

He leaned a hand on his thigh, feeling the bump of the marble in his pocket. What hurt most was knowing he'd given up all rights to the child he and Philadelphia had created together.

Low Down, or rather Louise, as she was now trying to think of herself, spent the morning down at the barn and corrals behind the main house. Preparations for the roundup were in full swing and were creating an air of anticipation and excitement that led to a lot of jokes that ended abruptly when the boys noticed her watching and listening. Then came a flurry of lifted hat brims and sheepish grins and a multitude of "sorry, ma'ams."

She didn't mind. This was the world she understood, the man's world of risque jokes and pride and posturing. A world of clear-cut goals where success or failure wasn't open to interpretation. Where a person was judged by his deeds and his character, not by what he wore or how pretty he spoke.

When Livvy called to her from the back stoop, she left the corrals with reluctance. She would far rather have joined the boys in their roundup preparations than climb up on the wagon with Livvy, Gilly, and Sunshine to drive to her new home.

Livvy took the reins, then pointed her chin toward the wagon bed where Gilly and Sunshine sat on a mound of hay. "Judging from those saddlebags, you don't have many clothes."

"Just this dress and one other."

"That's what I guessed. I put together a few things to make do until you can get more clothes. The skirts will be short but that can't be helped." Livvy flapped the reins across the horses' backs and urged the team out of the yard. "Do you sew?"

"I can darn socks and mend a seam." But she knew that wasn't what Max's mother was asking. Stamping down her pride, she looked at the short prairie grass running up to the wheel ruts. "Admitting this ain't going to make much of an impression, but I've never sewed a whole dress before. Didn't even wear dresses much until this week."

"I never met a grown-up lady who couldn't sew," Sunshine said.

"Well, now you have," Low Down said.

Gilly broke the following silence. "You'll need at least three everyday skirts and shirtwaists. A go-to-town skirt and jacket. Two good dresses and one party dress." She slid a glance toward Louise's hat. "Plus accessories."

"We'll have to go to town to buy material. Maybe while everyone's off on the roundup. Then we can get started. It might be easier and faster to send off for ready-made small clothes."

Louise was tempted to ask if Max had authorized them to spend his money left and right for new clothes for his temporary wife, but she kept silent, listening to the interplay between mother and daughter. She didn't understand what was meant when Gilly said, "Aunt Dilly was tall and braid looked smart on her. I think two spools." But Livvy nodded as if an entire discussion had preceded Gilly's comment.

When the conversation shifted to Wally and Philadelphia, her interest sharpened. But here, too, mother and daughter spoke in fragments and phrases that Louise didn't fully comprehend. But she understood the affection between them and was touched that neither questioned the decision to sew her some dresses. Nor did Livvy appear to object that Philadelphia would now be living with her in the main house instead of in Max's house. Louise wondered if all families absorbed blows like the McCords did.

"Mr. Houser seems to think hiding Philadelphia out here will avert most of the scandal." Livvy rolled her eyes toward a cloudless sky. "We're going to say that Philadelphia was engaged to one brother but loved the other and married him days before she should have married the first one. Then after she and Wally elope, she's coming out here to live on a ranch with both of them."

"Not both of them, Mama."

"Might as well be. Even with his own place, Max will still spend time up at the main house. He's been doing my accounts for years, no reason to change now. And there's Sunday dinner."

"Oh my." Gilly rubbed a gloved hand up and down on her forehead. "Sunday dinner."

"This misfortune is not going to break up my family," Livvy said fiercely. The quotation marks between her eyebrows deepened. "We'll continue to have Sunday dinner together."

Louise's heart sank, and she nodded when Gilly gave her a look of despair and rolled her eyes. In that instant, she and her new sister were in perfect accord. No one but Livvy was going to be happy about the whole family sharing Sunday dinner.

Livvy turned her head to look at Louise. "I don't think you've said three words since breakfast. Do you have an opinion about all this?"

"No, ma'am."

"I'm not ma'am, I'm Livvy." Livvy gave the reins an irritable flap. "Since we're going to have three Mrs. McCords, it'll go easier if we drop the formalities and use our given names. Are you agreeable?"

"I am. Except I don't feel like Louise. That doesn't seem like me." She couldn't remember back far enough to recall a time when anyone had called her Louise. And she didn't care much for the name. Louise impressed her as too soft and feminine for a rough number like her.

"Well, you can't be called Low Down. Max told me how you got that nickname," Livvy said, pressing her lips into a line. "I'm not going to have a daughter-in-law with a name that makes her sound worthless. You're a McCord now."

In fact, there was an element of safety and comfort in

her old name. No one expected much from a person called Low Down. She didn't expect much of herself. But Louise McCord . . . that was different. Louise McCord sounded like a woman of consequence who might be expected to know about things like sewing a dress.

"And you don't strike me as a person without opinions."

"I have opinions. But it ain't—it's not my place to jump into a family matter." Especially as she was acutely aware the trouble had begun with her.

But it was easy to be wise after an event. When this whole thing started, she'd had no inkling how many people would be affected by her longing to have a baby. Grinding her teeth together, she told herself that it was not her fault that Wally was about to marry the woman Max had wanted to spend his life with. She couldn't possibly have guessed that would happen.

"This is your family, too. And that means you have as much right to an opinion as anyone else." Irritation infused Livvy's voice and expression, and she released a long breath. "Nothing is working out the way I thought it would. Suddenly I'm going to have two new daughters-in-law. One's pregnant and wishes she wasn't. The other probably isn't and wishes she was."

"Mama," Gilly said, tapping Livvy on the shoulder. "Little pitchers have big ears."

"Sunshine isn't a fool. She knows things aren't working out the way anyone wanted them to."

The McCords were the only family Louise was likely ever to have. But that didn't mean they accepted her. Accepting the fact of Max's marriage was not the same thing as accepting the woman he'd married. She'd do well to keep that truth in mind.

Turning to glance at Gilly's softly rounded profile, she cleared her throat and remarked, "How long have you been married?"

"Mr. Weaver and I have been married for six years."

"Gilly, for heaven's sake. I think you can call him Dave in front of your sister-in-law."

"Six years," Louise repeated. But Gilly had only one child. That was discouraging. On the other hand, as nearly as she could piece together, Max had been with Philadelphia once and that had been enough. The whole business of sex and pregnancy was mysterious and frustrating.

"Well, here we are. Your new place."

As recently as this morning she had reread her copy of Max's letter describing the house, so she had some idea of what to expect. Nevertheless, the house surprised her. To her relief, it wasn't as large as she'd imagined or as she would have thought it was if she hadn't seen the main house first.

Max's house sat on a rise, and seemed tall and narrow with no landscaping in place to soften the angles. What Max had referred to in his letter as simple translated to clean lines and no wasted space.

"It's rather spare," Gilly murmured. "It will help if you plant some lilacs come spring and put in trees to break the wind."

"I like it," Louise said softly. The house didn't pretend to be grand or impressive. But it might become so in the future if wings were added to accommodate a growing family. But the future didn't concern her. For the moment, she was awed to think that she would be living in this house.

"Since you didn't come with a trousseau, I've brought extra linens and dishes and the clothing I mentioned earlier. Also, more food staples to get you started," Livvy said, walking around to the wagon bed and letting down the gate. She lifted Sunshine to the ground. "Don't anyone go inside empty-handed."

Carrying a box filled with pots and baking utensils, Louise climbed the porch steps of the house where she and Max would live for the duration of their marriage.

The foyer was large enough that she could have pitched her Piney Creek tent on the polished wood floor. A quick peek to the left revealed a parlor with a bay window. To the right was a dining room with a matching window. A staircase led upstairs; a paneled hallway ran back to a kitchen, pantry, and what Livvy called the mudroom.

"The kitchen is large and sunny," Gilly commented, placing a box of tablecloths and dish towels on a long wooden table.

"Uncle Max sent to Denver for the best appliances."

That he had. Louise had never seen anything like the gleaming six-hole, nickel-plated stove and oven. "And look at this," she said in a whispery voice. A pump handle overhung the sink. "Water in the kitchen. Can you imagine? You don't even have to go outside."

"We'll put everything away, and you can sort it out later. Right now, I imagine you want to have a look around."

"If you don't mind."

She was careful not to touch anything as she passed from room to room examining the furnishings and wallpaper and carpets. Since she'd seen Livvy's house and knew how things ought to look, she spotted blank areas, like the mantelpiece in the parlor. As everything else seemed complete, the blank spots puzzled her until the answer popped to mind. Probably it had been Livvy who furnished the house while Max was gone, and she had left space for Philadelphia's display items.

This was Philadelphia's house.

The rose-colored bedroom had been furnished with Philadelphia in mind. The paisley wallpaper and flowered carpets had been selected to please Philadelphia's taste and preference. The kitchen had waited for Philadelphia's dishes and pans and napkins and tablecloths. It should have been Philadelphia touring the house, marveling at all she saw.

Sobered and feeling a bit low in her mind, Louise

returned to the kitchen. Livvy and Gilly had donned aprons and were putting together a stew for supper. While Gilly peeled potatoes and Sunshine stood on a stool beside her, Livvy kneaded bread dough on the end of the long kitchen table.

"There's a rhubarb pie in the oven, and fresh coffee on the stove," Livvy mentioned, pushing the heels of her hands into the dough.

"I didn't realize I was gone so long."

"We planned to get supper started. You shouldn't have to cook the first night in your new home. You'll want to put away your things."

"That won't take long," Louise said, pouring herself a cup of coffee. She pressed the back of her hand to her forehead, then watched them working in her kitchen and taking time from their own homes to do it. "Why are you doing this?"

"Beg your pardon?" Livvy looked up from the lump of dough.

"You don't want me here. All I've done is cause the McCord family a lot of trouble. So why did you put together all these things?" She waved a hand at the now empty boxes. "Why are you cooking supper and planning to sew me some dresses? Why are you trying to help me?"

"Because you married Uncle Max and you're part of our family," Sunshine said, smiling the smile of youth and innocence. "We do too want you."

Livvy studied her for a moment. "Why did you stay in Piney Creek and nurse those men?"

"I honestly don't know. It just felt like the right thing to do."

After a shrug, Livvy slapped the dough down on the table and continued kneading.

Smiling, Gilly paused with a potato in one hand and a paring knife in the other. "If the McCords had a motto, it would be 'Do the right thing.' "

That could have been her motto, too. She understood the importance of doing the right thing. However, she noticed that only Sunshine had disputed her remark that she wasn't wanted here. No matter how Livvy and Gilly tried not to blame her for the scandal and misfortune pouring down on the family, on some level they did. Helping her originated in a sense of duty and an obligation to do the right thing for Max's wife.

After Livvy, Gilly, and Sunshine departed, she put away her few belongings, then fetched her everyday shawl and stepped outside the mudroom door. She sat on the top step of the kitchen stoop in a wash of afternoon sunshine, leaving the door open so she could smell the savory scent of stew simmering on the stove, and the yeasty fragrance of bread loaves cooling on the table beside the rhubarb pie.

There was space between the stoop and the clothesline for a kitchen garden, she noted. If she was still here come spring. And she identified a spot where the ground began to slope that would be convenient for pouring out sudsy laundry water.

To the west the land dipped and rolled like waves swelling toward the distant mountains. To the east the ground appeared flatter, bushier, but with fewer trees. She couldn't see the main house from here, didn't spot another rooftop or any signs of a nearby neighbor. If it hadn't been for voices calling back and forth down by the barn and storage sheds, Louise would have felt as if the world had dropped away, leaving only this house and this patch of ground.

A week ago she would have followed the voices and introduced herself and spent the rest of the afternoon getting acquainted with the hands. But everything was different now. Instinct warned that the boss's wife didn't lollygag around the barn with the hired men.

A deep sigh caused the shawl to slip off her shoulders. Well, she was accustomed to solitude. She had her songbook stories to think about, and after today she would be too busy to worry about being alone. Tomorrow she'd have chores—cooking and dusting and sweeping. And Livvy had mentioned that the hands had been feeding the chickens and milking the dairy cow, suggesting these were tasks Louise was expected to handle.

When the shadows lengthened and the air felt cool against her cheeks, she stood to return inside, pausing as she noticed a horseman trotting across the prairie range. Even from a distance she recognized Max by the way he sat Marva Lee and from the distinctively jaunty angle of his hat. She watched him lean forward in the saddle as Marva Lee sailed over a stone fence, then man and horse veered toward the barn.

Never had Louise expected to feel her heart constrict in a spasm of strange wild joy simply because a man rode toward her. But this wasn't just any man. Her husband was coming home for supper. And suddenly that seemed like a mighty fine thing.

She couldn't decide whether to curse Preacher Jellison for turning her life upside down or to bless him for giving her a taste of a life she would never have experienced otherwise.

She'd decide later. Right now she needed to give the stew a stir and set the table. Son of a . . . gun. She flat couldn't get over it. She had a husband, and he was coming home for supper.

Chapter 9

~❧───────────────────❧~

The original plan had included a wing extending to the south. The additional space would have added a sunroom, a library, and a family sitting room on the ground floor, a nursery and extra bedrooms above.

Before Max had departed for Piney Creek, he'd decided to wait and see how well Philadelphia adjusted to ranch living before adding the expense of the south wing. He had hoped that eventually she would share his love of the land and the pleasure of not dwelling eaves to porch rail with a neighbor. When that time came, if it did, then he'd construct the wing.

Now he studied the tall, narrow core of the house and conceded that Philadelphia would never have adjusted to an isolated location or to living so far from her father and friends and lady's clubs. Moreover, he'd neglected to provide quarters for a cook or maid, an oversight Max only now recognized as significant.

Absorbed in thinking about mistakes that seemed obvious in retrospect, he was almost to the barn before he saw Louise rise from the kitchen stoop and gather the edges of her shawl close to her breast. She stood straight and tall, not signaling, not seeming to expect anything, simply waiting and watching.

The barn called to him, but duty and guilt called louder. Swearing softly, he paused, then turned Marva Lee toward the house and rode up to the stoop, wondering what he could possibly say to her. To his relief she broke the silence first.

"Supper's ready whenever you are," she said, shading her eyes to look at him. She didn't castigate him for abandoning her as he'd half expected she might.

"I'd like to look at the barn and sheds, and speak to the boys." None of the hands were strangers, since most had worked for the McCords before Livvy parceled the ranch into fourths. They would expect him to say hello after a long absence.

"There's no hurry. Supper will keep." She dropped her hand and smoothed it across the front of an apron he'd seen his mother wear. "There's a basin of water in the mudroom where you can wash up." Late sunlight slanted across her face, finding gold in her hazel eyes, coaxing auburn highlights from her hair. "Max?" Color rushed into her cheeks and her voice sounded oddly shy. "This is a wonderful house."

From her perspective he supposed it was. Anything with solid walls and a roof would be an enormous step up from pitching a tent on the bare ground. She wouldn't notice the lack of an informal sitting room and servant's quarters.

Putting her out of his mind, he spent the next hour touring the barn, sheds, bunkhouse, corrals, and stock pond, and talking to Shorty, his foreman.

"Everything seems to be according to the plans," he said with satisfaction. He'd never doubted that it would be, not with Shorty Smith overseeing the barn raising and house building. Shorty had been his man on site, the person he'd trusted to make the day-to-day decisions and see that the job got done.

"I appreciate your diligence on my behalf," he said gruffly, shaking Shorty's hand. Spending the summer in the mountains would have been impossible without Shorty. His brother and Gilly's husband had their own operations to run, and he wouldn't have imposed by asking either to oversee an extensive building project.

"My pleasure, boss," Shorty said, puffing out his chest. "It ain't often a man gets to be part of a ranch right from the get go." He leaned on the top rail of the corral and slid Max a curious look. "I wish you and the missus every happiness on your new place."

Shorty wouldn't ask the questions flickering behind his sidelong glance, but it wasn't difficult to guess what they were. Cowboys were worse gossips than old women, and undoubtedly there was a great deal of bunkhouse speculation about Max coming home with one woman days before he was scheduled to marry another. By suppertime tomorrow the cowboy grapevine would be discussing what it meant that Wally had taken the gig to town wearing his Sunday best and toting a large traveling satchel. And before breakfast of the following day, the hands would notice that Wally wasn't participating in the roundup. By then they might have learned that Wally and Philadelphia had run off to Denver together.

Max bit down hard and faced toward a sunset blaze of red and orange. The days were getting shorter and the nights colder. "Tomorrow I'll bring Mrs. McCord down to show her the barn. You might tell the boys to shave and put on clean bandannas."

Having said all he intended to say, he headed toward the back of the house and the mudroom. The first time he entered his house should rightly have been through the front door so he could experience a first impression as others would. But having admitted the flaws, his impression of the house was soured.

"Is there a towel?" he called after washing up.

"Somewhere. But I don't . . . here, use this." Coming to the mudroom door, Louise glanced at the water dripping into the opened collar of his shirt, then pushed a dish towel into his hands.

The first thing he noticed after hanging his hat on a

peg and stepping into the kitchen was the stove. Iron with nickel trim and wood handles that stayed cool to the touch no matter how hot the firebox became. It burned wood or coal, soft or hard.

"Ain't it the grandest, shiniest stove you ever saw?" Louise said, following his gaze. "And look here. We have an icebox to keep things cool." Opening the icebox lid she removed a dish of butter. "There's no ice in it now, but come winter there will be." A stream of words poured out of her. "Your mother and sister prepared supper." She set the dish of butter on the table and stepped back, frowning. "Do I have to set out spoons even if we won't be using them? Oh, wait. I forgot about stirring sugar into coffee. Well, hell. I forgot to make fresh coffee."

"It doesn't matter." Remembering that he hadn't eaten since yesterday, he took a seat at the head of the kitchen table. "Louise," he said after watching her bounce from stove to pump handle to icebox as if she couldn't stop moving. "Will you sit down?"

"I dished out the stew, but I thought you'd want to see the rest of the house before you ate. I wasn't sure what to do."

"I'll see the house later." He swallowed a bite of stew, then reached for a fresh loaf of bread. "I'm sorry I disappeared last night and most of today. I knew Ma and Gilly would look after you."

"I don't need looking after," she said, bristling. "A lot happened last night and this morning. Your ma told me most of it." She pulled small pieces off a chunk of bread, rolled them into balls between her thumb and middle finger, and dropped the little balls into her stew bowl. "I guess you went crazy when you learned Philadelphia was pregnant."

Suddenly the food tasted like ashes. "There's nothing to be gained by talking about it." As the shadows deepened outside the windows, the lamp in the center of the table seemed brighter, spreading a soft glow over the tablecloth, smoothing the circles beneath Louise's lashes. He drew a breath. "I'll be gone about a week on the roundup."

Surprise lifted her brows. "I thought I heard Livvy mention the roundup would last longer than that."

"We won't bring in the cattle in one large herd, but in several smaller herds. I'll return with the first group and set up for branding and notching."

"At the main house."

He nodded. "Will you be all right staying here alone for a week? I could leave one of the boys to look after you."

Even the loose tendrils around her face seemed to stiffen with offense. "I don't need a nursemaid, damn it." Tilting her head, she glared at him. "A better idea would be to take me along on the roundup. I could learn how to chase down cows."

"You probably could." He smiled in spite of himself. "But I doubt the boys would appreciate having a greenhorn woman getting in the way."

"I'm no delicate little flower, McCord," she said, narrowing her eyes even farther. "I can do anything a man can do."

He thought again that he liked her best when her dander was up, and pride and bravado rose like mercury shooting up a thermometer.

"I won't argue the point," he agreed, reaching for more bread. "Ma and Gilly used to ride along before Gilly turned into a young lady. But Ma was never a greenhorn, she could bust mavericks out of the brush as good as any man. And I've seen Gilly hold a small herd together."

"Well, then." Triumph gleamed in her eyes. "I guess I can, too."

"Cow punching is something a person grows up with or grows into. It isn't something you learn in the middle of the fall roundup. You'd be a danger to yourself and others."

Maybe it was the play of lamplight across her features that made her expression so readable tonight. He saw her disappointment but also knew he'd struck the right chord when he explained that she might imperil others.

"You could go up to the main house and stay with Ma," he suggested after he'd finished the stew and she'd served him a slab of rhubarb pie. He wouldn't have left Philadelphia absolutely alone, and he was determined to offer Louise the same courtesies.

"I might visit, but I'll stay here." She continued to roll little bread balls, now dropping them on top of the pie she hadn't touched. "Somebody needs to feed the chickens and milk the cow. I guess that's me. Who knows? Maybe I'll ride out and find some cattle close in and practice driving them toward the barn."

This was what he didn't like. Her independence led to impulsive decisions. Patiently, he explained the foolishness of attempting to chase cattle out of the brush with no instruction and no one along to help if things went wrong.

"Suppose the steer charges your horse and your horse shies and throws you. You could be out there for a week with a broken leg and no water, and no one knowing where you are."

Raising her head, she gave him a long searching look. "I wouldn't think that would concern you overmuch," she said in an expressionless voice. "Nobody would shed a tear if I got thrown and broke my neck."

"No one would be happy about it, either," he snapped, returning her steady gaze. "What you do now doesn't alter a damned thing. Live or die. Stay or go. Wally will still be married to Philadelphia." Realizing he'd raised his voice, he leaned back in his chair and pulled a hand down his jaw, feeling the small pox pits beneath his fingertips. "Do you still want a baby?" he asked bluntly.

"Yes."

"Then stop feeling sorry for yourself, if that's what you're doing. I agree it wasn't much of a welcome, with Ma talking divorce before you even went inside the house, but the family's trying to do right, trying not to blame you for everything that's happened." He ignored the hissing sound of her breath and the way her spine went rigid. "But the truth is, a lot of lives have been changed or affected because you want a baby."

"Or because you wanted a summer in the mountains. Or because fate put a marble in your hand. Or—"

He raised his hand. "You're right. But the fact is Wally wouldn't have married Philadelphia today if you had wanted a piano or a house or something else. You and I are married because you wanted a baby. And so are Wally and Philadelphia."

"What are you trying to say?" she asked coldly.

"I guess I'm saying that I don't blame you, but you do bear some responsibility. I'm also saying that you can run off if you want to. You can risk your life on foolish, dangerous pursuits if you need to prove a point." He stared into her eyes. "Then nobody wins. Nobody in this whole mess gets what they want. Believe it or not, and I've told you this before, I don't want to see that happen. I'd like to think that at least one person finds something good in all of this. But I'm through begging you to stay, Louise. If you truly want to cut and run, then go. Nothing's holding you here, you're not a prisoner."

"I'm staying," she said, pushing up from the table. "I ain't changed my mind about a baby." Spinning in a swirl of skirts, she stormed toward the pump and worked the handle so vigorously that water gushed into the dishpan like a geyser. "I never said I expected a big welcome, and I never even hinted that your family hasn't treated me right! They've been polite, thoughtful, and nice as pie." She threw him a burning look. "They're treating me squarely, not for my sake, but for yours, and that's all right. But it's true that I could die right now standing here about to wash up the supper dishes, and no one would weep a single tear. That's how it's always been, and that's a fact!"

Abruptly Max realized that he had no idea what they were arguing about. Not an inkling. Standing, he decided now was a good time to inspect the rest of the house. For a moment he watched Louise furiously scraping the bowls and pie plates into the slop bucket, then decided he didn't have to explain why he was leaving the table. But he felt the need to say something.

"I've said all I'm going to on this subject, and don't you forget it." Hell, he didn't even know what the subject was.

"Oh, you can count on that!" she shouted as he left the kitchen and entered the hallway leading to the foyer.

He lit the lamps in the dining room and parlor and discovered that his instructions had been followed to the letter. The wallpaper reflected Philadelphia's favorite shade of crimson and the parlor sofa was upholstered in an offsetting dark blue. The colors were repeated in a flowered carpet and again in the fringe on the lampshades. Everything had turned out exactly as he had imagined when he'd designed these rooms. Except . . .

Frowning, he walked to the mantelpiece over the parlor fireplace. He'd pictured the heirloom candlesticks bequeathed to Philadelphia by her mother framing both ends of the mantelpiece, perhaps flanking an artful arrangement of figurines and velvet and silk flowers.

Instead, a solitary silver spoon stood against the wallpaper in the center of the mantel, propped against a scratched pewter watch case.

His impulse was to tuck the items into a drawer rather than give such shabby pieces a place of prominence. Displaying them was ludicrous. Embarrassing. Then he remembered Louise showing him the spoon at the campsite, something he'd forgotten. He covered his eyes and sighed.

For a while at least, this was her home, too. She had as much right to display her treasures as he had to display his collection of first editions in the glass-fronted bookcase. And that's what she had done.

Now he spotted a short stack of what turned out to be songbooks piled on top of the bookcase. Curious, he opened the bench seat in front of the piano and found more songbooks there. She'd placed a few with the piano and a few with his books as if unable to decide whether the songbooks were music or reading material.

Swearing, he thrust his hands deep into his pockets and found the green marble. Damn it. That's what he hated. About the time he was angry and feeling self-righteous and put upon, she said or did something that knocked the wind out of him.

After staring at the silver spoon for a full minute, he reluctantly returned to the kitchen and leaned in the doorway, watching her stack bowls on the drainboard. A dish towel was draped over her shoulder. "I'm not going to dry the dishes."

"I didn't ask you to."

"But I'll empty the dishwater in the yard."

"No, thank you. I'll do it myself," she said in a tight, clipped voice.

"I don't mind emptying the pan," he said, striving for patience.

"Well, I don't want you to do one damned thing for me!"

Max didn't understand why an angry woman refused to allow a man to do something helpful. Just as his mother had done when his father was alive, Louise bustled around the kitchen, wiping this, drying that, creating enough noise and commotion to make him feel that he was an idle lump of wood standing in her way.

"All right, what are you sore about?"

"Why would I feel sorry for myself?" She waved the dish towel and looked around with flashing eyes. "I never even knew a stove like that existed, and now I'll be cooking on it! And this house is the most beautiful place I ever saw. It will be a privilege to care for it and all the wonderful things in it. So don't you go accusing me—me!—of feeling sorry for myself, because I ain't! If it wasn't for you, I'd be as happy as a horse in high clover! You ask me, it's you who're feeling sorry for yourself!"

He saw it now. He'd insulted her or stung her feelings or maybe both when he said she was feeling sorry for herself. That's what the slamming and banging was all about.

"You think I'm feeling sorry for myself?" He didn't like hearing it either.

She leaned against the sink and crossed her arms over her chest. "There are going to be a lot of unhappy days for you, Max. When Wally and Philadelphia return to the ranch and the main house. The first time you see her as your brother's wife. The first Sunday dinner with everyone present. As you see her belly get bigger. The day she delivers."

"What's your point?"

"Making me feel bad isn't going to make you feel better."

Anger tightened his chest, and he pushed away from the doorjamb. Wives didn't speak to husbands that bluntly or critically. She had just given him one more reason to resent having married her.

"If you'll excuse me," he said coldly, "I'm going up to bed."

"You're excused!" She rolled her eyes and drew out the words. Then she picked up the dishpan and carried the dirty water toward the mudroom door. "I'll be up when I finish here."

He'd forgotten that only one bedroom had been finished. As Philadelphia had hinted that she would like rooms to furnish and decorate, he'd purposely left two of the three bedrooms empty. Like it or not, he and Louise would have to share a bed.

After lighting the lamps, he gazed unhappily at what was definitely a woman's bedroom. Rose paisley wallpaper. Ruffles and lace, lots of lace. A skirted vanity. Fringed tiebacks on the draperies. The decor had amused him when he'd planned it to surprise and indulge Philadelphia. Now it stifled and smothered.

Pressing his lips together, he glanced inside the dressing room, noting a row of his clothing on one side, and Louise's bought and borrowed items hanging on the other side.

By the time his unwanted wife came upstairs, he was in bed reading, and wearing a nightshirt, which was not his habit. Pretending to be engrossed in his book, he watched her enter the dressing room, then emerge a few minutes later completely covered by the voluminous tent-like nightgown. She'd taken down her hair and plaited it into a long braid that swung over her shoulder as she pulled back the blanket and sheet on her side then tucked herself and yards and yards of nightgown into bed.

Having arranged nightgown and covers, she pushed her pillow against the headboard and sat propped up as he was, her arms again crossed over her chest. A signal if he'd ever seen one.

"Is the light bothering you?" he inquired irritably. If she answered yes, as he expected she would, his choice would be to abandon the pleasure of reading before slumber or to ignore her wishes and be inconsiderate.

"Maybe I was feeling a little bit sorry for myself," she admitted in a low voice. "Your family's being nice, but I know they blame me for all the trouble." She cast him a quick hazel glance. "Then I start blaming myself and feeling bad and thinking that everything would have worked out a lot better, just like you said, if I'd picked a pi-ano or something else. But I didn't want a pi-ano, and everyone including you said I should pick what I wanted. It's just not fair, and I don't see an end to it. How long are we going to be fighting blame? That's what I want to know. A few weeks? Months? A year from Sunday?"

He closed the book with a snap and laid it on the bedside table. Concentration had been impossible; he doubted that he'd read two pages in the last forty minutes. He studied the wallpaper, trying to pick out the seams.

"Acknowledging your responsibility isn't the same as blaming you," he said finally. "If anyone's to blame, it's me. I should never have gone to Piney Creek."

"That occurred to me, too. So why did you?"

The answer wasn't simple. He'd failed to make Philadelphia understand his reasons; he doubted Louise would. But he told her about Jason McCord anyway, needing to remind himself what had driven him into the mountains despite Philadelphia's pleas that he stay here.

"I was born in Mexico," he said finally. "Wally was born in California. Gilly arrived in a mining camp near Central City. What those places have in common is gold or silver."

"Your father was a prospector?" Surprise caused her to shift on the pillow, and he felt her gaze on the side of his face. "I thought your pa was a rancher."

"No, it was Ma who grew up on a ranch down south. She met my father when he was working in a nearby town to earn enough to stake his next prospecting venture." Why two people with such different backgrounds, dreams, and personalities had fallen in love and married remained a mystery to Max. Maybe it had been a mystery to his parents, too.

"You remember the men in Piney Creek who brought their families to the diggings? My father did the same. In the early years maybe my mother enjoyed traveling to places she wouldn't have seen otherwise. Maybe living in mining camps felt romantic and adventurous. My father would have been content to chase the dream forever, but one day Ma realized she had three children growing up in rough camps. No house, no security. Only a hand-to-mouth existence and no future."

"Go on," Louise said. She'd propped her elbow on the pillow and rested her head in one hand while stroking the end of her braid across her cheek with the other hand. If he hadn't been focused on his parent's story, he might have laughed as the stubby end of her braid reminded him of a shaving brush.

"Ma started selling bread and pies out of the tent we lived in. She earned enough to buy a boardinghouse on Central City's main street. Three years later, she bought this land. A year after that she sold the boardinghouse and the four of us left Central City and came here to the ranch. We lived in a tent by the creek while the main house was being built."

"The four of you?" He heard a frown in her voice.

"My father stayed in Central City," he said, the words coming hard even now. "The dream was so strong that he let his family leave the mountains without him." And Max had been old enough to read the pain in his mother's eyes, old enough to feel himself abandoned and rejected.

"By the time he decided that being with his family was more important than searching for gold, the house was built and the range stocked. He came home hat in hand. But he never forgave my mother for finding riches in the mountains when he couldn't. Never let her or himself forget that she had bought the ranch with her earnings and he was living off the fruits of a woman's labor."

"Nothing costs so much as what is given us," Louise murmured with a sigh, and he looked at her, startled by her understanding.

"When Ma left the mountains and camps, she found stability and security in the land. But my father lost some vital spark. He never went into the mountains again, but he was never fully here, either. He left the better part of himself up there. And during the time they were apart, their marriage changed. Maybe Ma couldn't forgive him for choosing a sluice and a pan instead of her. Maybe she'd discovered she didn't need him after all. Maybe he blamed her for the loss of his dreams. Or maybe they were never suited in the first place."

"And you?" Louise inquired softly, her steady hazel gaze fixed on his face. "Did you forgive him for choosing a dream instead of you?"

"Good God," he whispered, staring at her in shock. When he looked down, he saw that his hands were clenched into fists. "I thought I needed this summer to understand him," he said slowly, his thoughts racing ahead of his words. "But you're right. That was only part of it."

Yawning, Louise plumped her pillow, then slid under the covers as if she hadn't just delivered a stunning insight. "I think you needed to go to Piney Creek. And this summer was your only chance to do it," she said in a sleepy voice, turning her back to him and the lamp. "Good night."

"Piney Creek was like Central City used to be, before the boom, before shaft mining," he said, speaking to her braid.

Long after he'd extinguished the lamp and Louise slept beside him, he sat in the dark remembering his childhood. Camping in a series of tents beside a series of creeks and streams. Helping his mother knead bread dough or roll out piecrusts. And later, emptying slop buckets in the boardinghouse, washing the stairs every morning before he gathered eggs for breakfast.

And then the ranch and his joy in the land—knowing the wandering had ended and he'd come home to a place where he belonged. Eventually the pain of missing his father knotted into anger so deep that he resented it when Jason McCord finally did rejoin his family.

Had he forgiven his father for letting them leave? For joining them eventually but leaving his heart beside a mountain creek? Not when he stood dry-eyed at the grave site, holding his mother's arm while the Reverend Dawson prayed.

But now? After his summer at Piney Creek?

After a time he stretched a hand to Louise's side of the bed and adjusted the blankets over her shoulder. It puzzled him that she understood so readily why he had needed a summer in the mountains, yet Philadelphia never had.

Philadelphia. Impossible as it seemed, he had forgotten for a while that tonight was Philadelphia's wedding night. He raised a hand to his eyes, and pain exploded behind his ribs.

She was Mrs. Wallace McCord.

By four o'clock, they were climbing the steps of the Denver County Courthouse. Within half an hour Wally had found a justice of the peace who married them in a dingy office that smelled of stale cigar smoke, glue, and ink. Minutes later they were again on the outside steps, dazed and awkward with each other, amazed that their lives could be forever altered in so short a time.

From there, they went to the telegraph office and dispatched announcements to Livvy McCord and Howard Houser. The carefully worded telegrams were targeted to Mr. Graham who managed the Fort Houser telegraph office and who was not known to respect the privacy of the telegrams that passed through his hands. By tomorrow the official story would be racing through Fort Houser like a prairie fire.

Wally then asked if she was hungry, and feeling confused and adrift, she had nodded yes although she felt sick inside and doubted she could swallow a bite.

He'd taken her to the dining room at the hotel where they had registered earlier, and they must have eaten although she couldn't remember what they had ordered. After coffee, they hailed a cab and attended the theater, where everyone wore evening dress except them, or so it had seemed. She couldn't recall one scene of the production.

Now they were back in the suite Wally had taken at the Denver City Hotel. He sat across from her holding his hat on his knees, looking younger than she knew he was and uncomfortable and very manageable.

She had already removed the fashionable wool cape that matched the smart blue-and-crimson-trimmed suit she'd chosen for the brief marriage ceremony. No, she absolutely would not think about the sugary confection of a gown hanging in her closet at home, the gown she would never wear.

Lifting her arms, she removed long pins, then placed her hat beside her on the settee. "I thank you from the bottom of my heart," she said in a low voice, smoothing the net and feathers and silk flowers trimming the brim of her hat. She cast him a quick peek, then lowered her eyelids. "I'm so ashamed." Tears welled in her eyes, sparkled on her lashes, then spilled to her cheeks.

The ability to weep at will was such a useful talent. Some women turned red and blotchy when they cried, but she did not. She knew she cried beautifully because she had perfected the art by practicing before a mirror.

Clasping her hands in her lap, she dropped her head and shoulders, creating a tableau of abject misery. "You must hate me," she whispered, letting tears fall on her hands. "You must hate it that you're stuck with a person of such low character."

In an instant he was kneeling in front of her, pushing his handkerchief into her hands. "Don't cry. I don't hate you, not at all." His hands lifted as if he wished to clasp her fingers, but he didn't yet claim the right to such intimacy. "You're not a low character." He drew a breath. "And I'm not stuck with you."

Now she covered her face with her hands and let her shoulders shake with sobs. "How kind you are. Oh how can I ever repay you for rescuing me from abandonment and scandal?"

"Philadelphia." It was the first time he had addressed her as anything other than Miss Houser. "Please look at me."

After patting her eyes with his handkerchief, she allowed herself to be coaxed into a sad gaze. He looked so earnest. So upset and eager to soothe.

"It's a bad beginning, yes," he said, trying to peer past her misery. "But others have made good marriages from bad beginnings. I intend to be a devoted husband and a caring father. You have my word on this." A wave of scarlet swelled up from his collar. "I hope someday you'll care for me as much as you—" Halting, he swallowed and knots ran up his jawline. "What happened before today doesn't matter. What happens from here on is what's important."

"Thank you," she murmured through the tears. Then she leaned forward and rested her head on Wally's shoulder, inviting him to offer comfort. After a moment, his arms came around her and he clumsily patted her back, whispering soft words and promises for the future.

Oh yes, he was manageable. Every man she had ever met was manageable. Except Max. Max was the only man who had ever said no to her. The only man who had not placed her desires before his own. She hated and loved him for that very reason.

Oh Max, she thought, and suddenly her tears were angry and genuine. It should have been you here tonight.

Chapter 10

❧━━━━━━━━━❧

Shorty Smith reminded Louise—she was still trying to think of herself as Louise—of Stony Marks, and another of the boys put her in mind of a fellow she'd known in the Dakotas. She took to the cowboys at once and would have liked to spend more time at the barn and corral except Max made it clear that the boss's wife could be friendly to but not friends with the hands. In a small act of defiance she spent the afternoon baking chokecherry pies sweetened with plenty of dark brown sugar. When they were cool, she delivered four of the pies to the bunkhouse.

Most of the day she devoted to discovering the nature of her wifely duties. No one had to explain, the chores swept her along. It was obvious that the bed needed making and breakfast needed cooking. First she had to go into the pearly dawn and rummage around beneath the hens to gather eggs for frying. Then bring in some kindling and stoke up the stove, something she would do before gathering eggs from now on so she could return to a warm kitchen. Before she cleaned up the breakfast dishes, she bundled up again and hurried down to the barn to milk Missy before Missy mooed the walls down. Then the cream had to be skimmed, and she had to decide if she needed to churn up some butter. Then turn Missy into the pasture before she washed out the bucket and dashed back to the house to tidy up the kitchen and start thinking about what she would feed

Max for dinner and supper. Knead some bread and put it aside to rise. Clean up the flour mess. And feed the chickens. She'd forgotten about the damned chickens.

After the barn tour, she fried up some ham and potatoes for Max's dinner. The bread wasn't ready to bake, so they had to do without. Then it was clean up the kitchen again and run through the house with a dust rag, doing a hurry-up job so she'd have time to pick the chokecherries she needed for the pies. And she didn't dare leave the kitchen while the pies were baking, not until she'd learned the quirks of the oven and if it cooked evenly or if she needed to turn the pans every few minutes.

Before she knew it, the sun was sinking and it was time to set the table again and the day was almost over.

"I'm plum tuckered out," she said to Max when they sat down to supper. The butter that Livvy and Gilly had provided was almost gone, and she gazed at the dish unhappily, wondering where she'd find time to churn up more. Heaven only knew what happened to the everyday chores on wash day.

"The boys were grateful to get those pies," Max mentioned, snapping his napkin across his lap in a way that made her remember the maître d' at the Belle Mark. "I guess it wasn't an inappropriate gesture. As long as you don't make a habit of it."

"I wasn't sure how the pies would turn out since I haven't baked in a real oven since I can't remember when."

Already she was wondering how she would accomplish all she needed to do tomorrow when Max and the hands left for the roundup. She'd need to care for her mule Rebecca and the horses they were leaving behind. More chores.

"I'm starting to think that shoveling gravel and panning for gold was a walk in the woods compared to being a wife."

Max smiled. "Is it really that difficult?"

"The work isn't hard; there's just so much of it. I feel like I'm cooking and cleaning up from cooking all day long and hurrying to do the other work in between cooking."

She hadn't yet gotten the hang of the stove or of using an oven. The beef was overcooked, and the potatoes were undercooked, errors in timing that wouldn't have happened if she'd been cooking over a campfire. There you could see the flames on the bottom of the skillet and raise or lower it accordingly. That the pies had come out well was something of a happy miracle.

Tonight she would have let Max throw out the dishwater, but he didn't offer. After supper he left the kitchen to sit in the parlor, which shocked her as she didn't think the parlor was for everyday use. When they went upstairs she hinted as much, talking to him while he was in the dressing room. Talking was better than silently imagining him naked behind the door.

"I needed to go over the expense figures for the house, barn, and sheds. Why are you smiling?" he added as he came into the bedroom.

"No reason." She hadn't figured him for a man who wore a nightshirt to bed. The long shirt ended at his knees and powerful calves emerged beneath the hem. "You could have spread out your papers on the kitchen table."

"Let's not start that business about not sitting on chairs. The chairs in this house are for sitting. Besides, I didn't want to disturb you."

"You wouldn't have disturbed me," she called from inside the dressing room. Now it was her turn to hide and don her nightclothes. "I was only cleaning up from supper and laying out the breakfast things." She stripped off one of the skirts and shirtwaists that Livvy had supplied, then dropped her nightgown over her head and returned to the bedroom.

When she brushed out her hair in the dark dressing room, she didn't do a good job of it. But she felt uncomfortable wandering around in her nightgown. Still, this was her bedroom, too, damn it. Studiously ignoring Max, she brushed her hair in front of the vanity mirror, then plaited it into a braid.

Tonight his habit of reading in bed didn't surprise her when she climbed in next to him. Earlier today she'd taken a minute to bring up the songbook given to her by the boys at Piney Creek so she could read, too.

"What?" Max asked after she laughed out loud. He lowered his book and looked at her.

"These are cowboy stories. Listen to this," she said, reading aloud. "Oh it's cloudy in the west and it's looking like rain and of course my old slicker's in the wagon again."

" 'The Old Chisolm Trail,'" he said with a half-smile.

"Oh, you know this story. Me, too, but I hadn't read that verse before. What are you reading?"

"*The Adventures of Tom Sawyer*. But my mind's drifting." Raising a hand, he rubbed the bridge of his nose.

There were many things that might distract him. The roundup that began tomorrow. Thoughts of Philadelphia. The papers he'd been studying in the parlor. She supposed it wasn't entirely impossible that he might be worrying about leaving her here alone, not that he needed to.

Closing the songbook, she set it aside and folded her hands on top of the ruffled spread. They sat close enough that she could feel the heat of his shoulder and inhale the good outdoors scent of him. Suddenly she realized that all day she'd been looking forward to this time with him. Even though she didn't care for the multitude of frills and ruffles, the bedroom was warm and cozy, and she could imagine the rest of the world had fallen away, leaving only them sitting against the pillows, reading together. It was a fanciful thought, but right nice.

"What's your mind drifting toward? If you don't mind my asking."

About the time she had decided he wouldn't answer, he said, "The papers I was examining show the expenses on this place were more than I figured. I'd counted on a salary at the bank to replenish any cost overruns."

"I'd forgotten about the bank position." She shook her head. "You just don't strike me as a banker type of man." Try as she might, she couldn't cast him in the role played by the fellow at the Colorado Merchant's Bank. Max belonged on the land.

"Maybe the only part of banking that I'll miss is a steady salary," he conceded. "I thought I could work in town and still keep up the ranch. Maybe it wouldn't have been as easily done as I'd hoped."

Louise agreed. "A man can't serve two masters. Eventually you would have had to choose." She was beginning to suspect that turning Max into a banker had been Philadelphia's idea, not his.

Yes, this was the very best time of day. Sitting close beside him in bed, discussing this and that. Enjoying the warm nearness of muscle and bone and the deep smooth timbre of his voice. If she moved her foot a few inches, she could touch his foot. She didn't do it, but she could have. And she thought about it. And she wondered—just a little—when they would get to the next poke. Which reminded her . . .

"Max?" She gazed down at her hands. "I've got something to tell you." Keeping her head down, she twisted her wedding ring around her finger, sliding the glow of lamplight along the gold circle. "I'm not pregnant. We're going to have to do, you know—it—again."

Max tilted his head back and turned his eyes toward the darkness outside the bedroom window. Louise didn't think it would have changed anything if they'd known she wasn't pregnant before Wally married Philadelphia, but she didn't know for sure.

"I'm sorry," he said finally.

"Me, too." She'd known yesterday, but it had taken until now to push her disappointment down far enough that she could tell him. It didn't seem fair that some people could get pregnant after one poke and other people couldn't.

"We both understood it might take a while." But the way his eyebrows knit together told her that he hadn't really believed it. He'd assumed, or more likely he'd hoped, that one poke had done the job. Naturally she had hoped that, too.

She slid a quick sidelong glance toward the crisp dark hair curling out of the collar of his silly nightshirt.

At some point she would have to force herself to submit to another poke. Heat flooded her cheeks, and her stomach rolled over in an odd way that almost felt like anticipation.

Max awoke before dawn and discovered himself wrapped around Louise, his legs tangled in the cursed nightgown. Paralyzed with surprise and dismay, he tried to think how this might have happened. The air in the bedroom was frigid because he liked to sleep with the window open a few inches. They must have rolled toward each other seeking warmth.

And she was indeed warm. The heat of her buttocks pressing against his groin caused an intimate stirring that grew stronger when he inhaled the warm sleepy scent of her hair and skin.

Embarrassed by his response, he carefully extricated himself and hastily slid out of bed, pulling the nightshirt over his head as he moved through the darkness to the dressing room. He dressed quickly, then carried his socks and boots downstairs to the kitchen where he discovered that Louise had brought in kindling the night before. In a moment he had the stove fired up but he didn't have to wait to shave as the water in the reservoir had stayed warm throughout the night.

As he shaved over a basin in the mudroom, he grudgingly conceded that Louise had the practical think-ahead mind that made for a good ranch wife. She'd brought in the kindling, filled the water reservoir, set the table for breakfast, laid out the skillet, and prepared the coffeepot. And this was only her second full day. He suspected she'd be handling her duties as efficiently as Ma or Gilly within a week or two.

Lowering the razor, he stared at his lathered face in the lamplit mirror.

She wasn't pregnant.

They would continue together, building habits, reaching small accommodations, learning to understand each other's foibles and strengths. It would happen merely by virtue of living together, regardless how either of them felt about creating a relationship.

The same process would occur with Wally and Philadelphia.

Placing his hands on either side of the basin, he dropped his head and leaned forward.

It would be Wally who sat down to supper with Philadelphia and praised her piecrust. Wally who watched her draw on her stockings and slide the garters into place. Wally who saw her with her hair down, who took the brush from her hand. Wally would learn her habits and mannerisms, would discover what pained or delighted her.

Not him.

By the time Louise passed through the mudroom on her way to collect eggs, he had finished shaving and had temporarily accepted what he could not change. He had tucked Philadelphia behind a mental door labeled: Forbidden.

The trick would be to keep that door shut.

* * *

Louise stood on the front porch, wiping her hands on her apron, and watched Marva Lee trot down the ruts that served as a road, heading toward the main house where the roundup would begin. In her opinion, no banker had ever ridden a horse the way Max did, as if he and Marva Lee were extensions of each other. Watching his straight back and broad shoulders was a pleasure that warmed her inside.

She was glad he was going.

Maybe some hard riding and hard work would knock the thoughts of Philadelphia out of his hard head. She knew when Max was thinking about that saintly paragon of womanly virtues, Miss Philadelphia Wonderful Houser, now Missus Wally McCord. A distracted look appeared in his eyes, and he turned cool and distant as he'd been at breakfast this morning.

Turning on her heels, she entered the house and returned to the kitchen. After pouring herself another cup of coffee, she reached in her pocket and removed her copy of the letter Max had written Philadelphia, then smoothed out the pages on the kitchen table.

She had memorized every sentence, but she read the letter anyway, feeling each word like a pin prick against her heart.

It was a happy letter, written by a man to a woman he deeply cared about. After describing parts of the house, Max gently chided Philadelphia for promising that he'd be sorry for abandoning her for the summer. He teased her about her pleasure in the wedding gifts that had begun to arrive. He called her dearest and said he was counting the days until she would be his.

When Louise had first read this letter, it hadn't affected her personally. She had simply liked the way the words flowed together and had wished someone would write her such a fine letter and call her dearest.

Then, after she and Max married, the letter had seemed

sad, evidence of fate's capriciousness. Now, it made her angry, although she couldn't have explained why.

Of course Max still thought about Philadelphia. He cared for her and he'd planned to share his life with her. Plus, a person couldn't turn his feelings on and off at will. He would probably grieve Philadelphia's loss for a long time, maybe forever.

She sipped her coffee, leaning back from the table to see out the window. This morning frost had sparkled on the range grass, and each day the leaves on the cottonwoods seemed a paler green, edging toward yellow. When she had visited the barn, she'd noticed the horses' hair was growing thick and long for winter.

Frowning, she gazed down at the letter. Keeping it didn't make her feel good anymore. Without considering what she was about to do, she crumpled the pages, then dropped them in the firebox of the stove and watched the paper curl to ash. And she fervently wished Philadelphia would disappear as easily.

There was another reason why she was glad to see Max leave for the fall roundup. Since marrying him, she hadn't had a single blamed minute to herself. She'd led a solitary life—she wouldn't exactly call it lonely—and she needed solitude to chew through the things that troubled her, to recall the items that gave her pleasure, and to make plans for tomorrow.

Standing, she gazed around her kitchen and decided the dirty dishes could wait. So could her other chores. What she needed now was a reminder that she was more than Max McCord's wife, she was still herself and she meant to stay herself.

Determined, she marched upstairs, threw off the too-short skirt and her shirtwaist. Then, because her prospector clothing had vanished, she chose a pair of Max's denims, rolled up the cuffs, and pulled them on. The waist was large enough that, without suspenders, the denims would have fallen around her ankles, so she borrowed a pair of suspenders, too. And a warm flannel shirt. And a hat and some riding gloves.

Feeling better than she'd felt in days, she strode down to the barn and corrals and looked over the horses that Max and the boys had left behind. Rebecca ambled over to the log rails, followed by a black gelding that was no longer young. She fussed over Rebecca a little then ran a hand along the gelding's winter-fuzzy neck.

"You don't like being left behind, huh?" she murmured before she climbed over the rails and dropped down beside him. "At your age you ought to know enough about cattle to teach me a little something."

The black quivered as she saddled and cinched him, as eager to go as she was. Once Louise was mounted, she let the gelding run off excess energy, laughing as he soared over the stone fence north of the barn.

For the next hour she rode aimlessly, enjoying the sunlight sparkling through brisk, chill air, getting a feel for the lay of the land, discovering draws and creek beds, wooded areas and open range. Occasionally she spotted a steer or cow and then the gelding's ears pointed sharply forward and she felt him tense beneath her, awaiting her signal.

"We'll get to that," she said, leaning to pat his neck.

Max would never approve of what she was doing, she knew. But she'd never been submissive, had never been afraid to take a risk, and she wasn't going to begin now. If she ended up injured . . . she'd deal with the situation if and when it happened. Just as she had dealt with unpleasant situations during all the years when she hadn't had a husband who thought he could tell her what to do.

"All right," she said to the gelding. "The next time we see a beeve, you do whatever it is you do, and I'll sit up here and observe and learn."

Almost at once the gelding leapt forward, galloping after a cow and calf that he spotted before Louise did.

There was no sitting and reflectively observing. It was all she could do to hang on as the gelding cut sharply in one direction, then whirled in another as the cow and calf tried to evade capture. If capture was indeed the objective, something Louise wasn't sure of at all. The gelding chased the cow at full gallop then cut directly in front of her and stopped hard, his head down, his front legs plowing out in front of him.

Louise sailed over his head and landed hard on her fanny.

She'd have some bruises to show, but she hadn't broken any bones, thank God, and the cow had missed trampling her. Grim-lipped and steely-eyed, she caught the gelding and swung up into the saddle again. By the time she looked up, the cow and calf had vanished. The likeliest place to hide was in a thick tangle of choke-cherries and other bushes she couldn't identify.

"You win this time," she shouted at the bushes, unwilling to prod the gelding into the thicket. "I'll catch you tomorrow."

The next time the black took after a lone steer, she had an idea what to expect and hung on longer, not trying to control the horse but just letting him work the beeve. Unfortunately, she ended as she had earlier, sprawled on all fours in the prairie grass.

At the end of the day, the gelding tossed her yet again, eyed her with what looked like disgust, then trotted toward the barn and corrals, leaving Louise to walk two miles back to the house. By the time she arrived, she was feeling the evening cold and aching in spots she hadn't known she had. After unsaddling the gelding and forking hay into the corral, she limped up to the house, anticipating a nice long soak in the wash tub. Among other things, she'd learned that chasing after cattle wasn't nearly as easy as she had supposed it would be.

By the morning of the fourth day she dared hope that

she was getting a handle on catching cows. Cows were more cunning than she would have believed and faster, too, which surprised her. Also, she had wrongly supposed they were as stupid as chickens.

She was heading out the back door when she heard Gilly calling from the front door.

"Louise? Are you there?"

A wide smile curved her mouth. She had never thought she would see a day when family came calling, but here it was. Pleased as all get out, she hurried to the front of the house. "Howdy!"

Gilly's mouth dropped when she saw the denims and suspenders. Flustered, she glanced down at Sunshine's wide eyes. "Mother and I were worried that Max didn't leave someone here to look after you, so I came by to check on you and bring a cake." She blinked and stared. "Louise, why on earth are you dressed like ... like *that*?"

"I'm learning to catch cows. But this is how I always used to dress," she explained cheerfully. "Come on in. And excuse the house. I ain't done my chores, but I'll catch everything up before Max returns." What was it about her new family that made her say "ain't" when she'd almost stopped using the word around Max? "It'll only take a minute to reheat the coffee."

Gilly picked up a basket at her feet and, holding Sunshine's hand, silently followed to the kitchen. "I don't think Max would approve of you chasing cows all by yourself."

Louise agreed, bringing two cups of coffee and a glass of milk to the table. "But if I wait for Max to teach me about cows, I'll still be waiting when the trumpet sounds."

Gilly smiled. "Dave's the same. He's always saying we'll do this or that, but he never gets around to it." She ran an eye over Louise's flannel shirt and suspenders, then cleared her throat. "Ma thinks we should go to town tomorrow to buy material for your new clothing. It needs to be tomorrow because two days after, Wally and Philadelphia will arrive home, and the first herd will be coming in. Me and Ma—and you, too, if you want to help—will cook for the boys since they'll need every man to hold the herd and do the branding and notching."

Louise cupped her hands around her coffee cup and nodded, absently thinking that Sunshine was a miniature vision of Gilly. Long chestnut curls hung beneath her neat little hat. Her eyes were a lovely clear McCord blue. "Tomorrow's fine. And of course I'll help with the cooking. I'll make pies." At least she knew she could make a credible pie.

Wally and Philadelphia were coming home. She didn't need a fortune-teller to predict that their arrival would shatter the fragile equilibrium she and Max had begun to establish.

"We'll come by for you tomorrow morning, and I'll tell Ma about the pies."

Lifting her arms, Gilly removed her hat, then took the cake out of the basket, followed by a pile of mending. And suddenly Louise realized Gilly meant to stay a while, which made sense when she thought about it. The drive would hardly be worth the considerable trouble if Gilly had delivered her messages and then turned around again and left.

Stepping to the window, she gazed toward the corral and pictured the black gelding waiting for her. He was out of luck. No horse could compete with a visit from family.

Grinning broadly, she returned to the table with a knife, plates, and forks, and suggested that Gilly cut the cake. Then, curious, she asked Gilly to describe her house. She made bread while Gilly talked and Sunshine played quietly with the doll that Max had brought her from Denver.

Louise laughed at Gilly's growing-up stories and told a few of her own. She asked about roundups and stampedes and caring for cattle through the winter. Gilly asked about prospecting and the people Louise met in the mining camp. They talked about the things all women have in common, homes and stoves, recipes and chores, until Gilly glanced at the kitchen clock, said, "Oh mercy me," and reached for her hat.

As Louise stood in the doorway and returned Sunshine's wave while Gilly's wagon headed up the rutted road, she realized she was sorry to see her niece and sister-in-law leave. She and Gilly were as different as a mouse and a moose, but they'd enjoyed each other's company and had found a few areas of shared interest. They hadn't discussed anything important, had avoided the problem areas, but they had made a beginning. Toward what, Louise didn't know, but she hoped it was a friendship. That would be mighty fine. She'd never had a woman friend before.

Chapter 11

The first person Philadelphia saw as she and Wally descended the staircase was her father, sitting beside one of the massive ferns, frowning and tapping a polished shoe as if he owned the hotel and itched to chastise someone. There was no surprise at discovering her father waiting in the lobby; it didn't occur to her to question his presence. Running across the marble tiles, she threw herself into his arms and clung there, fighting tears.

Howard Houser patted her back and murmured soothing sounds before he gently set her away and lifted an eyebrow in Wally's direction. "I'll take my daughter in to breakfast. You may return for her in two hours."

Coloring at the dismissal, Wally turned his hat in his hands like a rube, looking back and forth from Philadelphia to her father as if unsure what his response should be. His hesitation drove her mad. There had been nothing tentative about Max. And Max would never have allowed himself to be disposed of so easily. He would have stepped close and taken her arm, would have smiled his stubborn smile and made it obvious that any invitation included them both.

But Wally was not that sure of himself. And because he was already half in love with her, he'd become pathetically eager to please. As she might have predicted, he nodded and withdrew, ambling toward the street doors with the uncertain look of a man who had time to kill and no place to go.

Putting him out of her mind, Philadelphia tucked her arm through her father's and let him lead her into the hotel dining room. Instead of the midroom table where she and Wally had dined during the days they'd been here, the maître d' led them to a choice table beside a window overlooking the hotel's gardens. The gardens had been planned to offer a charming vista in any season, evidenced by a flaming plum tree that drew the eye away from bare flower beds covered with winter mulch.

Coffee for her father and tea for her appeared as if by magic, but her father waved aside the waiter who would have taken their order.

"By now you know if this solution is going to work. Will it?" her father asked bluntly.

She could smell the pomade slicking his hair back from a center part and the lingering scent of an English shaving soap, familiar smells that she associated with security, comfort, and indulgence. Among the shocks that had piled one atop the other during the past horrible week was the previously unthinkable realization that her father could not right every wrong, could not fix everything the way she wanted it fixed.

"You should have made Max marry me," she whispered. Tears of betrayal and accusation welled in her eyes.

"Now you know that's impossible. The son of a bitch already has a wife. If you'd waited for him to divorce that Jezebel, you'd have found yourself standing in front of a preacher holding a bastard in your arms. Is that what you wanted? To bear a child out of wedlock?"

Events had moved with lightning speed, beginning the moment Max related the story of his illness and subsequent marriage. A husband had been chosen for her, a hasty date selected for the elopement, a decision made as to where she would live afterward. And not once had anyone solicited her opinion.

"Of course not," she answered with a sigh. Several generations of proud Housers would roll in their graves if she shamed the family name by bearing a bastard. The scandal was bad enough without that. A drop of rain slid down the windowpane, followed by a thickening drizzle that obscured the plum tree. "Are people talking?" she asked, gazing out at the wet garden.

"Ridley reports that minutes after the telegrams arrived, the news of your elopement raced through town like a hot wind."

Philadelphia lowered her gaze and raised a hand to her forehead. "Is it known yet that Max has a wife?"

"That news created the first wave of scandal." He turned to the window and ground his teeth, sending knots rippling up his jawline. "The *Fort Houser Gazette* is running a quarter-page article today announcing your marriage to Wallace McCord. It's a straightforward piece presented as if Wallace was the man you always intended to marry. There's also a paragraph on a different page announcing the marriage of Max McCord. Needless to say, no at-home days are listed for either of the new Mrs. McCords."

His snappish tone informed her that his anger had not cooled. He still blamed her, at least partly. But it wouldn't do to permit him to see how his unfairness irritated her.

"What happens to the gifts? Given the circumstances, do you have to return them?" They had arrived addressed to her and Max. Strictly speaking, she supposed the gifts should be returned, but she didn't know the etiquette involved in this instance. The bride was still the bride. There had been a wedding.

"I have neither the time nor the inclination to sort out which gift returns to whom. I'd say keep them." He shrugged.

That was the answer she wanted to hear. She poured

another cup of tea, then led the conversation into the next area where she required assistance.

"Now that I've had a chance to think about everything, I've concluded I don't want to live on an isolated ranch. I never did." Sharing a home with Livvy McCord was a hundred times worse than living in the house Max had built for her. Livvy's sharp blue eyes made her uncomfortable, made her feel as if she didn't quite measure up. This was utterly ridiculous, and she resented it. "I want us to live in town with you, Daddy."

"There's enough scandal raging without everyone in town watching your belly grow," he snapped. "And you know they will. Besides which, when you do finally move to town, you need your own home, one that's equipped with a nursery."

She'd guessed that would be his position, and she'd thought about it; she had, in fact, put some subtly pointed questions to Wally. "Then I may be rusticating forever," she said, blinking at fresh tears. "Max sold enough cattle to at least build a house even if it is in the country, but Wally says he doesn't want to deplete the herd further. I can change his mind, of course, but it will take time. More time than I want to spend out there in the middle of nowhere." She let a tear slip down her cheek just as the waiter reappeared. Her father waved the man off with an annoyed gesture. "It's like you warned me, Daddy, ranchers are always short of ready cash. Unless you help, I'll never have a house in town."

"Damn it, Philadelphia. I can't make a banker out of every man who comes down the pike. I would have had to watch Max like a goddamned hawk to make sure he didn't give a loan to every rancher who'd fallen on hard times. Now you're hinting that I should turn Wally into a banker?" He shook his head and then finished his coffee, which had grown cold. "I doubt your new husband would recognize an amortization table if one fell on his face. There's nothing about him that makes me think he's suited for banking."

"I didn't ask you to take Wally into the bank," she murmured, leaving unspoken the words: You said it, not I. "But considering him for a position is an interesting idea. After all, you were willing to offer Max something. And a generous salary would go a long way toward a house in town." The conversation was boringly similar to a previous discussion, only then the subject had been Max. "I have no idea how Wally would take to the idea or if he'd be interested in finance." But she would bring him around as she had done with Max. "Naturally, I wouldn't expect you to act against your better judgment. You'll want to get to know Wally and consider carefully before making an offer. Frankly, I think you'll be surprised. I think Wally might take to banking."

"You are a caution," he said, shaking his head and looking at her across the table. "Sometimes you are so like your mother, may she rest in peace, that it's uncanny."

He referred to her ability to twist him around her little finger, of course. And her relationship with Wally would go the same way. Wally truly believed it was his decision not to claim his husbandly rights until well after the baby arrived. And when the time came he would believe that it was his decision to build a mansion equal to the home she had grown up enjoying. Wally McCord would do and believe whatever she wanted him to do or believe.

When she said nothing more, her father signaled the waiter, then urged her to order more food than she wanted. Unspoken was the admonition that she was now eating for two, but she understood the implication.

Finally she could think of the hated pregnancy without feeling sick inside and wanting to throw herself out a window. She still flogged herself for making a stupid,

stupid mistake, and everyone would eventually notice that the dates didn't work out. But when she felt a surge of panic close her throat, she had only to look down at the ring on her left hand and her thoughts grew calmer. Max might have betrayed her, but Wally would not. They were man and wife. He had no choice but to stand by her.

Turning to the window, she watched the cold drizzle slanting across the hotel gardens. At odd moments she found herself thinking about seeing Max again. How would they behave toward each other? What would they say? She wanted him to feel guilty and jealous; it was what he deserved. But she hadn't yet decided how to achieve that goal. She had to take into account that others would be watching and judging their reaction to each other.

"I want him punished," she said softly. The rain reminded her of all the tears she had shed. "He has to pay for what he did." She didn't have to identify whom she meant.

Her father nodded, and his eyes hardened like stones.

It didn't matter that she had engineered her own destruction and was more to blame than Max. She didn't see it that way. Max had betrayed her and refused to marry her. He had turned his back in her hour of need. The chain of events that ended with her pregnant and married to Max's brother had begun when Max refused to do as she wished. He should have stayed home instead of going to the mountains for the summer. Had he done as she'd asked, none of this would have happened. She would not be pregnant. The low creature Max married would have married someone else.

She wanted them both to suffer.

Like most western towns, Fort Houser spread outward from Main Street. Modest homes occupied the outskirts of town, while larger and more elaborate homes were found the closer one approached Main Street. Main Street itself was broad enough to easily accommodate two-way traffic, and was cobbled before the bank and the county courthouse. Livvy mentioned there were plans to cobble in front of the post office and town hall come next spring.

Louise, who believed she was not sensitive to such things, noticed that people stopped on the boardwalk to stare as the McCord women drove past on the wagon. She fancied that she drew the most intense attention. "Aren't there any saloons in this town?" A whiskey sounded good right now. Maybe Livvy and Gilly were thinking the same, given the way folks gawked at them.

"The saloons and parlor houses are located about a mile north of town." Livvy kept her gaze firmly forward, but her terse voice indicated her awareness of the interest they attracted. "The Ladies Society has been trying to close them down for years. So far it hasn't happened."

All right, Livvy and Gilly weren't thinking about whiskey. But the idea still sounded good to Louise.

The mature elms shading Main announced to all and sundry that Fort Houser was not a flash in the pan, but an established town worthy of the name. Brick storefronts imparted an impression of age and stability. Church steeples rising above the tree line suggested a settled, organized community. If Philadelphia's grandfather were still alive, he would have been proud of the town he had founded.

Livvy reined up before the Fort Houser Ladies' Emporium and set the wagon brake. "The first time is the hardest," she said quietly. "Both of you, hold your heads high and remember that you're McCords. Gilly, don't allow anyone to draw you into a discussion about what's happened. Louise, act like a lady and try not to look like a seductress."

"Me?" Her eyebrows soared, but she didn't laugh.

"Don't look hangdog, either. Not too assertive and not too apologetic." Livvy leaned across Gilly to look Louise in the eye. "I've noticed that you either thrust out your chin like you're spoiling for a fight, or you hunch up like you're hoping to disappear."

"I do?" But she knew that was exactly what she did.

"Aim for something in between," Livvy ordered, swinging down out of the wagon, then smoothing her skirts and straightening her hat. "And stick close by. Don't go wandering off."

The warm feeling of family cooled somewhat. Louise doubted Livvy would have thought it necessary to warn Philadelphia to act like a lady, or to tell her how to look, how to behave, and where to stand. Lips pressed together, she swung down from the wagon seat and conducted a quick inventory.

She was wearing one of the ensembles she'd purchased at the seconds shop in Denver. Comparing herself to Livvy and Gilly, she suspected her skirt and jacket were hopelessly out of fashion, but the length of her skirt was approximately correct, and the fit wasn't far off. She was clean and tidy. Her silly ladies' hat was almost the same color as her brown jacket. This morning she had carefully spit-shined her boots and had washed and ironed a fresh hanky.

Her chin came up, and her eyes hardened. Livvy and Gilly might not agree, but she didn't feel her appearance needed apology. She'd done the best she could with what she had to work with.

Gilly pressed her arm and gave her a look of encouragement. "With your hair and eyes, brown is a good choice. Don't you agree, Mama?"

Livvy was pushing at her gloves, studying the gold lettering curving across the emporium's display window. "Mmm. Green and gold would also be good." Sunlight dappled through the elm branches and lit the auburn strands threading the coil on her neck. Livvy McCord was a handsome woman; she must have been a beauty thirty years ago.

Livvy adjusted the strings of her purse, then lifted her head high and arranged a smile on her lips. "Gilly, I'm relying on you to select the trim we discussed." Stepping forward, she opened the door to the emporium. "Louise, you'll come with me. I want to hold the fabric near your face before we make any purchase. Gold may be as wonderful as I think, or it may make you look sallow. Of course, we won't know for certain until your tan fades. I suspect we'll have to take our chances."

A cheerful hum of voices greeted them when Livvy opened the door. As they stepped inside, however, a wave of silence began at the front aisles and rolled backward toward the bolts of material stacked up the far wall.

Had it not been for the silence, Louise doubted she would have noticed the tapping of their heels against a wooden floor. To her ears, their steps sounded like two deer and a horse clomping across a hard surface. Livvy managed to look stately and even a bit imposing as she moved toward the back. Gilly seemed delicate, and circles of pink burned on her cheeks, imparting an impression of fragility. Louise felt anything but stately or delicate. She felt tall and clumsy, big-handed, big-footed, a fit object for ridicule and scorn. When Gilly turned toward the trim department, Louise moved up next to Livvy.

"Get your chin off your chest and hold your head up," Livvy whispered from the side of her mouth. She smiled as she approached a woman standing behind a counter wearing a tape measure around her neck. "Mrs. McConigle, I hope you aren't too busy today, as we require your assistance for a rather large order." Withdrawing a list from her purse, she drew a breath and began. "If we put a ruffle around the hem of your everyday skirts, I think they'll do nicely," she said to Louise. To Mrs. Mc-Conigle, she added, "We'll need wash poplin and black broadcloth, enough for a half dozen ruffles."

Louise stood like a dolt, clutching her purse in front of her waist, gazing at the wide bolts of material. She recognized the serge and broadcloth, and velvet and cotton prints and gingham. There were lightweight wools that she hadn't seen before and many fabrics she didn't recognize.

"Whipcord serge in golden brown. That will do nicely for a suit." Livvy's pencil made a scratching noise against her list. "We'll want French taffeta for the holidays, I think." She eyed Louise as if seeing her for the first time. "Not a plaid, a solid. Green. Now how many yards, I wonder?"

"Do I have a say in any of this?" Louise inquired uneasily, shifting from one foot to the next.

"It's all been decided," Livvy answered in a frosty tone, indicating her list.

Mrs. McConigle pulled down a flat bolt of green taffeta and began to roll out the yardage. With a sly look she picked a newspaper off the counter and handed it to Louise. "Would you hold this for a moment? It's in the way, and we wouldn't want to smudge newsprint on the fabric now, would we?"

Louise glanced at the newspaper and sucked in a breath. It was folded back to a headline that read: Granddaughter of Founder Weds Rancher. Philadelphia's name jumped off the page. So did Wally's.

"When you've finished measuring out the taffeta, we'll need some chambray for shirtwaists in both plain and print, if you please." Livvy glanced at the newspaper in Louise's hands then made another checkmark on her list. "I hope Gilly can find bead trim for the taffeta. And I do hope dress stays are on her list." Only the crimson climbing her throat indicated she had read the headline.

And then the whispering began. Or perhaps it had begun earlier but only now moved close enough that Louise and Livvy could overheard a few words and phrases. As they were intended to overhear.

". . . his own brother's bride. Indecent is what . . ."

"She must have been carrying on with one brother while she was betrothed to . . ."

"Well, I think the oldest McCord jilted her and she ran off with the other one for spite. Look at the dates. The oldest one married first."

"That's her over there . . . the one who married Max McCord days before he was supposed to marry . . . what kind of hussy would . . ."

". . . don't know how they can show their faces as if nothing . . ."

It seemed to go on and on and on until Gilly appeared at the fabric counter, her cheeks pulsing with high color. "I believe I have everything. It's loaded in the wagon. Are you ready?" Her eyes pleaded with them to say yes.

"It will take all of us to carry these packages," Livvy said, hastily loading a multitude of string-tied parcels into Louise's and Gilly's arms.

She lifted a similar number of packages and started down the long aisle toward the street door. This time she didn't march silently. "Good morning, Mrs. Howard. Miss Greene." The ladies did not return her cool-eyed greeting. "A lovely day, Mrs. Peabody. Mrs. Johnson." Near the door she stopped suddenly and Louise almost ran into her. "Mrs. Halston, I haven't seen you in ages. May I present my dear daughter-in-law, Mrs. Max McCord." There was nothing warm in Livvy's voice. Her tone was steely and stubborn.

"Howdy do," Louise murmured, pasting a smile on her lips. She couldn't shake hands because of the parcels stacked nearly to her chin, and didn't know if women shook hands in any case.

Mrs. Halston pointedly ignored her. Cool, condemning eyes remained on Livvy. "Am I to assume there will be no wedding on Sunday, Mrs. McCord?"

"I believe today's *Gazette* answers that question, Mrs. Halston." Livvy's gaze was equally cool and unapologetic. "If you'll excuse us . . ." After nodding curtly, she swept out the door with Gilly and Louise trailing behind.

Silently they dropped their packages in the wagon bed, then climbed up on the seat. "Spines straight, heads high." Livvy released the brake and flicked the reins across the backs of the team.

When they reached the outskirts of town, Gilly raised a shaking hand to her forehead. "I've never heard you make an improper introduction before."

Livvy kept her gaze on the road and didn't answer.

"They kept whispering loud enough that I finally realized I was meant to overhear. I'm so glad I decided to leave Sunshine with Mrs. Radowitz. Glad she didn't hear any of this."

"What are the gossips saying?"

Gilly dropped her hand to her lap. "Philadelphia, who is blameless, is—"

"Philadelphia is not entirely blameless," Livvy snapped.

"—the villainess, stringing along both brothers, being no better than she should be. In another version, poor Wally is the cad. He was romancing Philadelphia all along behind Max's back and convinced her to betray his own brother. And there are those who believe that Louise is to blame. Louise worked her wiles on Max, dazzled him so thoroughly that he forgot about poor Philadelphia and married an adventuress. When Philadelphia learned she'd been jilted, she turned to Wally for comfort, then ran off with him out of spite."

"From now on scandal will be a constant part of our lives. Mark my words. The gossips will be counting the months until Philadelphia's babe is born. And then another wave of ugliness will begin while the rumormongers speculate on whose baby she's carrying. Well. I guess we don't have to worry about Louise or Philadelphia being inconvenienced by a stream of callers from town."

The distant mountains rose majestic and changeless above the tops of the cottonwoods dotted across the range. Louise gazed at the snowy caps and wished she could turn back the clock and return to Piney Creek and the celebration party at Olaf's cabin. If she could live the moment over again, she would ask the miners for a pouch of gold and call it good.

She genuinely liked Max and Livvy and Gilly. She expected to like Wally and Gilly's husband, Dave, when she knew them better. And she had brought all of them nothing but trouble and shame. That hadn't been her intention.

No one spoke until Livvy turned the wagon down the ruts leading to Max's house. Then Louise inhaled deeply, leaned forward, and said in a haughty voice, "Am I to assume there will be no wedding on Sunday, Mrs. McCord?"

Livvy and Gilly stared at her and immediately she regretted her impulsive imitation of the imperious Mrs. Halston.

Then, as Louise was starting to feel foolish, Gilly blurted, "Yes, you stupid cow, since everyone concerned is already married, you may assume there will be no wedding on Sunday."

Louise pushed the folded newspaper into Gilly's hands. "Perhaps you would like to read the full account, Mrs. Halston," she said, switching roles, "and see if you can figure out for your small mean self if there will be a wedding on Sunday."

"I already know the answer, Mrs. McCord," Gilly said with a sniff. She tilted her head back to look down her nose at Louise. "I'm only inquiring for the purpose of embarrassing you and calling to your attention the unforgivable behavior of those cads, your sons."

"And who is this?" Louise exclaimed, looking down at herself. "Could this be the irresistible temptress who started it all? The seductress no man can resist?"

"My heavens," Gilly gasped, drawing back in horror. "I believe it is. Have you no shame? How dare you show your face in public?"

"Because I don't give a flying—ah, fig—what you think, Mrs. Halston."

She and Gilly grinned, then they burst into laughter, falling on each other and laughing until tears ran from their eyes and their sides ached. Even Livvy was smiling when she wheeled the wagon to a stop in front of the porch.

"It was so awful!" Gilly gasped, pressing a glove to her ribs. "The whispering! The things they said."

"And the way they stood like stones as we were leaving. Nodding to thin air when Livvy said their names. And they didn't even glance at me!"

"Oh, they looked at you, all right."

"I'm glad you two find it amusing to be snubbed and scorned," Livvy said after setting the brake. She climbed to the ground and headed for the wagon bed. "Can you pull yourselves together long enough to carry these packages inside?" She loaded them both from waist to chin with parcels, then looked at Louise and seemed to consider for a moment.

Then her lips pulled down in contempt and she tossed her head. "Since you seem unable to comprehend the *Gazette* announcement, Mrs. Halston, perhaps you should drop by the church on Sunday. If there is no preacher, no guests, no bride and groom, then you may safely assume the wedding has been canceled." Pointing her nose at the sky, Livvy marched toward the door.

Louise's mouth dropped, and she blinked at Gilly. Then

they both laughed and followed Livvy into the house. Over coffee and cake, they examined the fabric and trim they had purchased before Livvy measured Louise every which way while Gilly wrote down waist size, bosom size, length of arms, length from waist to floor, length from shoulders to waist.

Louise hadn't known what to expect from this day, but she had sensed that appearing in town would be difficult for Livvy and Gilly and therefore for her. And so it had.

But it had also turned into a happy day. She picked up the cake plates and dropped them into the dishpan, then brought the coffeepot to the kitchen table, refilling cups as Livvy and Gilly sketched suits and dresses on the parcel wrappings.

Before the women departed, they glanced into the parlor and noticed Louise's silver spoon. It was impossible not to notice it since the spoon was the only item on an otherwise bare mantelpiece.

"That's a very pretty spoon," Gilly said after a moment of surprised silence.

"Is it an heirloom?" Livvy inquired politely before she recalled Louise's background. "No, not an heirloom then." When Louise said nothing, Livvy crossed to the mantel and picked up the spoon, turning it between her fingers. "I have some polish that will remove the tarnish lickety-split. The next time you're up at the house, remind me and I'll send some back with you."

Blinking hard, Louise nodded. In the last minute she had experienced an array of emotions. First, embarrassment sudden and hot, that all she had of her own to display was a tarnished spoon. Then defensiveness. The spoon was the only nice thing she owned, and she didn't care what they thought. Damned if she was going to explain. And finally, a rush of gratitude powerful enough to close her throat. They hadn't laughed. They hadn't dismissed her spoon with ridicule or contempt.

When she stood in the doorway watching them drive away through a moist blur, she wondered if she really would choose differently if she could relive that moment of decision on the mountainside in front of Olaf's cabin.

Max reined up next to Dave Weaver, pushed back his hat, and wiped dust from his forehead. "Does it seem to you that the herd is only half what it was last year?"

He had agreed to return to the main ranch with the first herd and brand any beeves they'd missed in the spring. But until today it hadn't seemed necessary to split the cattle into smaller herds. Today they'd added another eighty beeves, and splitting into two herds would make each herd more manageable. Strictly speaking, it wasn't really necessary. The boys were handling all the beeves with no particular difficulty.

Dave nodded. "I'm not sure this is the best year to split out the beeves. No one's going to end up with a decent-sized herd." Rocking back in the saddle, he frowned at the cattle grazing on dry yellow grass. "We sold too many in the spring. Course, no one could have predicted this would be a drought year or that we'd lose so many."

The judge who'd adjudicated Jason McCord's will had insisted the cattle be counted and branded according to ownership, thus ensuring that no dispute would arise later among Jason McCord's heirs. This had been done, but Dave Weaver and the McCords had continued to work the four land parcels as one ranch.

Early this spring they'd held a family meeting and agreed that operating four ranches as one was not an efficient long-term arrangement. Whose hired hands should hay the cattle during the winter? To whom did the spring calves belong? Who was responsible for what chores and expenses? Moreover, Dave and Max had both pledged cattle as collateral to build their places. The bank reasonably wished to know how many cattle each man owned. In the end, it was agreed to split the main herd as soon as each place was fenced. Dave was prepared to move his and Gilly's cattle onto their range. Max's ranch was ready enough that he'd agreed to bring his beeves to his place and Shorty and the boys would be responsible for feeding them over the winter.

The bank. Max lit a cigar and waved out the match.

This spring he'd sold fifty winter-thin beeves for about half the money he could have gotten for the same cattle if he'd sold them now. But he'd needed cash money then to put against the loan to build his house, barn and out-buildings, and begin the fencing.

Cost overruns hadn't concerned him much. When he'd ordered the best stove and oven on the market, when he'd decided on top-grade wallpaper and when he'd bought a piano for the parlor, he'd thought of the salary he'd earn at the bank and planned to put most of it against the house loan. The terms of his loan were gener-ous, and he hadn't supposed Howard Houser would be too particular about the date he paid it off.

Now he gazed at the herd and imagined it divided into fourths. The result was sobering. Happily, his note at the bank wasn't due until the first of June next year. Therefore, he had some time to find a solution for pay-ing off his loan. This was about the only happy thing he could think of at the moment.

The day after tomorrow he'd have to face his brother and the woman who was carrying his child.

Chapter 12

Much as it pained Louise to conduct herself as a real wife, she felt Max deserved to return home to a clean house. Therefore, she pinned up her hair, tied on an apron, and eventually, grudgingly, conceded some satisfaction in scrubbing floors and polishing surfaces until they gleamed. Next in her preparations, she put up a wash, laundering the items she'd borrowed from Max's side of the dressing room along with the rest. She suspected it would be a long time before she'd again enjoy the comfort and convenience of trousers.

Once the laundry was flapping on the line, she took a couple of pie apples down to the corral to give Rebecca and the black gelding. "It'll be good to have the boys back," she said, offering the apples. She couldn't quite bring herself to state aloud that she'd missed Max and would be glad to see him again.

Tugging her shawl close against a cold wind and leaning against the corral rails, she squinted up at the house. In her time she'd ridden past hundreds of houses with lines of wash waving in the yard. Sometimes laughing children ran in and out between freshly laundered sheets, and that was nice to see.

There was nothing that spoke so powerfully of family and home as a line of wash, that snowy proof of a woman's labor on behalf of those she loved. Home was where a person could hang out the wash without fear that someone would steal her shirts and long johns.

Home was also where the squeak of a windmill was a comfort and not a lonely sound. And home was where you planted flowers in the expectation that you would be there to see them bloom year after year.

Louise had never had that kind of home, and she doubted she'd be here in the spring to plant flowers around the front porch. But she'd already realized part of a dream she hadn't known she'd dreamed. She was looking at a house with wash on the line, and, miraculously, it was hers. That was her petticoat pinned next to Max's nightshirt, and her everyday stockings flapping against his heavy boot socks. If a solitary figure were to ride past and wonder what sort of woman lived in the house with the wash in the yard—this time the woman would be her.

A shine of moisture filmed her eyes. Oh Lord. How could she have wanted this so much and not have known it?

Almost running, she returned to the warmth of the kitchen where she focused on peeling the apples Livvy had sent over. And while her pies baked, she leaned in the mudroom doorway, drinking coffee and watching the wash flutter on the line even after it was dry and ready to come inside.

Louise awoke well before the rooster crowed. As she had done all week, she rolled to Max's pillow to inhale the scent of him, but the laundered case now smelled of soap and fresh air. Rising in the dark, she dressed quickly in old clothing, heavy boots, and a thick shawl to protect her from the frosty air as she went about her morning chores. When she returned with a basket of eggs and a bucket of milk, the water she'd left on top of the stove was hot enough to fill the wash tub and have a bath.

Once she was clean and glowing from a good scrub, she sat near the opened oven door, drying her hair and

wondering if she should wear the black dress she'd
worn to dinner in Denver. Or if it would be more appropriate to wear one of the too-short skirts, a shirtwaist, and a jacket.

When she realized what she was thinking, she rolled
her eyes toward the ceiling and threw up her hands.
No one she had ever known—including herself—would
believe that Louise Downe would waste two minutes
trying to decide which lady ensemble might make her
appear the most attractive.

But Max was coming home today.

And so was Philadelphia.

Before she dressed, in one of the too-short skirts
and a somber dark shirtwaist, Louise hitched up the
wagon and loaded her pies. The crusts on a few were
brown around the edges, but all in all she wouldn't
have to hide her face when the boys tucked into them.

Until she drove away from the house, she hadn't noticed that autumn was making inroads. Gumweed and
rabbit brush continued to bloom, but drifts of red and
rust climbed the foothills. Seemingly overnight the cottonwoods were turning to gold, and here and there a
maple or an ash flamed orange like a column of fire. She
also spotted wild turkey, pheasant, and a family of quail
not far from the road. If she'd been wearing her pistol,
she could have filled the larder for a week.

So far no one had suggested that putting meat on the
table was a wife's chore, and that was good because a
woman had to draw the line somewhere. Sure as hell if
she brought home one pheasant, she'd be expected to
provide all the small game. Thinking about it made her
angry, and she held on to the feeling since anger was
something she understood a lot better than the fluttery heat that erupted deep in her stomach when she
thought about seeing Max again.

Pressing her lips together, she tightened her grip on
the reins as she pulled up in front of the main house and

set the brake. Gilly had already arrived and hurried outside to lend a hand. They carried the pies into Livvy's kitchen, which smelled of baking ham and yeasty bread and the beans and bacon bubbling in a large pot on top of the stove.

"What can I do?" Louise inquired, removing her hat and jacket.

"You could peel potatoes." Gilly tossed her an apron before she returned to shucking corn. "One of the boys rode in about thirty minutes ago and said the first herd will arrive before dinnertime. We should have plenty of food here for dinner and supper."

"Hello, Aunt Louise." Sunshine ran in the back door and smiled. "You're wearing lady clothes."

"I was hoping to see you. I brought you something."

"Is it candy?"

"Much better than candy. I brought you a rock."

"A rock? Oh." Sunshine tried not to show her disappointment, and Gilly hid a smile.

Louise reached in her pocket then bent over and placed an egg-sized rock in Sunshine's small hand. "Look," she said, kneeling and tracing her fingernail along a streak the width of a thread. "That's gold."

"Real gold?" Sunshine whispered, her blue eyes widening. Now she inspected the rock with genuine fascination.

"Real gold. Just like your grandpa searched for way back when, and like your uncle Max was trying to find this summer."

"You panned for gold, too," Sunshine said, staring at the rock.

"Yes, and me, too."

"I never had gold before. Mama, can I take this down to the barn and show Mr. Deke?" When Gilly nodded, Sunshine threw her arms around Louise's neck and kissed her on the cheek. "Thank you, Aunt Louise! This is the best gift I ever had. Real gold!"

Standing, Louise touched her fingertips to her cheek. Sunshine had kissed her. And had called her aunt.

"You have a way with children," Gilly observed. "Sunshine is very fond of you. She says you make her feel grown up."

The compliment made her face grow hot. "Where is Livvy?" she asked, changing the subject before she filled the lap of the apron with potatoes then sank to a low stool and pulled the slop bucket in front of her to catch peels.

"Ma's upstairs seeing to the room that will be Wally and Philadelphia's."

"Oh." From now on, nothing would be the same. Philadelphia would live here, and she would bring a new element to the fragile relationships Louise had begun to form. Livvy and Gilly would be Philadelphia's family as much as they were Louise's. And Philadelphia would be Sunshine's aunt, too.

Frowning, she scraped the blade of the paring knife across a potato and swore she would say nothing. "What sort of person is Philadelphia? What does she look like?" Well, damn it anyway. Her mouth wouldn't mind her brain.

"Her eyes are blue or green, depending on what she wears and the light," Gilly said after a pause. "She has blond hair. I guess Philadelphia's about my height, maybe a bit shorter, but not by much."

Louise suppressed a sigh. In her heart she had already guessed that Philadelphia would be one of those little, dainty, ultrafeminine women who made women like Louise feel clumsily gigantic and about as womanly as a fence post. Initially Gilly had caused the same effect, and still did to some degree, but Gilly's kindness helped Louise ignore or forget their differences in size and grace.

"Philadelphia is quite stylish. Everyone in Fort Houser looks to her for the latest mode. She receives fashion news from Paris, France, and she buys all her hats and footwear in Denver." Carefully Gilly stripped strands of corn silk from a pale white ear. "As for what she's like . . . her mother passed when Philadelphia was about twelve, I believe. Early on she stepped forward as her father's hostess, and she's quite accomplished in that area."

Louise told herself to stop here. Just keep her mouth closed. "What exactly does a hostess do?"

Gilly shrugged. "Mr. Houser entertains a lot of important guests in town and from out of town. Financiers, other bankers and politicians, people he's met during his business travels. Philadelphia chooses the menu for dinner parties, decides the seating arrangements, directs conversation and keeps it flowing. After dinner a hostess might entertain her guests at the piano or with song. Perhaps she would invite musicians to perform. Philadelphia also hosts exquisite teas and luncheons for the clubs and societies she belongs to."

"Do tell," Louise murmured, mimicking a say-nothing phrase she'd heard Livvy employ when they were buying fabric at the Ladies' Emporium. One thing she'd learned from listening to Gilly's explanation: she hoped Max never asked her to do any hostess chores because she didn't have a single hostess skill.

"As Mr. Houser's official hostess, I believe Philadelphia also takes his associates sight-seeing or shopping, and she entertains them if Mr. Houser is otherwise occupied. For instance, she brought one of Mr. Houser's guests to the Fourth of July picnic and celebration."

So Philadelphia was charming and gregarious. In addition to being tiny, a fashion plate, and an accomplished hostess. How nice for her, Louise thought sourly.

"Actually, I don't know Philadelphia all that well. I'm twenty-six and she's only twenty. We don't really have the same friends. And Philadelphia is very social whereas I'm not."

This made Louise seven years older than Miss Wonderful. She was old, plain, tall and big, clumsy and graceless, without an accomplishment to her worthless name. When she looked down, she discovered she had whittled a potato into a sliver.

Livvy bustled into the room bringing the scent of lemon polish and lamp oil, a dust rag over her shoulder. "Did Deke ride back to the herd, or is he still about? I want him to set up the long table outside. Far enough from the corrals to escape the dust and stink of cattle, and close enough to the kitchen that we can get the food on the table while it's still hot." She pressed Louise's shoulder on the way to the table to inspect the pies. "You're learning," she said with a smile. "Sprinkle enough sugar on top and no one will notice if the outer crust is a bit brown."

"I doubt I'll ever be much of a cook."

"Nonsense. You'll get the way of it. All women can cook. It comes natural, like getting up in the morning, like having babies, like living a life."

This life was so different from any Louise had lived that nothing about it felt natural. And deep down she didn't want it to. The day this life became second nature was the day she couldn't go back to what she had been. She didn't dare let herself change that much. If she did, she was just begging for heartbreak.

By the time Livvy returned from searching out Deke and getting the table set up, Louise and Gilly had the potatoes and corn almost cooked and ready.

"We'll keep the potatoes hot until it's time to mash them," Gilly said as Livvy popped her head in the kitchen door.

"Better get started. The herd is behind the barn now, and Max and the boys are cutting out the calves and beeves that need branding. Once they're in the pens, the men will come up to the house for dinner."

Max was here. Instantly Louise's face felt feverish

and fluttery heat exploded in her stomach. She tucked her hands in the folds of her apron so Gilly wouldn't notice a sudden tremble. But that didn't help her. As she needed to keep busy, she volunteered to mash the potatoes and pounded them with the masher until her whole arm began to ache, going after the lumps like she was killing snakes.

"I'll slice up the bread, if you'll take the butter dishes out to the table," Gilly said twenty minutes later. "I think Sunshine set out the salt and pepper, but it wouldn't hurt to check. I don't know where she's got to."

Swirls of dust hung over the pens when Louise stepped outside and peered toward the barn. By the time she reached the table and looked up again, the men had emerged from the dust and were walking toward the house.

Her gaze flew straight to Max. Tanned face, blue eyes, dark curly hair. Broad shoulders and narrow hips. A man handsome enough to set a woman on fire. Hastily, she pushed at the wisps of hair floating around her flushed face, and swore softly when she noticed a greasy stain on her dark shirtwaist, probably butter. Damn. Well maybe he wouldn't notice.

Max lifted his head toward the house, and she caught a quick breath and held it as his gaze touched her. But it was only a touch that continued past her. His step faltered. For a moment Louise believed he had tripped over something, then she saw his expression go slack and his chest hitch.

Feeling her throat close, knowing what she would see, she followed his stare and watched Wally and a woman who could only be Philadelphia come around the side of the house and into view. Philadelphia was as Gilly had described her. Small, perfectly groomed, and exquisitely dressed in a forest green traveling suit with matching hat and cape. She was beautiful.

Against her will, Louise's heart sank into a swamp of

jealousy. Philadelphia was everything any woman would want to be, everything Louise could never be. Max's family accepted her. Max loved her. And she was carrying his baby.

Philadelphia's step also faltered, and she halted abruptly as if the sight of Max had thrown up a wall of shock and pain. Her face paled, and her eyebrows slanted in a helpless expression of deep sorrow and longing that swiftly altered to anguish. Blindly, she reached for Wally, curling toward his body where she pressed her forehead against his shoulder and raised her gloves up beside her cheeks. Wally's arm came around her in a protective gesture.

Then Livvy appeared as if by magic, all bustle and good cheer, welcoming home the newlyweds while everyone took a deep breath and struggled to compose themselves.

Louise stood beside the table, watching the drama unfold as Max and Wally stared hard at each other before Max thrust out his hand and Wally gripped it. Philadelphia stepped back, visibly collected herself, then turned to clasp Livvy's hand. She didn't look at Max nor did he look at her, but the sadness had returned to her gaze.

When Gilly and Sunshine joined the group at the side of the house, Louise picked up a butter dish because she needed something to do with her hands, needed to pretend that she was doing something useful.

Livvy must have seen her bend over the table and remembered her, because Livvy leaned close to Philadelphia and gestured over her shoulder. Philadelphia shuddered and raised her gloves as if warding off a blow and she shook her head no. Now Louise understood and she shuddered, too. Oh God. Livvy was going to insist on an introduction.

Despite the uncharacteristic pangs of jealousy, Louise truly regretted hurting Philadelphia. Philadelphia was least deserving of the disasters that had befallen her, and she had and would suffer the most. Philadelphia had lost the man she loved, and she had lost him when she needed him most, while carrying his baby. She'd been forced to marry a man not of her choosing, and the wrong man would raise her child. For the rest of her life, she would be the target of gossip and whispers. And all of this had happened because a woman she didn't know and had never met wanted a child of her own.

Since Philadelphia refused to go to Louise, Livvy scowled and urgently beckoned Louise forward. Louise would rather have stepped off a cliff.

But the moment had to come, she knew that. Inevitably she and Philadelphia had to meet. They were both part of the McCord family. It would be impossible to avoid each other.

Reluctantly and filled with dread, she pushed dragging feet toward the group at the side of the house. She had almost reached Livvy and Philadelphia when she realized she was still clenching one of the butter dishes and her thumb was firmly imbedded in the butter. She threw Max a despairing glance over the top of Philadelphia's hat, but he was no help. He and Wally were both staring blankly at Sunshine and the rock she showed them. Both held their faces carefully expressionless.

Livvy introduced Louise and Philadelphia and prattled on to say that three Mrs. McCords were too confusing, therefore they would immediately jump to the intimacy of using first names. Then Livvy took Gilly's arm and moved toward her sons, leaving Louise and Philadelphia alone together.

Louise spun out a string of silent cuss words and wished she were anywhere but here, wished there was some place to put down the damned butter dish. She drew a breath and released it slowly, then she did the right thing. All her life she'd tried to do the right thing, which usually meant doing the hard thing.

"I know it doesn't help, and it doesn't change anything, but I'm truly sorry that I set in motion all the bad things that have happened to you. I never meant to hurt you or anyone."

Philadelphia's eyes glittered like shards of glass. "I know all about you, *Low Down*." She spat Louise's name and made it sound like an insult. "You immoral piece of garbage! You didn't care which man drew the marble; you would have slept with any of them! You're an affront to decent women. You're not fit for respectable company!"

All right, she'd known this meeting would not be congenial. Philadelphia had every reason to despise her, and no reason at all to be cordial or forgiving. But Louise had always assumed that genuine ladies conducted themselves as Mrs. Halston had. Cold and distant with no flash of emotion, as if true ladies floated above the crass passions of inferior persons. In the true-lady world, an icy invisible barrier kept the riff raff at bay. Thus shielded, a true lady conducted herself with scathing politeness no matter the circumstances. This was Louise's uninformed opinion, and Livvy McCord's conduct had seemed to bear it out.

Louise didn't think grand ladies spoke as Philadelphia just had. And she didn't think grand ladies got themselves pregnant before marriage, no matter how sick in love they were. People with backgrounds like Louise's thumbed their noses at convention, but ladies and gents were the ones who set the conventions and followed them to the letter. Or maybe she just wanted to find something about Philadelphia to criticize.

She moved her thumb in the butter. "I don't know what to say."

"Say nothing! Don't speak to me. Stay out of my sight!" Spinning from Louise, she called to Livvy. "Mother McCord, might I be shown to my room? Our journey was tiring and," she spread her hands and darted a quick glance at Max, "and our homecoming upsetting. I'd like to lie down if I may."

"Of course. Your room is ready." Linking arms with Wally and Philadelphia, Livvy walked them toward the front porch with Sunshine right behind. Gilly looked back and forth from Max to Louise, then excused herself and hurried back to the kitchen.

Max watched Philadelphia walk away. Maybe he studied the single brave feather quivering on her hat, or maybe he watched the sway of her stylishly draped bustle. All Louise knew for certain was that he seemed unaware of his own wife who stood in front of him with her hair a mess, a stain on her shirtwaist, and her thumb in the butter.

"Are you all right?" Louise asked in a low voice. It had to hurt to see the woman he wanted walking off to inspect a room she would share with another man.

Max looked at her without a flicker of recognition. When his vision cleared and his gaze sharpened, he swore, then pulled off his hat and raked his fingers through his hair. "How's everything out at the place? Did you have any problems?"

"Of course not. Everything is right as rain."

Dust had collected in the creases on his forehead and fanning from his eyes. Louise experienced an absurd urge to stand close to him and wipe the dust away with her fingers. She wanted to press her nose against his throat and inhale the scents of horseflesh and cattle and man sweat. Wanted to touch him and shake him and say, Look at me. Please look at me.

"You have your thumb in the butter," he said suddenly.

"I know. Will you be home tonight? Or will you stay here with the boys?"

If he hesitated, she didn't notice. "I'll be home after supper," he answered, looking at the butter dish and her buried thumb. Then he muttered something about washing up and walked away from her. She watched him go as he had watched Philadelphia, with loss and longing in her eyes.

The dark, sweet scent of whiskey reeled through her senses even before she entered the shadowy kitchen. Seeing Max's deeper shadow at the table, she walked past him to fetch her shawl from the mudroom, then went to the shelves near the sink. Enough moonlight filtered through the frost on the window glass that she had no difficulty finding a glass to take to the table.

"There's no reason for you to be up," he said when she reached for the bottle and poured herself a drink.

"I know." The whiskey scalded the back of her tongue, flowed toward her stomach like liquid fire. Raising her knees, she propped her bare feet on the edge of the chair and tucked her nightgown in around them. "I hope it doesn't snow before the rest of the herd comes in and the branding is finished. Feels like it could, though."

The bottle clinked against the lip of his glass, then silence. She didn't mind. It was nice to sip good whiskey and quietly share the darkness. Good companions didn't need words.

"There's a mystery down at the corral," he said eventually.

"Do tell." On the other hand, words were fine, too.

"Eight beeves wandered into the corral and closed the gate behind themselves."

She swallowed another fiery sip of whiskey. "Is that so."

"And there must have been a hell of a windstorm while I was gone, strong enough to blow hay in the corral to feed those beeves."

"Well, that is a mystery, now ain't it."

"So which horse did you use?" he asked after another silence.

"The black gelding."

"That's Hoss. A good choice if you can stay on top of him."

"I spent some time picking myself out of the dirt." With the comfort of the dark and the whiskey and the faint glow of embers in the firebox, she knew he wouldn't chastise her for rounding up a few cattle on her own. It wasn't that kind of moment. Plus, he could see that she hadn't broken any bones. And all's well that ends well.

"I imagine the only reason you didn't brand the two calves is because we have all the irons up at the main ranch." A hint of amusement softened the sharpness of his words.

"Max? Is this here going to be a habit? Sitting up in the middle of the night drinking?"

This time the silence stretched so long that she decided he was through talking.

"I thought I was doing what I needed to do," he said defensively. "I thought I had to spend the summer at Piney Creek to understand. I think Pa dreamed of succeeding big at something he loved to do, and he didn't want to leave the mountains until he did. I think it broke something inside when Ma succeeded but he didn't. And every time someone praised him about the ranch, whatever was broke cracked a little more."

So that's what had occupied his thoughts during the roundup. Going over and over his summer in Piney Creek, seeking to justify the decision that had ended by changing lives. She poured another splash into her glass and leaned back in her chair.

"The thing is, I could have figured that out without ever leaving Fort Houser." Disgust roughened his voice.

"Max? You've got a long day tomorrow. You need some sleep."

"I was dead set on going. It meant there wouldn't be any engagement parties, no prenuptial celebrations, none of the bridal fuss that women like. It meant leaving

Shorty to build the house and ranch. How did walking away from my responsibilities ever seem reasonable?"

"If you'd known Philadelphia was pregnant, you would have left the mountains like a shot."

"I don't know why she didn't tell me. I had her letters in a packet inside my vest when I took sick. They were burned with my clothing. But I go over and over them in my memory, wondering if I missed a hint I was intended to see. But I don't recall anything like that. She wanted me to come home, but hell, she didn't want me to go in the first place. She never wrote there was a special reason why I should come back."

"You're beating a dead horse, Max. It's done and over." The words were harsh, but she spoke them softly.

"Damn it, I'm so black-bile-up-to-here fricking angry." Sitting forward, he propped his elbows on his thighs and dropped his head in his hands.

"I know."

She understood feeling angry and being helpless to do anything about it. She'd felt that way today after Philadelphia spoke to her. She'd felt that way so many, many times in her life. There wasn't anything that would fix Max's anger or alter the injustice of everything that had happened. But it wasn't in Louise's nature to sit idly by and do nothing in the presence of pain and need.

Sliding her bare feet to the cold floor, she stood, thought a minute, then fetched Max's winter duster from the mudroom and spread it on the kitchen floor. She folded her shawl for a pillow.

Then she moved to stand in front of him, and tapped him on the head to get his attention. "I ain't got much to give to take your mind off hurting, but I'm offering you what I got."

Reaching down, she lifted the bottom of her night-gown with the intention of pulling it over her head. The wretched thing swallowed her up, and she thought she never would get it off. Swearing and slapping at volumes of material, she shoved it down and tried opening the drawstring at her neck. Better. She got one arm and shoulder through the opening, then the other, and she pushed the gown to her waist.

Max drew a sharp breath, and she realized she stood silhouetted by the moonlight falling through the frosted window. Now was not the moment to go timid, she reminded herself. This was her idea—in for a penny, in for a pound.

A push and a wiggle eased the nightgown over her hips and she let it drop around her ankles. "Last time anyone saw me buck naked I was a baby," she said uncomfortably, resisting an urge to clap an arm over her breasts and a hand over her private parts.

Nobody thought she had any standards, but she did and modesty was one of them. Standing in front of a man while naked as a jaybird, even if the man was her husband, meant standing on a mound of anguish. But this wasn't the night to expect Max to battle the nightgown; she had to undress herself. The point here was to ease his anger, not add to it.

He didn't say anything, didn't do anything. And she suddenly wondered if offering herself had been a terrible mistake. Worse, there was naught to do but go forward. Tentatively, she reached a hand to his hair, paused, then drew him toward her.

A sound erupted from deep in his throat, and his arms came around her waist so tight she thought he'd crush her, and he pressed his face hard against her bare stomach. "Damn."

"It's all right," she whispered, stroking his head, holding him against her.

She had a sense that he resisted but lost the battle. Releasing her, he bent to yank off his boots, then he stood and ripped open his shirt, sending buttons flying every which way before he jerked open his belt and shoved down his denims.

His skin was pale in the frosty moonlight, and she supposed hers was, too. But his eyes burned at her through the darkness, and she gasped and didn't feel the chill.

When they were both naked, they stood looking at each other, peering through shadow and dim glow. Not touching. Just looking, seeing with incomplete memory and imagination.

When Louise thought her racing heart would pound through her chest, Max finally reached a hand to her throat and drew his fingertips down between her breasts, down to her waist. Swaying on her feet, she followed his lead and stretched a trembling hand to his bare chest, stroking her palm down washboard muscles that tightened at her touch.

The strangeness of being naked in front of someone and of touching the firm warmth of a man's skin imparted a dreamlike quality. Whatever they did tonight would not seem real tomorrow. Thus she could kneel on the duster she had spread across the chilly planks and reach a hand to pull him down beside her. She ran her hands from his jaw to his shoulders and felt the tension and anger bunched beneath her palms. And when she gazed at his face, into his eyes, she understood that she had to lead and offer permission each step of the way because he feared the anger that had led them here.

Gently, she caught his hands and curved them around her breasts, heard the hissing noise he made at the back of his throat. "You won't hurt me," she whispered, knowing it was true. He would use her tonight and use her roughly and selfishly; she understood that, and it was what she offered. But he would never hurt her. He was not that kind of man.

Eyes locked to his, she shook the pins from her hair and felt the coils tumble down her back, instinctively sensing this was something he wanted. Then she lay back on the duster and cushioned her head on her folded shawl. Even though it felt as if they moved in a dream, she still burned hot with embarrassment and had to close her eyes when he rocked back on his heels to stare at her nakedness.

A low groan rumbled up from his chest, a growl of pain and fury and desire and hunger. The sound shot lightning through her body, flashing fire that lit her from within and tingled and burned and made her whimper and writhe beneath his stare.

When she could stand it no longer, she opened her arms and he came to her with the same primitive sound, covering her with the hard heat of male muscle and sinew. His mouth ravaged her breasts, his hands plundered at will. And he took her as she had known he would, thrusting hard and deep and furiously, spending his anger as he spent himself.

Afterward, when they had returned to the bedroom and Max slept beside her, Louise touched her stomach through the folds of her nightgown. She hoped they had made a baby tonight on the kitchen floor.

It seemed that a woman should remember the night a new life began inside her. Such a miracle should not be the result of routine or an ordinary coming together. Life should begin in a cataclysm of heat and fury bathed in the sweat of passion and urgency.

Tonight had been all of that, and she would never forget it.

Chapter 13

Philadelphia's father brought trunks of clothing and personal items to the ranch and stayed for an hour on the second day. On the third and fourth days, Philadelphia pressed and put away her clothing, annoyed there was no maid to perform the tasks for her. On the fifth day she had nothing to occupy her time except embroidery, and that was of no interest. She was so bored with her self-imposed seclusion that she wanted to scream, but she refused to go downstairs while that creature was in the house.

Irritated and feeling out of sorts, she stood beside the bedroom window where she couldn't be seen, and peered through lace curtains down at the long table where the hands would eat their dinner. Occasionally Gilly or the creature passed in and out of view, setting up utensils and condiments and carrying out dishes that didn't require heating.

Philadelphia could not keep her eyes off the Low Down person when she appeared. The nasty creature was tall and raw-boned and moved with purpose instead of grace. Given her shocking and disreputable background, there was no reason to suppose she would have any sense of fashion, and she didn't. Her skirts were six inches too short, revealing indecent glimpses of thick everyday stockings, and the shirtwaists she wore were dark, utterly plain, and totally lacking any stylish detail. If the creature spent twenty minutes arranging her hair, Philadelphia would be surprised, as Low Down's hair was just twisted into a utilitarian coil at the nape of her neck.

Still, she wasn't entirely as unappealing as Philadelphia had hoped she would be. Her features were regular if not delicate. She had well-shaped brows and especially fine clear eyes, a light brownish color flecked with green and gold if Philadelphia remembered correctly. Even without a corset, her figure was molded to a desirable hourglass shape. The creature was not pretty except when she smiled, but she possessed an indefinable quality that drew one's attention. She was what Philadelphia's father referred to as "a handsome woman" or "a woman of presence."

What made Philadelphia feel sick inside was noticing the creature's only jewelry, a gold wedding band.

This plain, immoral opportunist was the no-account woman Max had married instead of her. She didn't care that Low Down had nursed Max through his bout of small pox. She didn't care how the marriage had come about. The fact was, Low Down had taken Max. Philadelphia didn't believe for a single instant that chance had determined the outcome. The creature had decided she didn't want the other miners and had somehow arranged for Max to draw the scratched marble. Philadelphia felt certain of this. And Max had obliged by forgetting his bride and his upcoming wedding. He had thrown her aside rather than appear less than fair and noble before a group of strangers he would never see again. It would have been better if he had died of the pox. It would have served him right.

Well, she thought furiously, no doubt Max regretted his choice every time he glanced at his debauched, graceless wife. And every time he thought of the woman he could have had instead. Every time he remembered their evening together and considered her pregnancy and how he had walked away from his responsibility. She hoped guilt and remorse gnawed at him day and night.

Pushing the door open, Livvy popped her head inside. Instantly, Philadelphia stepped away from the curtains, irritated at being caught peeping at the dinner preparations below.

"Are you ill?" Livvy inquired, entering without an invitation.

"Not at all. Why do you ask?"

"I rapped at the door several times." Again without a by-your-leave, Livvy seated herself in one of the chairs flanking a small fireplace and brushed a strand of hair off her cheek. "I've been so busy cooking and cleaning the last few days that I haven't had an opportunity to speak to you regarding some personal and practical matters."

This was exactly the sort of comment that annoyed her most about Livvy McCord. A faint hint of criticism underscored Livvy's mention of being busy, but surely she didn't expect Philadelphia to cook for and clean up after a motley crew of cowhands?

Gracefully, Philadelphia sank to the facing chair and folded her hands in her lap. Casting her eyes down in an expression of modesty, she murmured, "If you're referring to Wally's decision to sleep in his old room and leave this lovely guest room to me, I admit I readily agreed. I've never shared a room with anyone, and we just thought, well, we decided to sleep apart until we know each other better." She had no intention of sharing her room with a man, not now or ever.

"Sleeping arrangements between a husband and wife are their private affair," Livvy said crisply. Her gaze slid from Philadelphia's face to her waist. "We need to discuss clothing."

This was a pleasant surprise. Heavens knew her mother-in-law could use some fashion advice. Even around the house, one didn't need to look indistinguishable from a servant. Before Philadelphia could decide on a tactful way to say so, Livvy was talking again.

"Although you don't look it, I figure you must be about four months along. Very soon you'll need clothing to accommodate your condition. Have you given any thought to alterations?"

Philadelphia stared, then blinked rapidly. It just didn't go away. There were long stretches when she forgot her condition, then something jolted the pregnancy back to the front of her mind. "I don't think I'm that far along."

"You must be close. Max departed for the mountains on May 30, and as I understand it, you and he . . ." Livvy coughed into her hand. "I'm counting from May 29." Now she frowned. "My dear, you really should stop lacing so tightly. I realize you didn't want anyone to guess, but you're safely married now, and it isn't good for the baby to lace so tightly. I'd recommend that you stop wearing a corset entirely."

"Perhaps." Again she cast her eyes toward her lap and fidgeted with her fingers.

"Meanwhile, we can begin letting out the waists on some of your dresses and ensembles and sewing up anything new you need. Gilly and I are doing some sewing for Louise; we can work on your requirements as well."

"I wouldn't dream of putting you to any trouble. Whatever alterations are necessary can be done by my seamstress." In fact, she would indeed need additional dresses, a thought that lifted her spirits somewhat. She'd have Wally take her back to Denver for a shopping excursion.

Livvy fell silent for a full minute. "Perhaps I should remind you that Wally is not a wealthy man. Surely he's mentioned that we won't be sending many cattle to market this year."

"Oh, I'm certain we'll manage." She didn't wish to offend the famous McCord pride by mentioning that her father would pay her seamstress as he always had. And she counted on the fact that the Houser pride would ensure that her father also paid for the Denver excursion rather than subject her to the indignity of appearing in altered clothing. The Housers weren't the sort to make do.

"There's something else we need to discuss." Livvy clasped her hands in her apron lap. "I suspect you've kept to your room since you arrived because Louise has come every day to help with the cooking. Is that correct?"

"I don't wish to see or speak to that person," Philadelphia said coldly. "I won't be in the same room with an immoral creature such as she. No decent woman would."

Livvy reached across the space that separated them and took her hand. "Philadelphia. The worst thing that can happen is to have this family split down the center." She drew a deep breath. "I know everything that's happened is deeply painful to you. I certainly understand how you would focus blame on Louise. But I beg you to rise above these feelings if you possibly can. For the sake of the family."

Withdrawing her hand, she stood abruptly and returned to the window. Staring through the lace, she watched the men striding toward the house from the barn and corrals. If she'd opened the window, she knew the air would stink of dust and scorched cowhide. Truly, she didn't know how she could endure living on a ranch. None of the outside smells were pleasant.

"The whole family will have dinner here every Sunday. For the sake of unity and harmony, I ask that you tolerate Louise for a few hours every Sunday and on holiday occasions."

After the countless concessions she had already made, expecting her to share a table with a woman no better than a whore added insult to injury. Her frown settled on Max and Wally, walking behind the cowboys toward the house. Both were flushed and tight-jawed as if they'd been arguing.

"You ask too much, Mother McCord. As a tribute to the decent women in this family, you should instruct Max to leave Low Down at home on Sundays and come to dinner alone."

"Her name is Louise," Livvy said sharply. "If I close my door to Louise, I also shut out Max, and rightly so. I would expect both of my sons to turn their backs on any person or place that does not welcome their wives. It would kill me if any of my children ever felt unwelcome in this house."

Livvy paused, clearly wanting Philadelphia to bend to her wishes. Too angry to speak, Philadelphia remained silent.

"Holding the family together depends on you. I wish that burden weren't yours to bear. I wish things were different, but they're not. If you can move ahead with your life and focus on Wally and your child instead of dwelling on past hurts and betrayals, then the McCord family has a chance to come through this intact. And if you can find it in your heart to treat Max and Louise politely if not warmly, you'll go a long way toward settling much of the gossip and scandal."

Down by the barn Max and Wally halted and turned to face each other. Philadelphia couldn't hear what they shouted, but she saw their clenched fists and braced postures. She saw the cowboys look back from the table, saw the creature and Gilly stop with bowls of food in their hands.

When she looked at the brothers again, Max and Wally were hitting and punching each other, going at it as if they were the worst of enemies.

"This breaks my heart," Livvy whispered at her side.

* * *

It was a stupid argument that should never have escalated into a fistfight. What did Max care if Wally ended with a few more beeves than he did? He didn't even know if that was the case because they hadn't yet taken a final count. Also, Dave Weaver was recording the preliminary tally and dividing the herd into fourths, not Wally.

He'd made an offhand comment about Wally ending up with more calves, and Wally had reacted as if Max had accused him of stealing. By the time Max explained that he'd simply made an observation, Wally was beyond reason and fighting mad. In Max's opinion, Wally had been spoiling for a fight ever since he'd returned from Denver.

"That's a damned lie," Wally objected, spitting the words and glaring at Max over Livvy's head. "But if I were mad, I'd say I have reason. You leave here for months, then walk in and expect to take over like you've only been gone five minutes. You don't know what it was like to watch the streams and creeks dry up this summer. You don't know how it felt to ride out and find the dead beeves by following circling buzzards. If you'd been here like you should have—"

"That's enough, both of you. Sit down, Max. You, too, Wally."

They were in the kitchen where Livvy had cleaned and doctored split lips, a couple of black eyes, and various scrapes, scratches, and bruises. Gilly had cast them a despairing look before heading to the corrals to find Dave, and Louise had given Max a long, unreadable stare before she followed Gilly. As for Philadelphia, Max guessed she was upstairs. He'd seen the curtains twitch at the window of Gilly's old bedroom, otherwise he hadn't glimpsed hide nor hair of her since the day she'd arrived.

"The two of you should be ashamed of yourselves," Livvy snapped. When they were boys, they had called the look she gave them now her fire-and-brimstone look. It began with her fists on her hips and her eyes narrowed to slits, and occasionally it had ended with a switching. "Fighting like two mad dogs, and doing it in front of your hands."

"Hell, they enjoyed it," Wally said sourly, staring at his outstretched legs.

Max agreed, remembering the cheering and hollering.

"I imagine they also enjoyed watching your wife wade in and stop the carnage," Livvy stated coldly.

Max frowned down at his bruised knuckles. He'd managed to pull his punch a second before he would have laid Louise out on the ground. Jumping into the middle of a fistfight was a damned foolhardy thing for her to do, and he still could hardly believe that's what she'd done. But she had walked between them without a hint of fear or hesitation, and she'd smacked them both with the heels of her hands, knocking them backward. Curling her lip, she'd said with disgust, "You're acting like you ain't in long pants yet! Now get your butts up to the house and apologize to your ma for shaming her in front of the hands."

"Aren't you the focus of enough gossip and talk without adding to it?" Turning her back to them, Livvy walked to the window and glared outside. "Every person who hears this tale will believe the two of you were fighting over Philadelphia. And that's the story the boys will tell in the saloons tonight."

"It was about cattle," Max insisted firmly. Wally nodded.

"You two haven't fought each other since you were in your early teens, and now you go at it over a few calves?" Turning from the window, Livvy leaned against the sideboard and folded her arms across her chest. "Well, I hope blacking each other's eyes and bruising each other's ribs got it out of your systems. Because I don't want to see this happen again, do you hear me?"

The air went out of Max's chest, and he covered his eyes with a hand. No one would believe that he and Wally had fought over a couple of calves. Of course it was more than that.

"This can go one of two ways," Livvy said. "We can accept that things got turned around and didn't work out the way we planned. We can put the past behind us and make this situation work for everyone. Or," she stared at them, "the two of you can destroy our family. Is that what you want? To live within shouting distance of each other and fill the space with animosity? Do you want to tear your sister in two pieces? Never mind what it will do to me if you two can't accept the decisions you made. If you want to throw away a lifetime of caring about each other because of a woman, I can't stop you. But think about it and be sure that's what you really want."

She looked like she wanted to switch them, but they were grown men so she walked outside instead, slamming the door behind her.

"Hell," Max said after a minute, touching his fingers to his cracked lower lip. "Where'd you learn to throw a punch like that?"

"From you." Leaning back in the chair, Wally gingerly placed a hand against his ribs. "Damn. I'm not going to be able to take a deep breath for a week."

They sat in silence taking inventory of minor injuries.

"I guess this had to happen," Max said in a low voice. He hated it that Wally had married Philadelphia, hated that Wally was falling in love with her, and hated it that Wally would make her a good and devoted husband. Hated to think that Philadelphia might return Wally's love someday. He hated it that he couldn't place his hand on her stomach and feel his child kicking inside. Hated it that he would never know his son or daughter the way a father should. For a few violent moments he had needed to punish Wally for all of his own mistakes.

"I've been wanting to knock you into next Sunday, waiting for a chance to do it," Wally admitted, considering the hole in his pants above his knee.

Max nodded. Wally hated it that he'd saved the family honor at the cost of choosing his own bride and his own future. He hated it that Philadelphia had loved Max and Max had been there first. He had to hate it that his wife was carrying his brother's child.

"I'm through," Max said firmly. "As far as I'm concerned, it's finished."

"Same here."

"Have we talked about this enough, or is there anything more you want to say?"

"We've covered it," Wally said. "We know where we stand and what we're going to do about it."

They stood, gazed hard into each other's eyes, then shook hands, holding the grip longer than was necessary.

It occurred to Max that if he repeated this conversation to Louise, she would blink and claim they hadn't talked at all. But she would be wrong. They had said it all with their fists, and Livvy had added the postscript. Now the air was clear, and they could go on. They slapped each other on the back and returned to the corral to wrap up the branding and ear notching.

While he worked, Max decided that Livvy was right. There was no woman worth losing his brother over. His feelings wouldn't change overnight, but for the first time since he had looked down and found the scratched marble in his palm, he understood that he'd only paid lip service to the fact that he had to let Philadelphia go. On some level he had stubbornly believed that eventually, somehow and someway, everything would work out as it should have. But it wasn't going to. He had to accept that, completely and finally, or lose his brother.

* * *

They didn't discuss the dreamlike evening on the kitchen floor or the fight between Max and his brother. There was no need because Louise understood that Philadelphia stood squarely at the center of both events. To state it mildly, Philadelphia was not her favorite topic despite the amount of time she wasted thinking about the woman. Half a dozen times a day she recalled her meeting with Philadelphia and thought about all the things she might have said in response to Philadelphia's remarks.

The only reason she'd taken Philadelphia's comments lying down was because she felt sorry for her, and because she knew Livvy McCord desperately did not want an open breech within the family. For Livvy's sake, Louise had decided that she would do whatever it took not to cause further trouble. If that meant letting Philadelphia walk all over her, well, so be it. There was nothing Philadelphia could say to her that she hadn't heard before.

Besides, if she ever let herself cut loose, she could outdo Philadelphia any day of the week when it came to insults. If living in a man's world had done nothing else, it had taught her how to cuss and hurl insults alongside the best of them.

There was another, less noble reason why she hadn't given Philadelphia a hard verbal slap. A little matter of the truth.

Pausing with her dust rag on the piano keys, Louise reluctantly conceded that Philadelphia was right. Louise hadn't been choosy about who drew the scratched marble. To get a baby she would have slept with just about any of the prospectors.

But she wasn't a whore as Philadelphia believed. She wasn't promiscuous either. At age twenty-eight, she'd been with two men, and one of them she'd married. If that made her an affront to decent women—if wanting a baby to love and raise wasn't something respectable folks could understand—then she didn't want to be decent or respectable.

Be who you seem to be. That was one of the proverbs she tried to live by. She didn't put on airs, didn't gussy up her background, didn't apologize for who she was or how she lived. She tried to do right and stay out of trouble. She lived what she considered a decent life, though it might not seem so to someone like Philadelphia.

There were about a million rules in the Good Book and in society, and she tried to obey those that made sense. But it never should have been a rule that a woman became indecent if she was willing to accept just about any man in order to make a baby. Some women were never going to catch a husband or didn't want one. That didn't make them in-damn-decent.

Raising a hand, she banged her fist down on the piano keys, striking a jarringly discordant sound. After she did it again, Max appeared in the parlor archway, startling her. She hadn't realized he'd come inside.

"What are you doing?"

Her chin came up and she glared. "Everyone in the McCord family can play a stupid pi-ano except me. Even Sunshine can pick out a tune; she told me so." When Max smiled and pointed out that neither he nor Wally played the piano, she snapped at him. "You know what I mean."

"I'm sure Gilly would be delighted to teach you."

"Well, maybe I'll just ask her about that." After closing the lid over the keys with a bang, she swished her skirts past him and headed for the kitchen. "Or maybe I won't. Maybe I think a person can be decent without knowing how to play a single damned note. What are you doing here anyway?"

"I came up to the house for dinner," he said patiently, following her into the kitchen.

"Oh Lord. Is it dinnertime already? Seems I just finished putting away the breakfast fixings." Her face flamed as she walked across the section of floor where they had lain together, and she didn't dare look at him. They had done . . . it . . . on the kitchen floor. If she were still a cussing woman, she would have spun out a string of awed swearing, yes sir.

"Just give me some bread and gravy. That'll be fine."

"A man ought to have more than bread and gravy for his dinner." He was standing too close, and that flustered her. In all her born days, she didn't think she'd ever met a man who smelled as wonderful as Max did. He smelled like lots of good things. Leather and smoke, horseflesh and cowhide. Soap and fresh air, earth and sun. Sometimes he smelled of whiskey, and sometimes he smelled like the apples she kept in a basket near the mudroom door. Sometimes she smelled lamp oil on his hands, sometimes coal or pine resin. If she sniffed him before he washed up at night, occasionally she caught the tang of good honest man sweat.

"Louise . . ."

They stood gazing into each other's eyes, close enough that her skirt wrapped his legs. And his intense speculative look suggested that he, too, remembered what had happened in this spot a few nights ago.

"Mr. McCord? Max? Are you in there?"

Louise gave him a faint smile and stepped backward, folding her shaking hands in her apron.

"That you, Shorty?" Max called toward the mudroom door. He placed a fingertip at the corner of Louise's lips.

His touch was light, but it shot a spear of fire down to her toes and pinned her to the floor.

"You and me," Max said quietly. "We got some talking to do. I'll be back after I find out what's on Shorty's mind."

Nodding, Louise leaned against the sink and wet her lips. There were a dozen things he might want to discuss. Piano lessons, expenses, the roundup, the weather, his black eye. But the hot tingle in her stomach and the accelerated thump of her heartbeat suggested that she hoped it was none of those things.

When the strength returned to her legs, she stood up straight and blinked at the bacon drippings on the stove shelf, then toward the sideboard where she kept the flour sack. She tried to think about gravy, but her heart and ears listened for Max's voice. Even so, she had the skillet out and on the stove before she realized the voices outside were too loud. Frowning, she hesitated, then moved the skillet off the heat and wiped her hands in her apron. All she had to do was stand in the door to the mudroom and she could hear Max and Shorty.

"I'm sorry, Mr. McCord. You got to know we wouldn't walk out on you if there was any choice."

Louise pressed a hand to her mouth, smothering a gasp.

"I'd appreciate it if you'd give me a few days to work this out." Anger shook Max's voice.

"There's nothing you can do. This ain't going to work out. The boys are cleaning the bunkhouse now. We'll ride out after we finish the day's chores." A silence ensued, broken by the sound of throat clearing, spitting, and boot scuffing. "I'm sorry. I felt like I was part of this place. Wanted to watch it grow."

"If things change, there'll always be a place for you here."

"I hope they do change, boss. I surely do."

There was time for them to shake hands, time for Shorty to walk away before Max slammed into the house, strode past her, and dropped heavily into a chair at the table.

Louise poured a cup of coffee and placed it in his hand. "What was that? I heard the end of it, but not the beginning."

"The boys went into town last night to spend their wages and let off a little steam."

"And?"

"Nobody in town would take their money. They were either ignored or told to get out. They couldn't buy a drink or a woman, couldn't get a shave or a shine. No restaurant would serve them. The hotel told them to move on and use someone else's hitching rail. One of the sheriff's deputies followed them everywhere they went. Watching them and how they were treated. Smiling when it became apparent that Shorty and the boys couldn't buy the time of day."

"But why?" Louise's eyes widened and she spread her hands. "Why would any establishment turn away business?"

He stared at her. "Because the owners were told to."

"But who . . . ?" Then it came to her. "Oh." Silently she returned to the stove and poured another cup of coffee for herself.

"As long as Shorty and the boys work for me, they're pariahs in town."

Louise sat at the table and shoved back the hair falling across her forehead. "Surely Howard Houser doesn't hold the mortgage on every business in Fort Houser," she said angrily.

"There's one bank in town, and Houser owns it. I've seen the file room. Hundreds and hundreds of folders. Mortgages, loans, investment accounts, savings, you name it. If someone makes a financial transaction, you can bet that Howard had something to do with it. If he doesn't hold the mortgage directly, he probably has dealings with the establishment's suppliers, and so on."

"The hell with him. We'll hire new hands."

"Who's going to sign on? The word will get out, if it hasn't already, that working for Max McCord is like working for free because no one in town will accept money from one of my hands. I might as well pay their wages in dried peas for all the good my money does them."

The ripples continued to widen, rolling outward from

a moment on a mountainside above Piney Creek. Swearing softly, Louise watched Max drag his fingers over the pits marking his jaw.

"Would it do any good to speak to Houser?" Even as she asked the question, she knew any appeal would be futile.

"Houser knows what he's doing. The ostracism will continue until he decides I've been punished enough."

"This isn't fair," Louise said furiously. "If you won't believe me, then believe your ma. Livvy said you did the right thing. She knows what happened wasn't your fault."

"That was before anyone knew about Philadelphia's pregnancy. The pregnancy is my fault. That's what Howard can't move past." He pushed a hand through his hair. "I'd feel the same if I had a daughter and some bastard got her pregnant."

Maybe Max did have a daughter, Louise thought, looking away from him. Maybe the child Philadelphia carried was a girl.

"Well," he said after a full minute. "I can't feed a herd by myself. And I know Howard Houser. If I spread my herd among Dave, Ma, and Wally's herds, their hands won't be able to buy so much as a plug of tobacco, either." He stared at a point in space, his face hard and resigned. "There's nothing to do but sell out. I'd rather sell the herd now than watch them starve over the winter."

"You're talking about giving up your ranch?"

What more did Max McCord have to lose before the reverberations ended from that day on the mountainside? He'd lost his bride, his child, a future in banking. Before it was over, he might lose his brother and now his ranch. She'd be damned before she let that happen. It ended here, now. Max was not going to lose anything more.

"Like hell," Louise said, leaning forward. Her eyes glittered. "You got me. And I'm worth three hands any day. You and me, we can get those beeves through the winter."

He stared at her. "You don't know what you're saying. Getting a herd through the winter is hard work. The cattle don't stop eating when a blizzard blows. We'll have to keep the stock ponds from freezing over. I can't ask this of you."

"You ain't asking. I'm volunteering. We're not giving up without a fight."

Chapter 14

"I'm sorry, but I never interfere in Papa's business." How many miserable hours had she now spent staring out of her bedroom window? She hated living here, loathed it. The daily monotony and idleness were driving her mad.

"I'll ride into town tomorrow and speak to your father myself." Bending at the hearth, Wally banked the logs in her bedroom fireplace. "Trying to ruin Max is small-minded and serves no purpose. This has to stop."

Small-minded? She certainly hoped he displayed more tact when he spoke to her father.

"Did Max ask you to intercede on his behalf?" Ironically, if Max lost his ranch, he'd have to move into town as she had wanted him to do in the first place.

"No. Would you like to come to town with me?" Wally asked. He looked quite handsome today, dressed and groomed for Sunday dinner. If she had her way—and eventually she would—he'd never wear flannel and everyday denims again. "You said something about wanting to stop by Mrs. Dame's."

The at-home dresses and wrappers Mrs. Dame was sewing for her were shapeless sacklike things that she could not imagine wearing. On the other hand, her regular clothing was beginning to fit snugly at the waist. Every day she checked her stomach in the mirror, detesting the roundness she saw reflected. Knowing it would get worse, knowing she would bloat up like a frog and lose her figure was a dismal fact she refused to contemplate.

"The garments Mrs. Dame is making don't require much fitting." Outside, a cold wind plucked at browning leaves then chased the leaves toward the barn. Philadelphia wished herself a thousand miles from this window.

"I know how bored you've been. I could drop you at Mrs. Dame's, then maybe you'd like to do some shopping at the Ladies' Emporium or visit friends. There's no hurry to get back."

She wasn't about to put herself through another trip to the emporium. Last week she had wheedled Wally into taking her to town and she'd received one nasty shock after another. Women she had known all of her life had cut her in the emporium. And when she called on ladies she considered friends, their doors had been closed to her. Even the Grayson sisters had instructed their housekeeper to say they were out, as if Philadelphia didn't know they received every Wednesday afternoon.

The injustice of it made her shrivel inside. Apparently the scandalmongers believed she had been seeing both the McCord brothers, playing them one against the other. This is what came of her father and Mrs. McCord deciding on the story to be put about and not involving her in the process. They hadn't spared her from scandal; they had, in fact, made her a social persona non grata and had given her one more cross to bear. The same humiliation would have resulted if the full truth were known, but in that case at least a few of her friends and acquaintances would surely have pitied her and understood she was a victim, not a villainess.

"No," she decided, hating it that she was truly a prisoner here. "I'll stay at the ranch. I cannot endure it that I—I!—have been smeared in this affair." Angry tears welled in her eyes and she stamped her foot. "It isn't fair!"

"No, it isn't." Wally came to her and clasped her

hands in his, stroking her fingers. "It might take your mind off things and make time pass a little quicker if you gave Ma a hand in the kitchen. . . ."

Cats would bark before she turned herself into a household drudge. "Did Livvy ask you to say that? Has she complained about me?"

"Not at all," Wally hastily assured her. "But Ma's doing all the cooking, cleaning, washing, and ironing."

"Are you implying that because your mother won't tolerate servants in her house, I should become a housemaid? I'm a guest here!" Offended, she tried to withdraw her hands, but he held on.

"I'm only suggesting that keeping busy might relieve the boredom for you, and Ma would undoubtedly appreciate the help." A certain timidity crept into his voice when he wanted her to do something that he sensed she didn't wish to do. The signal gave her a moment to prepare her response.

"Oh Wally. Is that the next humiliation, the next punishment? That I should sink to the level of a servant?" Tears spilled beautifully over her lashes, and she accepted the handkerchief he pushed into her hand. Blotting her cheeks, she prevented teardrops from spotting the bosom of her Sunday taffeta. "If you insist, I'll debase myself but . . . how much must I bear?"

"Of course I'm not insisting. I was merely offering a suggestion, that's all." Gently, he guided her into his arms and caressed her back. "My poor brave darling."

"It never ends," she whispered against his throat. Her breath on his freshly shaven skin caused his body to tighten. In a week or two she might allow him to kiss her cheek. She knew he wanted to. After the baby arrived, she would consider kissing him back as a reward if he did something to please her. "I suppose my eyes are red and I'm a mess now," she said, pulling away to dab her lashes.

"You're beautiful."

"Do you know if *she's* coming to dinner this week?"

Of course she was. Last Sunday Philadelphia had feigned illness and Wally had brought dinner to her room. She hadn't enjoyed a single bite knowing the creature was at the table with the rest of the family, undoubtedly gloating and telling herself that Philadelphia feared to face her. Which was a lie. No respectable woman had anything to fear from a fallen woman who knew nothing of decency.

"I'll stay by your side every moment," Wally promised gruffly. "In time, family gatherings will get easier. Until they do, just ignore Louise."

He could count on that. As far as she was concerned, the creature did not exist.

Once they had their own house in town, she would begin to wean Wally away from the McCords and the intolerable family gatherings. Unfortunately, a house in town was not yet a real consideration, but it would be. Her father had grudgingly promised that the next time he spoke privately to Wally, he would discuss a position at the bank. Moving Wally away from ranching was the first step on the road to molding him into what she wanted. But nothing would happen until after the baby was born. Her ordeal would continue for months yet.

Taking Wally's arm, she collected herself and lifted her head. Together they descended the staircase.

At the bottom of the stairs, Gilly's daughter, Sunshine, ran out of the parlor—the girl never seemed to walk—and threw her arms around Philadelphia's waist.

"You look so pretty, Aunt Philadelphia! Are you feeling better this week?"

Gently she removed the child's arms. "Darling, you mustn't embrace me like that; you'll crush my skirts."

The careless child was witless enough to look confused. "But Aunt Louise likes it when I hug her."

"As we can all observe, Low Down lacks beauty and style, and her skirts are as ugly as she is. No one would notice if the material was wrinkled, not even her. Women of Low Down's ilk don't care about appearances."

A man cleared his throat, and when she looked up, Max and Low Down were standing in the foyer watching. Max stared at her with a flat, unreadable gaze. An infuriating half-smile curved the creature's lips, but bright pink blazed on her cheeks. So what if the creature had overheard her comments, Philadelphia thought with satisfaction. She hadn't spoken a word that wasn't true.

As if to prove Philadelphia's remarks, Low Down knelt with no thought for wrinkling her plain, unattractive skirt, then she opened her arms and smiled at Sunshine. "I do like hugs. And your aunt Philadelphia is correct that I don't care diddly how I look. Never have."

Sunshine danced across the foyer and wrapped her arms around Low Down's neck. "Oh, you smell good. Like apple cider."

The creature laughed, a husky sound that belonged in a smoky saloon. The vulgarity of it grated across Philadelphia's nerve endings. "I used the last of the apples to make pies. I imagine that's what you're smelling." The creature glanced at Max and nodded at Wally standing silently at Philadelphia's side before she took Sunshine's hand. "Let's go to the kitchen and see if your grandma needs any help."

Apple cider, indeed. Philadelphia moved forward and demurely lowered her eyelids as Wally shook hands with Max. But she stood close enough that Max couldn't help inhaling the fragrance of rosewater and the rose petal sachet tucked inside her corset.

"Hello, Philadelphia."

"Good morning, Max."

Today they would begin to establish the habits that would govern their behavior toward each other for now and all time.

"Are you feeling well?" A lack of expression concealed the tumult of emotion he must be experiencing, exactly as she was.

"Yes, thank you," she murmured. Wally moved closer and placed a proprietary hand against the small of her back. "And you?"

"Quite well, thank you."

The banality of the exchange deadened her mind. Was this how it would be? Dull, meaningless politeness? Never before had they gazed at each other and found themselves at a loss for words. She let him see her despairing stare at his mouth, then she touched the tip of her tongue to her upper lip. They had to pretend now, but she had forgotten nothing, nothing at all.

Still Max's expression didn't change, but his shoulders stiffened and he closed his hand into a fist around something in his pocket.

"I'm going to speak to Howard Houser tomorrow," Wally said, "and insist that he lift the ridiculous ban on accepting your hands' money."

A flash of anger knit Max's eyebrows. "I appreciate your concern, but you're wasting your breath. Stay out of it, Wally."

"Philadelphia and I don't think this is fair treatment. We should put the past behind us."

Max gave her a narrowed look of speculation, and she felt her skin tingle and her stomach spun into a slow roll. His gaze dropped to her waist before sliding away.

She released a breath she'd unconsciously been holding. Next to Max, Wally was but a pallid shadow. Where Max stood immovable as a rock, her husband was like a malleable child.

"Dave's out back, waiting to show you two his new saddle," Gilly called with a smile, walking toward them from the kitchen. "Hello, Philadelphia, you're looking well today."

To her dismay, the men moved toward the door. "How long before we eat?" Wally asked Gilly. Wally had promised to stay by Philadelphia's side, but the frantic signals she sent him sailed past his thick head. He would hear about this later.

"About twenty minutes." When the door closed behind the men, Gilly wiped her hands in the folds of her apron while Philadelphia tried to recall when last she had seen Gilly or Livvy without the ubiquitous apron. "Would you like to join us women in the kitchen?"

She didn't know the first thing about kitchens, nor did she have the slightest notion how to prepare a meal. This was no oversight; she didn't wish to know. Most particularly, she was unwilling to provide an opportunity for Livvy to make her feel inadequate or useless. Livvy McCord might believe a woman's place was in the kitchen, but true ladies decidedly did not. And finally, the creature was in the kitchen.

"I prefer to wait in the parlor," she said pleasantly. "Perhaps you'd care to join me?" A bit of company would be welcome.

"I'd enjoy that I'm sure, but I'm in the midst of filling the salt cellars." Gilly gave her a smile and a shrug, then returned down the hallway toward the kitchen.

Shocked by Gilly's casual dismissal, Philadelphia did not move for a long moment. She stood excluded and abandoned in the chilly foyer with teeth and hands clenched. Finally she spun in a furious swirl of taffeta and marched into the parlor, where she occupied the time until dinner by counting the days until she could escape from here.

Dinner, of course, was precisely the ordeal she had expected. First, in an aggravating breech of convention, Sunshine was permitted to dine with the adults. Worse, the child chattered incessantly and no one ordered her to be silent; it was enough to give one a headache. The men talked politics and cattle and the weather. Livvy and Gilly discussed the clothing they were sewing for the creature. The creature spoke only once. She answered yes when Gilly inquired if she still intended to drive to Gilly's home after dinner for a dress fitting.

As for herself, Philadelphia finally abandoned any effort to introduce refined topics and concentrated on setting a silent example of grace, delicacy, and good manners. Occasionally she lifted her lashes to peek down the table at Max, hoping that he noted the vast contrast between good breeding and Low Down's boorish manners. Twice she caught Max staring at her, and she smiled inside her mouth.

Although she never glanced at Low Down or acknowledged her presence, she was very aware of the creature. From the corner of her eye, she noticed a deferential expression when the creature gazed at her betters. Which was as it should be. It gave great satisfaction to know Low Down understood she didn't belong among superior decent company. She was a misfit, an abomination.

After dinner the men stepped outside to smoke their vile cigars, and Low Down immediately jumped up and collected several dessert plates before she left for the kitchen. The creature's transparent desire to flee was gratifying and raised a flush of righteous triumph to Philadelphia's brow.

"I declare," Gilly commented, watching Sunshine skip toward the kitchen. "That child dotes on Louise." She cast Philadelphia a guilty look and hastily added, "and you, too, of course. Sunshine says she wants to be as beautiful as her aunt Philadelphia when she grows up."

"I've always had a way with children," she admitted with a modest smile. In the past, this response had contained little real meaning, but now it did as she abruptly recalled her pregnancy and her smile faded.

"When I was as far along as you, I was already wearing loose clothing," Gilly commented. "Mama thought I was surely going to have twins," she added with a smile.

Livvy raised her coffee cup, and her eyes sharpened. "Did I overhear Wally say he intends to speak to your father about driving off Max's hands?"

She was not going to allow herself to be drawn into a discussion of Max's punishment. Instead she lowered her voice and leaned forward, imparting a confidence. "Wally doesn't know this, but I believe Daddy intends to extend a job offer tomorrow."

"Do you think Wally will accept the offer?" Livvy inquired.

"Of course he will."

Pushing up from the table, Livvy carried her coffee cup to the dining room window. In the ensuing silence, Philadelphia overheard Low Down and Sunshine laughing in the kitchen.

"In some ways, Wally will make a more successful banker than Max would have," Livvy said eventually. She frowned at the men smoking outside, their backs to the wind. "Wally isn't as quick at ciphering, but he'll be more comfortable working for someone else. Max needs to be his own boss."

"Wally isn't as tied to the land as Max is," Gilly offered after a minute. "Since he hasn't built on his parcel, he wouldn't have to divide his time between ranching and banking. We could split his herd between our hands and the hands at the main ranch . . ."

"Was this your idea or is it your father's belief that he can turn anyone named McCord into a banker?" Livvy put the question without turning around.

As usual, Livvy didn't display the deference she should have toward a Houser. Philadelphia's grandfather had founded Fort Houser, her father was its most prominent citizen, and until Livvy McCord's son had betrayed her,

Philadelphia Houser had served as society's reigning belle. Truly, her mother-in-law was an infuriating woman.

She forced herself to smile. "I can't deny that it would please me to see my husband move up in the world, but I assure you I do not dictate my father's decisions."

Gilly cast an uncomfortable glance toward her mother's rigid back, then politely shifted the focus of the conversation. "Will you accompany Wally into town?"

"I guess you didn't hear about my horrible experience last week." Blinking at brimming tears, she told Gilly about the cuts and snubs directed her way. Gilly murmured sympathetic sounds, but Livvy remained as unmoved as she had initially. Philadelphia dabbed her eyes with a scrap of lace. "It's unbelievable that this is happening to me! The scandal was supposed to be diverted; instead my good name is ruined!"

Now Livvy turned. "In view of the circumstances, your good name would have been ruined no matter how the situation was handled."

Shock widened her eyes. "You can't possibly be suggesting that I am in any way to blame!"

"Allowances can be made for the unfortunate fact that you had no mother to guide and advise you. But your father must also be aware that my son did not abuse you. Your predicament is the result of a consensual act, and, therefore, you do, of course, share responsibility for the loss of your good name, as you put it. Perhaps the scandal would be easier to bear if you acknowledged your part in causing it!"

"That is outrageous! That horrible Low Down person is to blame, not me!" Philadelphia came to her feet, her hands shaking. Heat flooded her face, and her lips trembled. "I don't know why you've turned against me. My only crime was loving Max McCord. I don't deserve any of the hideous things that happened to me, and I am in no way whatsoever at fault!" Tears swam in her eyes as she gathered her skirts and fled to her room.

She slammed the bedroom door then quietly opened it and tiptoed to the head of the stairs to eavesdrop.

"Weren't you a bit hard on her, Mama?"

"I suppose I'll have to apologize," Livvy admitted with a sigh. The aggrieved tone announced that any apology would not be sincere. "If you'd conceived before marriage—God forbid—I know you wouldn't have denied responsibility. You would have admitted to as much wrongdoing as Dave."

"You know she's spoiled. She's always been coddled and catered to, and I doubt she's ever had to face her mistakes. If she truly believes that she shares no blame, then it must hurt terribly to be treated as a pariah. And Mama, she'll never escape the taint of this scandal. Surely you can find it in your heart to pity her."

Spoiled! Coddled and catered to!

Well, so what if she was? She was a Houser, after all, not some nobody with no name or background. Everyone knew she could have married far higher than a McCord. Who were they, after all?

"One thing is abundantly evident. Weekly gatherings are too great a strain on everyone. As much as I dislike the necessity, I think from now on we'll have a family dinner only once a month."

"She means well, Mama."

"Then why isn't *she* speaking to her father about Max? Houser would relent if Philadelphia asked him to end his vendetta."

The men returned then, and shortly afterward Gilly and Dave and Max and Low Down collected jackets, hats, and gloves, and said their good-byes. Lifting her skirts, Philadelphia moved silently to the hallway window that overlooked the front road.

After a minute the couples emerged, walking toward their respective wagons. She paid no attention to Gilly and Dave, but watched sharply as Max assisted Low Down up on the wagon seat.

And she gasped as Low Down said something, then placed her gloved palm against Max's cheek. They looked into each other's eyes, then Max laughed and tucked Low Down's skirts around her legs before he climbed into the driver's seat.

Oh, dear heaven. They were lovers.

Feeling sick inside, Philadelphia pressed a hand hard against her mouth. It had never occurred to her, not once, that Max would actually bed the creature. Naturally, she had assumed that he would remain faithful to her. Yes, he'd made that stupid promise to give Low Down a baby, but no one expected him to keep a commitment made under duress. As for her father driving off Max's hands, he had to know he deserved punishment, but surely he also understood that someday they would be together again. She had never intended to make him angry or drive him into the creature's arms. Never that.

Reeling with shock, she stumbled back to her room and fell across the bed in a storm of furious weeping. Damn him.

When Wally came upstairs, she threw herself into his arms and sobbed on his shoulder. After he had anxiously inquired over and over as to what had put her in such a state, she explained, "Your mother hates me! She said such mean things. . . . I'm sure she didn't mean it but . . . Oh Wally." Easing back in his arms, she turned swimming eyes up to his face. "Will you do something for me?"

"Of course, dear. Anything!"

"Kiss me."

He blinked hard as if he'd been poleaxed. Then he looked delighted. He wet his lips and gently drew her forward as if she were made of thin glass that might shatter beneath his hands.

His kiss was soft and tender. Utterly boring. When it

ended, Philadelphia pressed her head into his shoulder to smother her sigh and conceal her despair.

Since Max was not present to agonize over his brother kissing her, the kiss was wasted. She'd gained no advantage by granting it.

She wished to heaven that she had not seen Max tuck the creature's ugly skirts around her legs. Damn him, damn him.

"I loved listening to Dave strum his guitar. And Gilly plays the pi-ano without even looking at the sheets of music!"

Max nodded and glanced at the main house as he drove past on the way home. The front of the house was dark. As the window of Wally and Philadelphia's room opened to the back, he couldn't tell if their lamps were lit or if they were still awake.

"It was a fine evening," Louise added cheerfully, pressing her thigh and leg against his. The temperature hovered around freezing, so the sensible course was to share each other's warmth. Nevertheless, he was aware of her closeness and her scent. Sunshine had been right that she smelled like apple cider.

"You didn't speak three words until we reached Gilly and Dave's place." He guessed he knew why.

"I didn't have anything to say." She kept her gaze fixed on the inky road ahead.

By now he should have known she wouldn't complain, but he'd thought she might make a reference to Philadelphia's appalling rudeness. But she hadn't, not during the drive to Gilly and Dave's, nor during the return trip. Now he understood that she wouldn't mention Philadelphia throughout the remaining three miles to their house.

All week he had dreaded seeing Philadelphia. He kept thinking if things had gone differently, they would have been in Denver now on their wedding trip. But any thoughts of what might have been had evaporated when he watched her protect her skirts by pushing Sunshine away. Never would he have guessed that she would value the drape of her skirts more than a child's embrace.

Moreover, he would have sworn Philadelphia incapable of delivering scathing remarks and then smiling when she discovered the object of her scorn, Louise, had overheard her comments. Worse, she had tossed him a quick triumphant glance as if they were conspirators and she expected him to applaud.

Granted, Philadelphia had no reason to exude warmth and kindness toward Louise. But Max would have wagered everything he owned that Philadelphia Houser would never ostracize a person seated at the same table. She wouldn't knowingly cause the rest of the dinner company a moment's discomfort. He had expected chilly politeness but certainly politeness. He had not expected pointed rudeness or the slashing remarks aimed at Louise. Definitely he had not anticipated that he would gaze down the dinner table at the woman he would have married and feel defensive and angry.

Thinking about it now, he experienced a stab of shame that, aside from one brief moment in the foyer, he had forgotten that she was pregnant. How in the hell could he have forgotten even for an instant? He'd worried all day yesterday that his feelings of tenderness toward the mother of his child would be uncomfortably evident to everyone at the table. And then he'd forgotten. Truly, he was a bastard, and she was better off without him.

"It's a beautiful night, ain't it?" Louise said at his side.

"Isn't—not ain't," he said automatically.

"Isn't it. The stars look close enough to grab."

Another thing that bothered him was wondering if Philadelphia had always been as self-absorbed as she had seemed today. Was this a recently acquired trait? Perhaps a symptom of her condition? Or had he been so blinded that he hadn't looked beyond flirting eyes and dimpled cheeks? Abruptly he recalled teasing her about doing and saying whatever she pleased and the devil take the consequences. Today he'd observed a manifestation of the same thoughtlessly selfish behavior, but this time he had judged it harshly.

"Now who's being quiet?" Louise asked, nudging him with her shoulder.

"Thank you for going with me to Ma's for dinner," he said after a minute. She must have dreaded today's dinner as much as he had.

"I wasn't sure if I'd like your family, but I do. There was one time when I looked around the table and I thought, son of a bitch, here I am. . . ." She halted abruptly and drew a breath. "And I thought, my stars, here I am having dinner with a real family, and I have as much right to be here as . . . you know, anyone else." Ducking her head, she pushed at the fingers of her gloves. "Anyway. It was a good moment, as fine a moment as I can recall."

"You keep that in mind," he said firmly, peering ahead into the cold darkness. "You do have a right to be there." He understood Philadelphia wanting to punish him, but Louise had nothing to do with Philadelphia's pregnancy or her marriage to Wally. It wasn't right to punish someone else for his faults.

"Did you know that Gilly wants another baby?"

"She hasn't said anything, but it doesn't surprise me."

"She and Dave have been hoping for three years, but it hasn't happened yet. It doesn't seem fair that some folks get pregnant just like that, and others have to wait for years."

Instantly he remembered the amazing night on the kitchen floor and felt his thighs tighten. As long as he lived, he would never forget the moment when her nightgown dropped to her waist and he realized what she intended. And then seeing her in the frosty moonlight that gave her body a shimmer of silver. She wasn't small or delicate, but she was perfectly and beautifully proportioned. Small waist, full breasts, long, strong legs. Her skin had been taut and hot, smooth and firm to the touch.

Muscles tight, he pulled the wagon around the house to the mudroom door. "I'll put the wagon away. Do you need assistance?"

She laughed and scooted across the seat. "I can climb down without your help."

Cold wind rushed to fill the vacancy against his thigh and leg, but he didn't release the brake. When she reached the stoop, he called into the darkness. "Louise?"

"Yes?"

"I've been thinking . . . this might be a good night for you not to wear that damned nightgown."

"Tonight?" Surprise lifted her voice.

"Unless you'd rather not."

"I sure didn't think . . . I mean with you seeing . . . Listen, are you just feeling sorry for me, or—"

"Louise? It's cold sitting here. Could you just say yes or no?"

"Yes!" Her laugh was throaty and floated on the frosty air with the warmth of a promise. "Yes, yes, yes!"

As he drove the wagon toward the shed, it occurred to him that he'd made love to her with reluctance, and he'd made love to her in anger. Tonight was the first time he would make love to her because he truly wanted to. And damned if he wasn't as surprised as she that it would happen tonight.

Anticipation made his fingers tremble as he unhitched the wagon and turned the horses into the corral. He was so intent on the image of finding Louise naked in his bed that he didn't consider the significance of the snowflakes silently spinning out of the black sky. He didn't think of anything but her.

When he entered the bedroom, she was in bed, the covers pulled up under her chin, her brown hair loose on the pillow. Red tinted her cheeks, and her eyes were wide and round.

"You aren't hiding that wretched nightgown under those blankets, are you?" Smiling, he sat on the vanity bench and pulled off his boots and wiggled his toes with a sigh of pleasure.

"I'm naked as the day I was born," she whispered. The red in her cheeks turned fiery.

What an odd woman she was, he thought as he pulled off his trousers and unbuttoned his shirt. She dressed and undressed in the closet, didn't display an inch of flesh if she could cover it. She was not flirtatious or a tease. In fact, he would have said that modesty formed one of her defining traits. Yet, in his dark moment she had bared herself to him and given him the most erotic evening of his life. He would never forget that night on the kitchen floor. He wanted to give her a night that she wouldn't forget.

Sliding beneath the blankets, he spooned his body around her to warm the chill on his skin. Instantly he felt himself respond to the firm heat of her nakedness.

"Louise?" he murmured against the nape of her neck after he pushed aside her hair. "There's going to be lots of dawdling tonight."

"What does that mean?" Suspicion placed a wobble in her voice, and he felt her stiffen.

"You'll have to wait and see." He let his breath flow across the tender skin beneath her ear, and he slipped an arm around her waist, drawing her closer into the hard curve of his body.

"You didn't blow out the lamp."

"No, I didn't." He ran his hand along the curve of her thigh, dipped to the hollow of her waist, then teased his fingers up her rib cage, moving his palm to her arm

and up to her shoulder. A little puff of breath blew between her lips and he knew she had expected him to
touch her breasts. And he would. Eventually.

Nuzzling her, he moved his lips on the nape of her
neck, traveling to her ear, then rising above her to follow the line of her jaw. She smelled like apple cider as
she had earlier, but there was another scent, a deeper
fragrance that was hers alone. It was a warm earthy
scent that aroused him on a primitive level, the scent of
woman. Turning her beneath his hands, he followed her
jaw with his lips, kissing the corners of her lips, pulling
slightly away when she would have returned his kiss.

Now, his mouth found her collarbone and traveled to
the hollow of her throat. He pressed his tongue against
the wild throbbing of her pulse.

"Oh my God." Her hands started to rise, but he gently
pressed them back to her sides. "Am I supposed to do
something?" she asked in a husky murmur.

"Just relax." Lifting away from her, he gazed down at
her full, magnificent breasts. Then he stroked his thumbs
across budding nipples and felt them harden like stones.

She made a choked sound. "How am I going to relax with you doing . . . what you're doing!" Her back
arched, lifting her breasts to his hands, but he lowered
his mouth instead. "What are you . . . ? Oh Max! Oh
my!" Heat flooded her skin, and her hands made a helpless fluttering motion near her waist.

"Shhh," he said, smiling as he drew her nipple into
his mouth and heard her gasp. Her fingers found his
hair and dug into his scalp. As he stroked his tongue
across and around the tip of her breast, he heard her
breathing grow ragged, and she couldn't hold her body
still. Her fingers flew around his head and shoulders;
her hips rocked and tried to turn toward him.

When her skin felt hot enough to burst into flame, he
ran his hand across her lower belly and teased his fingers through the soft brown curls between her legs.

"Oh!" She tried to sit up, but he pressed her back, and returned his hand to the hot, moist mystery. "Oh Max. Oh Max."

He caressed her, stroked her, teased, and tasted until her body trembled and her breath came in mindless gasps midway between a sob and a moan. She no longer tried to pull the blankets over them, no longer resisted his mouth and hands as he explored her.

There was joy in awakening her body, and in taking her mind to the edge of new and vivid, feverish sensations, then easing away and rising to kiss her lips and gaze into her stunned eyes. "I'm going to kiss every inch of you," he whispered against her lips.

Her eyes flared wide. "Every inch?" She wet her lips. "Every . . . no, no, don't do that."

But he did, taking his time, tasting deep of her, leading her along paths she had not traveled. And when he felt her shudder deeply and cry his name, he held her tightly in his arms until the shudders subsided and she lay limp against him, her eyes dark with amazement.

"My Lord," she whispered, staring in wonder. "If I'd had any idea that dawdling could be like *that*, I never would have objected!"

Laughing, he kissed the sweet valley between her breasts. She was so responsive and uninhibited, so wonderfully willing and giving.

"Max?" she said after she'd caught her breath.

"Hmm?" He was almost asleep, enjoying her silky hair pressed to his cheek and the warm fullness of her body curved into him.

"Tonight was . . . it was just . . . well, I never imagined . . ." Her voice trailed, and he smiled against the top of her head. "What I'm trying to say is . . . I think I'd like to kiss you all over, too."

Instantly all thoughts of sleep vanished from his mind, and his body rose to full, rampant attention. Her fingers explored beneath the blankets and found him, and he heard her soft laugh.

"Seems like you wouldn't say no to a little dawdling yourself," she said, curving her fingers around him. "You feel like velvet, did you know that?"

He made a strangled sound of pleasure. "You are amazing."

Later, before they fell asleep tangled in each other's arms, he chanced to glance at the window and noticed snow melting against the panes.

The smile vanished from his lips.

Chapter 15

Since Max had offered to milk Missy while he was in the barn feeding the horses, Louise returned directly to the house after gathering eggs. In the mudroom she removed Max's old winter duster, knocked the snow off, and hung it on a peg. After shaking snow off the shawl she'd tied over her hair, she blew on her cold fingers and hurried into the kitchen to fry up breakfast.

The kitchen was warm and rich with the fragrance of boiling coffee. Louise turned off the lamps, then stood before the window watching the sky brighten above whirling snowflakes tumbling lazily toward earth. Most of the flakes were enormous and reminded her of the lacy center of the doilies that Livvy and Gilly crocheted for tabletops and furniture arms.

Yesterday the thick, wet fall of snow had seemed beautiful as the first snow always was. But today she frowned as she noticed her tracks from the henhouse were rapidly filling and Max's trail to the barn had vanished. Yesterday the cattle could still find grass; today six inches of snow concealed the forage. Today she and Max would have to feed the beeves.

She'd seen it coming and had prepared by cooking all day yesterday. Extra loaves of bread filled the breadbox. She had plenty of butter; there were boiled eggs and pickles for something quick. They might get weary of ham, but she'd baked enough to see them through several days if need be. And finally she had crowded the icebox with raisin pies and vanilla pudding.

Thick slices of ham sizzled in the skillet, the gravy was bubbling, and the biscuits ready to come out of the oven when she heard Max enter the mudroom and stamp the snow off his boots.

"Something smells good."

Snowflakes still clung to his eyelashes when he entered the kitchen, carrying the bucket of milk. Louise watched as he spooned cream out of the bucket and into his coffee cup. "Do I have time to shave before breakfast?"

"The biscuits are ready now." She didn't like beards because they hid too much of a man's face. And a mustache caught food and concealed the shape of the upper lip. She preferred a man to be clean-shaven so she could see who she was talking to and dealing with. But there was something ruggedly appealing about Max before he stropped up his razor and shaved. She wouldn't have believed that a time would come when she found herself mooning over a man's morning whiskers. She didn't like to admit it, even to herself.

"Damn."

"What's wrong?" Max asked, wiping snow off his face with her dish towel. "Do you regret volunteering to hay the cattle? I wouldn't blame you if you did."

She hadn't realized she'd spoken aloud. "I was just thinking what a foolish woman I am. But not because I volunteered to be a ranch hand. Sit down so I can dish this up."

"You're a lot of things, darlin', but not foolish. Aside from Ma, you're the least foolish woman I've ever met."

The bones melted in her hand, the pan tipped, and biscuits rolled across the plank floor.

Son of a bitch. He'd called her darlin'. The word just rolled off his tongue as easy as pie, like it had been waiting there for just this moment.

"Did you burn yourself?" He jumped up from the table and took the pan out of her hand, dropping it into the sink.

"The biscuits are ruined." It had to be a mistake. He hadn't meant to call her darlin'. Or he didn't mean it as an endearment, it was only an expression. Very likely he addressed a lot of folks as darlin' and wasn't aware that he did. And she hadn't noticed until now.

"A little grit won't hurt." Leaving her rooted to the floor, Max bent to pick up the biscuits, putting them in a bowl. He turned his head sideways. "You're wearing a pair of my trousers under that apron."

"Well, you didn't think I was going out there to feed cows wearing a skirt, did you?" For no reason at all she was suddenly angry enough to bash him over the head with the skillet. Gripping the handle, she stared down at him, wanting to smack him one.

What was this darlin' business, anyway? She did not want to moon around over his unshaved whiskers, and she did not want him calling her darlin'. No sir. When it was time to walk away from here, she wanted to do it without a pang. Without regret, without a single backward glance. And without hearing the wind whistle through a hole in her heart.

Releasing the skillet, she slammed the oven door, then forked up ham slices and slapped them on the plates. Grits slopped over the pan when she ladled out a couple of scoops and smothered the grits and ham beneath a river of red-eye gravy. Not a single egg yoke survived an assault with the spatula.

"Louise?" Max leaned back when she banged his plate down in front of him. "What happened here? Why do you suddenly have a burr in your blanket?"

"Just eat your breakfast. And don't go calling me darlin' anymore. I mean it."

He blinked. "I called you darling?"

"Damned straight you did, and I don't like it!"

He sat down and snapped a napkin across his lap. "Exactly when did this terrible offense occur? Last night?"

A rush of color heated her cheeks. The last two nights had been, well, spectacular. She wasn't sure how she felt about that, either. It troubled her that she'd done a complete about-face and was starting to enjoy poking so much. And kissing. Kissing was more thrilling than she had ever dreamed it could be.

"Not last night. You said it just now." She'd been right, he didn't even know he'd called her darlin'. On the one hand, that lessened the offense. On the other hand, that he didn't even know he'd said something nice was pretty insulting.

"Now, I'm not saying you're wrong to be angry and offended. But it seems to me there are a lot worse things one person could call another person than darlin'."

When she looked up, his eyes were sparkling and his lips twitched at the corners.

"In fact, if you wanted to call me darlin', I think I could stand it. I imagine I'd shudder the first time, maybe take offense. Then I think I'd settle down and decide that darlin' was a lot nicer than, oh, something like 'you bastard.' "

She narrowed her eyes and stared at him suspiciously. "You're joshing me, right?"

His eyes twinkled and danced above those twitching lips. "Now would I tease an angry woman?"

Good Lord. That's exactly what he was doing. Louise leaned back in her chair. She didn't think anyone had ever teased her before.

"Darlin'," he said, drawing out the word, "finish your breakfast. Time's wasting. We need to get out there in the storm and find out if we've made a mistake or if we're going to be able to feed those beeves all winter."

"Of course we are," she snapped, staring at him. Her mind had turned mushy. She didn't know if she was still pissy that he'd called her darlin', or if she was flattered and pleased that he'd teased her. Well, damn. Here she went, mooning around again. "How are we going to do it?"

"Have you pitched hay before?"

"I've seen it done. You want more coffee?"

"Watching it and doing it are two different things. Yes, thank you, I'd like more coffee."

"Well, get it yourself and I'd like some, too." The way she was mooning around and falling into wifely service was enough to gag a cat. Most of the time she didn't even notice the bad habits she was developing. If she didn't nip this in the bud, pretty soon she'd be polishing his boots and saddles. "How much hay pitching are we going to be doing?"

He blinked and ran his fingers over the pox marks on his chin, then he got up and poured them both more coffee. "We have to fork the hay out of the stack and onto the sled. Then you drive the team and I'll pitch hay off the back. When the first load is distributed, we'll drive back to the haystack and load up again. We'll know more after this morning, but I figure we'll need at least five or six loads."

Louise smiled and relaxed in her chair. "That doesn't sound too hard."

She was dead wrong.

By the time she finished washing the breakfast dishes, bundled up, and trudged out behind the barn, Max had hitched the team and was already pitching hay onto the flat bed of the sled. Like her, he wore a bandanna tied over his hat and knotted under his chin to hold his hat in place. But he'd thrown off his duster. After a few minutes Louise threw off her duster, too. Pitching hay was hard labor, and within minutes she'd worked up a sweat. Long before the sled was loaded she thought her arms were going to fall off her body. Only pride and willpower kept her wielding the pitchfork.

Once the sled was mounded, they stopped to wipe their foreheads and catch their breath. In less than a minute, Louise felt the cold seep through her shirt and trousers and settle in her sweat-damp long johns.

In silence they brushed snow off their shoulders and shrugged on their dusters, then Louise took the reins and Max vaulted onto the back of the sled. Squinting, trying to peer through the thickening snow, she drove the sled out onto the range behind the barn and sheds. She drove slowly so Max could fork hay without falling off.

What surprised her was how scattered the cattle were. She had assumed they would bunch up against the weather. Instead, there were a few beeves here and a few beeves there. None of them were smart enough to walk up to the haystacks and pull off a bite. No, someone like her had to take their meal to them. And they weren't all that easy to spot as snow blanketed their backs and ice rimmed their nostrils. They were easy to mistake for bushes until they shifted weight.

On their second trip out to the range, they stopped at the stock ponds so Max could knock ice away from the edges and keep the access clear. Louise waited with the team, willing her arms to stop twitching and pretending she wasn't cold to the bone.

After a third bout of pitching hay onto the sled, her long johns were soaked and so was her shirt. Her shoulders and back ached like she'd taken a beating. This time when she gripped the reins and led the team into the storm, the cold found a way inside the duster and formed a thin layer of ice on her wet shirt.

Her teeth chattered during the fifth and sixth drives out to the range, and each time it took longer to load the sled. Louise heard cussing from the back, but she didn't turn around. She muttered a few curses herself.

She didn't know why Max worried about the herd being small this year. It seemed to her there were millions of cows out here in the snow, all hungry and unable to feed themselves, and all of them too dumb to stay close to the barn where a person might hope to easily locate their butts.

When they finally finished, the morning was gone and it was nearly noon. She helped Max unhitch the team then left him to rub down the horses. Lowering her head against the falling snow, she returned to the house and carried in enough wood to stuff the stove's firebox.

When Max came in the door and fell onto a kitchen chair with a low sound, she stood stripped down to her long johns, hunched over the warmth of the stove examining the blisters bubbling up on her palms.

"Well, you know what they say. It's not work that kills, but worry." She stared at the blisters. "I was getting soft."

"Who says that?"

"Whoever makes up proverbs. There's always a proverb to make a person feel better about whatever."

"I don't know who I'm madder at. Howard Houser or Shorty Smith." He closed his eyes and stretched his neck against his hand. "Don't go to any trouble over dinner. I'm too tired to eat. Let's just have whatever's left over from breakfast."

"If you can find the energy to slice the ham and bread, I'll stir up some fresh gravy. Lord a'mighty, I'm glad we're finished with that!"

"Darlin', you do know that we have to feed them again before it gets dark."

She groaned, and the string of cuss words that spun out of her mouth would have done a mule skinner proud. But

Max was too tired to object to her cussing and she was too tuckered out to object to his calling her darlin'.

After they finished eating in their long johns, they sat in silence, hands cradled around their coffee cups, sober faces turned to the snowy window.

It was going to be a long, hard winter.

On sunny days, Louise asked in a hopeful voice whether they still had to feed the cattle, as if Max might announce that beeves didn't get hungry when the sun shone. Like it or not, the snow pack was here to stay until the spring melt, and that meant the cattle couldn't graze, and that meant he and Louise had to feed them. Twice a day. Every day.

Blurred by exhaustion, the days blended into weeks and the sole purpose of life became feeding. Feeding the horses, the chickens, the cattle, themselves. There wasn't time or energy for much of anything else. He and Louise rolled out of bed and were dressed before dawn; they dropped back in bed shortly after a hurried supper, so fatigued they didn't often try to read but fell asleep within minutes.

Each of them performed only the most necessary chores. The barn didn't get mucked out daily as it had when Shorty was foreman. The only fence lines Max rode were those nearest the house and barn. He chopped enough wood to keep the firebox blazing but couldn't find time to stack logs or chop kindling for tomorrow.

Louise kept them fed and washed what clothing they needed on a piecemeal basis. Housework fell by the wayside except for one item. Every day when she returned from driving the sled, she polished her silver spoon.

On the positive side, Livvy understood they had no spare time for family dinners. For that, Max was grateful and imagined everyone else was, too. But he did make a point of riding up to the main house once a week to check on his mother and make sure her foreman and hands were taking care of business. Ordinarily Wally would have kept an eye on things, but Wally was riding into town every day to his job at Howard Houser's bank.

Twice Max had seen Philadelphia, but they hadn't spoken. Both times she'd been sitting in the parlor, hands folded in her lap, facing the foyer when he walked in the door. And each time they had stared at each other and he had remembered her running into his arms when he returned from Piney Creek.

Today when he stepped into the foyer and glanced toward the parlor, she wasn't there. Relief or disappointment, he couldn't be sure which, tightened his jaw as he hung up his coat and hat, then went through the house to the kitchen where Livvy waited with coffee and biscuits.

"Eat something," she ordered, sitting at the kitchen table across from him. "I know you miss your dinner when you come over here."

"Just coffee. I had a bite with your hands down at the bunkhouse." Every time he came to the main house, he caught himself listening for footsteps overhead. And sniffing the air for traces of rose petals. "This situation is never going to seem natural if Philadelphia runs and hides every time I ride down your road. Tell her that she can continue cooking or ironing or sewing or whatever she's doing to help you."

Livvy folded her arms on the table and gave him a long unreadable stare. "Philadelphia's in town visiting her father," she said finally. "That's good, because you and I have some things to talk about."

He knew that tone of voice. "Am I going to wish I was holding a shot glass instead of a coffee cup?"

"I've talked to Wally. I wasn't sure if I should mention this to you. I'm still not sure if it's the right thing to do."

"The right thing is to tell me what's troubling you. This family has never had secrets."

Livvy moved her coffee cup in circles on the table, then looked up at him. "I think there's something amiss with Philadelphia's pregnancy. I don't think she'll carry to term."

Max released a breath. "Why do you say that?"

"She's five and a half months along, but no one would know it to look at her. She said she was picking up some waiting clothes today at Mrs. Dame's, but she really doesn't need them. Something's wrong, Max. This baby isn't developing like it should."

He knew as much about pregnancy as most men, which was to say he knew next to nothing. He spread his hands. "You're saying she should be larger?"

His mother shoved a lock of hair off her forehead with an exasperated motion. "Philadelphia insists she's gained considerable weight and seems astonished that I don't see her belly. She believes she's enormous and has lost her figure, but I sure don't see it. I've almost begged her to consult Doc Pope, but she won't. So far no one in Fort Houser knows of her pregnancy, and she doesn't want them to. I believe Doc Pope would be discreet, but if she doesn't agree, then I think she should consult a doctor in Denver. But she refuses."

"Do you want me to speak to her?"

"Good Lord, no! Stay out of this, Max. I'm telling you only because it's your baby and you have the right to know there may be something wrong. If anyone tries to talk some sense to her, it should be her husband. Wally's doing what he can, but she's headstrong and so far he hasn't been successful."

Wally, not him. Lowering his head, he rubbed his knuckles across his forehead. "Is her life or health in danger?" He would never forgive himself if something terrible happened to Philadelphia because of him.

"That's what's so frustrating! I don't know. She needs a doctor to check her. She looks healthy, you know that, but something is definitely not right."

Max stood and moved to stare out the kitchen window. Knots rippled along his jawline like beads on a string. Every instinct urged him to ride into town right now, find her, and take her to Doc Pope's. She would listen to him.

"No, Max. I know what you're thinking, but you don't have the right to interfere," Livvy said softly. A sigh lifted her shoulders. "Either Wally will convince her to see a doctor, or he won't. In either case, I think she's healthy and she'll come through with no lasting ill effects." After a long pause, she stood and checked on something in the oven. "Maybe I shouldn't have mentioned this."

"No, you did the right thing."

"It just makes a hard situation harder." She returned to the table and sat down. "Which brings me to the next thing. I guess you already know that Wally spoke to Howard, but Howard brushed him aside. There isn't a cowboy in the region who will sign on with you if he wants to spend his wages. But a lot of people are watching what's going on out at your place."

Then it wasn't his imagination that the traffic had increased on dry, clear days. "Why would anyone care?"

"About half the town believed Louise seduced you into jilting Philadelphia and Philadelphia ran off with Wally out of spite. When word got out that you might lose your cattle, folks pretty much figured you and Louise got your just desserts. That attitude is changing. Those who have seen Louise when she goes in to buy provisions don't see a woman who looks like a temptress. They see a polite, no-nonsense woman who couldn't be flirtatious if you gave her lessons. And when a few folks rode past your place to gloat, they saw you and your wife working like dogs to keep your cattle alive. People are talking. Eventually, Howard will be forced to back off his position."

"It won't happen before spring."

"Probably not," Livvy agreed. "But it will happen. In the meantime, Wally has told Howard that he and Dave intend to help you on Sundays so Louise can have a day free from men's work. Howard objected, but Wally backed him down by saying you're his brother and that's how it's going to be. Gilly and I will come, too, and help Louise cook ahead so it'll be easier during the week. Wash and mend and clean. Whatever needs doing." She didn't mention Philadelphia.

Max rocked back on his boot heels and pushed a hand in his pocket, catching the green marble between his fingers.

"Wally is living my life," he said softly, keeping his gaze on the snowy ground outside the window.

"And he's thriving," Livvy agreed in a crisp voice. "Wally has found his calling, and it's banking. When he puts on that starched white collar every morning, he sees a circle of power, prestige, and influence. What would you have seen, Max? I don't think it would have taken long for you to start looking at that starched collar as a noose. Or a leash."

"Who knows?"

"In your heart I think you do. It wasn't a banker who built that house five miles outside of town."

Stubbornly, he set his jaw and said nothing.

"As long as we're speaking frankly, there's something I want to say to you." She drew a breath. "I wasn't happy when you brought home a wife named Low Down who'd been willing to bear a child out of wedlock and wasn't particular who the father was."

Max continued to stare out the window and roll the marble against his palm. The person his mother described sounded like a stranger. It was hard to reconcile the woman he had believed he'd married with the woman who worked beside him every frigid morning, pitching hay.

"I'll tell you something that I've thought a lot about," Livvy said. "I don't know three women who would have stayed through a smallpox epidemic no matter how desperately the victims needed her. And I don't know three women who would work as hard as Louise is doing no matter if it's sunny out there or a blizzard is raging. Without her, Max, you'd lose those cattle."

He nodded, his eyebrows clamping in a frown.

"I've always known what you were thinking. You're squeezing that marble in your pocket and you're thinking your cattle wouldn't be at risk if it weren't for Louise. And maybe you're right. But take a hard look, son. When you see that woman working up a sweat pitching hay like a hired hand . . . you're looking at character.

"And if we ever have another family dinner that goes like the last one did, you pay attention. I have an idea that your Louise doesn't sit still for too many insults, and I imagine she could cut someone down to size in about three sentences if she wanted to. But she sat silent while Philadelphia ridiculed and belittled her. Louise did this out of respect for you and this family. That is also character.

"Maybe you really believe Wally is living your life. If so, then you haven't been honest with yourself. And you haven't taken a good hard look at the life you have. Mark my words, Max. Someday you're going to hold that marble, and it won't be a symbol of all you lost. That marble will be the gold you went to Piney Creek to find. It will be the most precious thing you own. I say this because I didn't raise any stupid sons."

"Maybe you did," he said finally.

He knew what his mother was advising, but it would

never happen. He might forget for a while that Philadelphia would bear his child and another man would raise it. But the knowledge was always there, weighing down the back of his mind, ready to raise up and strike him with guilt and remorse every time he touched Louise or appreciated her or enjoyed her company.

"I'm bored and I'm perishing of loneliness! I *want* to move back home. Livvy doesn't fold my handkerchiefs like Pansy does, and she makes me feel guilty and inadequate in the bargain."

Her father leaned back in his chair and watched her pace in front of his desk. "The decision that you and Wally should live at the McCord ranch was made for excellent reasons that have not changed."

"There is absolutely nothing to do out there! How many pillowcases can a person embroider? How many stupid books can I read? If we moved to town, I'd have callers. But no one is going to drive clear out there." She glared at him, then resumed pacing.

"It isn't the distance, my dear. Perhaps you've forgotten, but you're in the center of a scandal that is going to worsen when you start—" He waved a hand at her stomach.

"You could make people call on me, you know you could. Whatever threats you used to drive off Max's cowboys, you could use to make people receive me!"

"I learned something a long time ago, Philadelphia. Society is the province of women. They guard their realm zealously and brook no interference. The surest way to ruin my bank is to pressure the clientele to force their wives and daughters into making social choices to please me. Those wives and daughters will make my clients' life hell on earth until they move their accounts to a bank in Denver that will not dictate their women's guest list. While we're on this subject, you are not the only person feeling the effects of the scandal. The bank has lost a few accounts over this. Not many, but there will be more once your pregnancy is known."

She stamped her foot to point out that he was digressing. And she let tears well and swim in her eyes. "You don't know what I have to endure out there! I overheard Mrs. McCord and her insipid daughter talking about me. They think I'm coddled and spoiled. And that's not all. As shocking and unbelievable as it sounds, I sometimes think they prefer the company of that debauched creature who stole Max!" She stared at him. "Well? Do you really want me to live with people like that?"

He came around the desk, patted her back, and said, "There, there." Such mild comfort infuriated her.

"I don't want to hear 'There, there.' I want you to fix this! I want you to get me away from the ranch!"

"Nothing can be done until after the baby is born. Then we'll talk about the future." He set her back from him and lifted her chin. "Now dry your eyes. Your husband is waiting to take you to luncheon."

She found one of Livvy's poorly folded handkerchiefs in her beaded fringed bag and dabbed her lashes. It had been her suggestion to have her noon dinner with Wally at the hotel. She'd harbored some nebulous idea about letting everyone see her hold her head high. She'd hoped to encounter a few previous friends and shame them for deserting her in her time of trouble.

"Wally is doing very well, by the way. Exceptionally well. Your husband is a natural-born banker. He's taken to it faster than I could ever have imagined. In fact, in many ways he reminds me of myself at that age."

Philadelphia looked up, and her mouth dropped. She had never dreamed that Wally would actually succeed. Therefore, hearing the praise and pride in her father's voice confused her. Certainly she was pleased that Wally's performance exceeded anyone's expectations. But she suddenly experienced an unpleasant vision of a future wherein her father discussed business with Wally and ignored her.

Absently patting her hand, he led her to his office door. "From my point of view, you married the right man. This one is a banker, by God!"

She stared at him in horror. Wally was not the right man for her. Max was and always would be.

Chapter 16

Winter stormed down from the north and punished the plains with a vengeance. Blizzards pounded the range with a frequency and ferocity that surprised even the old-timers. In December, the temperature plummeted and didn't rise above zero for three weeks.

On bitterly cold mornings Louise and Max sat beside the kitchen stove, drinking coffee and waiting for dawn, dreading the necessity of going out into the driving snow to search for cattle in a blizzard. Many nights they half pushed, half carried stiff, half-frozen beeves into the barn and desperately tried to save them from freezing to death. Sometimes they succeeded; sometimes they didn't. It was an exhausting, heart-wrenching experience no matter how the effort ended.

All week Louise fervently looked forward to Sunday when the family came. Then she put on her lady skirts and shirtwaists and worked at preparing for the hard week to come. The work went easier when shared. This was the day the butter got churned, the laundry got washed, the rips and tears got darned and mended. On Sundays, she cleaned house from top to bottom, usually with Sunshine wielding a dust rag alongside her. Then before the men went back out to feed the beeves in the early evening, they all sat down to a late-afternoon meal. Afterward, Gilly played the parlor piano loud enough for Livvy and Louise to enjoy the music while they tidied up the kitchen.

No one mentioned Philadelphia except to comment occasionally that her father had sent his carriage to take her into town; otherwise Louise assumed Philadelphia stayed at the main house alone.

Louise didn't really expect Philadelphia to visit the man she should have married in the house he had built for her. Her presence would have made everyone acutely uncomfortable. But it was also true that Philadelphia's refusal to join the family created a subtle tension that ran beneath the Sunday gatherings like a dark undercurrent.

"Aunt Louise?"

Abruptly she realized that Sunshine had called her twice. "Sorry, I guess I was woolgathering."

"Mama has lots of items on our parlor mantel, but you only display that one spoon. Why don't you put out other things, too?"

They had finished dusting the piano and parlor furniture, and now Louise was polishing her spoon. She liked to feel the cool smooth weight in her hand, liked to polish and rub until her reflection peered back at her in the shiny bowl.

"This is the nicest thing I ever owned, and it's special. It's the only thing I have that's good enough to display."

"Why is the spoon so special?"

"I'd like to hear the answer to that," Max said, appearing in the archway.

Snowflakes sparkled in his dark hair and on his lashes. Melting snow had dampened his shirt collar, and his cheeks glowed pink with cold.

Louise decided yet again that he was the handsomest man she had ever laid eyes on. It amazed her, simply knocked the air out of her chest that this splendid man was her husband. She could not believe that in a few hours they would climb into bed together and share each other's warmth and bodies. A flush heated her cheeks, and she looked away from his smile and back down at her spoon.

"This spoon reminds me of a schoolhouse and your uncle Max. I like to look at it and hold it in my hands."

"That old spoon?" Sunshine asked, puzzled.

She nodded, avoiding Max's steady gaze. "The boys up at Piney Creek gave it to me. No matter how low I feel or how tired or how cranky or lonely, I feel better when I look at my spoon." Now she lifted her head and slid a quick glance toward Max. "No matter what else I may have done, this spoon reminds me that once upon a time, I did one good thing."

Now Sunshine laughed. "You do lots of good things, Aunt Louise! I 'spect you always have."

"I 'spect so, too," Max said quietly, gazing at her above Sunshine's head.

Her stomach tightened, and her heart pounded against her rib cage. His expression was unreadable, but he looked at her as if he really saw her, as if his sharp blue eyes penetrated to regions others couldn't see. Or maybe she'd been reading too many romantic songbooks.

"Well, you're both wrong," she said firmly, raising her fingertips to the heat pulsing at the base of her throat. If Sunshine hadn't been standing beside her, she might have dropped in a cuss word to emphasize her point. "I'm mean and selfish. I'm cantankerous, stubborn, and willful. So don't go hanging any halos on me." She replaced the spoon on the mantel and stepped back to admire the soft shine as she always did. "Every man for himself and the devil take the hindmost. Those are words to live by, and I do. But once," she said, her voice going soft, "I did a good thing. And I'm proud of that."

"You are so funny, Aunt Louise. Ain't she, Uncle Max?"

"Isn't," Louise said automatically. "Not ain't."

Max leaned in the archway, continuing to regard her in that peculiar, penetrating way. "Ma says she knows you don't have an extra two minutes, but she wonders if you could find time to bake mincemeat pies for Christmas Eve. She says your pies are as good as anything she can make."

That news made her smile. She'd made wonderful progress on cooking now that she had a real stove at her disposal and was using it every day. "I'll find time."

"Oh, she's mean and selfish and cantankerous, isn't she?" Max said to Sunshine. He had that sparkly-eyed, twitching-lips look. "Always seeing to her own self-interest. Just can't get her to do one thing for the family or to help out someone else."

"That's not Aunt Louise, that's Aunt Philadelphia," Sunshine said, speaking with the careless honesty of children. She beamed at them. "I can play a new song on the piano. Would you like to hear it?"

"Very much," Louise said, clearing her throat. "You can serenade me while I finish dusting and sweeping in here."

Max watched Sunshine climb up on the piano bench, then he straightened in the doorway with a frown. "I came to tell you that Wally, Dave, and I returned to the house to get warm, but we're going out again. I spotted a cow about a mile north that looked like she was in trouble. I'll bring her in while Wally and Dave see to those sick beeves in the barn."

Louise's gaze went to the window. A blizzard raged beyond the glass. If the storm didn't blow through in the next hour, she suspected everyone would stay overnight. Already she was counting linens and pillows in her mind, trying to figure where she would put everyone. The men could make up the beds in the bunkhouse and sleep there. The women would have to share the only bed in the house. Gilly and Sunshine could climb in with her, and she'd put Livvy on the cot.

If this were a real marriage and this were really her house, she'd inform Max that the other two bedrooms had to be furnished before next winter. It would be good to have them available for emergencies.

Max coughed in his hand, then tugged his shirt collar. "I assumed you'd had that spoon for a long time. I didn't know the prospectors gave it to you." Turning his head, he gazed at Sunshine, who concentrated on coaxing music out of the piano. "I remember the schoolhouse and the first time I saw you. I thought I was on fire, and you put a cool wet rag on my forehead. I opened my eyes, and I truly thought I was looking at an angel."

"An exhausted angel with matted hair, dirty clothes, and probably wearing vomit on her boots," Louise said with a smile. She reached a finger to the mantel and touched the spoon. "The first time I saw you, you were in Dovey Watson's saloon, drinking whiskey with Stony Marks."

"That's odd." His eyebrows rose. "I don't recall seeing you before I got sick."

"There's no reason you'd remember." Tilting her head, she considered asking a question that she wasn't sure she wanted answered. "Max? I've been wondering. Why did you keep the green marble?"

Weeks had passed before she figured out what it was that he transferred from one pair of trousers to another, what it was in his pocket that he gripped like a lucky charm. Except she doubted he considered the green marble lucky.

"I keep the marble to remind me how quickly a person's life can change," he said finally. "To remind me to expect the unexpected. I keep it because it represents everything that's happened since I got sick in Piney Creek."

She nodded slowly, pulling the dust rag through her fingers. "I guessed it was something like that."

What he didn't say was the marble reminded him their marriage was only temporary. But she sensed that was also one of the functions the marble served. Eventually, he'd have his freedom.

"Did you like my new song?" Sunshine asked, turning on the bench to smile at them.

"Absolutely." Louise set aside her dust rag to applaud. "I liked it so well, I'm hoping you'll play it again."

Wally's voice called from the kitchen, and Max leaned into the hallway to say he'd be right along.

"Be careful out there," she said softly.

His gaze traveled slowly across her bosom before he met her eyes again. Butterflies exploded in her chest and banged around her rib cage. And she hoped to high heaven that he had no inkling of his power to reduce her to pudding with a glance.

"We'll be back for supper in about an hour."

Neither of them moved until Wally called again. They stood transfixed, each studying the other's tired face. Louise couldn't guess what Max was thinking, but she was thinking about the marble in his pocket. He was right about life changing quickly. That tiny scratched marble had instantly given her a family, and a husband she was beginning to love.

Moisture glistened in her eyes, and she turned away before he saw. Oh Lord. She didn't want to love him or his family.

With a sinking heart, it occurred to her that the future held nothing but heartbreak. She could see it coming.

It was Max who ran into trouble. And it wasn't his heart that broke, it was his arm.

Wally and Dave brought him back to the house and sat him on the edge of the kitchen table after Livvy hastily cleared away pans and mixing bowls. "What happened?" she demanded, gingerly helping Max out of his heavy coat.

"Marva Lee didn't clear the stone fence," Wally explained. "We're going to need some whiskey to take care of this."

"Under the dry sink," Louise said. Someone, Gilly or Sunshine, threw open the cabinet doors. She kept her gaze on Max who sat white-faced, his teeth clenched, holding his arm close to his chest.

Wally took the whiskey bottle from Gilly, pulled the cork with his teeth, and handed it to Max. "If the snow wasn't so deep, Marva Lee would have broken a leg and we'd have had to put her down. And Max would have a whole lot more broken bones than he does."

"You jumped a fence?" Louise stared in disbelief. "In this weather? You dumb son of a—" Remembering Sunshine, she halted and bit her lip. The urge to yell at him sent a flood of crimson rising up her throat, and her hands curled into fists.

"It wasn't the smartest thing I ever did," Max agreed. He took a long swig from the bottle, then blinked at his mother. "Ma? You going to set this?"

Livvy threw up her hands and stepped backward. "Lord! I was never good at doctoring when it meant hurting one of my children. Wally, you do it."

"I don't know anything about setting an arm. Dave?"

"I guess I could," Dave said unhappily. Moving forward, he took off his hat, hesitated a minute, then ripped Max's sleeve up to the elbow to get a look. "That's a bad break."

Louise frowned. "That isn't so bad. When the bone's sticking out of the skin—now that's bad. But I don't see any bones sticking out." Everyone in the kitchen stared expectantly. "Oh hell. All right, I'll do it." She pushed up her sleeves and moved next to Max. "Take another deep drink, darlin', this is going to hurt like all get out."

"Oh it's darlin', now, is it? I'm offended." Looking straight into her eyes, he took a long pull from the bottle.

"You keep drinking just as fast as you can." Bending

over him, she probed the break with her fingertips, closing her ears to the hisses and gasps Max made through his teeth. "Not too bad at all. Wally, we're going to need some splints. Sunshine, help your ma rig up a sling. Dave, get Max off the table and into that end chair."

"What can I do?" Livvy asked crisply.

"You can open another bottle and pour whiskeys for everyone, starting with me."

"Here." Max thrust the bottle into her hands. She took a deep swallow, letting the heat scald down to her nerve endings. "I'm sorry, Louise."

She knew what he was sorry about. Feeding the cattle had been her first thought when he came through the door holding his arm.

"It's over now. All these weeks have been for nothing. Give me back the whiskey."

The situation demanded some serious swearing and bullying, but she couldn't let herself cut loose, not with Sunshine in the kitchen. Having a child nearby placed a severe crimp in her style.

"You are full of . . . horse feathers, cowboy." Leaning over him, she stared hard into his eyes. "I didn't work like a damned dog out there and freeze my butt off—excuse me, Sunshine—so we could just let those damned— 'scuse me, Sunshine—stupid cows starve or freeze. And we aren't going to find a buyer for them now, that's for damned sure—excuse me, Sunshine."

He took another pull at the bottle, then pushed it back into her hands. "We can't manage it. I won't be able to lift a damned pitchfork until the end of January. Excuse me, Sunshine."

"You ain't losing those cows, Max." Tossing her head back, she swallowed liquid heat, then shoved the bottle toward his good arm. "I'll load the sled and do the forking. You can drive. Hell, the horses can practically do it alone. They know the routine. All you have to do is sit there and hold the reins in your good hand."

A chorus of voices objected, but she stared everyone into silence. "I hear what you're saying, and I know it isn't going to be easy. I don't know how I'll manage it, but I will. I can do this. Because we ain't losing those cows," she repeated stubbornly. "That's too high a price for a good man to pay! Now you," she said to Max. "Rest your arm on the table. Let's get this done."

She glanced at Livvy, who moved around behind Max and murmured to Wally and Dave. Thin-lipped and grim-eyed, they moved forward and each clamped a hand on Max's shoulders.

Watching her with narrowed eyes, Max lifted the whiskey to his lips and swallowed heavily before he set the bottle on the table. "Seems like you're in charge here, so what are you waiting for? Do it."

"I'm so mad at you for jumping a fence in the middle of a blizzard that I'm going to enjoy this."

She didn't. As Livvy had said, hurting someone you loved was a hard, hard thing. The only positive aspect of setting Max's arm was that she was strong and experienced, and it happened fast. She nodded at Wally, who slipped his hands down around Max's upper arm, then she pulled Max's arm straight out, doing it swiftly, pulling hard. She didn't set it properly on the first attempt, but she heard and felt the bones align on the second try. Max's eyes fluttered up and Dave caught him as he toppled over.

A body hit the floor behind her, and Sunshine cried, "Mama!"

"Give me the splints, Wally. Livvy, I need some strips to tie the splints in place."

When she had his arm wrapped and the sling packed with snow, she fell into a chair and lifted the whiskey bottle to her lips. "You folks better stay here tonight rather than risk traveling in a blizzard in the dark." She looked up at Wally and Dave. "You gents take Max down to the bunkhouse before he wakes up. Get a fire going in the potbelly, and it'll warm up in a hurry. Give me a few minutes to calm down, then we'll bring some food to you."

Dave pulled on his coat and gloves, but Wally didn't move. He stood staring like he hadn't seen her before. "I owe you an apology," he said quietly.

"No, you don't."

"Oh yes, he does," Livvy said, slapping corks back into the whiskey bottles.

"It's all right." Louise suspected she knew why Wally felt he should apologize. Someone had told Philadelphia about her being Low Down, had told Philadelphia her whole worthless life story. Early on, Livvy had probably related Louise's story to Wally, but Livvy would never have discussed her with Philadelphia. She was sure of that. But someone had.

"I haven't treated you as well as I should, Louise. Maybe I can make up for that a little by reminding you that you're not in this alone." Wally looked so much like Max tonight. Handsome. Determined blue eyes. "You have family. Somehow we'll work this out. We'll help you feed those beeves."

The last thirty minutes had been emotional and draining. Undoubtedly, that's why her eyes swam and she had to blink hard.

"I'm not so stupid or so proud that I'd turn down a helping hand. Thank you, Wally. You, too, Dave."

She had family.

"Aunt Louise! You're crying."

"No I ain't, honey." She swiped a hand across her eyes and watched Wally and Dave take hold of Max by the ankles and under his arms and carry him outside. "We better see to your ma." Gilly was sitting sprawled on the floor, propped against the bottom of the sink cabinet. She clutched a whiskey glass against her chest and she was staring at Louise with awe and amazement.

Louise laughed. Shaking her head, she threw out her

hands in a helpless gesture. "That crazy bastard. 'Scuse me, Sunshine. Jumping a fence in a blizzard! What in the hell was he thinking of? I swear, sometimes I suspect God didn't give men but half a brain. Would any of us do a damned fool thing like that?"

Livvy smiled and Gilly giggled, and then they were all laughing, great gusts of side-holding laughter that left them breathless and wiping tears from their eyes and cheeks. None of them could have explained why they laughed until they cried except they all felt better afterward.

Later, when Louise and Gilly pulled a sled laden with food down to the bunkhouse, a frozen wind drove snow and ice particles into their hair and faces. But Louise didn't feel the cold. She was warmed by the memory of Wally saying she had a family now. She wasn't alone anymore.

The new schedule was far from ideal. Dawn had already broken by the time Dave Weaver arrived to help with the morning feed. And since the days were short, it was dark before Wally arrived, and then he had to change out of his banker's togs and into work duds.

Max drove the sled and in the evenings he held a torch so Louise and Wally could see to work. While he stood watching, frustrated and angry, he relived the decision to jump the stone fence. Actually it hadn't been a conscious choice. He hadn't thought about the jump at all. Now his family was paying for his carelessness. And no one paid a heavier price than Louise.

When she wasn't pitching hay or feeding all the mouths on the ranch, she was shoveling a path to the barn and henhouse, chopping firewood, and milking Missy. She helped Max get dressed in the morning and undressed in the evening. She stropped his razor and shaved his face as if she'd served an apprenticeship in a barbershop. As if that weren't enough, she dragged half-frozen cows into the barn and rubbed them dry, gave them warm water to drink, and bullied them into a healthier state. Max marveled that she didn't keel over in exhaustion. He felt like she was working herself half to death on his behalf.

"What else can we do? We can't go back and change what happened," Louise pointed out. "So stop stewing around. You might as well enjoy your time off."

He slapped his book shut and shifted on the pillow to glare at her. Lamplight softened her wind-chapped cheeks and gleamed in the braid that lay across the shoulder of the cursed nightgown. But even in the mellow flattering light, deep circles were evident beneath her lashes and fatigue dulled her eyes.

"That's ridiculous. I can't enjoy anything when you're working harder than most men." Watching her chop wood or shovel a path, watching her work until her legs shook and she could hardly stand ate him up inside.

"It's not so bad," she insisted, setting aside her songbook. "We're managing. I don't mind the extra work."

"Well, I mind."

When she came up to the house after feeding the beeves and cracking ice off the stock ponds, her arms were trembling and twitched so badly that she had to steady her coffee cup with both hands to keep the coffee from spilling. Worst of all, two nights ago the temperature had fallen to fifteen degrees below zero. Tears of frustration and determination had frozen on her cheeks before they reached her chin. He'd seen the little beads of ice in the torchlight, and he'd gone crazy inside.

"I'll make this up to you," he promised grimly. "I swear it, Louise."

"Well, there is something you could do for me. I'd sure like to have a baby," she said in a soft voice, looking down at her hands. "But with you all busted up . . ."

"Louise Downe McCord!" He sat up, and a slow

grin replaced his frown. "Damned if you aren't turning into the temptress that half of Fort Houser thinks you are."

A sparkling glance chased the fatigue from her eyes. "I'm afraid it's finally happened. I've turned into a wanton woman."

"Absolutely debauched."

"Without shame. Too bad your arm's in a sling and you can't take advantage of my fallen state."

"My arm's busted, darlin', but everything else still works."

She had a wonderful laugh, husky and unselfconscious. "Do tell," she said when she'd caught her breath.

"There are ways to manage this where my arm wouldn't be in jeopardy."

Curiosity flickered in her hazel eyes. "If you want to elaborate on that statement, I'm listening."

"The man doesn't always have to be on top."

"Oh!" She blinked, thinking about it. "Well, nothing ventured, nothing gained. I suppose we could give that a try."

Now he laughed. She was so knowledgeable and experienced in some areas, so innocent in others. "If you're willing, as tired as you are, I'm willing, too." In fact, his body had proven itself ready, willing, and able several minutes ago. "But you have to take off your nightgown. Pitching a tent in a high wind is easier than fighting that damned nightgown."

Thirty minutes later, she slept with a smile on her lips, her head resting against his good shoulder. He needed to get up and turn off the lamps, but he knew how exhausted she was and couldn't bring himself to disturb her.

Despite what she had said the day he broke his arm, there were so many good things about Louise. If he had a herd left after this hard bitter winter, it would be because of her. To say he was grateful would be to understate his sentiments by a country mile.

Not for the first time, he decided that she reminded him of an egg. Hard-shelled on the outside, soft on the inside. She blustered and swore and slammed things around in the kitchen when she was angry. Stuck out her chin and dared the world to take a swing. But she didn't sulk, didn't pout, didn't attempt to manipulate. And although he tried, he couldn't recall ever hearing her complain. She had a remarkable ability to accept whatever life tossed her way and find something positive.

But beneath that hard, defensive shell, was a vulnerable woman who couldn't see her own worth. Others did. Even Sunshine grasped that Louise's opinion of herself was nowhere near who she really was.

And now, in the silence of a cold black night, thoughts of betrayal crept into his mind.

Philadelphia would never have volunteered to help him save his herd. If he tried for a hundred years, he wouldn't be able to imagine her pitching hay in below-zero weather with tears freezing on her cheeks, or working until she shook with exhaustion and couldn't hold a coffee cup between her blistered palms.

Philadelphia would not have stepped forward to set a broken bone. If she had remained in the room, she would have fainted as Gilly had. It was impossible to imagine her nursing a stream of men filling a schoolhouse with the stench of pus and vomit. Philadelphia would have been among the first to flee at the initial whisper of disease.

Further, he could not visualize Philadelphia ever throwing off her nightgown and her inhibitions as Louise had done tonight. Philadelphia would always be the rigidly delicate and modest lady who submitted and endured and participated as little as possible because joy and enthusiasm in the bedroom would damage her dignity and self-image. He couldn't know for certain, but he suspected Philadelphia would view sex as a manipulative tool, dispensing her favors as a reward or in exchange for favors granted.

Frowning, he stared at the icy frost patterns laced across the windowpanes, and he remembered Philadelphia ridiculing Louise in front of Sunshine, and again in front of the family at dinner. He remembered countless incidents of pouting lips and copious tears and a stamping foot. Oddly, he did not remember laughter in their relationship. He remembered his goals and her goals, but no common goals or shared viewpoints.

What on earth had drawn them together?

Lowering his head, he rubbed his fingertips across his forehead. Damn it. How could he criticize the mother of his child? How could he justify such disloyalty? Without the intervention of one green marble, it would have been Philadelphia sleeping beside him now. It would have been him fastening a stiff starched collar around his neck and riding into the bank every day. Not so long ago, that's what he had believed he wanted.

But his worst betrayal came when he smiled at Louise and realized with sudden guilt and astonishment that he could love her. And when he understood that he respected and admired this unusual woman, and he genuinely enjoyed her company.

When these insights occurred, his mind instantly backed away and his thoughts shut down. What kind of bastard would love one woman while another carried his child? Tar and feathers were too good for such a man.

And there was the fact that Louise would leave him once she became pregnant. This was their agreement. Through trial and error and compromise they were managing to live together and doing it successfully, in his opinion. But she'd said nothing to indicate that anything had changed. Their agreement held.

He gazed down at the top of her head and the curve of her cheek. Studied her work-roughened hand rising and falling on his chest. Once he had believed that smooth pale hands with manicured nails were beautiful. Now his eyes had opened to the aching beauty of bruised knuckles, blunt nails, and callused palms.

If it hadn't been for Philadelphia and the child she carried . . . if he and Louise hadn't agreed their marriage was only temporary . . .

But he would never know what might have happened. He could allow himself to respect Louise and enjoy her company, but he could not permit his regard to deepen into anything more than admiration and esteem. Not when mere months ago, he would willingly and happily have married someone else. Not while that someone else grew large with his child.

Chapter 17

❧━━━━━━━━━━❧

"I don't believe I've seen you this excited," Max mentioned after he'd apologized for not assisting her up the veranda stairs. One arm was in the sling, and in his free hand, he carried a cloth bag filled with gifts.

"This is my first real Christmas," Louise explained. "For people without a family, Christmas doesn't mean much." That's how it had always been for her, just another day. But not this year. She lifted her hem away from the snowy steps and looked up with eager, sparkling eyes. "Oh Max, I can't wait to see the tree. Will there be candles on it?"

Once she had believed life couldn't offer a better moment than the party in her honor on the day the prospectors burned the schoolhouse. But the night at the Belle Mark with Max had eclipsed the party in her honor. And now she was positive that her first Christmas Eve with a real family would be the best evening in her whole life.

Max smiled. "There'll be candles on the tree. And ornaments and strings of popped corn and cranberries. We'll stuff ourselves on Ma's famous divinity and the fudge Gilly always brings. Gilly will play carols on the piano, and we'll try to sing along. We'll all eat and drink too much, and go home loaded with gifts."

She held her breath, listening, then slowly exhaled. "Oh! It sounds so wonderful. Like everything I ever imagined, but better."

269

At the door, Max inclined his head in a gesture that was almost a bow. "I'm sorry to ask you to knock, but . . ."

He was being overly solicitous, but instead of annoying her, his attitude seemed proper tonight. This was a very special occasion, and she wanted it to feel that way in every respect.

Before she rapped on Livvy's door, she brushed damp snowflakes off the shoulders of Max's best coat before she lowered the hood of her cape and wiggled to dislodge any clinging snow.

"Oh my, don't we look grand!"

Good Lord, he was handsome, peering at her with those delft-blue eyes from beneath the brim of a rakishly tilted Stetson. Tonight he wore a starched white shirt and a dark tie and vest over good wool trousers and his Sunday boots.

She didn't look too shabby herself. Tonight she wore the stylish green taffeta that Gilly had sewn up for her. Yards and yards of material floated around her new shoes and swept toward a handsome bow topping her bustle. The green taffeta crackled and whispered in a wonderful way when she walked.

This was the first time ever that she had owned a dress that wasn't too big here and too small there; the green taffeta fit her perfectly. She had a lovely new dress, she was going to a party, and this year she would have a Christmas. Thrilled with everything, she'd taken extra care with her appearance. She'd rubbed lotion into her cheeks and throat, and she'd brushed her hair until it gleamed before she coiled it on top of her head. She had even cut a sprig of holly and pinned it at the back of her hair for a festive touch.

The door swung open, and Livvy beamed and wished them a merry Christmas. "I thought I heard you two out here. Come in, come in." The black velvet Max had purchased in Denver had been put to good use, sewn up into a lace-trimmed dress that was soft yet distinguished. And for tonight's celebration, Livvy had pressed waves in her graying auburn hair where it curved back toward the knot on her neck. Looking at Max's mother now, it was hard to believe that only yesterday Livvy had stood in Louise's kitchen wearing a soiled apron, peeling potatoes, and telling a hilarious and slightly risque story about a bull that had gotten into the bunkhouse.

"You look wonderful!" Louise said.

"Oh my, so do you." Livvy hung their coats on the rack. "Turn around so I can see how the bow turned out. Well, I declare. Gilly could make a living with her needle!"

Sunshine ran out of the parlor and halted abruptly. "Oh, Aunt Louise!" Her eyes rounded. "You look beautiful!"

Laughing, Louise waved aside the compliment. "Well, now, look at you! You're the one who's beautiful tonight. Spin around and let me see."

Hair and ribbons flying, Sunshine spun fast enough to flare black velvet around her stocking-clad calves. "Mama trimmed my dress in the scraps from yours. See?" She touched her collar, then held out green taffeta cuffs for Louise to admire.

"I don't suppose you'd like to put these gifts beneath the tree, would you?" Max asked, smiling.

"Oh yes, I would. But first, look up there. It's mistletoe! You have to kiss Aunt Louise, and I get to watch."

"So do I," said Livvy, winking at Sunshine.

"Only a fool would miss an opportunity to kiss a pretty woman." Max slipped his good arm around her waist and grinned. "Looks like we've been ambushed."

Laughing, Louise wound her arms around his neck, careful not to bump the sling across his chest. But when she saw Max's expression, her laughter hitched on a quick intake of breath. There was something different in his eyes, something she had never seen there before.

Something deep and clear and intense that made her gasp and caused her knees to tremble.

"You have beautiful eyes," he said in a low, gruff voice. "Tonight your eyes are more green than hazel, as green as the early spring grass."

"Good heavens," she whispered, amazed. "I didn't know I had any beautiful parts." And until now she hadn't heard him express the pretty words she knew were inside him. Certainly she'd never imagined that she might inspire such words. Lordy, Lordy. For the rest of her life she would remember that Max McCord had said she had beautiful eyes, as green as the early spring grass.

Her hips pressed to his, and her gaze dropped to his mouth. And suddenly she wished they were home alone in their bed.

Leaning forward, Max brushed warm lips across hers, a kiss so soft and fleeting that it was almost a tease. When she opened her eyes, he was staring at her. Then he moved his hand on the small of her back and drew her tighter against his body, and he kissed her again, this time with a deep hunger that suggested he'd forgotten they had an audience.

"Well, my, my," Livvy murmured, using another of her phrases that said nothing but in this case managed to convey interest, amusement, and approval.

Sunshine clapped and laughed, then caught Louise's hand. "Come look at my present to you and see if you can guess what it is." Her eyes danced with excitement. "You'll never guess!"

Before Louise allowed Sunshine to pull her to the parlor, she asked Livvy, "Do you need any help with supper?"

"Everything's under control. When you're ready for coffee or something cool, and a break from a certain imp's chatter, come back to the kitchen." She winked at Max. "I had to move the pies you brought yesterday to make room for Dave. He's taken over the pantry to make his special Christmas punch. He's been waiting for you and Wally to serve as official tasters."

Before Sunshine tugged her into the parlor, Louise glanced over her shoulder at Max. He returned her gaze, wearing that same intense, almost smoldering expression. She couldn't decipher what it meant, but the smoky speculation in his eyes sent a warm shiver thrilling down her spine.

Then both he and Livvy turned to look up the staircase.

"I have half a mind not to go downstairs at all!" Leaning toward the mirror above the vanity table, Philadelphia patted one of the curls on her forehead, then turned her head from side to side to admire the flash and sparkle of the diamond earrings her father had given her last Christmas. She expected him to give her a matching bracelet tomorrow when she and Wally drove in to have Christmas dinner at home. "Your mother insisted on ham tonight even after I mentioned that I prefer turkey."

"We've always had baked ham on Christmas Eve."

She glanced at him in the mirror, irritated that he stood before the window with his back to her. So rude.

"My family has turkey on Christmas Eve." Thinking about diamonds led her to wonder if Wally had repaid her father for her wedding ring. She supposed it didn't matter. "I'm sure your mother means well, but really. Ham?" Looking into the mirror, she studied the set of his shoulders, trying to judge how far she could take any criticism of his mother. Perhaps it was enough to plant a seed here and a seed there.

On the other hand, she was in a strange and rebellious mood. Before this tedious evening ended, she might tell Wally exactly what she thought of his judgmental family.

Leaning to the mirror, she pinched color into her cheeks, then ran her fingertips along the silk roses trimming her neckline. "I haven't decided yet if I'll go downstairs."

She'd like Max to see her looking as beautiful as she did tonight, but it was an affront to decency to expect her to be in the same room as Low Down. She had promised herself it would never happen again.

"I insist that you join the family tonight."

Insist? Her eyebrows rose and she turned on the vanity bench. "I beg your pardon," she said coolly. "You *insist*?"

He continued to stand with his back to her as if there were something fascinating down below in the dark snowy yard.

"Aside from the fact that I'd find it humiliating to have Christmas alone while you're here upstairs, we need to discuss your refusal to make yourself part of the family. There are times when I wonder if I really have a wife."

"And sometimes I wonder if I really have a husband, since you're never here! You leave for town before I'm awake, and you don't return from Max's place until I'm ready to retire for the evening, and then you go out to the barn. On the weekends, you abandon me and return to Max's, and you stay there all day long!"

Now he turned and looked at her for a long moment before he lifted a piece of kindling from her fireplace and lit a cigar. She hated it when he smoked in her room. Eventually, she would have to abandon hints and address the problem directly, which irritated her. It was so much nicer when people anticipated her wishes.

"If you want me home in the evenings and on the weekends, all you have to do is ask your father to lift the restrictions on Max's employees. Howard will listen to you."

"If I've told you once, I've told you a dozen times. I don't interfere in Daddy's business." She did not like the way he was looking at her through the nasty smoke curling up from his cigar. Like she was to blame for this, that, and the other thing.

"Then nothing is going to change. I understand why you don't want to accompany me to Max's place when everyone goes there to help on Sundays. But you need to understand that holding yourself aloof places you outside this family. I don't like that, and I'm sure the family doesn't like it."

She stiffened in disbelief. "Have you forgotten what your brother and his doxy did to me?" Standing abruptly, she presented her profile and thrust out her stomach. "Take a good look, Wally." Mrs. Dame had let out the seams as far as possible, but even so, the gown's waist was uncomfortably snug.

"I haven't forgotten anything. How can I when you keep reminding me how badly you've been wronged."

She stared. "What on earth has gotten into you tonight?" When reason failed, tears generally succeeded. She blinked until she felt moisture wet her lashes. "Why are you saying mean things to me? Why are you being so hateful?"

Ordinarily he rushed to comfort her, but astonishingly he remained at the window. She had to find one of her own handkerchiefs to dab her eyelids.

"It will take time for our situation to seem normal and for everyone to feel comfortable. But that time will never come if we don't make a beginning."

"You don't mean we. You mean me!"

"All right, I mean you. Hiding or refusing to speak to Max when he comes here doesn't make things easier for anyone. All it does is keep the situation in front of us all."

Which was exactly why she let Max see her only occasionally. She wanted him constantly aware of "the situation." She wanted him always thinking about her and feeling sick with guilt.

"What kind of family life can we hope to enjoy if you

refuse to be in the same room with Louise? We must get past this, Philadelphia. I know it isn't easy for you, but you need to accept how things are and make the best of it."

Fury burned circles on her cheeks. "Low Down has the manners of a creature raised in a pigsty, the grace of a peasant, and all the charm you might find in a brothel! She's gauche and utterly lacking in morals, without a shred of decency. I will never spend one minute with *her* unless it is absolutely and totally unavoidable!"

"Her name is Louise. Not Low Down. Not that creature." Never before had he spoken so sharply or stared with such cold eyes.

Astonishment dried her tears. "My God. You're defending that, that . . ."

"It's Christmas Eve. A night to celebrate love and family." His gaze narrowed. "I expect you to join me in the festivities, and I expect you to be cordial to all members of my family. That includes my brother and his wife."

"Oh my heavens." She stared at him as a terrible thought occurred. "Did you purchase gifts for Max and *her*?"

"We are giving Max a leather vest, and Louise a pair of fleece-lined gloves."

"We?" Her voice spiraled into shrillness. "You signed the tags from both of us? You had no right to do that!" Furious, she stamped her foot, but that wasn't enough. Frantically she looked around, then grabbed a china figurine from the top of the bureau, and hurled it to the floor. "Now look what you made me do!" The shattered pieces raised genuine tears to her eyes. "I loved that piece!"

When he didn't come to her, didn't bend to pick up the pieces of china or offer to glue them, she peeked at him through her lashes. Incredibly, he'd turned his back again and stood gazing out the window. She could not believe it.

He drew on his cigar and blew a smoke ring at his reflection in the panes. "It's getting late. After you pick up your mess, we'll go downstairs."

A scream of outrage and fury rushed up her throat, but she checked herself. She needed to figure this out.

What had changed his attitude? When had his puppy-like adoration become judgmental?

It had to be the bank. He wouldn't dare treat her like this if he feared her father or if he believed her happiness essential to his future.

She half sat, half fell onto the vanity bench. She could not spend thirty minutes with her father without having to listen to paeans of praise for Wally's success at the bank. Wally had a remarkable grasp of finance and the financial markets. Wally's tact and diplomacy made him a natural for dealing with difficult patrons. No one could have learned all the facets of banking any faster than Wally McCord. She was sick and tired of hearing about Wally's exploits at the bank. It was almost as if he were her father's favored son and she was merely the wife he had married.

Good God. Her eyes widened, and she stared at the back of Wally's head. That was exactly the problem. When she married Wally, she had given her father the son he had always wanted.

Wally may have received his position at the bank because she wanted it so. But he had swiftly proven his worth and firmly established himself in her father's dazzled eyes.

Shocked and tight with resentment, she stood, then kicked the broken pieces of the figurine beneath her bed.

The first thing was to endure and get through tonight. Next, she had to endure and get through the delivery of the baby. Until then, she had to endure an unwanted marriage to the wrong man.

But once the baby was born and she no longer needed this Judas who had usurped her place in her father's heart, then, step by step, she would shed a marriage she didn't want and seize the marriage she did want.

As for Wally McCord, he held his position at the bank because she had wished it, and he could lose that position because she wished it. In time, he would discover this.

Refusing to speak to him, she slapped his arm away and walked to the top of the staircase as if he were invisible and she didn't see him beside her. She had lifted her skirts to descend when she saw Max and the creature standing in the foyer beneath a sprig of mistletoe.

Max had one hand on Low Down's cheek and he gazed into the creature's eyes as he had once gazed into hers, with tenderness and the smoky heat of desire. Philadelphia inhaled sharply and felt the blood rush to her face as he drew the creature hard against him and kissed her as if Sunshine and Livvy were not looking on with encouragement and approval. He kissed the creature as if she were a beautiful, desirable woman and not a coarse vulgarian trespassing where she was not wanted and didn't belong.

What was it about this plain graceless woman that made Max's eyes soften as he watched her follow Sunshine into the parlor? Why on earth would Wally rise to such a person's defense? Mystified, Philadelphia struggled to find an answer. But she could think of no reason why anyone would give Low Down a second glance or a second thought.

The creature's hands and cheeks were chapped and wind-reddened, her hair dressed plainly and unimaginatively. She hadn't the faintest notion of style or etiquette. Her background was deplorable, her morals shocking. There was nothing whatsoever appealing about this no-account person. If she had not tricked Max into marriage, Low Down would never have attracted a man.

Philadelphia seethed as Low Down turned in the parlor doorway and gazed back at Max with shining eyes. Even a fool could see that she loved him. It was in her gaze, on her flushed cheeks, at the trembling corner of her lips.

What the stupid creature didn't grasp was that Philadelphia could take Max away faster than she could snap her fingers. Max didn't care two jots about a nobody like Low Down. He had to pretend in front of his family, and Philadelphia understood this. But he loved her, and she could have him anytime she wanted. When the time was right, she would.

Pasting a bright smile over her anger, she lifted her skirts to descend the stairs. "Merry Christmas," she called gaily. Max had always liked her whimsical moments. He'd teased her about her daredevil ways, but she knew he found her boldness charming.

Ignoring Livvy's wary regard, she swirled into the foyer, letting a lacy edge of petticoat flash beneath rose-colored satin skirts. She whirled to a stop before Max, bringing with her the rose petal scent of her signature fragrance.

Dimpling up at him, she opened her fingers across her bosom and noticed the mistletoe. "Oh! We're standing beneath mistletoe." Expectancy and a breathless suggestion hung in the observation. She let him see the wicked twinkle in her eyes, let him recognize an open dare.

Without looking, she sensed Livvy's shocked disapproval and the heat of Wally's anger. Well, Wally had wanted her to behave naturally, to pretend there was no Situation with a capital *S*. He'd wanted her to join the family and not run away from Max. In fact, Wally's advice worked to her advantage. Kissing Max beneath the mistletoe would punish Wally and remind Max of what he had given up. If she touched her tongue to his lips, if she could be that daring, he would understand that she still wanted him and that she knew he wanted her, too.

She moved forward until she could feel the heat of his body, then she lifted her face and closed her eyes. And finally, finally, his warm hard hand curved around her waist for the first time since that terrible night when he had betrayed her.

"No woman should be ignored beneath the mistletoe," Max said smoothly. Deftly, he turned her beneath his hand to face Wally. "Little brother, your wife is awaiting her Christmas kiss."

His hand dropped from her waist, and he moved away. The only thing that softened her fury was recognizing the strain in his voice. He had wanted to kiss her, but he wouldn't risk it in front of his mother and brother.

Stepping forward, Wally bent and brushed chill lips across her cheek before he turned to his mother. Philadelphia didn't care that he was angry. It served him right. Tossing her curls, she followed Max into the parlor. Immediately she knew she'd made a mistake.

Low Down turned from admiring the tree. "Howdy, Philadelphia. Merry Christmas."

The creature didn't smile, didn't lower her eyelids or nod her head in a partial bow. There was not the slightest hint of deference in her posture or expression. She stood before the Christmas tree with Sunshine at her side and gazed at Philadelphia with bland curiosity, like a cow waiting to be slaughtered. Well, Philadelphia was happy to oblige.

Lifting a critical eyebrow, she scanned the creature's dress. "Ah, green. The color of envy. It's a difficult color to wear," she explained to Sunshine. "Green makes most people look so sallow and sickly, but you can see that for yourself." She directed a smile of withering pity at Low Down. "Good heavens! What on earth is that awful thing hanging off the back of your head? Something you dug out of the snow in your yard?"

"Actually, it is."

Max started to say something, but Philadelphia cut

him off. "How amusing. I wonder what you'll dig out to wear next? Twigs? Dead soggy leaves?" If she hadn't been a refined lady, she would have mentioned horse droppings.

The creature's eyes narrowed, and she tilted her head as if considering a reply. Then her shoulders relaxed, and she smiled down at Sunshine. "Well, let's see. What might I dig out of the yard next? If I found a horseshoe, I could wear it as a bracelet. Or as a tiara. If I found a length of rope, I could trim my cape or maybe use the rope for a belt."

Sunshine laughed in delight. "If you found a dead rabbit, you could make a fur collar."

"I think we should go help your grandma in the kitchen." She extended her hand. "Now, if I found a cow bell, I could wear it as a necklace, and then you would always know where to find me." She paused in front of Max and met his eye before she and Sunshine left the parlor, prattling on about things to be found in a yard.

"You have no quarrel with Louise," Max said quietly. "Leave her alone."

"How gallant of you to defend your Low Down." She spat the name out of her mouth as if it tasted bad.

"Put your anger where it belongs. It's me you despise, not Louise."

It occurred to her that this was the first time since the night before he left for Piney Creek that they had been alone together. This opportunity might not come again soon, and they were wasting it talking about Low Down.

"Oh Max. You know I don't despise you." She lowered her hands to her stomach, deliberately directing his attention to her pregnancy. "If only—" She didn't know what she might have said next if she'd had the chance, but Wally appeared in the doorway.

Wally looked from her to Max. "Dave is waiting for us to sample his punch."

"Excuse me." Max dipped his head to her, then walked out of the parlor.

Wally stared as if he'd eavesdropped on every word she had spoken, then, without speaking, he turned and followed Max.

And there she stood, deserted in an empty parlor while everyone else talked and laughed in the kitchen. It was so rustic to entertain in the kitchen, for heaven's sake. So crude and low class. And it was so unforgivably rude to abandon a guest. Well, she had intended to allow herself to be persuaded to play the piano tonight, but why should she entertain people who treated her so insultingly? She wouldn't.

Eventually, Livvy announced dinner—ham—and everyone sat down. Not a hint of decorum prevailed. They laughed about the evening Max had broken his arm, teasing him and Low Down, too. And there was some unseemly tale about a bull getting into Livvy's bunkhouse. Dave and Max exchanged comments about the mustache she had convinced Wally to grow.

Tonight Low Down didn't sit in awkward silence as she had the last time she and Philadelphia were forced to share the same table. The creature chattered as constantly as Sunshine. Her eyes sparkled with pleasure, and her laughter came frequently.

Slowly Philadelphia began to grasp the point Wally had made earlier. Low Down had become a member of the McCord family in a way that Philadelphia had not. The insidious creature was building a shared history, was claiming a role in new family stories.

Throughout supper, Low Down and Gilly chatted easily about sewing and visits back and forth to fit the green taffeta. She teased Dave about some incident involving a broken guitar string. She even told some foolish story about Wally falling off the hay sled that made everyone laugh. As for Livvy, she praised Low Down's pies to the sky and reminded the creature of plans to drive into town after the first of the year.

Shocked and disbelieving, Philadelphia began to realize if there was a belle at this party, it was Low Down.

Too stunned to speak, she sat in resentful silence through the lighting of the tree candles and the dispersing of gifts. To her disgust, she watched Low Down turn teary over a supposedly pretty rock that Sunshine gave her. A rock! Which the creature promised to display on her parlor mantelpiece. How did Max endure this woman? She was an embarrassment.

Low Down's hardened background made any tears suspect. Yet every gift brought a gush to her eyes and a hitch to her voice. It was a clumsy performance, and Philadelphia doubted anyone was deceived. People didn't weep with joy over a rock or a songbook. The creature didn't even play the piano. But she wiped tears from her eyes and bubbled with appreciation and thank-yous.

When Philadelphia could endure no more of this farce, she pushed her gifts off her lap and stood. Placing one hand at her waist and raising the other to her temple, she excused herself, "I'm exhausted, and I don't feel well."

Wally silently accompanied her up the staircase to the door of her room. "Can I bring you anything?"

"Nothing. I want to leave early tomorrow."

Her father would have turkey for dinner and a few valued clients as guests. She would serve as hostess, of course. The conversation would be decorous and refined. Later, she would open her gifts in the family parlor and find delights more interesting than a wool scarf and embroidery patterns.

"Do you like the cradle I made for you?" Wally asked.

"Well, the cradle isn't really for me. It's for the baby. But I liked it." Why would he think she'd be excited about a piece of furniture that wasn't even for her? The cradle did, however, explain what he'd been doing in the barn every night until after midnight.

"Thank you for the vests and the shirt studs." Leaning forward, he kissed her on the forehead, his lips warmer and more forgiving than they had been beneath the mistletoe.

She watched him descend the staircase before she went into her bedroom and closed the door. The first thing she saw was the shattered figurine. This was the worst Christmas Eve she'd ever spent.

Max gently shook Louise awake. She was dozing on his shoulder, her arms wrapped around the gifts piled in her lap. "We're home."

"Already?" Yawning, she gave her head a drowsy shake.

"It's after midnight," he said, smiling. "Dawn is going to arrive in an eyeblink."

"And I will turn from a princess to a hay-pitching peasant," she said with a laugh. "Oh Max. I truly did feel like a princess tonight. Tonight was the most wonderful, the most beautiful, the absolute best evening of my life! It's so amazing. I don't think I've received three gifts in my entire life and then in the last few months, I've received a box full. First from the boys at Piney Creek, and then tonight from your family." Starlight glistened on damp eyes. "Do you think everyone liked the things we gave them?"

"Absolutely. You know, I was wondering . . . did you receive a gift from me?"

She turned her face toward the house. "I didn't expect anything. Just having tonight is enough. I'll never forget it."

"Well, damn it all. I must have forgotten to take your gift to Ma's." He grinned at the look of surprise she turned on him. "You go on inside where it's warm. I'll put the horses away and be there in a few minutes."

"I could help."

"No need. I managed to hitch them, I think I can un-hitch them. It'll just take some time."

"I'll wait. That will give me a chance to look at each gift slowly and think about the person who gave it to me."

"Louise? Thank you for the book and the razor. I always wanted an ivory-handled razor."

Her face lit with delight. "Livvy suggested the razor and when I saw it, I knew you'd like it! And the teacher at the school helped me order the book. She said you'd like that, too!"

"I know I will, I've read Twain before. Stoke up the fire and heat the coffee. I'll be there as soon as I can."

He wouldn't forget tonight, either. Observing her joy had brought an odd ache to his heart unlike anything he remembered experiencing. And he'd glimpsed a reflection of his feelings on the faces of his mother and sister. Even Dave and Wally had smiled with soft eyes at Louise's excitement when she opened her gifts. The McCords had made this a wonderful Christmas for her. His family wasn't the kind who could say straight out that things had changed and that they respected and admired who and what she was. But they could show her—and him—in a hundred small ways. This Christmas had been for her.

When he entered the kitchen, he noticed she had removed the sprig of holly from her hair, but she still wore the green taffeta dress that displayed her splendid figure to lush advantage.

"Would you like something to eat? I saved back one of the mince pies for us."

"Lord, no. I'm so full I won't be able to eat for days."

"Well, then." Her eyes sparkled and danced. Truly, he'd never met anyone with eyes as beautiful or as expressive. "Give me my present."

Laughing, he returned to the mudroom and reached

to the highest shelf where he withdrew a flat box from beneath a stack of coats and blankets.

"What can it be?" Sitting down, she took the box and turned it between her fingers, shook it next to her ear, then ran her palms over the top as if she could sense what might be inside.

He brought her a cup of coffee. "Open it. You're making me crazy."

"No, I have to guess what it is. I think it's . . . an apron. Is that it?"

"Louise, open the box."

Finally, she lifted one corner and peeked inside, then burst into laughter. "It's a nightgown!"

"A skinny nightgown," he said, grinning with pleasure.

"A beautiful nightgown," she whispered. Standing, she shook it out and held it against her body. "There's real lace around the neck and the cuffs! Did you see that?"

"I saw it," he said, laughing. "Now sit down again because we're going to have a little ceremony."

Going back to the mudroom, he withdrew the cursed nightgown from its hiding place and carried it back to the kitchen.

"I'll make rags out of the material," Louise said.

"I'm not taking any chances that this thing will turn up in my bed ever again." He opened the lid of the firebox and stuffed the cursed nightgown inside. And stuffed and stuffed, making it appear more bulky and more unwieldy than it was until she was laughing and cheering for him to win the battle.

"And now," he said after replacing the lid over the burning nightgown. "A toast." He raised his coffee cup and so did she. "Out with the old nightgown and in with the new!" He saw her gazing back at him with soft, shining eyes. "But not tonight," he added in a husky voice.

"No," she whispered. "Not tonight."

She came to him and wound her arms around his neck. Tonight there was no Philadelphia, no baby, no guilt or feelings of betrayal. Tonight was enchanted, a night set apart from the life they would return to in a few short hours. Tonight was theirs alone, a night for joy and tenderness and the greatest gift of all, the giving of themselves.

Chapter 18

⌘

"The people you're harming most are my wife and my family."

"Now you know how it feels to stand by and watch someone you love suffer."

Max stood before Houser's massive cherry wood desk, gripping his hat in his hand. If the only person being hurt had been himself, nothing on earth could have made him ride in to the bank and humble himself in front of Howard Houser.

But it was Louise out there in the dark cold and blowing snow every morning and every evening. Louise staying up all night with half-frozen beeves. Louise, so exhausted she staggered. One night shortly after the new year, she had fallen asleep at the supper table.

And it was Dave, leaving his own ranch and family to help out. Wally, giving up his evenings to work in the ice and cold.

"What will it take to end this? What do you want from me? Whatever it is . . ." He swallowed his pride. "I'll do it."

Howard leaned back in his chair and smiled, noting the sling across Max's chest.

"It doesn't end until you're ruined. It doesn't matter if you get those cattle through the winter because I can guarantee you won't find a buyer come spring. And without a buyer, you won't have funds to retire your mortgage. You'll lose your ranch in June. The first thing I plan to do after foreclosing is burn your house and barn to the ground."

Slowly, Max nodded his head. This was what he had expected from Houser, but he'd had to give it a try for the sake of Louise and his family.

"Just so you understand, McCord. In retrospect, I don't entirely fault you for marrying that woman. I don't agree with the choice to put yourself in the drawing, but I understand why you thought you had to do it. I'm going to destroy you because you seduced an innocent young woman and ruined her life. You tarnished her name and placed her at the center of a scandal.

"Right now, my daughter is a prisoner in your mother's home. The last time she came into town was on Christmas Day. She won't come again because she rightly believes her condition will be noticed. My man Ridley informs me there are already whispers. Perhaps they originated with your mother's cowboys, or maybe Mrs. Dame, the seamstress, has been indiscreet. It doesn't matter. Sooner or later my daughter's condition will be noticed and remarked upon. If the law permitted, I would kill you for destroying her innocence and her illusions. I'd shoot you dead for placing a blot on the Houser name. As justice is denied me, I must satisfy myself by destroying you. And I will. Now get out of my office."

Wally looked up from a stack of papers piled neatly on his desk as Max strode through the lobby. He started to rise, but Max shook his head and continued toward the door. There was nothing to discuss. Wally had known as well as he that an appeal to Houser would be futile.

Before he pushed through the heavy glass doors, Max took a moment to look back into the lobby. A short line of patrons waited before the teller's cages, but their low voices didn't disturb a reverential hush. And though tall reinforced windows faced the street, very little light illuminated the gloom within.

He had believed he wanted to spend his days here.

When Wally stood, Max stared as if observing a stranger dressed in stiffly formal attire. He noted the gold chain across his brother's vest, a gift from Howard and exactly like the chain Howard wore. He remembered the rash on Wally's neck caused by the chaffing of his high starched collar. He studied the fulsome dark mustache that Philadelphia had wheedled and coaxed his brother to grow.

And he saw himself as he might have been, refashioned to please a woman. Dressed as a somber dandy in uncomfortable clothing and shoes and wearing an itchy mustache.

Whatever expression constricted his features caused Wally to flush deeply and turn aside, and he regretted that. Tonight, when Wally came to help Louise, Max would make things right. He would tell Wally that the right brother had taken the bank position. He would express his genuine pride in his brother's success and rapid rise and wholeheartedly wish him well. And he would silently thank God that he was not spending his days in this airless, musty countinghouse.

Once outside, he breathed deep of the fresh cold air and settled his hat on his head before he reached into his pocket and gripped the green marble. A moment later he was astride Marva Lee and heading out of town.

Every day he exercised his arm and every day his arm became a little stronger. It wouldn't relieve Louise's burden when he returned to work, and he hated that, but soon he'd be able to spare Wally and Dave.

Recently Livvy had taken to serving tea and toast in the parlor every afternoon at three. Philadelphia couldn't guess why her mother-in-law had decided to do this, but she was embarrassingly grateful for something to look forward to as a break in her long, boring day. Sometimes Gilly and Sunshine rode to the main house to join them, but more often, like today, she and Livvy were alone.

"Are you feeling well?" Livvy inquired, studying Philadelphia across the tea table. Livvy was an overbearing and unpleasant woman, but she had her moments. It was annoying, but kind of her to worry about Philadelphia's health.

"Really, Mother McCord, there's nothing to be concerned about. My back aches, and it's difficult to find a comfortable sleeping position. Otherwise I feel fine."

"I know you're tired of hearing this, but I wish you would consult a doctor."

This subject again. Striving for patience, she explained her position yet another time. "First, I couldn't endure being examined by a man. Second, I don't trust Dr. Pope's discretion. Finally, I don't want to risk my condition being noticed by going into town."

"I'm deeply worried about you and the baby."

To conceal her irritation, Philadelphia lowered her head over her teacup. Livvy seldom had time to read, so they couldn't discuss literature. Her mother-in-law sewed, but she didn't do embroidery or fine work. Livvy had little appreciation for china painting, and they had few acquaintances in common. There was little they could talk about except the baby.

"I'm quite strong, I assure you, and I feel fine." She searched her mind for a topic of mutual interest but could think of nothing.

"The thing is, you have no experience." Frowning, Livvy tilted her head to one side. "You're due to deliver in about six weeks, but anyone looking at you would assume you're two or three months from your delivery date. That's why I'm concerned."

Six weeks? Tea slopped into the saucer as she counted in her mind. She hated her predicament so much that she ignored it to the best of her ability and seldom thought about the delivery or the delivery date. Though she knew it was ridiculous, she cherished a secret hope that if she didn't acknowledge her swelling belly, her pregnancy would disappear.

"I don't wish to alarm you," Livvy continued, hesitating. "But I feel I should mention that sometimes our first pregnancy doesn't end as happily as we would wish."

Philadelphia raised her eyebrows.

Reaching across the table, Livvy set aside Philadelphia's cup and saucer and then clasped her hands.

"I lost two babies before Max was born. Both times I suspected something was wrong because, like you, I didn't go into maternity clothing until late, and I wasn't nearly as large as I should have been. As it turned out, both babies were weak and puny and died shortly after delivery."

She had no idea what to say. "I'm sorry."

"I mention this only because I know you must be concerned as I was. And because it might go easier if you prepare yourself for all possibilities. It occurred to me that you have no one to answer whatever questions you may have. I apologize that I've been remiss in this regard. I urge you to ask anything you like, and I'll answer as frankly as I can."

"Well, there is something . . . do babies always come when they're supposed to?"

Livvy released her hands and poured more tea for them both. "Not always. First babies in particular often arrive early."

"But they can come later than expected?"

"Gilly arrived ten days later than I'd calculated." She smiled. "The midwife said Gilly came close to setting a record. But she'd tended one delivery where the baby was nearly two weeks overdue. That doesn't happen often, I would say."

"I see. How long did it take you to regain your shape?"

"It took less time with each baby. Probably because I was that much busier." Livvy gazed at a point in space, smiling at memories. "We couldn't afford help in those days. I had my babies, and three days later I was on my feet again."

Philadelphia shuddered. "I've heard the mother should rest in bed for at least two weeks."

"Ideally, yes. And you should plan on that. Fortunately, you have Gilly and me to help out until you and Wally can get settled in your own home."

"That can't happen soon enough!" When she realized how insulting that sounded, she dimpled and waved a hand. "We don't wish to impose on you any longer than necessary." It was one of those moments when she suspected Livvy saw through her, but she really didn't care. She just wanted out of here.

After tea, she sat in her room beside the fireplace and considered the cradle on the floor beside the wall.

Six weeks.

Very soon she simply had to speak to Wally and her father about a house in town. If her father truly didn't want the inconvenience of living in a house with a new baby, then he could find a rental for them until their own home could be built.

Wally would object, of course. He had mentioned several times how fortunate they were to have his mother's help with a newborn. She would point out they could hire a nursemaid. He would say he needed to live out here to keep an eye on his holdings and Livvy's. She would remind him that he and Livvy shared a foreman. If more supervision was required, Wally could call on Max. Max owed him for going over there night after night after night.

The problem was she could no longer predict with certainty if Wally would do what she wanted. Initially, she had believed he would be easily managed, but, surprisingly, that wasn't always the case. Occasionally, he turned stubborn and couldn't be manipulated to do things her way no matter what she tried. The first incidence had occurred when he insisted on helping Max and Low Down feed their cattle. Then again on Christmas Eve when he had insisted that she go downstairs.

His refusal to do what she wanted infuriated her and made her hate him for a while. But there was also an intriguing little niggle of a challenge, as there had been with Max.

Resting her head against the back of the chair, she closed her eyes. Why, against all sense and logic, was she drawn to Max, the only man she couldn't wrap securely around her little finger? And why had fate seen fit to shackle her to another man fashioned in Max's image? In the entire county there were only two men who had ever said no to her. She was in love with one and married to the other. It was so unfair.

She stared at the cradle, and tears of self-pity slipped down her cheeks.

Six weeks.

In late January a warm spell sent daytime temperatures into the mid-forties. Patches of dry ground appeared, and the ice thinned on the stock ponds.

"It's been almost a week since we've had to bring any beeves into the barn for the night," Louise mentioned, climbing into bed. She leaned against her pillows with a sigh of pleasure. Her back ached tonight. "We can get a full night's sleep."

Max straightened his arm out in front of him, clenched his fist and drew it toward his shoulder. "As good as new."

"Haste trips up its own heels."

"Now what does that mean?"

"It means you could have taken another week before deciding you can pitch hay with that arm. Wally and Dave wouldn't have minded."

"I mind."

"It won't do anyone any good if you injure yourself again because you went back to work too soon."

Turning, he placed a hand on her cheek and leaned forward to brush his lips across hers. "Darlin', I suspect all women want to protect and nurture, but if it was up to you, I'd still be wearing the sling come summertime."

She stared at him, then dropped her head and plucked at the bedcovers. "Maybe so."

"All right, let's have it. You've been brooding about something for almost three weeks. What's bubbling in your pot?"

There were two things. The first she had decided not to mention until they no longer had to feed the beeves. The second item she'd decided not to mention at all.

But since he'd noticed her distraction, she changed her mind. "Gilly said Dave told her that Wally told him that you went into town and talked to Howard Houser about dropping his vendetta and letting you hire some hands."

He gave her a long steady look. "Can't a man do anything in this family without every damned person knowing about it?"

"Well, this damned person wants to know why you didn't tell her about it your own damned self."

"There was nothing to tell. I asked Howard to drop the restrictions so I could hire on some men, and he refused. That's all there was to it. Nothing new."

"That's not what I heard."

"Well, I don't know what . . . oh. You mean the part about foreclosing my ranch and burning it to the ground?"

She rolled her eyes and threw up her hands. "You didn't think that part was important enough to mention? Why didn't you tell me?"

"What's the point? Houser is going to make sure I can't find a buyer for my cattle, so I won't be able to pay my mortgage. He knows Wally needs to hang on to his money for a house in town, and Ma and Dave are cash poor. Even if I were willing to drag the family further into my problems, which I'm not, they don't have the ready money to loan."

"How much do you owe?"

"That's the frustrating part. It's a small mortgage."

"How small?"

"About three thousand dollars. Makes you want to laugh, doesn't it? You and I knew men who panned that much out of Piney Creek in a day."

"I'll give you the money for the mortgage."

"No!"

The answer came so quickly and with such vehemence that Louise drew back against the pillows.

"Max, please listen. I have the money. It's in a bank in Denver. I've got three thousand and more. I never told you about the money because . . ." It seemed ridiculous now that she had once worried that he might take her money.

"Stop. Don't say another word." His chin came up, and his eyes narrowed into slits. "We aren't going to talk about your money. Not now, not ever again."

"But how are you going—?"

"Howard is a force in Fort Houser. But he may not have as much influence in Denver as he thinks he does. But if no one in Denver will buy my cattle, then I'll drive them all the way to Chicago myself if that's what I have to do."

No man could drive a herd by himself. He knew it, and she knew it.

"Max—"

"I won't take a cent from you, Louise. Not under any circumstances. If you don't drop this subject, I'll leave the house and sleep in the bunkhouse. That's how strongly I feel about this. I mean it. I won't listen to another word."

By now she knew when she could roll by him and

when she couldn't. Knew when he'd dug in his heels and wouldn't be budged.

In tense silence, they sat side by side in bed, pretending to read for another twenty minutes before they blew out their lamps.

Tonight was the first time in weeks that Max had not kissed her before extinguishing his lamp. The first time in weeks that he'd turned his back instead of spooning around her body.

Wide awake, Louise stared at the dark ceiling and reviewed every word they had spoken since she climbed into bed, looking for the moment when things had gone sour. Offering him money had been the kicker. That's when everything went drastically wrong.

As she thought about it, she began to understand.

Max had never intended to tell her about the house mortgage or Houser's threat to foreclose. Losing the ranch was his problem; it had nothing to do with her. Besides, she might be gone before June when the mortgage came due. And if he had accepted her offer, he would have insisted that the money be a loan not a gift. But he couldn't do that because a loan would mean an ongoing tie between them, and they wouldn't be able to make a clean break when she left.

For a woman who had always prided herself on not being a crier, she had sure shed a lot of tears since Christmas. Pulling a hand out from under the blankets, she wiped her eyes and her nose.

Maybe Max had guessed the other thing she had to tell him, and that's why he was so adamant about not taking the money. No, if Max had guessed, he'd let the beeves starve before he'd allow her to work as hard as she did twice a day.

That's why she hadn't told him that she was two months pregnant.

She wasn't going to leave him while he needed her. She wouldn't leave until the range began to green up and the cattle could graze. Oh God. Thinking about it made her stomach cramp.

She didn't know how she would find the grit to honor her agreement and ride away from here. This was her home now. She had scrubbed its floors, washed its windows, shoveled snow off the porch, bathed in the kitchen. She knew the corner where the house had settled. Knew how to make the oven bake evenly. If she wasn't here, who would take care of her chickens? Who would pin the laundry on the line when she was gone?

Thinking of the house was easier than bearing the pain that knifed through her body when she thought about Livvy and Sunshine and Gilly. They were so much a part of her life now, so much a part of who she had become since she tumbled out of the wagon in front of Livvy's veranda.

The thought of finding a family and then having to leave them behind ripped at her heart.

But that pain was only a fraction of the agony she would feel when she kissed Max for the last time. When they sat in bed together, their shoulders touching, for the last time. When he took her in his arms for the last time.

She had sworn she would never love him, but she did. Oh God, she did. She loved every single thing about him. She loved the way he tried always to do the right thing, and how he felt about his family. She loved the gentle way he treated his animals and the moments when he gazed at her with tenderness and understanding. She even loved him when he turned stubborn and pushed out his chin.

How could she live without his touch and his kisses and the sound of his laughter?

But every day brought the moment of departure closer. For weeks she could forget that their marriage wasn't real. Then something like tonight happened, and she was jolted back to reality. She might have forgotten their marriage was only temporary. But Max had not.

Slipping her hands beneath the covers, she gently placed them flat on her stomach. This is what she had dreamed of and had longed for. Carrying Max's baby under her heart should have made her happier than anything else ever would. Instead, she turned her face into her pillow to muffle her sobs and wept until she'd cried herself dry.

The warm spell didn't last. Arctic air sank down from the north and gripped the plains in an icy stranglehold. Blizzards froze cattle where they stood, and cattle froze on clear days when the pale sun's thin warmth couldn't penetrate the lid of frigid air. Temperatures plummeted and stayed low, not rising above twelve below zero during the first ten days of February.

Finally, toward the end of the month, the numbing cold receded and patches of bare ground slowly reappeared. Crocuses pushed out of the ground on the sunny side of the barn and beside the veranda steps. During the last week, the red foxes returned, and a bluebird was spotted near the bunkhouse.

Philadelphia watched it all from her bedroom window.

While she did nothing but pace and wait, Wally went into town every day. Livvy kept house and her accounting ledgers, went to Max and Low Down's place every Sunday. Max and Low Down worked their ranch and fought to keep the cattle alive. Heaven only knew what Gilly did every day, but she and her family also drove to Max's house every Sunday.

Everyone had things to occupy their time except her. She had not gone into town since Christmas, two months ago. And no one had come here to call on her.

She, who not long ago had been society's undisputed leader, was now being shunned. How could this happen? People had clambered for an invitation to her musicals and her receptions. Her presence had guaranteed an event would be a success. The door knocker rapped all afternoon during her at-home days. She had been the person who decided who was the crème de la crème and who should be dropped from guest lists.

Now, unbelievably, she had been dropped. When she let herself think about it, rage made her ill, and she had to lie down.

It never should have been this way. She and Max should have been the toast of the town. Young newlyweds at the peak of society, swirling from one engagement to another, setting the pace and the mode, the envy of everyone.

And that's how it would be once the problems were fixed.

Turning from the window, she frowned across the room at the cradle against the wall.

The only thing anyone could talk about was the baby, the baby, the baby. And Livvy watched her all the time. Her mother-in-law studied her color, stared at her stomach, observed how she sat and walked and what she ate.

And every day it got worse. Every morning Livvy smiled broadly and said the same thing. "We could have a baby any hour now." Then Wally would look startled and ask if he should ride into town or stay here with his wife.

This morning Livvy had pointed out that Philadelphia was two days overdue, hinting that Wally should stay home. But Philadelphia had eventually persuaded him to go on into town. And then she'd had to listen to Livvy thanking heaven that she'd carried to term and hadn't miscarried.

Two days overdue.

Wally would be distracted at the bank, awaiting word. So would her father. And so would Max. Livvy had three cowboys waiting, ready to ride to the bank, to Gilly's, and to Max's the instant her labor began.

Two days overdue.

First babies often came early, but they were seldom more than two weeks late.

She could wait another week, but what was the point? Delay wouldn't make what she had to do any easier.

Brooding and angry, she shoved her nightgown in the laundry bag and made certain a fresh gown lay near at hand. Then she removed all jewelry except her wedding band. After she brushed her hair into a simple knot at the nape of her neck, she lifted her head high and walked out of her bedroom to the top of the staircase.

There was no choice.

She drew a deep breath and placed a hand over her thundering heart. And then she threw herself down the staircase.

Chapter 19

Wally and Howard Houser jumped out of Howard's carriage and rushed toward the door as Max and Louise followed Gilly's horse into the yard of the main house.

Livvy met everyone at the front door and ushered them into the parlor where she quickly related how she'd heard Philadelphia's scream, followed by a horrifying racket. When she reached the foyer, she found Philadelphia sprawled unconscious at the foot of the staircase.

Howard started up out of his chair, but Livvy raised a hand. "She's in bed now, resting. She could have broken her neck, but she didn't. She has a cut on her forehead and a sprained wrist and ankle. She may get a black eye, and she'll certainly be bruised."

"And the baby?" Howard demanded.

"I'm guessing that's why she came to the stairs. To call me because her labor had begun." Livvy clasped her hands in front of her waist. "Frankly, I don't hold much hope for the baby," she informed them, speaking slowly. "Philadelphia's contractions are weak and she's been bleeding since she fell." She stared hard at Howard and Wally. "If either of you can talk sense to her, I beg you to urge her to allow us to send for Dr. Pope or a midwife. She won't listen to me. Each time I mention outside assistance, she becomes hysterical."

"Where's my daughter?" Howard stood, a bloodless scowl clamping his expression.

"She's upstairs. I'll go with you." Wally and Houser hurried out of the parlor.

Every instinct urged Max to follow, but his mother's gaze pinned him and warned that he would not be welcome. Because he couldn't remain seated, he added wood to the parlor fire and knelt before the flames. Frustration rolled his stomach in knots, and he thought the top of his head would blow off.

He was to blame for whatever happened today. Philadelphia's pain, the birth or loss of a child. His child. If Philadelphia died, he would never forgive himself. It was hard enough already. But if his lust had put her in a position where she died . . .

"I left Sunshine with Dave," Gilly said when the silence became oppressive. "I didn't think she should . . ."

"You made the right choice," Livvy agreed absently, her gaze on the staircase.

Louise studied Max, then turned to Livvy. "What can we do to help?"

"Gilly is no good in a medical situation. We'll put her to work in the kitchen. Gilly, you know where I stacked the diapers and blankets. Get them ready. Also, we'll need a supply of towels. And there'll be wash to do."

"I assume the 'we' you keep mentioning means you and me?" Louise inquired, raising an eyebrow.

"I'm guessing you've attended a birthing or two?"

"Several," Louise admitted. "Most of them sudden. Where there was no one to help but me." She glanced toward the hearth, concerned by the pain in Max's eyes. "But I doubt Philadelphia wants me to help with her delivery."

"If Mr. Houser and Wally can persuade her to allow a doctor, I'll assist him alone. If not, I need you no matter how she feels about it." Livvy dusted her hands together, the matter decided.

Twenty long minutes later Wally and Howard Houser returned to the parlor. Houser walked directly to the window and glared through the panes. "That is the most stubborn woman. . . . She has some damned idiotic idea that no one will learn about the baby if she has it alone. But every person in Fort Houser will know if we send for Dr. Pope."

"Like you said, Ma, she gets hysterical about having a doctor present." Wally pushed both hands over his forehead and through his hair. "But she agreed that if something goes wrong and it looks as if she might die, then we can send for Doc Pope. But we had to promise not to do it until she gives the word."

Livvy blinked hard. "Philadelphia is in no fit state to make this decision. I implore you to send for Doc Pope right now!"

Howard answered without turning from the window. "This day will be hard enough without beginning it on a broken promise. This pregnancy began in betrayal, it isn't going to end that way. When my daughter tells me to fetch Dr. Pope, I will. But not before." When he faced into the room, his gaze hardened on Max. "Why is he here?"

"I sent for him," Livvy said sharply.

"I have a right to be present," Max insisted. But it was Wally he faced. They stared at each other. "After this baby is born, I'll step back and relinquish any claim, as I promised. But today, I need to be here as much as either of you."

"And I need Louise's help. She's assisted at birthings before. Oh. You haven't met Max's wife." Hastily Livvy introduced Louise to Howard Houser.

"Howdy do," Louise said solemnly. In her old life she would have stuck out her hand to shake. But she didn't have to strain to know what to do in this situation. Philadelphia's father wore his superiority like a shield to ward off people like her.

Howard Houser looked her up and down, and his

eyebrows soared as if he were surprised to discover that she was clean and tidy and modestly dressed.

Louise was surprised by him, too. She'd expected the man who was making a misery of her life and Max's would look like the ogre he was. But Houser was her height, balding, and he looked more ordinary than she had imagined. Right now, he was a man half-sick with worry for a beloved daughter.

"Shouldn't someone be with her? She's alone."

As the sharp words were directed to her, Louise supposed the statement indicated his grudging approval. Howard Houser would have welcomed the devil if the devil could help his daughter.

Now Houser flicked a hand at Wally. "It's early, but I could use a drink. It's going to be a long day."

"We all could," Wally said, meaning the men.

Before she hurried after Livvy, Louise sought a quick word with Max. He stood before the fireplace as if he'd taken root there, staring into the flames.

"You haven't said two words."

He didn't look at her. "If she dies . . ."

"She ain't going to die, Max. I promise you, I won't let her die." Philadelphia was the mother of his child, and she should have been his wife. He loved her. Never had Louise been more aware of that than now as she watched knots ripple up his jaw, saw his hand working the green marble in his pocket.

"How soon will something happen?" he asked in a low voice.

"I imagine it'll be several hours yet."

He nodded. "Tell Ma I'm going to borrow one of her horses. I need to do something or I'll lose my mind."

She didn't let herself dwell on his feelings because it would hurt too much. And she walled off her own emotions because they hurt, too. To get through today, she needed to forget that her husband loved Philadelphia and that Philadelphia would give him a child before this day ended.

There was something else that she didn't let herself think about, although she knew she would later. Philadelphia's child would be half sister or half brother to the child that Louise carried. It was another reason, maybe the best reason, to do everything she could to help mother and child come through the delivery safely.

Livvy waited outside Philadelphia's bedroom door. "I'm sorry to ask you to help after the abominable way Philadelphia has treated you. But there's no one else."

"It doesn't matter." She gave Livvy a steady, direct look. "Now the whole truth."

"I had an idea you'd know there was more." Livvy shook her head and wrung her hands together. "I don't know what to make of this. I ran to the barn and brought back two cowboys to help me get her upstairs and into bed. That's when I noticed that she was bleeding profusely. Once I got her into a nightgown and lying down, the bleeding slowed. I packed her with absorbent cotton."

"You've got a rubber sheet on the bed?"

Livvy nodded. "We've been ready for a couple of weeks. And I have plenty of sheets. We're going to need them since we'll have to remake the bed periodically, especially if the bleeding continues." Livvy glanced toward the bedroom door. "She's having chills and stomach pain down low. Some nausea."

Louise's thoughts raced. "After a fall like that, I'd expect labor to begin at once, particularly since she's overdue. But you're describing—"

"Take a look and tell me what you think."

The instant Louise walked into the room, she smelled the thick coppery scent of blood. Philadelphia was curled on her side in bed, shivering, her arms wrapped around her stomach. Louise exchanged a glance with Livvy before she approached the bed.

"Howdy, Philadelphia. You look like hell."

One eye was swelling and beginning to discolor; she was going to have a dandy of a black eye. And the cut on her forehead would leave a scar. It had bled into her hair and the blood had dried there. Her wrist was wrapped in a stiff bandage to hold it steady, but Philadelphia seemed unaware of wrist pain as she cupped her stomach. That indicated greater pain in her stomach than in her wrist.

Her eyes fluttered open. "You! Get out of my room!"

Louise pulled back the covers and examined Philadelphia's bloody nightgown and the bloody sheet beneath her hips. She raised her head and stared at Livvy. "Someone should fetch Doc Pope right now."

"That's what I've been saying!"

"No!" Philadelphia glared at them with burning eyes. "It's not your decision! No, no, no!"

"Is the pain constant or intermittent?" Louise snapped.

"Constant. Oh God, it's constant. It doesn't let up. Give me back the blanket, I'm so cold."

"Let us have a minute or two to clean this up and get you into a fresh nightgown, then you can have the blanket," Livvy said soothingly. To Louise she added in a lower voice, "We can fold a sheet into a pad and put that beneath her so all we have to change next time is the pad instead of the whole bed."

Fifteen minutes later, they had the mess cleaned up, the bleeding slowed, and Philadelphia into a clean nightgown and wrapped in an extra blanket. Louise carried the bloody sheets into the corridor with Livvy right behind her. "Well?" Livvy said.

"If I didn't know better," Louise answered slowly, puzzled, "I'd say we were dealing with a miscarriage, not a birth. She's having chills, constant pain. . . . I'd give her a few grains of gallic acid every few hours to arrest the bleeding, and advise her to stay in bed for the next two months and hope she carries to term."

"It can't be a miscarriage." Livvy frowned back into the bedroom, her eyes on Philadelphia, writhing beneath her blankets. "The one thing there's no doubt about is the date of conception. May 29. She's not early; she's overdue."

"And that means we have a situation here that sure ain't good. She must have hurt herself inside when she pitched down the staircase."

"Or maybe it's the baby that's hurt and bleeding."

"Either way, Livvy, this isn't a normal delivery. We need the doctor."

They stood in silence, staring into the bedroom.

"We'll alternate sage tea and tansy tea for the bleeding," Livvy said finally. "I've got some laudanum if the pain gets unbearable. If we can't slow or stop the bleeding, then I'll insist that Howard or Wally send for Doc Pope. I'll throw them both out the door if I have to."

"You fix the tea tray, and I'll stay with her." Shaking her head, Louise entered the bedroom and pulled a chair next to Philadelphia. "Is the pain still constant?"

"You have no right to be here, and I want you gone. I detest you! Get out, get out, get out!"

"Do tell." Louise reached for the basin on the bed table beside her and held it as Philadelphia vomited. When Philadelphia fell back on the bed, Louise wiped her face with a damp cloth and gave her a glass of water to rinse her mouth.

"To tell you the truth, I don't know why I'm trying to help you. You're about as worthless a person as I ever met. But I'm here for the duration. I guess tending sick folks or folks in pain is a flaw in my character. Now do you want to know what's happening to you, or not?"

They stared at each other, then Philadelphia fell back on her pillow. "I wish it was you lying here suffering. I wish you'd never been born."

"I've wished that myself a few times. Now. You've lost

a lot of blood. That tells us something is bad wrong. You're also sick to your stomach, shivering, and experiencing continual pain. None of that is usual for a delivery. If Livvy and I can't slow down the blood loss or stop it, we're sending for Doc Pope."

"I'd rather die than send for a doctor!"

"Well, it might happen that's going to be the choice. Death or a doctor. You might be stupid enough to let yourself die because you have some crazy damned notion that a doctor is going to tell everyone that you have a baby everyone will hear about anyway, but I ain't going to let that happen. I can't promise anything about the baby—that ain't looking good—but I can promise that you are not going to die! Long before that happens, a doctor is going to be standing here working on you."

"Never! My father promised! Oh! Oh!"

Leaning forward, Louise placed her palms on Philadelphia's stomach. It was a contraction, but weak. After glancing at the clock with the intention of timing the contractions, she explained what had just occurred.

"Where is Livvy?" Philadelphia asked when she'd caught her breath. "I want her here, not you."

"She's downstairs fixing tea."

Philadelphia grimaced and clenched her teeth, then she exhaled slowly. "Max will never love you. Not ever. He loves me, and he always will!"

Louise gazed at the blankets mounded over Philadelphia's belly and unconsciously her hand dropped to her own stomach.

Philadelphia smiled. In the midst of her pain and nausea, she smiled. "Anyone with eyes can see that you love him. That's good. Because when I take him, I want you to suffer like you've made me suffer!"

"Philadelphia? Shut up."

"*What?*"

Louise narrowed her eyes down to slits. "Do you have

trouble understanding English, or are your ears bad? I said, shut up. We aren't going to talk about me, and we aren't going to talk about Max. The only person we're going to talk about today is you. You ought to like that since that's your favorite subject."

"Nobody talks to me like that!" Bubbles sputtered up at the corners of her lips.

"Now here's how it's going to go." Reaching, she picked up the basin again and caught another gush of vomit. "The only way you get rid of me and I get rid of you," she paused to wipe Philadelphia's mouth and hand her the water, "is after you produce that baby. So here's what you do. The next time you have a contraction, you concentrate on making it stronger and harder. When the time comes, I'll tell you to push, and you better damned well do it."

"I don't take orders from you. I'll do what I please!"

"Not today you won't. Today, me and Livvy and Mother Nature are going to dictate what you do. Now let go of those covers. I need to see if you're leaking blood again."

"No, you don't," Philadelphia snapped, baring her teeth. "If you think I'm going to let you inspect my bottom—"

"Before today is over, I'm going to be sick of looking at your bottom." Louise preferred a male patient every time. Women could be such a pain in the butt. She sighed. "Let go of the covers, or I will break your fingers."

"What?" Shock widened Philadelphia's blue-green eyes, and her mouth dropped open. "What did you say?"

"I said I am going to check and see if you're bleeding again. If you resist, I'll break your fingers. And I'll enjoy doing it." Louise pried up one finger, pulling it back far enough that Philadelphia screamed and snatched her hand away.

"That's better."

"I . . . I can't . . . you . . ."

"I've been told my bedside manner stinks," Louise commented, hauling down the covers for a look. She didn't spot blood on the pad, or the cotton packing Livvy had put between Philadelphia's legs. "Coddling only makes it harder to get things done."

Philadelphia screamed. "Livvy!"

Louise pulled up the covers and sat down. "I expect Livvy isn't one for coddling either, although I could be wrong."

"Not by much," Livvy said, carrying a tea tray into the room. Her nostrils pinched, and she glanced toward the vomit basin. "We'll start with sage tea, see where we go from there."

And so began six hours of vigilance, worry, work, and a growing sense of helplessness. Louise and Livvy took turns rubbing Philadelphia's back, wiping sweat from her forehead, or wrapping her in extra blankets when the chills shook her. They brought her tansy tea and sage tea, gave her cold water when she demanded it, and held the bedpan when the urge inevitably came. They changed the bloody sheets and Philadelphia's nightgown about once every hour and a half. Afterward, one of them would take the sheets and nightgown and the vomit basin downstairs where Gilly waited with a laundry tub and hot, fresh coffee.

When it was Louise's turn, she lingered, glad to escape the odors in the bedroom upstairs. Glad to sit for a minute and rest her own back.

But this time she strode into the kitchen too spitting mad to think about coffee or a minute's rest.

"What's happening up there?" Max asked. "It's been hours."

"Shut up," Howard snarled, then asked Louise the same question. An hour ago, Livvy had implored Howard to send for Doc Pope, but he'd refused. Until Philadelphia sent for him and asked him to fetch the doctor, he would not break his promise.

Furious, Louise walked up to him, slammed her fists on her hips, and leaned into his face. "Listen to me, you son of a bitch. Your daughter has been losing blood for six goddamned hours. She's weak, she's sick, she's in pain. And she is going to die if you don't get a doctor out here and damned soon! Whatever is happening up there, it's beyond what Livvy and I can handle. Now I don't like Philadelphia; I don't like one damned thing about her. But I promised Max that she isn't going to die, and she goddamned well isn't! So. Are you going to send a cowboy to fetch the doc, or do I have to go out there, climb on a horse, and go get the doc myself! I promise you, somebody is going to town to get the doctor and right now. The question is, who's it going to be?"

"It's going to be me," Max said grimly. Long ago the men had shed jackets and ties and rolled up their sleeves. Max pushed down his cuffs and headed toward the back door where he'd hung his jacket.

"You're not going anywhere, McCord. This isn't your decision. Nobody goes for the doctor until I talk to my daughter first."

Louise ignored him. "Don't waste a minute, Max. She's in a real bad way."

"I'm going, too," Wally said, jumping to his feet. "I can't sit here doing nothing. I'm going crazy."

"You stay where you are! I'm going upstairs to speak to my daughter, then we'll decide."

"No, you're not going upstairs. Sit down, Mr. Houser." Louise gave him a push on his chest, and he was startled enough to sit down hard. "Believe me, you don't want to go up there. Give me that whiskey bottle. Gilly? I need a glass."

Gilly brought three glasses, dropped into a chair, then poured for herself, Louise, and Howard Houser. "The clothesline is full of frozen sheets. All I can do now is wash them, wring them out, and stack them in the box over there in the corner. I don't know what we'll do about nightgowns. We've gone through all of Philadelphia's, and we've started on Mama's." She gave Louise a look of anguish. "I'm so scared. Is Philadelphia going to die?"

Louise tossed back the whiskey, then studied the bottom of the glass. "Philadelphia's lost a lot of blood. She's very sick and very weak. I hope the doctor can save her, but I guess it could go either way."

Houser propped his elbows on the table and dropped his head in his hands. "You're not a doctor; you don't know. What you are is a vulgar-mouthed interfering woman."

"I've been called worse."

He lifted his head and rubbed his eyes. "She's my only child. I've tried never to let her down. Now, because of you, I've broken my promise." His furious expression promised that she would regret crossing him.

"So what will you do, Mr. Houser? Will you punish me for trying to save your daughter's life? Punish Max for riding hell-bent for leather to fetch the doctor? What can you do to make our lives harder or make us more miserable than you've made us already?" Reaching for the bottle, she refilled her glass and then poured more whiskey for Gilly and Houser. "Maybe you won't wait until foreclosure to burn down Max's house. That would teach us not to interfere, wouldn't it. Or maybe you could send one of your minions to shoot what's left of Max's cattle. Yeah, that would teach us a lesson."

A deep plum color infused his cheeks, and he leaned toward her. "Whatever happens is well deserved. Whose fault is it that my daughter may die?"

"I'm not sure," Louise said thoughtfully, moving her glass in damp circles on the table. "Maybe it's Philadelphia's fault for not saying no when she should have.

Maybe it's your fault for not setting limits and for letting her believe rules don't apply to her. Maybe it's Max's fault because he loved her too much. Maybe it's your wife's fault for dying too soon. Maybe it's my fault for marrying Max when I didn't even want to. Maybe it's Livvy's fault for buying land outside Fort Houser and making it possible for her son to meet your daughter. Maybe the weather is to blame for providing a warm spring evening conducive to poking. I don't know who or what is to blame. What difference does it make? Will assigning blame change anything?"

"That's enough!" he said, speaking through his teeth.

"Yes, it is," she said wearily, pushing up from the table. "Gilly, we'll need a stack of fresh towels for the doctor. Your mother said to tell you to put out the roast beef for supper. People can eat if they feel like it."

Without glancing at Houser, Louise walked out of the kitchen and up the stairs and back into the oppressive and frightening odors and the sight of blood and pain. Livvy looked up with a worried and helpless expression and shook her head.

"I hope the doctor gets here soon."

"I do, too." She wanted Philadelphia to live. She had promised Max.

An endless hour elapsed before the downstairs door finally banged open and Max, Wally, and Dr. Pope ran up the staircase. The doctor strode in the room, but Max and Wally halted at the door and their eyes widened before they turned away.

"Oh Jesus."

"God!"

"Damn it, get out of here," Louise said, pushing them into the corridor. "Go downstairs," she ordered before she shut the door on them. "We'll tell you the minute we know anything."

Dr. Pope set down his bag, threw off his coat, and

rolled up his shirtsleeves. "I'm told she's full term. She fell down the staircase and that's when the bleeding began. Is there anything else I need to know?" After Livvy described what had happened throughout the last seven hours, he nodded briskly.

"I want to die," Philadelphia whispered. She blinked dazed eyes at the ceiling.

"We're going to try to prevent that," Dr. Pope said, bending to open his bag. "You ladies might want to step outside for a minute or two. I think our little mother would appreciate some privacy during the examination."

"Oh. Of course." Taking Louise's arm, Livvy headed for the door. She sagged against the corridor wall. "I am so thankful that he's here. Whatever you said to make this happen, I bless you for it."

After a few minutes, Louise frowned. "What's taking so long? Did he forget we're waiting out here?"

"I didn't forget," Dr. Pope said, stepping into the corridor and pulling the door shut behind him.

"How is she? Will she be all right?" Livvy inquired anxiously.

"I'd say so. She'll need complete bed rest and a lot of care, but she's young and healthy. I expect her to recover."

"And the baby?" Louise asked.

"We'll know in a few minutes, but my informed guess is the baby will not survive. You said this was a full-term baby, but it isn't. She's only seven months along. Being eight, maybe nine weeks premature, plus the fall . . ." He shook his head.

"That's impossible," Livvy stated flatly. "This isn't a premature baby. It can't be."

"Mrs. McCord, I've been delivering babies for thirty-five years. I know how far along a woman is, and I know the difference between a delivery and a miscarriage. This is a miscarriage." He spoke with the full authority of his title and experience. "Whichever one of you is going to assist, we'll begin now." He pushed open the door and walked back into the bedroom.

"Seven months," Livvy whispered. "No wonder she didn't want a doctor." Her eyes rounded, then narrowed. "You and I didn't understand what we were seeing. We dismissed a miscarriage because it wasn't possible." Hot color rose in Livvy's cheeks, and her shoulders stiffened. "She damned near got away with this. It wouldn't surprise me if falling down the stairs was no accident."

"Livvy, what are you saying?"

"Think about what a seven-month baby means." Striding forward, she entered the bedroom and closed the door with an angry click.

Before Louise could think about anything, she needed to tell the others that Doc Pope was confident Philadelphia would survive. She found everyone sitting around the kitchen table waiting in worried silence. They gazed at her with anxious, expectant eyes.

"There's nothing much to report yet. Livvy and the doctor are with her."

"What are they doing?" Howard demanded.

"I don't know. My impression is that Doc Pope will deliver the baby." She didn't tell them the baby was two months premature. "The doctor expects Philadelphia will fully recover."

"Thank heaven," Gilly whispered.

But Max was the person she spoke to, the only person she saw. He dropped his head in his hands and didn't move. She guessed he was praying, thanking God. And then she remembered Philadelphia saying that she would take Max away. If she ran off with Max, it would break Wally's heart. All Louise had to do was glance at Wally's white, drawn face to see that he loved his wife. But Philadelphia had said she would take Max.

Smothering a sigh, she placed her hands against the

small of her back and stretched. "I'll return when there's more news."

There was a wooden bench in the corridor outside Philadelphia's bedroom, and she sat there to wait, leaning her head back against the wall.

Seven months ago Max had been in Piney Creek. She knew he hadn't left camp during the summer because she'd been aware of Max by then and had kept an eye on him. There was no possibility that Max could be the father of Philadelphia's child.

Lowering her head, she rubbed the bridge of her nose with thumb and forefinger. Livvy was right. Now they knew why Philadelphia had taken such an adamant position against seeing a doctor. She might deceive Livvy and Louise, and almost had, but a doctor would know at once that she was not as far along as she claimed.

The scope of Philadelphia's deceit was staggering to think about. She would have married Max and let Max raise another man's child while believing it was his. And Wally. Wally had married Philadelphia to give a McCord child the McCord name. If Philadelphia had told the truth, Wally's life would have been very different now.

Finally, to protect her deception, Philadelphia must have deliberately fallen down the staircase, hoping to induce labor when labor should have begun if the baby had been Max's. She must have known that she might seriously injure herself and her baby, but she had done it anyway.

Louise shuddered and pressed a hand to her stomach as the door opened and Livvy emerged, holding a bundle in her arms. She jumped to her feet. "The baby lived!"

"Only for a few minutes. It's a boy," Livvy said in a flat voice.

"Where are you going?"

"This is not a McCord. I want the men she deceived to see this baby and know what she did."

"Livvy, wait." Louise caught her mother-in-law's arm. "There's no reason to tell anyone about this baby. You'll only bring pain to those who love her. They don't have to know." She didn't want Max to learn that Philadelphia had betrayed him with another man. It would hurt too much. "Please, don't do this. We can keep her secret for the sake of those we love."

Anger flashed and burned in Livvy's gaze. "She betrayed Max. And she intended to pass another man's by-blow off on my son to raise as his own. Wally didn't have to marry her; he could have had his own life, could have chosen his own bride. Then she allowed her father to punish Max when Max had nothing to do with this pregnancy. And she dared—she dared—to call you indecent! She did these things to my family, and by God in heaven, I will not protect her. Get out of my way."

Livvy carried the baby down the stairs and into the kitchen. Circles of scarlet flamed against her pale cheeks as she told Max, Wally, Howard Houser, and Gilly what she had come to say.

"That is a filthy lie!" Houser stood abruptly, shaking with anger. "How dare you suggest that my daughter had sexual congress with another man only two months before her wedding?"

Livvy's chin came up. "Doc Pope will confirm this child was premature." Livvy turned back the blanket that had hidden the baby's face. "If you still doubt, then look at this child. See for yourself that this is not my son's baby."

Louise drew a sharp breath. From where she stood, she could see a shock of black hair and the baby's face and chest. His skin was the color of coffee with cream.

Howard Houser stared, then he threw out an arm to catch himself. Leaning, he steadied himself against the kitchen wall. "Luis Delacroix," he whispered, blinking at the bundle in Livvy's arms. "That son of a bitch!"

Max met his mother's gaze; then he stood abruptly and walked out the back door, letting it slam behind him.

Chapter 20

❧────────────────❧

She floated through laudanum dreams for fourteen hours before she awoke with a dry mouth and severe anxiety. Pretending to sleep for another thirty minutes, she considered her circumstances and reluctantly concluded that she was backed into a corner. Though it wasn't fair, she was going to be blamed.

"Philadelphia?" Gilly's soft voice called from the side of the bed. "Are you awake? Here, let me help you sit up."

"Oh!" Pain radiated through her body. Every stiff, sore muscle protested the slightest movement. She must have bruises all over, and her wrist and ankle hurt. Her bottom ached with a dull pain that would remind her for several days of yesterday's ordeal. "May I have my mirror, please? It's on the vanity."

Gilly fetched the mirror, but Philadelphia wasn't sure she had the courage to look. First she sipped a glass of water. Then she smoothed back her hair and explored her swollen left eye with her fingertips.

Finally she raised the mirror and gazed into the glass. A long shudder passed down her spine. Her eyelid was the worst, black and purple and more puffy than her fingertips had told her. A raw gash cut across her forehead from eyebrow to hairline, and a large bruise covered most of her jaw. She hadn't knocked out any teeth, thank heaven, nor had she broken her nose, a possibility that had worried her for several days. She had been very fortunate, but then, she usually was.

Slowly, her pulse calmed. Her injuries were minor and would heal. In the meantime, the cuts, bruises, and her black eye would garner sympathy.

Gilly sat down beside her. "When you feel up to it . . ." She cleared her throat and studied her hands. "Everyone wants to speak to you."

"I'd like to wash my teeth and brush my hair."

"While you're seeing to your toilette, I'll bring you coffee. Or would you prefer chocolate? You can have toast but no other solid food until the day after tomorrow. I made some chicken broth yesterday. Should I bring you—"

"Just the hot chocolate." Sudden hope flared. The way Gilly prattled on made Philadelphia wonder if perhaps Dr. Pope had not betrayed her after all. "The baby died," she said, testing the waters as Gilly stood.

"Yes. Here's your hairbrush and your tooth powder."

That didn't tell her much. "What did the doctor say? About the baby?"

At the door Gilly looked back, and there was no sympathy in her gaze. "You had a seven-month miscarriage yesterday. The baby you lost was not fathered by Max," she said coolly, shutting the door behind her.

The air went out of Philadelphia's body, and her hands clamped into fists. The worst had happened. Exactly as she had feared, the doctor had been her undoing.

What she hated most was the realization that she might as well have spared herself the fall down the staircase, since everyone had found out anyway. Lifting the mirror, she studied the cut on her forehead. Possibly it would leave a scar.

On the positive side, she could toss away the shapeless sacks she'd been forced to wear. Best of all, the gossips who were speculating about her hasty marriage to Wally would see her in town as soon as she could get up and about, and they would see her as slender as ever. Whispers might circulate that she'd lost a baby, but no one really listened to cowboy gossip. The whispers would fall silent when she showed herself in the Ladies' Emporium.

She brushed her hair but didn't pin it up. Instead, she arranged a long golden curl over one shoulder. It made her look younger, more fragile.

Beginning to feel anxious again, she wondered who would appear first. When the rap came on the door, her nerves twitched and she thrust the mirror beneath the covers. "Come in."

Max opened the door, but he didn't step into the room. Morning light turned his face haggard, illuminating dark circles beneath his eyes and washing the color from his lips. Still, he had the power to stir her in ways no other man ever had.

"One word." His voice was low and hoarse. "Why?"

This wasn't a question she had anticipated since the answer was obvious. "Everything that happened is your fault, Max. I implored you not to leave me alone all summer. I begged you to stay, but you wouldn't listen. Even after I gave myself to you, you wouldn't do as I asked." Surely he understood the reason she had surrendered her innocence was to induce him to stay in Fort Houser. It had stunned her when he left anyway.

"I was hurt and lonely. Shocked that you would disregard my wishes and use me so badly. In July the son of an acquaintance of Father's stayed with us for two weeks." Accusation gleamed in her eyes. "*He* paid attention to me."

She waited for Max to say something. But he didn't comment, didn't mention the cuts and bruises on her face. He stared as if she were a puzzling stranger who touched nothing inside him.

If she'd been standing, she would have stamped her foot. "I was angry, Max. You deserted me to go live with a grubby passel of prospectors. I missed all the engagement parties people would have hosted for us if you'd stayed here. Luis understood that. He said he would never have behaved so thoughtlessly or so selfishly toward his future wife!"

As she watched his eyes and his expression harden, she sensed that discussing Luis might be unwise. She also sensed that her explanation was going badly, but she didn't know why.

She fluttered her fingers in a dismissive gesture, tilted her head, and gave him a sad, brave little smile. "That's behind us now. I forgive you. All in all, everything worked out for the best. The baby just complicated everything. Now it's simpler. Now there's no rush, no time constraints. We can dissolve marriages we don't want and start over. It can be the way we both want it to be."

Max stared as if he didn't grasp anything she'd said. His behavior was beginning to annoy her.

"Max?"

Without a word, he turned on his heel. A moment later she heard his boots on the staircase.

Well, he needed time, that's all. Very likely he hadn't accepted responsibility for driving her into Luis's arms. But he would. Max was fair, and doing the right thing was important to him. By the time she regained her health, he would have considered everything she'd said and he'd be ready to apologize and they would pick up their lives together.

Before her next visitor, she had a moment to rest and enjoy the pleasure of flattening her palms on her stomach. In no time at all she would have her figure back.

"Mrs. Weaver sent you a pot of chocolate," her father said, entering without knocking. He placed a tray on her bedside table and the aroma of toast and hot chocolate wafted toward her.

"Would you pour me a cup? Please, Daddy?" she asked in a little-girl voice.

Like Max, her father appeared to have spent a sleepless and difficult night. He wore the same clothing he'd worn yesterday, and he hadn't shaved, leading her to guess that he hadn't gone home last night but had stayed here at the McCord ranch.

He gave her a cup of chocolate, then sat heavily on the chair Gilly had vacated. "I don't know where to begin."

"I wanted to confide in you, but I just couldn't." That's what would hurt him most. She hadn't come to him with her problems.

"It was Luis Delacroix," he stated flatly. "That son of a bitch was a guest in my home. I've known his father for twenty years."

"He overpowered me, Daddy." Tears wet her eyes. She saw Luis in her memory, imagined the scene so vividly it could have been true. "I resisted, but—"

"Really?" A chill hardened his tired gaze. "You didn't cry out? Told no one afterward? I'm willing to accept that Delacroix seduced you, but I won't accept that he did so against your will. You'd already been with one man; you knew what was happening. I remember watching you flirt with him, Philadelphia. I remember thinking you were too innocent to understand what you were doing." He made a sound of disgust deep in his throat.

"Please don't blame me." Tears spilled out of her swollen eye. "It was only once. An accident. Afterward I felt so ashamed, so frightened. I didn't know what to do."

"You've hurt so many people." He rubbed the salt-and-pepper stubble on his jaw, then straightened against the back of the chair. "I've apologized to Max and his wife. Naturally I'll end the restrictions against any hands they hire. When I return to the bank, I'll mark Max's mortgage paid and return his note. I've told him if he needs a loan to buy more cattle, he can name his own terms. Maybe that will make up in some small way for . . ." He lifted a hand and let it fall back to his lap.

"You apologized? To Max and that creature?" She couldn't believe it. "He may not have been the one who . . . but he jilted me!"

"I wouldn't blame Wally if he decides to divorce you."

She gasped and stared. Divorce would be her decision, not Wally's.

"If he divorces you, I'll buy you a small house in Denver."

"I don't want to go to Denver! I want to stay in Fort Houser. This is my home!"

He shook his head. "You're my only child, Philadelphia, and I don't intend our estrangement to be permanent. But I don't want to see or speak to you for a long while. Perhaps we'll correspond from time to time." He rose to his feet. "If I'm not present to solve your problems, maybe you'll have a better chance to grow and grow up."

Stunned and speechless, she watched with her mouth opened in disbelief as he left the room. An estrangement? He was banishing her? But why? Truly, she didn't understand.

Before she could reach any conclusions, Wally entered the room and came to her bedside. "How are you feeling?"

Finally, someone thought to ask about her. "I'm sore and weak." Gingerly, she touched her black eye.

"I'll come right to the point." Wally pulled the chair closer and reached for her hand. "Your father has made a very generous offer. He's proposed that I open a new bank in Santa Fe."

"Oh please, Wally. I don't want to hear about business."

"Just listen. Your father will pay moving expenses. He'll build us a suitable house near the town square. I'll receive a handsome salary plus stock bonuses. Eventually, I'll own the bank."

Us? Could he or her father really believe she would move a thousand miles away from her home? With Wally?

"Or," he said, meeting her gaze, "since I entered into this marriage based on a false premise, I can divorce you. Your father made it clear that the offer in Santa Fe is firm whether or not you and I remain married."

She would speak to her father about *that*.

"Everyone seems to believe that I should divorce you. But I've thought about it, and that isn't what I want. I think you and I can make a fresh start. I think we could learn to love each other. But you may not agree; you may wish to regain your freedom. Therefore, I leave the choice to you. If you prefer a divorce, I won't object if you go to Wyoming and begin proceedings. You can claim that I've deserted you. Or you can come to Santa Fe with me, and we'll start over."

Of course it was her choice. And she had already decided what she and Max would do.

"If you choose to come to Santa Fe, then we need to set down some ground rules. We will never discuss this period of our lives again. I don't want to know who the man was or why you became pregnant by him. That's behind us and forgotten."

He looked down at his thumb stroking the back of her hand. "We will not have separate bedrooms. We will always dine together. We will visit your father and my family twice a year, and they will always be welcome in my home. That includes my brother and his wife, whom you will treat with respect."

"Do you have other demands?" she asked coldly.

"Very likely I will. If you can't abide by a few simple rules or if you can't take no for an answer, then go to Wyoming." He shrugged and gazed at her. "You're selfish and self-centered, Philadelphia. Capable of cunning and deceit if it serves your purpose. I don't know why I think I could love you or why I find you challenging. But I do."

"No one speaks to me like that!"

Standing, he gazed down at her. "I don't expect you to make up your mind immediately. I won't be leaving for Santa Fe until the end of the month. You have until then to decide what you want to do."

"I can tell you right now!"

"I don't want to hear it now. I want you to think about everything, and be sure. Seems to me that you need to choose between making our marriage a real one, or facing the scandal of a divorce."

The word "scandal" gave her pause. He was right, of course. A divorce would finish her if she wasn't ruined already. Clearly, she could not remain in Fort Houser. But that didn't matter. She and Max would start over in some place new and fresh.

No one came to sit with her after Wally left. If she listened hard, she could hear faint sounds of conversation drifting from the kitchen, but the distance was too great to make out words. They were probably talking about her. Criticizing her. Making it sound like everything that had happened was her fault.

A genuine tear trickled down her cheek, followed by another. There hadn't been a choice. Anyone would have done what she did.

Max would understand. He just needed a little time.

Chapter 21

It seemed to Louise that a weight had lifted from Max's shoulders and left him so light of foot that a spring appeared in his step. After a week of moody silence, he became a different person. For the last two weeks, he had whistled in the mornings on his way to the barn. He seemed easier in his mind and didn't lose his temper with the new hands even when Louise thought he should have.

When she asked why he hadn't jumped Merdock's butt the morning Merdock slept late, Max had just shrugged and explained he was so grateful to have the boys back that he didn't care if Merdock was late getting to work. Then he'd laughed and predicted his attitude would change, but right now he thanked heaven that the bunkhouse was full. And he thanked God that Louise no longer had to labor like a hired hand.

Tears had sprung into her eyes, and she had rushed from the room because she understood what he was saying. He didn't need her anymore. And now that Philadelphia's pregnancy had been resolved, old doors had opened. New options were possible.

It was time for Louise to leave.

Though it made her feel foolish to think about it now, for a while she had hoped they might forget about their agreement. Just set it aside. They got along well; they had fallen into a comfortable routine that seemed to suit them both. To her amusement and amazement, she had turned into a real wife and secretly liked caring for a house and a husband.

And the nights. How she loved the nights when they read together in bed, shoulders touching, sharing bits from his book and her songbook. That's where they discussed the important things, the events or emotions they didn't share with others. And that's where he reached for her and slid her new nightgown up to her hips and kissed her until she was dizzy with loving him and wanting him.

But reality had slapped her hard the day of Philadelphia's labor. She had gazed into Max's eyes and saw a reflection of the woman he loved, and it wasn't her. She had listened to Philadelphia's threat to take Max away, and she'd felt the bitter sting of truth.

Oh Lord, she was crying again. And Gilly would be here any minute. In fact, she thought she'd seen Gilly ride in, but Gilly wouldn't have gone directly to the barn. Livvy must have come to speak to Max.

Today she and Gilly were going into town to choose birthday gifts for Sunshine. They had decided Sunshine should have at least one or two store-bought gifts. Perhaps an embroidery hoop, maybe new Sunday shoes.

"Louise?"

"Come in." Grabbing a dish towel, she wiped her eyes and shouted toward the front door. "I'm in the kitchen."

Smelling of fresh, cold air and the light verbena scent she favored, Gilly bustled down the hallway and straight to the coffeepot hissing and bubbling on the back of the stove. "Mama's watching Sunshine so you and I are footloose and fancy-free today." She smiled. "Your wagon's out front, but I don't think the horses would mind if we have a cup of hot coffee before we leave."

"Max said he'd hitch the wagon. I didn't know he'd already done it."

"Louise McCord! Have you been crying?"

"No."

Gilly peered into her face. "You are crying!" A sudden smile replaced her frown. "And if my suspicions are correct, I think I know why. Stand up and let me take a good look at you."

Pulling Louise to her feet, Gilly gazed hard at her waist and then studied her wet, anxious face. A radiant smile lit her expression. "My heavens! Mama is going to be so happy, and so am I!" Throwing out her arms, she clasped Louise in a tight embrace. "When are you due? Does Max know yet?"

"Oh Lord, it shows then?" She sat at the table and pressed the dishcloth to her eyes. If Gilly knew, then she couldn't put off telling Max. And then . . .

"Absolutely," Gilly said with a laugh. "Tears are a dead giveaway, especially for a strong woman like you."

"I don't know what's wrong with me. I sure don't feel strong. Everything makes me cry!" Fresh tears drowned her eyes when she thought about never seeing Gilly again. Or Sunshine. Or Livvy. Max, she couldn't bear to think about at all. Every time she imagined telling him that she would be leaving as they had agreed, her heart hurt so badly that she backed away and told herself: One more day.

"I didn't want to tell Max—"

"While you were feeding those cattle," Gilly guessed. She sighed. "That's how it is in a good marriage. You want to help your man. And he wants to protect his woman. If Max knew you were pregnant, he would have let those beeves starve before he'd let you work that hard."

A good marriage. Oh Lord, here came the tears again. "I can't talk about Max. It makes me cry." She blew her nose in her hanky and blotted her eyes with the dish towel. "I'll get my hat and coat, then we'll go down to the barn and tell him we're leaving. Gilly, promise we won't talk about Philadelphia today."

Gilly's eyebrows lifted. "You aren't worrying about her, are you? Oh Louise. If Max had married Philadelphia, it would have been a disaster. And I'd wager the earth that Max has known that for a long time."

Louise wished she could believe Gilly's airy dismissal, but she didn't. Where there was smoke, there was fire. And there was plenty of smoke between Max and Philadelphia. Moreover, she had heard Mr. Houser tell Wally that he would understand if Wally divorced Philadelphia. But she had thought about it and had concluded that Philadelphia would be the one to seek a divorce. Philadelphia would travel to Wyoming as soon as she could. And Max would go with her.

Because now the only thing standing between Max and Philadelphia was Louise. If she weren't in the way, they could be together as they had always wanted to be.

"If you're feeling even a tiny bit jealous of Philadelphia, well, you're just being silly," Gilly insisted as they left the house and walked toward the barn.

Louise wanted so much to believe what Gilly said. Her heart leapt on any small scrap of hope, and she tried hard not to see what was right under her nose.

But when they had almost reached the barn door, when they were close enough to see inside, they both stopped abruptly. Just beyond the door, Max held Philadelphia tightly against his body. He lowered his head and kissed her.

A hot knife sliced through Louise's body. The pain of seeing them holding each other was worse than anything she had ever experienced, worse than anything she could have imagined. Her fingers dug into Gilly's arm, and she made a strangled sound.

Then she turned and blindly ran back to the house.

The men in the barn looked toward the door, then faded away like snowdrifts beneath a warm wind. Puzzled, Max straightened in the stall he was mucking

out and glanced around to see what had caused the
boys to leave so hastily.

Philadelphia stood in a bar of sunshine just inside the
door. She'd tossed back a short cape to reveal a dark
riding jacket that curved over her breasts and nipped
her waist. She wore a small feather-trimmed hat atop a
mass of golden curls.

"Max?" She peered into the barn, but she didn't step
out of the rectangle of light.

Slowly, he put down his shovel, dropped his gloves in
the straw, and walked toward her. With the sunlight
in her curls, shimmering and glowing around her, she
looked like an ethereal creature sketched by imagination, too perfect to be real.

Halting a few feet from her, he thrust a hand into his
pocket and grasped the green marble. So much had happened since the first time he had gripped this marble. He
wasn't the same man he'd been that day on the mountainside. Nor did the marble represent the same things to him
that it had then.

"I've waited for you to come to the main house," she
said, pushing her lips into a pout. "Then I realized *she*
must be keeping you here. So I came to you."

If not for the green marble, he would have married
this woman.

"I'm leaving for Fort Laramie next week. I need to
know when you'll join me."

She believed nothing had changed between them.
There wasn't a doubt in her expression or her gaze.

"I'm not going anywhere." He spoke softly, gently.
Once she had been important to him. Once he had held
her and believed he loved her.

"Don't tease, I'm upset enough. My father will only
speak to me through his attorney. The day after tomorrow Wally is leaving for Santa Fe. Your mother scarcely
talks to me, and she's been rude twice. Gilly avoids me.

None of my friends or acquaintances will call. I need you."

"You don't need me, Philadelphia. Whatever was between us has been over for a long time." They had never needed each other, had never understood each other. "If we had married, it would have been a mistake."

"I don't know how you can say that, because you're wrong. I love you, Max. And you love me."

"You're mistaken on both counts."

Her gaze flicked to something behind him, then she rushed forward and pressed against his body, lifting her hands to his face. "Kiss me and then tell me you don't love me. If you can."

Confidence sparkled in her eyes before her lids closed and her arms wrapped around his neck. She pulled his head down and lifted on tiptoe to kiss him.

And as he'd expected, he felt nothing. Absolutely nothing.

Placing his hands on her waist, he moved her away from his chest and hips. "Go home," he said quietly. "You have a good husband who wants to love you. I genuinely believe you could be happy with Wally if you'll give him and your marriage a chance."

"I don't want Wally. Why do you think I'm willing to endure the scandal of a divorce? It's because I want *you*!" She stamped her foot, and her eyes flashed.

He almost smiled because he knew her well enough to know that once she understood he wouldn't follow her to Fort Laramie, she would stay with Wally rather than open herself to more scandal. With a bit of luck, she and Wally could create a satisfactory marriage, maybe even a happy one.

"Listen to me," he said, placing his hands on her shoulders and looking into her eyes. There was no way to soften the blunt truth, but he tried by speaking in a gentle tone. "I don't love you, Philadelphia, and I don't want to marry you. I love Louise." He touched her cheek with his fingertips. "Louise is the best thing that's ever happened to me, and every day I thank God for giving me such a blessing. I hope one day you'll say the same thing about Wally."

She jerked backward as if he had struck her. "You're telling me that you love that creature?"

"With all my heart," he said simply. He'd known it for a long while, but this was the first time he'd tested the words on his tongue. A grin curved his lips. Now that he'd stated his love aloud, he wanted to shout it from the barn roof.

"I don't believe this! You're advising me to remain married to your brother?"

"I have no right to advise you, and whatever you decide is none of my business. But . . . do you really want to exchange a man who loves you for the shame and disgrace of a divorce?"

"I don't want to stay with Wally. He's changed. He isn't as easy to manage as I thought he would be!"

Max smiled at her expression. "That's exactly the kind of man you need." Any small doubt faded. She would accompany Wally to Santa Fe. And Wally would provide the challenge she couldn't admit she wanted and needed. Theirs would be a volatile union, a constant struggle for control. But he suspected Philadelphia and his brother would find such a marriage stimulating and exciting.

Taking her arm, eager to send her on her way, he turned her toward the doorway, intending to walk her to her horse. "Gilly!" At once, he knew his sister had seen and overheard most of what had happened in the last few minutes. And she wouldn't have come to the barn alone. He swung a quick frown toward the house.

"For a bad minute, Max, I thought you'd turned stupid." Anger burned in the scorn Gilly leveled on Philadelphia. "And you dared to judge Louise. You don't know the meaning of decency!"

"Where is she?" His stomach cramped, and his hands curled into fists. He knew what Louise would think if she'd seen Philadelphia in his arms. Damn it.

"By now I imagine she's left you and is on her way to Denver."

Breaking into a run, he raced toward the house. Surely Louise understood that Philadelphia's kiss didn't mean anything.

His chest tightened around a kernel of panic. Curse his hide, he hadn't told her that he loved her. He'd been waiting for her to say it first, too proud to lay his heart on the line until she did.

But she had to know, didn't she? She was angry and hurt by seeing Philadelphia kissing him. But she wouldn't up and leave him. She'd at least give him a chance to explain.

He strode through the mudroom door and went straight to the parlor. His heart sank.

Her silver spoon was gone. She wasn't coming back.

He who is born a fool is never cured. She'd forgotten the truth in that proverb. Cursing, she wiped tears from her cheeks with the back of her hand.

She gave the horses their heads, too wild inside to care how recklessly she was driving over snow-packed, icy roads. She'd go to Denver. She had enough money in her bag to get a room for tonight. Tomorrow, when there were no more tears to cry, she would decide what to do next. How did people live when they no longer had a heart?

The horses galloped past the outskirts of Fort Houser and she dashed a hand across her eyes, blinking hard.

How could she have been such a blind fool? She *knew* Max wanted Philadelphia. He always had. Hadn't she reminded herself of this fact only an hour ago?

But she hadn't wanted to believe the raw emotion

she'd seen in Max's eyes the day of Philadelphia's labor. She had wanted Gilly to convince her that Max never thought about Philadelphia, didn't pine for her, didn't wish it was Philadelphia he'd married. No, that wasn't true. She had wanted *Max* to convince her of these reassuring lies. But deep in her heart she'd known how he really felt. She was nothing but an obstacle standing between him and Philadelphia; that's what she had always been to him.

Well, not anymore. She would vanish into the streets of Denver. Or maybe she would withdraw her money from the bank and take a train west until she ran into an ocean. She'd buy a little house and spend her life raising their child and trying to forget a tall, lanky cowboy with pox marks on his chin and a blue gaze that sent shivers down her spine. Max would always be the best part of her. She would see him in every blue-eyed man. Would find him in the face of her child.

"You idiot," she whispered, whipping the reins across the horses' backs. It was her fault that she was dying inside. She had forgotten who she was.

She had let herself be lulled and seduced by the luxury of a real mattress, warm food three times a day, and the joy of caring for a home. She had even given names to the stupid chickens. How dumb could she be? Very dumb. Dumb enough to appropriate Max's family and love them and try to make them her own. When she thought about never again seeing Livvy or Gilly or Sunshine, her ribs felt as if they were cracking.

But the worst, the very worst, most stupid and foolish thing she had ever done in her whole life was to fall deeply, crazily in love with Max McCord.

She had never had a chance. Her love was hopeless from the beginning. She could never be a lady like Philadelphia. She couldn't even be Missus Louise McCord; that wasn't who she was.

She was just plain ole Low Down. Low-down, good-for-nothing, never amount to a hill of beans, worthless, just taking up space in the world. That Low Down.

Hot tears stung her eyes, and her chest hurt. She'd forgotten who she was, had forgotten that names and nature do often agree. It was certainly true in her case. But oh, how she had wanted to be someone else. How she had longed to be Missus Max McCord. Hearing the words had made her feel proud inside.

"Louise!"

Blinking hard at the dampness scalding her eyes, she thought for an instant that she had imagined Max's shout. Then he yelled again, and she turned to see him riding hell-bent for leather alongside the wagon.

"Go away!" She didn't know what he was doing here, but she resented his chasing after her. It would have been better if they didn't actually have to say good-bye.

"You're driving like a damned maniac! Louise, stop the horses!"

She shouted back. "The only thing I have to say to you is good-bye. I've said it now, so get on home."

"I didn't kiss Philadelphia, she kissed me." Marva Lee ran full out, her mane fluttering and her tail rippling behind her. Max had one hand on his hat and one hand gripping the reins. His duster flapped behind him. "She blindsided me. Just jumped on me. I didn't want her kissing me, didn't ask her to do it. Most important, I didn't like it."

How dumb did he think she was? "I don't care who the hell kissed who, the fact is the two of you were kissing," she shouted, fighting tears and the reins. "And it sure looked to me like you were enjoying it. Well, you can have Philadelphia, I don't care. It's time I left anyway."

He eyed the team as if he might be thinking about doing something foolish like jumping down between them and trying to stop them. Instead he brought Marva Lee up close beside the wagon seat.

"You can't leave. In fact, you have to pull over and stop," he demanded, shouting at her. "I'm making a citizen's arrest!"

"What? What are you talking about?"

"I'm arresting you. You're stealing my wagon and my horses."

At first she thought she had misunderstood, and that was possible since the wheels and harness were rattling and squealing, making it hard to hear. Then she realized he had a valid point. She'd taken his wagon and horses without his permission. "I'll send you payment from Denver."

He was riding forward over Marva Lee's neck, his head turned to glare at her. "If I wouldn't take your money to save my ranch, what makes you think I'd take your money now? I saw what taking a woman's money did to my father. I'm never going to accept a dime of your funds for anything!"

Louise's mouth dropped, and she stared at him. That's why he'd refused her offer, not because he didn't want to be tied to her, but because he didn't want to end like his father, resenting his wife for bailing him out. The instant he said the words, it sounded so obvious.

What other mistakes had she made?

"Louise, slow down before you break your neck. We need to talk!"

No sooner had he shouted the warning than she felt the back wheels lock and spin into a sickening icy slide. She was skilled enough to save the team from wrecking, to hold the wagon steady until it straightened again, but she wasn't balanced well enough to save herself. The wagon seesawed and pitched her into the road, where she banged down on the ice and rolled across the snow pack into a drift.

Quicker than she could sort out what had happened, Max was off Marva Lee and pulling her out of the snowbank. He propped her against the drift and ran his strong work hands over her neck, down her arms, and across her rib cage. When he threw up her skirt and moved his hands from her ankles to her knees, she slapped down her skirts and wiggled away from him.

"Here. Sit on my duster," he insisted. "Are you hurt?"

"I'm not hurt." Probably badly bruised, but not actually injured. Her skirt was torn, and her hat had gone missing.

"It's a miracle you aren't dead. I never saw anybody drive a wagon that recklessly!"

She blinked at the road. "Where are the horses?"

"Probably halfway to Denver. We'll send someone to look for them later. Right now you and I have some things to talk about." He sat on the snow facing her and tried to take her hand, but she snatched it away.

She was going to have to swallow her pride and ask him to take her to a hotel in Fort Houser. Damn.

"I know what you're going to say," she said, lifting a hand and cutting him off. "You're a good man, and you and I have become friends so you want to make this as easy as possible for me. And I appreciate that, but I know what I saw and I know how you feel." She looked down at her hands twisting in her lap.

"No you don't."

"And if you're mad about me just running off, well, I'm sorry about that. It was cowardly. And I didn't think about stealing your horses and wagon." She looked at him. "But it's time I left, Max. I've overstayed my welcome."

"Louise, listen to me. I don't care about Philadelphia. She doesn't mean a thing to me. Whatever I felt for her died a long time ago."

"We haven't lied to each other, let's not start now. I saw your face when Philadelphia was in labor, and your expression said it all." She hated to remember that day. "You were worried to death about her. And you were devastated when you learned she'd been with another man."

"Damned right I was worried. Weren't you? Wasn't everyone? I didn't want her to die; I didn't want a death on my conscience. As for being devastated that she'd been with another man, hell yes, the news shocked me. I never expected such a thing. And it made me furious. I'd been flogging myself that I'd betrayed Philadelphia by taking my wife—you—to bed. And all the while she had betrayed me weeks before." He sat on the snow facing her with his legs tucked up under him Indian fashion. "Call it pride, call it stupidity, but of course I was furious that she was pregnant by another man. But Louise . . . that has nothing to do with you."

He looked at her sitting on the side of the road, as unaware of the snow and cold as he was, her heart swimming in her eyes. It was so like her to think of other people's happiness and run off to clear the way for him and Philadelphia. Despite her bluster and bravado, despite the chip she sometimes wore on her shoulder, there wasn't a selfish bone in this woman's body.

"I love you, Louise Downe McCord. You drive me absolutely crazy sometimes, and this is one of those times, but I love you."

Her eyes widened in surprise, and she gripped her hands tightly in her lap.

"If you hadn't run off when you did, if you'd stayed a few more minutes, you would have heard me tell Philadelphia to go home. You would have heard me tell her that I love you with all my heart and that you're the best thing that ever happened to me and I thank God for you every day of my life."

"You told Philadelphia all that?" She stared. "Well, damn it, Max, I ought to smack you hard. Why'd you tell her all that instead of telling me?"

"I planned to tell you. I was getting around to it." He cleared his throat and wished his hair was combed and wished they weren't sitting on the snowy ground by the side of the road. This wasn't the ideal circumstance in which to commence a long-overdue courtship. "Mrs. McCord, I love you," he said, making a beginning. "I've tried to identify the moment when I first knew you had captured my heart."

She stared at him with such an odd expression that a stab of fear pierced his chest. What if she didn't love him back? What if she'd run away, not because of what she'd seen in the barn, but because she was tired of him and didn't want to be married anymore? Then he would just have to woo her and win her.

"I think I fell in love with you that amazing night on the kitchen floor. Or maybe it was the evening you stepped up and set my arm." Testing things, he reached for her hand, and, to his joy, she glared, but she let him take it. "Or maybe the night I knew I loved you was when I kissed you under the mistletoe on Christmas Eve. It's hard to say because I look at you now and it seems to me there's never been a time when I didn't love you."

He clasped her hands hard. "Don't ride out on me, Louise, I need you. I couldn't stand losing you. I'm laying my heart on the line. I'm saying I love you and no man ever meant those words more. I think we can make a good life together; we've already started. Let's forget about an agreement we made before we knew each other. I want you with me always." A sigh lifted his chest, and he gave her a look of exasperation. "Are you ever going to interrupt this speech and tell me that you love me? Or are you going to torture me by keeping me in suspense?"

"I'm bad tempered and stubborn, Max. I'm never going to be a lady. I doubt I'll ever in my life invite someone to tea or be invited to such an event. I don't have any fashion sense, and I'll never be beautiful."

"What are you talking about?" he asked, frowning. "You're the most beautiful woman I've ever seen. How can you not know that?" When she stood naked before him like a young Venus, he was struck dumb with awe. And when she smiled at him across the bedcovers, the shine in her lovely eyes took his breath away. He told her what he was thinking. "And you have a wonderful mouth just made for kissing and laughing."

She studied him with suspicion, then amazement. "Good Lord. You really mean it! You honestly think . . . Oh Max. You're the only person in the whole world who thinks I'm beautiful!" Moisture jumped into her damp eyes. "And I love you for it. I love you so much, more than you could possibly know!"

Lunging forward, she threw her arms around his neck and knocked him flat on his back. Lying on top of him, she smiled down into his face. "I guess I'm not going to leave you after all."

"Good." If anyone rode up on them and saw them carrying on like this, there would be a scandal to end all scandals. He didn't care. He wrapped his arms around her and kissed her until she was breathless.

"All my life I dreamed of having someone think I was beautiful," she whispered.

Had he ever thought she wasn't? If so, he didn't remember it. Tenderly, he kissed her again and again. "Nothing in my life would mean anything if you weren't here to share it. There'd be no reason to get up in the morning without you to light the sun with your smile."

"Oh Max! Oh my. You have such beautiful words inside you." She wrapped her arms around his neck and pressed her nose against his neck so she could smell him. "Will you write me a letter someday and say all those pretty things?"

"I'll write you a hundred letters."

They kissed and whispered love talk and made a shocking spectacle of themselves if there had been anyone to see. When Max's breath was ragged and he thought he'd go crazy with wanting her, he drew her to her feet and into his arms.

"I've been thinking. I want you to give me your silver spoon," he said gruffly. "I'm going to frame it in a shadow box along with the green marble." He kissed her deeply and deliberately, knowing there was still more to talk about, knowing they would never run out of things to say to each other. Most important, he knew this splendid woman was his. "Someday our grandchildren will ask why we framed an old silver spoon and a scratched marble, and why we display them in a place of honor on our mantel." He caught her face between his hands. "And I will tell them the spoon and the marble are the most valuable and precious items that you and I ever owned."

She gazed at him with luminescent eyes, radiant as if she were lit from within. "I have something to tell you."

"Will it keep until we get home? Right now, all I can think about is taking you to bed and showing you how much I love you."

"My news will keep," she whispered, her gaze loving him.

He swung into the saddle, then pulled her up behind him. Louise wrapped her arms around his waist and held him close, her eyes turned toward the distant mountain peaks.

A light breeze swept down from the snowcaps, across the foothills and onto the plains, bringing the scent of spring and a promise of new beginnings. Louise smiled through a shine of joyful tears. She'd been wrong about so many things. Most of all, she had been wrong about herself.

She wasn't Low Down anymore. She would never be Low Down again. Eyes focused on the mountains, she whispered good-bye to the sad, scruffy, rootless, and lonely woman she had left in Piney Creek.

Then she snuggled close to her husband's back, thought of the precious child she carried, and turned her face toward family and home.

Three brides plus one groom equal nothing but trouble. Read on for a sneak peek at I DO, I DO, I DO, the delicious romance by Maggie Osborne. Available in bookstores everywhere.

Only one woman climbed out of the stage, which made Clara decide that she had sold the inn not a moment too soon. In her papa's time, the stage had arrived twice daily and deposited a half dozen guests on the inn's doorstep at each stop.

"She's the only one?" Clara asked Ole Peterson after he'd placed the woman's tapestry bags on the veranda.

"The rest of the passengers are continuing on," Ole said. He sounded apologetic.

Clara nodded and wished him a safe trip, hesitated, then walked across the lawn to join her guest. "It's beautiful, isn't it?" she asked pleasantly, glancing toward the ocean.

"It's amazing, Wonderful. Magnificent. Words fail me." The woman glanced at Clara, then back at the ocean. "My husband promised I would love the sea, but I never imagined it would be so big, so overwhelming, or so fascinating."

As the Pacific had always been in Clara's backyard, she tended to take it for granted. Seeing the landscape anew through her guest's eyes was always a refreshing experience.

"Well," Clara said, watching dots of color burning on the woman's cheeks. "Please come inside. I have a room I think you'll find to your liking. Dinner will be served in the dining room promptly at seven. You'll have time to freshen up."

"You are the proprietor?"

"Yes." Until tomorrow, when the new owners arrived.

She led the way past Papa's cuckoo clocks and Mama's collection of tiny china cups into a homey lobby, where she set down the tapestry bags and stepped behind the counter.

Apparently the woman from the stage hadn't arranged her own accommodations often enough to be comfortable with the process. She blushed deeply and didn't meet Clara's gaze.

"I wonder . . ." The color deepened in the woman's cheeks and she blinked rapidly, her words coming in an anguished rush. "I know this will sound like a strange request, but I wonder if I might examine your guest book from nine months ago. You see, there's someone who might have stayed at your inn. It would be helpful to me to know if he did stay here."

All was explained. Clara would have wagered the money in the cash drawer that the woman's husband had left her and she was attempting to find him. She had heard this sad tale before. There wasn't much that she had not seen while growing up in the hostelry business.

Sympathy softened her gaze. The poor soul wasn't a beauty, but who was? She was pretty in a cautious sort of way, as if she felt it more virtuous not to turn men's heads.

Clara turned the register to face the woman and extended a pen, saying, "Of course you can examine the register from last year. I'd be happy to show—" She stopped talking and stared.

The woman's horrified gaze had fixed on Clara's wedding ring. She gripped the edge of the counter as if to hold herself upright and the color abruptly drained from her face, leaving her as white as a new towel.

"Your ring!" She sounded as if she were strangling.

"It's my wedding ring," Clara explained slowly, wondering if the woman was having some sort of fit. "It's a family heirloom. My husband's grandfather designed the ring and his grandmother wore it all her married life, then his mother wore it."

The woman shook her head. "No. This can't be. No."

"Ma'am? Can I get you something? A glass of water?"

"You don't understand. But look." She tore at her gloves, clawing at her left hand. "It has to be a coincidence. Yes, that's it, it must be a very strange coincidence." She thrust out a shaking hand and the counter lamp gleamed down on her wedding ring. Clara gasped and her heart stopped beating. Her eyes widened until they ached.

The woman wore the same ring as she was wearing. Two bands of twisted silver enclosing filigreed silver hearts. But how could the rings be identical? Jean-Jacques had said the ring was one of a kind, an original design.

"Oh!" Clara reeled backward a step, vigorously shaking her head in denial. "No. This cannot be. I won't believe this."

"Please," the woman whispered. "Tell me your husband's name."

"Jean-Jacques Villette." The name choked her; one look at the woman's sickly, ashen face confirmed an unfolding nightmare. "*Mein Gott!* We're married to the same man!" The words came from a great distance. Her ears rang and her knees shook. She felt nauseous.

If ever a situation had called for someone to faint, this was it. So Clara was glad to see the other Mrs. Villette sink below the countertop and hit the floor.